Child's Play

Child's
Play

Reginald Hill

FELONY & MAYHEM PRESS • NEW YORK

CHILD'S PLAY

A Felony & Mayhem mystery

PRINTING HISTORY
First UK edition (Collins): 1987
First US edition (Macmillan): 1987
Felony & Mayhem edition: 2010

ISBN: 978-1-934609-61-3
Manufactured in the United States of America

Library of Congress Cataloging-in-Publication Data

Hill, Reginald.
  Child's play / Reginald Hill. -- Felony & Mayhem ed.
    p. cm.
  ISBN 978-1-934609-61-3
  1. Dalziel, Andrew (Fictitious character)--Fiction. 2. Pascoe, Peter
(Fictitious character)--Fiction. 3. Police--England--Yorkshire--Fiction.
4. Yorkshire (England)--Fiction. I. Title.
  PR6058.I448C45 2010
  823'.914--dc22
                        2010037702

Contents

The icon above says you're holding a book in the Felony & Mayhem "British" category. These books are set in or around the UK, and feature the highly literate, often witty prose that fans of British mystery demand.

⸺•◆•⸺

For information about British titles or to learn more about Felony & Mayhem Press, please visit us online at:

www.FelonyAndMayhem.com

Or write to us at:

Felony and Mayhem Press
156 Waverly Place
New York, NY 10014

Other "British" titles from

FELONY&MAYHEM

MICHAEL DAVID ANTHONY
The Becket Factor
Midnight Come

ROBERT BARNARD
Corpse in a Gilded Cage
Death and the Chaste Apprentice
Death on the High C's
The Skeleton in the Grass
Out of the Blackout

DUNCAN CAMPBELL
If It Bleeds

PETER DICKINSON
King and Joker
The Old English Peep Show
Skin Deep
Sleep and His Brother

CAROLINE GRAHAM
The Killings at Badger's Drift
Death of a Hollow Man
Death in Disguise
Written in Blood
Murder at Madingley Grange

CYNTHIA HARROD-EAGLES
Orchestrated Death

REGINALD HILL
A Clubbable Woman
An Advancement of Learning
Ruling Passion
An April Shroud

A Killing Kindness
Deadheads
Exit Lines
Death of a Dormouse

ELIZABETH IRONSIDE
The Accomplice
The Art of Deception
Death in the Garden
A Very Private Enterprise

BARRY MAITLAND
The Marx Sisters
The Chalon Heads

JOHN MALCOLM
A Back Room in Somers Town

JANET NEEL
Death's Bright Angel

SHEILA RADLEY
Death in the Morning
The Chief Inspector's Daughter
A Talent for Destruction
Fate Worse than Death

LESLIE THOMAS
Dangerous Davies

L.C.TYLER
The Herring Seller's Apprentice
Ten Little Herrings

LOUISE WELSH
Naming the Bones

Child's Play

PROLOGUE

Spoken by a member of the company

> A simple child, dear brother Jim,
> That lightly draws its breath,
> And feels its life in every limb,
> What should it know of death?

Wordsworth: *We are seven*

Death? Not much. Not then; not now. What is it? You here, I there: you stopping, I going on? Unimaginable! But I can imagine dying and the fear of it. The love of it too. I can imagine a corvette in heavy seas—a bathtub vessel in harbour, but let a gale come howling up the Tyrrhenian, then in the twinkling of a dog-star, its steel sides are changed to perilous cliffs and the dinghy far below bounces on the wild waters like a baby's teething-ring.

I can hear what the wind sings! At home, a father's anger and a mother's tears; at school, nipping draughts and stumbling repetitions, dreadful doubts and tiny triumphs...the sum of the squares...*Lars Porsena of Clusium*...a spot on the nose...a place in the Eleven...how to mash a girl...*arma virumque cano*!

Now I seize the rope and feel its fibres burn my frozen palms. With what strange utterance the wind resounds against this metal cliff; arms and the man, it sings...*you 'orrible sprog*!...*move to the right in threes*!...*hands off cocks and on to socks*!...*squeeze it like a tit*!...a pip on the shoulder...a place on a course...how to kill a man...

Italiam non sponte sequor!

And now at last the gaping O receives me and suddenly it is once more a dinghy and the wind is just a wind. Master of myself finally, and of these men who kneel around me, I give commands. Eyes gleam white as fish in sea-dark faces, paddles plunge deep, and my buoyant craft drives over the grasping waves towards the sounding but unseen, the undesired but never to be evaded Ausonian shore.

Fanciful, you say? Romantic even? Oh, but I have still darker imaginings. Time blows like mist in a wind, parting and joining, revealing and concealing, and now the wind is a wind of Autumn bearing with it not the salt spume of foreign seas but the bright decay of fallen leaves and the peppery scent of heather and the dust of limestone tors.

There is noise in it too, animal noise, a breathing, a coughing, an uneasy shuffling of feet as I pass over the dew-damp grass towards the darkling house. A window stands carelessly open… reckless I enter and the wind enters with me…slowly I move across the room…along corridors…up stairs…uncertain, hesitant, yet driven on by a gale in the blood stronger than any fear.

I push open a bedroom door…a nightlight shines like a corpse-light…but this dimly apprehended shape is no corpse.

Who's there? Is there someone there? What do you want?

It is time to speak into this light which shows so little.

Mother?

Who's there? Closer! Closer! Let me see!

And now the wind is a burning wind of the desert in my veins, and it sobs and it shrieks, and the house bristles with light, and I reach for the saving darkness as the helpless, hopeless sailor embraces the drowning sea…

SECOND ACT

VOICES FROM THE GRAVE

Sweet is a legacy, and passing sweet
The unexpected death of some old lady.

—Byron: *Don Juan*

CHAPTER 1

No one who attended Gwendoline Huby's funeral would soon forget it.

Her eighty-year-old frame was lighter by far than the ornate casket that enclosed it, but the telekinetic weight of resentment from the chief mourners was enough to make the bearers stagger on their slow path to the grave.

She was buried, of course, in the Lomas plot at St Wilfrid's in Greendale, an interesting specimen of late Norman church with some Early English additions and a pre-Norman crypt which the vicar's wife (in a pamphlet on sale in the porch) theorized might have been the work of Wilfrid himself. Such archaeological speculation was far from the minds of the bereaved as they processed from the dark interior to the brilliant autumn sunlight which traced out the names on the tombstones of all but the most eroded and deepest lichened dead.

The surviving relatives were few. To the left of the open grave stood the two London Lomases; to the right huddled the four Old Mill Inn Hubys. Miss Keech, successively nurse, house-keeper, companion, and finally nurse once more at Troy House, essayed a crossbench neutrality at the foot of the grave, but her self-effacing tact was vitiated by the presence at her shoulder of the man generally regarded as the chief author of their woes, Mr Eden Thackeray, senior partner of Messrs Thackeray, Amberson, Mellor and Thackeray (usually known as Messrs Thackeray etcetera), Solicitors.

'*Man that is born of woman hath but a short time to live and is full of misery,*' intoned the vicar.

Eden Thackeray who had thoroughly enjoyed the greater part of his fifty-odd years composed his face to a public sympathy with the words. Certainly if several of those present had their way, there'd be an extra dollop of misery on his plate shortly. Not that he minded. Misery to lawyers is like the bramble-bush to Brer Rabbit—a natural habitat. As the old lady's solicitor and executor, he was confident that any attempt to challenge the will would only serve to put money in the ever receptive coffers of Messrs Thackeray etcetera.

Nevertheless, unpleasantness at a funeral was not, how should he put it? was not *pleasant*. He hadn't relished being greeted by Mr John Huby, nephew to the deceased, landlord of the Old Mill Inn and archetypal uncouth Yorkshireman, with a look of sneering accusation and the words, '*Lawyers?* I've shit 'em!'

It was his own fault, of course. There had been no need to reveal the terms of the will until after probate, but it had seemed a kindness to pre-empt any anticipatory extravagance on the part of John Huby by summoning little Lexie from her typewriter and explaining to her the limits of her family's expectations. Lexie had taken it well. She had even smiled faintly when told of Gruff-of-Greendale. But all smiles had clearly stopped together when she bore the news back to the Old Mill Inn.

No! Eden Thackeray assured himself firmly. This was the last time he let a kindly impulse move him off the well-worn rails of legal procedure, not even if he saw one of his own family chained to the line ahead!

'Thou knowest, Lord, the secrets of our hearts...'

Aye, Lord, mebbe thou dost, and if so, nivver hesitate to pass them on to that silly old bat if she happens to drift in thy direction! thought John Huby savagely.

All those years of dancing attendance! All those cups of watery tea, supped with his little finger crooked and his head nodding agreement with her half-baked ideas on Lord's Day Observance and preserving the Empire! All those Sunday afternoons spent crammed—no matter what the weather—into his blue serge suit, the arse of which always required a good hour's brushing to remove the thick layer of cat and dog hair it picked up from every seat at Troy House! All that wasted effort!

And worse. All those debts run up in the expectation of plenty. All those foundations already dug and equipment already ordered for the restaurant and function room extensions. His heart fell flat as a slop-tray at the thought of it. Years of confident hope, months of tremulous anticipation, and barely twenty-four hours of joyous attainment before Lexie came home from that bloodsucking bastard's office and broke the incredible news.

Oh yes, Lord! If like the vicar says, thou knowest what's going on in my heart, then pass it on to the silly old bat pretty damn quick, and tell her if she hangs around a bit, she'll likely catch Gruff-of-sodding-Greendale coming up the chimney at the Old Mill after her!

'Forasmuch as it hath pleased Almighty God of his great mercy to take unto himself the soul of our dear sister here departed...'

The pleasure, dear God, is entirely yours, thought Stephanie Windibanks, née Lomas, first cousin once removed of the dear departed, as she grasped a handful of earth and wondered which of those around the grave would make the best target.

That low publican, Huby? Rod's suggestion that she should console herself with the thought that she had been dealt with no worse than that creature had only fanned her resentment. To be put on a par with such an uncouth lout! Oh Arthur, Arthur! she apostrophized her dead husband, see what a pass you've brought me to, you stupid bastard! At least, dear God, do not let them find out about the villa!

But what was the use of appealing to God? Why should He reward faith when He was so reluctant to reward works? For it had been hard work cultivating the Yorkshire connection all these years. Of course, it might be pointed out that she had long been aware—who better?—of Cousin Gwen's central dottiness. Indeed, she had to admit that on occasion she had even actively encouraged it. But who would have guessed that when it pleased Almighty and entirely Unreliable God of His great mercy to take Gwen's soul unto himself, it would also amuse him to leave her dottiness wandering loose and dangerous on the terrestrial plane?

God then her target, rather than Huby? But how to strike the intangible? She wanted a satisfyingly meaty mark. What about God's accomplice in this, that smug bastard Thackeray? It would be nice, but long experience of the world of affairs had taught her that lawyers loomed large in the ranks of the pricks it was fruitless to kick against.

Keech, then? That down-market Mrs Danvers, peering with myopic piety at a point a little above the vicar's head as if hoping to see there and applaud the ascension of her benefactress's soul…

No. Keech had done well, it was true, but only in relation to her needs. And think of the price. A lifetime of those creatures and that smell…! It required the soul of an ostler to envy Miss Keech!

This then was the worst moment of all, the moment when you realized there was no one to vent your rage on, a nothingness as insubstantial as the spirit of that silly old woman doubtless smiling smugly in her satin blancmange mould six feet below!

She hurled the earth with such force against the coffin lid that a pebble rebounded straight up the vicar's cassock, producing a little squeal of shock and pain which translated the *sure and certain hope of the Resurrection* into the *sure and certain hype of the Resurrection*. No one was surprised. Was not this, after all, the age of the New English Prayer Book?

'I heard a voice from heaven, saying unto me, Write…'

Dear Auntie Gwen, thought Stephanie Windibanks's son, Rod Lomas, Mummy and I have come up to Yorkshire for your funeral which has been rather Low Church for my taste and rather low company for Mummy's. You were quite right to keep these Hubys in their place, as dear Keechie puts it. They are the product of very unimaginative casting. Father John looks too like a bad-tempered Yorkshire publican to be true, and Goodwife Ruby (Ruby Huby! no script-writer would dare invent *that*!) is the big, blonde barmaid to the last brassy gleam. Younger daughter Jane is cast in the same jelly-mould and where this superfluity of flesh comes from is easy to see when you look at the elder girl, Lexie. In shape no bigger than an agate stone on the forefinger of an alderman, I swear she could enter an ill-fitting door by the joint. With those great round glasses and that solemn little face, she looks like a barn-owl perched on a pogo stick!

But all this you know, dear Auntie, and much else besides. What can I, who am *here*, tell you, who are *there*? Still, I must not shirk my familial obligations, unlike some I can think of. The weather here is fine, corn-yellow sun in a cornflower sky, just right for early September. Mummy is as well as can be expected in the tragic circumstances. As for me, suffice it to say that after my brilliant but brief run as Mercutio in the Salisbury Spring Festival, I am once more resting, and I will not conceal from you that a generous helping of the chinks would not have gone astray. Well, we must live in hope, mustn't we? Except for you, Auntie, who, if you do still exist, must now exist in certainty. Don't be too disappointed in our disappointment, will you? And do have the grace to blush when you find what a silly ass you've been making of yourself all these years.

Must sign off now. Almost time for the cold ham. Take care. Sorry you're not here. Love to Alexander. Your loving cousin a bit removed,Rod.

'Come ye blessed children of my Father, receive the kingdom prepared for you...'

I hope the preparation's a bit better than yours was, Dad, thought Lexie Huby, sensitive, as she had learned to be from infancy, to the rumbles of volcanic rage emanating from her father's rigid frame. She had giggled when Mr Thackeray had told her about Gruff-of-Greendale but she had not giggled when she broke the news to her father that night.

'Two hundred pounds!' he'd exploded. 'Two hundred pounds and a stuffed dog!'

'You did used to make a fuss of it, Dad,' Jane had piped up. 'Said it were one of the wonders of nature, it were so lifelike.'

'Lifelike! I hated that bloody tyke when it were alive, and I hated it even more when it were dead. At least, living, it'd squeal when you kicked it! Gruff-of-sodding-Greendale! You're not laking with me are you, Lexie?'

'I'd not do that, Dad,' she said calmly.

'Why'd old Thackeray tell you all this and not me direct?' he demanded suspiciously. 'Why'd he tell a mere girl when he could've picked up the phone and spoken straight to me? Scared, was he?'

'He were trying to be kind, Dad,' said Lexie. 'Besides, I were as entitled to hear it as you. I'm a beneficiary too.'

'You?' John Huby's eyes had lit with new hope. 'What did you get, Lexie?'

'I got fifty pounds and all her opera records,' said Lexie. 'Mam got a hundred pounds and her carriage clock, the brass one in the parlour, not the gold one in her bedroom. And Jane got fifty and the green damask tablecloth.'

'The old cow! The rotten old cow! Who got it, then? Not that cousin of hers, not old Windypants and her useless son?'

'No, Dad. She gets two hundred like you, and the silver teapot.'

'That's worth a damn sight more than Gruff-of-sodding-Greendale! She always were a crook, that one, like that dead husband of hers. They should've both been locked up! But who does get it then? Is it Keech? That scheming old hag?'

'Miss Keech gets an allowance on condition she stays on at Troy House and looks after the animals,' said Lexie.

'That's a meal-ticket for life, isn't it?' said John Huby. 'But hold on. If she stays on, who gets the house? I mean, it has to belong to some bugger, doesn't it? Lexie, who's she left it all to? Not to some bloody charity, is it? I couldn't bear to be passed over for a bloody dogs' home.'

'In a sense,' said Lexie, taking a deep breath. 'But not directly. In the first place she's left everything to...'

'To who?' thundered John Huby as she hesitated.

And Lexie recalled Eden Thackeray's quiet, dry voice... *'the rest residue and remainder of my estate whatsoever whether real or*

personal I give unto my only son Second Lieutenant Alexander Lomas
Huby present address unknown…'

'She's done what? Nay! I'll not credit it! She's done what?
It'll not stand up! It's that slimy bloody lawyer that's behind it,
I'll warrant! I'll not sit down under this! I'll not!'

It had been an irony unappreciated by John Huby that in
the old church of St Wilfrid, what he had sat down under was a
brass wall plaque reading *In Loving Memory of Second Lieutenant*
Alexander Lomas Huby, missing in action in Italy, May 1944.

It was Sam Huby, the boy's father, who had caused the
plaque to be erected in 1947. For two years he had tolerated his
wife's refusal to believe her son was dead, but there had to be an
end. For him the installation of the plaque marked it. But not for
Gwendoline Huby. Her conviction of Alexander's survival had
gone underground for a decade and then re-emerged, bright-eyed
and vigorous as ever, on her husband's death. She made no secret
of her belief, and over the years in the eyes of most of her family
and close acquaintances, this dottiness had become as unremark-
able as, say, a wart on the chin, or a stutter.

To find at last that it was this disregarded eccentricity which
had robbed him of his merited inheritance was almost more than
John Huby could bear.

Lexie had continued, 'If he doesn't claim it by April 4th in
the year 2015, which would be his ninetieth birthday, that's when
it goes to charity. There's three of them, by the way…'

But John Huby was not in the mood for charity.

'2015?' he groaned. 'I'll be ninety then too, if I'm spared,
which doesn't seem likely. I'll fight the will! She must've been
crazy, that's plain as the nose on your face. All that money… How
much is it, Lexie? Did Mr sodding Thackeray tell you that?'

Lexie said, 'It's hard to be exact, Dad, what with share prices
going up and down and all that…'

'Don't try to blind me with science, girl. Just because I let you
go and work in that bugger's office instead of stopping at home and

helping your mam in the pub doesn't make you cleverer than the rest of us, you'd do well to remember that! So none of your airs, you don't understand all that stuff anyway! Just give us a figure.'

'All right, Dad,' said Lexie Huby meekly. 'Mr Thackeray reckons that all told it should come to the best part of a million and a half pounds.'

And for the first and perhaps the last time in her life, she had the satisfaction of reducing her father to silence.

'The grace of our Lord Jesus Christ...'

Ella Keech's gaze was not in fact focused on some beatific vision of an ascending soul, as Mrs Windibanks had theorized. Myopic she was, it was true, but her long sight was perfectly sound and she was staring over the clerical shoulder into the green shades of the churchyard beyond. Money and descendants being alike in short supply, most of the old graves were sadly neglected, though in the eyes of many, long grass and wild flowers became the lichened headstones rather more than razed turf and cellophaned wreaths could hope to. But it was no such elegiac meditation which occupied Miss Keech's mind.

She was looking to where a pair of elderly yews met over the old lychgate forming a tunnel of almost utter blackness in the bright sun. For several minutes past she had been aware of a vague lightness in that black tunnel. And now it was moving; now it was taking shape; now it was stepping out like an actor into the glare of the footlights.

It was a man. He advanced hesitantly, awkwardly, between the gravestones. He wore a crumpled, sky-blue, light-weight suit and he carried a straw hat before him in both hands, twisting it nervously. Around his left sleeve ran a crape mourning band.

Miss Keech found that he became less clear the closer he got. He had thick grey hair, she could see that, and its lightness formed a striking contrast with his suntanned face. He was about the same age as John Huby, she guessed.

And now it occurred to her that the resemblance did not end there.

And it also occurred to her that perhaps she was the only one present who could see this approaching man...

'...*the fellowship of the Holy Ghost be with us all evermore. Amen.*'

As the respondent amens were returned (with the London Lomas party favouring *ā* as in 'play' and the Old Mill Huby set preferring *ah* as in 'father') it became clear that the fellowship of the newcomer was not so ghostly as to be visible only to Miss Keech. Others were looking at him with expressions ranging from open curiosity in the face of Eden Thackeray to vacuous benevolence on the face of the vicar.

But it took John Huby to voice the general puzzlement.

'Wha's yon bugger?' he asked no one in particular.

The newcomer responded instantly and amazingly.

Sinking on his knees, he seized two handfuls of earth and, hurling them dramatically into the grave, threw back his head and cried, 'Mama!'

There were several cries of astonishment and indignation; Mrs Windibanks looked at the newcomer as if he'd whispered a vile suggestion in her ear, Miss Keech fainted slowly into the reluctant arms of Eden Thackeray, and John Ruby, perhaps viewing this as a Judas kiss, cried, 'Nah then! Nah then! What's all this? What's all this? Is this another one of thy fancy tricks, lawyer? Is that what it is, eh? By God, it's time someone gave thee a lesson in how decent folks behave at a funeral!'

So saying, and full of selfless eagerness to administer this lesson, he began to advance on Eden Thackeray. The lawyer, finding himself in the Court of Last Resources, attempted to ward him off with the person of Miss Keech. Side-stepping to get at his proper prey, John Huby's foot found space where it looked for terra firma. For a second he teetered on one leg; then with a cry in which fear was now indistinguishable from rage, he plunged headlong into the open grave.

Everyone froze, then everyone moved. Some pressed forward to offer assistance, some pressed back to summon it. Ruby Huby leapt into the grave to succour her husband and landed with both knees in his kidneys. Eden Thackeray, no longer needing Miss Keech for ægis, released her and was then constrained to grab her again as she too started the easy descent into the pit. The vicar stopped smiling comfortingly and Rod Lomas looked across the grave, caught Lexie Huby's eye, and laughed aloud.

Gradually order was restored and the unquiet grave emptied of all but its proper inmate. It was only now that most of those present realized that at some point in the confusion the catalystic stranger had vanished. Once it was ascertained that the only permanent damage was to John Huby's blue serge, Miss Keech, still leaning heavily on the arm of Eden Thackeray, signalled that the obsequies were back on course by announcing that a cold collation awaited those who cared to return with her to Troy House.

Walking away from the graveside, Rod Lomas found himself alongside Lexie Huby. Stooping to her ear, he murmured, 'Nothing in Aunt Gwen's life, or her fortune for that matter, became her like the leaving of it, wouldn't you say?'

She looked at him in alarmed bewilderment. He smiled. She frowned and hurried on to join her sister who glanced back, caught the young man's eye, and blushed beneath her blusher at his merry respondent wink.

CHAPTER 2

The facade of the Kemble was a mess. To rescue the old theatre from Bingo in these hard times; to renovate, refurbish and restore it; to divert public money and extort private sponsorship to finance it; these had been acts of faith or of lunacy depending on where you stood, and the division in the local council had not been on straight party lines.

But the will had been great and the work had been done. Creamy grey stone had emerged from beneath a century of grime and Shakespeare's numbers had triumphed over the bingo-caller's.

But now the huge eye-catching posters which advertised the Grand Opening Production of *Romeo and Juliet* had been ripped down, and what caught the eye now were aerosoled letters in primary colours taking stone, glass and woodwork in their obscene stride.

GO HOME NIGGER! CHUNG = DUNG! WHITE HEAT BURNS BLACK BASTARDS!

Sergeant Wield took a last look as he left the theatre. Council workers were already at their priestlike task of ablution, but it was going to be a long job.

When he got back to the Station, he went to see if his immediate superior, Detective-Inspector Peter Pascoe, was back from the hospital. Long before he reached the inspector's door, a dull vibration of the air like thunder in the next valley suggested that Pascoe was indeed back and was being lectured, doubtless on some essential constabulary matter, by Superintendent Andrew Dalziel, Head of Mid-Yorkshire CID.

'The very man,' said Dalziel as the sergeant entered. 'What odds is Broomfield giving against Dan Trimble from Cornwall?'

'Three to one. Theoretical, of course, sir,' said Wield.

'Of course. Here's five theoretical quid to put on his nose, right?'

Wield accepted the money without comment. Dalziel was referring to the strictly illegal book Sergeant Broomfield had opened on the forthcoming appointment of a new Chief Constable. The short list had been announced and interviews would take place in a fortnight's time.

Pascoe, slightly disapproving of this frivolity when there was serious police business toward, said, 'How was the Kemble, Wieldy?'

'It'll wash off,' said the sergeant. 'What about the lad in hospital?'

Pascoe said, 'That'll take a bit longer to wash off. They fractured his skull.'

'The two things are connected, you reckon?' said Dalziel.

'Well, he *is* black and he *is* a member of the Kemble Company.'

The attack in question had taken place as the young actor had made his way to his digs after an evening out drinking with some friends. He'd been found badly beaten in an alleyway at six o'clock that morning. He could remember nothing after leaving the pub.

The trouble at the Kemble had started with the controversial appointment of Eileen Chung as artistic director. Chung, a six-feet-three-inch-tall Eurasian with a talent for publicity, had gone instantly on local television to announce that under her regime, the Kemble would be an outpost of radical theatre. Alarmed, the interviewer had asked if this meant a diet of modern political plays.

'Radical's content, not form, honey,' Chung said sweetly. 'We're going to open with *Romeo and Juliet*, is that old-fashioned enough for you?'

Asked, why *Romeo and Juliet*? she had replied, 'It's about the abuse of authority, the psycho-battering of children, the degradation of womanhood. Also it's on this year's O-level syllabus. We'll pack the kids in, honey. They're tomorrow's audience and they'll melt away unless you get a hold of them today.'

Such talk had made many of the city fathers uneasy, but it had delighted a lot of people including Ellie Pascoe who, as local membership secretary of WRAG, the Women's Rights Action Group, had quickly got in touch with Chung. Since their first meeting, she had talked about the newcomer with such adulation that Pascoe had found himself referring to her in a reaction, which privately at least he recognized as jealous, as Big Eileen.

It was after her television appearance that trouble had started in the form of obscene phone calls and threatening letters. But the previous night's attack and vandalization had been the first direct interpretation of these threats.

'What did Big Eileen have to say?' inquired Pascoe.

'Miss Chung, you mean?' said Wield correctly. 'Well, she was angry about the paint and the beating-up, naturally. But to tell the truth, what seemed to be bothering her most was getting someone to replace the lad in hospital. He had an important part, it seems, and they're due to open next Monday, I think it is.'

'Yes, I know. I've got tickets,' said Pascoe without enthusiasm. It was Ellie who'd got the tickets and also an invitation to the backstage party to follow the opening. His objection that there was a showing of Siegel's *The Killers* on the telly that night had not been sympathetically received.

'Do we count it as one case or as two, sir?' inquired Wield, who was a stickler for orderliness.

Pascoe frowned but Dalziel said, 'Two. You stick with the assault, Peter, and let Wield here handle the vandals. If they tie in together, well and good, but at the moment, what've we got? Someone gives a lad a kicking after closing time. Happens all the time. Someone else goes daft with a spray can. Show me a wall where they haven't! It's like Belshazzar's Feast down in the underpass.'

Pascoe didn't altogether agree but knew better than to argue. In any case, Dalziel didn't leave a space for argument. Having disposed of this policy decision, he was keen to get back to the main business of the day.

'Who's Broomfield making favourite, Wieldy?' he asked.

'Well, there's Mr Dodd from Durham. Two to one on. Joint.'

'Joint? Who with.'

'Mr Watmough,' said Wield, his craggily ugly face even more impressive than usual. It was well known that Dalziel rated Watmough, the present Deputy Chief Constable, as a life-form only slightly above the amœba.

'*What*? He wants his head looked! Find out what he'll give me against our DCC finding his way out of the interview room without a guide dog, Wieldy!'

Wield smiled though it hardly showed. He was smiling at Dalziel's abrasive humour, at Pascoe's faintly pained reaction, and also just for the sheer pleasure of being part of this. Even Dalziel would only speak so abusively of a superior before subordinates he liked and trusted. With a slight shock of surprise, Wield found he was happy. It was not a state he was much used to in recent years, not in fact since he had broken up with Maurice. But here it was at last, the dangerous infection breaking through, a slight but definite case of happiness!

The phone rang. Pascoe picked it up.

'Hello? Yes. Hang on.'

He held out the phone to the sergeant.

'For you, they say. Someone asking for Sergeant Mac Wield?'

The note of interrogation came on the *Mac*. This was not a name he'd ever heard anyone call Wield by.

The sergeant showed no emotion on his rugged face but his hand gripped the receiver so tightly that the tension bunched his forearm muscles against the sleeve of his jacket.

'Wield,' he said.

'Mac Wield? Hi. I'm a friend of Maurice's. He said if ever I was in this neck of the woods and needed a helping hand, I should look you up.'

Wield said, 'Where are you?'

'There's a caff by the booking office at the bus station. You can't miss me. I'm the suntanned one.'

'Wait there,' said Wield and put down the receiver.

The other two were regarding him queryingly.

'I've got to go out,' said Wield.

'Anything we should know about?' said Dalziel.

Mebbe the end of life as I know it, thought Wield, but all he said was, 'Could be owt or nowt,' before turning away abruptly and leaving.

'*Mac*,' said Pascoe. 'I never knew Wield had Scottish connections.'

'I don't suppose they know either. He gives nowt much away, does he?'

'It was probably a snout and we all like to keep our snouts under wraps,' said Pascoe defensively.

'If I looked like Wield, I'd put my snouts on display and keep my face under wraps,' growled Dalziel.

Thank you, Rupert Brooke, thought Pascoe, regarding the Superintendent's huge balding head which his wife had once likened to a dropsical turnip.

But he was careful to sneeze the thought into his handkerchief, being much less sure than Sergeant Wield of his ability to shut his mind against Dalziel's gaze which could root up insubordination like a pig snuffling out truffles.

Wield's capacity for concealment was far greater than anything Pascoe ever suspected.

Mac, the voice had said. Perhaps it had served him right for relaxing his guard and letting happiness steal in like that, but such instant retribution left the courts for dead! That a voice would one day call to change his life as he had chosen to live it had always been possible, indeed likely. That it should sound so young and speak so simply he had not anticipated.

I'm a friend of Maurice's. That had been unnecessary. Only Maurice Eaton had ever called him Mac, their private name, short for Macumazahn, the native name of Allan Quatermain, the stocky, ill-favoured hero of the Rider Haggard novels Wield loved. It meant *he-who-sleeps-with-one-eye-open* and Wield could remember the occasion of his christening as clearly as if... He snapped his mind hard on the nostalgia. What had existed between him and Maurice was dead, should be forgotten. This voice from the grave brought no hope of resurrection, but trouble as sure as a War Office telegram.

When he reached the café, he had no problem in picking out the caller. Blue-streaked hair, leg-hugging green velvet slacks and a tight blue T-shirt with a pair of fluorescent lips pouting across the chest, were in this day and age not out of the ordinary even in Yorkshire. But he'd called himself the suntanned one, and though his smooth olive skin came from mixed blood rather than a Mediterranean beach, the youth would have been impossible to miss even if he hadn't clearly recognized Wield and smiled at him welcomingly.

Wield ignored him and went to the self-service bar.

'Keeping you busy, Charley?' he said.

The man behind the counter answered, 'It's the quality of the tea, Mr Wield. They come here in buses to try it. Fancy a cup?'

'No, thanks. I want a word with that lad in the corner. Can I use the office?'

'Him that looks like a delphinium? Be my guest. Here's the key. I'll send him through.'

Charley, a cheerful chubby fifty-year-old, had performed this service many times for both Wield and Pascoe when the café had been too full for a satisfactory *tête-à-tête* with an informant. Wield went through a door marked TOILETS, ignored the forked radish logo to his left and the twin-stemmed Christmas tree to his right, and unlocked the door marked *Private* straight ahead. It was also possible to get into this room from behind the bar, but that would draw too much attention.

Wield sat down on a kitchen chair behind a narrow desk whose age could be read in the tea-rings on its surface. The only window was narrow, high and barred, admitting scarcely more light than limned the edges of things, but he ignored the desk lamp.

A few moments later the door opened to reveal the youth standing uncertainly on the threshold.

'Come in and shut it,' said Wield. 'Then lock it. The key's in the hole.'

'Hey, what is this?'

'Up here we call it a room,' said Wield. 'Get a move on!'

The youth obeyed and then advanced towards the desk.

Wield said, 'Right. Quick as you like, son. I've not got all day.'

'Quick as I like? What do you mean? You don't mean...? No, I can see you don't mean...'

His accent was what Wield thought of as Cockney with aitches. His age was anything between sixteen and twenty-two. Wield said, 'It was you who rang?'

'Yes, that's right...'

'Then you've got something to tell me.'

'No. Not exactly...'

'No? Listen, son, people who ring me at the Station, and don't give names, and arrange to meet me in dumps like this, they'd better have something to tell me, and it had better be good! So let's be having it!'

Wield hadn't planned to play it this way, but it had all seemed to develop naturally from the site and the situation. And after years of a carefully disciplined and structured life, he sensed that what lay ahead was a new era of playing things by ear. Unless, of course, this boy could simply be frightened away.

'Look, you've got it all wrong, or maybe you're pretending to get it wrong... Like I said, I'm a friend of Maurice's...'

'Maurice who? I don't know any Maurices.'

'Maurice Eaton!'

'Eaton? Like the school? Who's he when he's at home?'

And now the youth was stung to anger.

Leaning with both hands on the desk, he yelled, 'Maurice Eaton, that's who he is! You used to fuck each other, so don't give me this crap! I've seen the photos, I've seen the letters. Are you listening to me, *Macumazahn*? I'm a friend of Maurice Eaton's and like any friend of a friend might, I thought I'd look you up. But if it's shit-on-auld-acquaintance time, I'll just grab my bag and move on out. All right?'

Wield sat quite still. Beneath the unreadable roughness of his face, a conflict of impulses raged.

Self-interest told him the best thing might be to spell out what a misery the boy's life was likely to be if he hung around in Mid-Yorkshire, and then escort him gently to the next long-distance coach in any direction and see him off. Against this tugged guilt and self-disgust. Here he was, this youth, a friend of the only man that Wield had ever thought of as his own friend, in the fullest, most open as well as the deepest, most personal sense of the word, and how was he treating him? With suspicion, and hate, using his professional authority to support a personal—and squalid—impulse.

And also, somewhere down there was another feeling, concerned with both pride and survival—an apprehension that sending this boy away was no real solution to his long-term dilemma, and in any case, if the youth meant trouble, he could as easily stir it up from the next phone box on the A1 as from here.

'What's your name, lad?' said Wield.

'Cliff,' said the young man sullenly. 'Cliff Sharman.'

Wield switched on the table lamp and the corners of the room sprang into view. None was a pretty sight, but in one of them stood an old folding chair.

'All right, Cliff,' said Wield. 'Why don't you pull up that chair and let's sit down together for a few minutes and have a bit of a chat, shall we?'

CHAPTER 3

As soon as Pascoe walked through the door, his daughter began
to cry.

'You're late,' said Ellie.

'Yes, I know. I'm a detective. They teach us to spot things
like that.'

'And that's Rosie crying.'

'Is it? I thought maybe we'd bought a wolf.'

He took off his jacket, draped it over the banister and ran
lightly up the stairs.

The little girl stopped crying as soon as he entered her room.
This was a game she'd started playing only recently. That it was
a game was beyond doubt; Ellie had observed her deep in sleep
till her father's key turned in the lock, and then immediately she
let out her summoning wail and would not be silent till he came
and spoke to her. What he said didn't matter.

Tonight he said, 'Hi, kid. Remember last week I was telling
you I should be hearing about my promotion soon? Well, the bad

news is, I still haven't, so if you've been building up any hopes of getting a new pushchair or going to Acapulco this Christmas, forget it. Want some advice, kid? If you feel like whizzing, don't start unless you can keep it up. Nobody loves a whizz-kid that's stopped whizzing! Did I hear you ask me why I've stopped? Well, I've narrowed it down to three possibilities. One: they all think I'm Fat Andy's boy and everyone hates Fat Andy. Two: your mum keeps chaining herself to nuclear missile sites and also she's Membership Secretary of WRAG. So what? you say. WRAG is non-aligned politically, you've read the hand-outs. But what does Fat Andy say? *He* says WRAG's middle-of-the-road like an Italian motorist. All left-hand drive and bloody dangerous! Three? No, I've not forgotten three. Three is, maybe I'm just not good enough, what about that? Maybe inspector's my limit. What's that you said? Bollocks? You mean it? Gee, thanks, kid. I always feel better after talking to you!'

Gently he laid the once more sleeping child back on her bed and pulled the blanket up over her tiny body.

Downstairs he went first into the kitchen and poured two large Scotch-on-the-rocks. Then he went through into the living-room.

In his brief absence his wife had lost her clothes and gained a newspaper.

'Have you seen this?' she demanded.

'Often,' said Pascoe gravely. 'But I have no objection to seeing it again.'

'*This*,' she said, brandishing the *Mid-Yorks Evening Post*.

'I've certainly seen one very like it,' he said. 'It was in my jacket pocket, but it can hardly be the same one, can it? I mean your well-known views on the invasion of privacy would hardly permit you to go through your husband's pockets, would they?'

'It was sticking out.'

'That's all right, then. You're equally well known for your support of a wife's right to grab anything that's sticking out.

What am I looking at? This Kemble business? Well, the chap who got kicked is going to be all right, but he can't remember a thing. And Wield's looking into the *graffiti*. Now why don't you put the paper down...'

'No. It wasn't the Kemble story I wanted you to look at. It was *this*.'

Her finger stabbed an item headed *Unusual Will*. Published today, the will of the late Mrs Gwendoline Huby of Troy House, Greendale, makes interesting reading. The bulk of her estate whose estimated value is in excess of one million pounds is left to her only son, Alexander Lomas Huby, who was reported missing on active service in Italy in 1944. Lieutenant Huby's death was assumed though his body was never found. In the event that he does not appear to claim his inheritance by his ninetieth birthday in the year 2015 the estate will be divided equally between the People's Animal Welfare Society, the Combined Operations Dependant's Relief Organization, both registered charities in which Mrs Huby had a long interest, and Women For Empire, a social-political group which she had supported for many years.

'Very interesting,' said Pascoe. 'Sad too. Poor old woman.'

'Stupid old woman!' exclaimed Ellie.

'That's a bit hard. OK, she must have been a bit dotty, but...'

'But nothing! Don't you see? A third of her estate to Women for Empire! More than a third of a million pounds!'

'Who,' wondered Pascoe, sipping one of the scotches, 'are Women For Empire?'

'My God. No wonder they're dragging their feet about promoting you to Chief Inspector! Fascists! Red, white and blue, and cheap black labour!'

'I see,' said Pascoe feeling the crack about his promotion was a little under the belt. 'Can't say I've ever heard of them.'

'So what? You'd never heard of Bangkok massage till you married me.'

'That's true. But I'd still like to know which of my world-wide sources of intelligence I can blame for my ignorance. Where did *you* hear about them?'

Ellie blushed gently. It was a phenomenon observed by few people as the change of colour was not so much in her face as in the hollow of her throat, the rosy flush seeping down towards the deep cleft of her breasts. Pascoe claimed that here was the quintessence of female guilt, i.e. evidence of guilt masquerading as a mark of modesty.

'Where?' he pressed.

'On the list,' she muttered.

'*List?*'

'Yes,' she said defiantly. 'There's a list of ultra-right-wing groups we ought to keep an eye open for. We got a copy at WRAG.'

'A list!' said Pascoe taking another drink. 'You mean, like the RC's Index? Forbidden reading for the faithful? Or is it more like the Coal Board's famous hit-list? These organizations are the pits and ought to be closed down?'

'Peter, if you don't stop trying to be funny, I'll get dressed again. And incidentally, why are you drinking from both those glasses?'

'Sorry,' said Pascoe handing over the fuller of the two. 'Incidentally in return, how come at nine-thirty in the evening you're wearing nothing but the *Evening Post* anyway?'

'Every night for what seems weeks now you've been staggering in late. Rosie instantly sets up that awful howl and you stagger upstairs to talk to her. I dread to think what long-term effect these little monologues are having on the child!'

'She doesn't complain.'

'No. It's the only way she can get your attention for a little while. That's what all this is about. The next stage is for you to stagger back downstairs, have a couple of drinks, eat your supper and then fall asleep beyond recall by anything less penetrative than Fat Andy's voice. Well, tonight I'm getting in my howl first!'

Pascoe looked at her thoughtfully, finished his drink and leaned back on the sofa.

'Howl away,' he invited.

The *Unusual Will* item had caught other eyes that day too.

The *Mid-Yorks Evening Post* was one of several northern local papers in the *Challenger* group. The *Challenger* itself was a Sunday tabloid, published in Leeds with a mainly northern circulation though in recent years under the dynamic editorship of Ike Ogilby it had made some inroads into the Midlands. Nor did Ogilby's ambitions end at Birmingham. In the next five years he aimed either to expand the *Challenger* into a full-blown national or use it as his personal springboard to an established editorial chair in Fleet Street, he didn't much care which.

The other editors within the group were requested to bring to Ogilby's notice any local item which might interest the *Challenger*. In addition Ogilby, who trusted his fellow journalists to share a story like the chimpanzee trusts its fellow chimps to share a banana, encouraged his own staff to scan the evening columns.

Henry Vollans, a young man who had recently joined the staff from a West Country weekly, spotted the piece about the Huby will at half past five. Boldly he took it straight to Ogilby who was preparing to go home. The older man, who admired cheek and recognized ambition to match his own, said dubiously, 'Might be worth a go. What were you thinking of? Sob piece? Poor old mam, lost child, that sort of thing?'

'Maybe,' said Vollans who was slim, blond and tried not unsuccessfully to look like Robert Redford in *All the President's Men*. 'But this lot, Women For Empire, that rang a bell. There was a letter in the correspondence column a couple of weeks back when I was sorting them out. From a Mrs Lætitia Falkingham. I checked back and it had the heading. She lives at Ilkley and calls herself the founder and perpetual president of Women For Empire. The letter was about that bother in Bradford schools. She seemed to think it could be solved by sending all the white kids to Eton and educating the blacks under the trees in the public parks. I checked through the files. Seems she's been writing to the paper off and on for years. We've published quite a few.'

'Yes, of course. Rings a bell now,' said Ogilby. 'Sounds nicely batty, doesn't she? OK. Check it out to see if there's anything there for us. But I suspect the doting mum/lost kid angle will be the best. This racial vandal stuff at the Kemble theatre looks more interesting.'

'Could be if there's some bother on the opening night,' said Vollans. 'Shall I go? I could do a review anyway.'

'Theatre correspondent too,' mocked Ogilby, admiring the young man's pushiness. 'Why not? But talk to me again before you do anything on Mrs Falkingham. We're treading very warily about Bradford.'

Bradford's large and growing Asian community had high-lighted by reversal the problems of mixed race schooling. It was the usual question of how best to cater for the classroom needs of a minority, only in this case the minority was frequently white. The *Challenger*'s natural bent was conservative, but Ogilby wasn't about to alienate thousands of potential readers right on his doorstep.

'OK, Henry,' said Ogilby dismissively. 'Well spotted.'

Vollans left, so pleased with himself that he forgot his Robert Redford walk for several paces.

Nor did interest in the will end there.

A few hours later the telephone was answered in a flat in north Leeds, quite close to the University. The conversation was short and guarded.

'Yes?'

'Something in the *Mid-Yorks Evening Post* that might interest. Women For Empire, that daft Falkingham woman's little tea-circle out at Ilkley, could be in for a windfall.'

'I know.'

'Oh.'

'Yes. You're way behind, as usual. All that's long taken care of.'

'Oh. Sorry I spoke.'

'No, you were right. You're in a call-box?'

'Natch!'

'Good. But don't make a habit of calling. 'Bye.'

'And up yours too,' said the caller disgruntedly into the dead phone. 'Condescending cunt!'

Not far away in the living-room of his small suburban flat, Sergeant Wield too reclined on a sofa but he was wide awake, the *Evening Post* with its news of wills and vandals lay unopened on the hall floor, and the ice cubes in his untouched Scotch had long since diluted the rich amber to a pale straw.

He was thinking about Maurice Eaton. And he was marvelling that he had managed to think so little about him for so long. Lovers beneath the singing sky of May, they had even wandered once close to the decision, momentous in that time and at that place and in those circumstances, of openly setting up house together. Then Maurice, a Post Office executive, had been transferred north to Newcastle.

It had seemed a God-sent compromise solution at the time—close enough for regular meetings but far enough to reduce the decision on setting up house to a problem of geography.

But even small distances work large disenchantments. Wield had once been proud of his fierce fidelity but now he saw it as a form of naïve self-centredness. He recalled with amazement and shame his near-hysterical outburst of jealous rage when Maurice had finally admitted he was seeing somebody else. For thirty minutes he had been the creature of the emotions he had controlled for as many years. And he had never seen Maurice again since that day.

The only person who ever got a hint of what he had gone through was Mary, his sister. They had never spoken openly of Wield's sexuality, but a bond of loving understanding existed between them. Two years after the break with Maurice, she had left Yorkshire too when her husband was made redundant and decided that Canada held more hope for his family than this British waste-land.

So now Wield was alone. And had remained alone, despite all temptation, treating the core of his physical and emotional being as if it were some physiological disability, like alcoholism, requiring total abstinence for control.

There had been small crises. But from the first second he had heard Sharman's voice on the phone, he had felt certain that this was the start of the last battle.

He went over their conversation again, as he might have gone over an interrogation transcript in the Station.

'Where'd you meet Maurice?' he'd asked.

'In London.'

'London?'

'Yeah. He moved down from the North a couple of years back, didn't you know that?'

It was a redundant question, the boy knew the answer. Wield said, 'New job? Is he still with the Post Office?'

'British Telecom now. Onward and upward, that's Mo.'

'And he's…well?'

Perhaps he shouldn't have let the personal query, however muted, slip out. The boy had smiled as he replied, 'He's fine. Better than ever before, that's what he says. It's different down there, see. Up North, it may be the 'eighties in the calendar, but there's still a ghetto mentality, know what I mean? I'm just quoting Mo, of course. Me, this is the first time I've got further north than Wembley!'

'Oh aye? Why's that?'

'Why's what?'

'Why've you decided to explore, lad? Looking for Solomon's mines, it is?'

'Sorry? Coal mines, you mean?'

'Forget it,' said Wield. 'Just tell us why you've come.'

The boy hesitated. Wield read this as a decision-making pause, choosing perhaps between soft-sell and hard-sell, between free-loading and blackmail.

'Just fancied a change of scene,' said Sharman at last. 'Mo and me decided to have a bit of a hol from each other...'

'You were living together?'

'Yeah, natch.' The youth grinned knowingly. 'You two never managed that, did you? Always scared of the neighbours, Mo said. That's why he likes it down there. No one gives a fuck who's giving a fuck!'

'So you decided to take a trip to Yorkshire and see me?' said Wield.

'No! I just set off hitching and today I got dumped here and the name of the place rang a bell and I said, hello, why not get in touch with Mo's old mate and say hello? That's all.'

He didn't sound very convincing, but even if he had, Wield was not in a convincible mood. Hitch-hikers didn't get dropped at bus-stations.

He said, 'So Maurice told you all about me?'

'Oh yes,' said Sharman confidently. 'He was showing me some old photos in bed one night and I said, *Who's that?* and he told me all about you and the thing you had together and having to keep it quiet because you were a cop and all that!'

The real pain came at that moment, the pain of betrayal, sharp and burning still as on that first occasion, an old wound ripping wide.

'It's always nice to hear from old friends,' said Wield softly. 'How long are you planning staying, Cliff?'

'Don't know,' said the boy, clearly puzzled by this gentle response. 'Might as well take a look round now I'm here, see the natives sort of thing. I'll need to find somewhere to kip, not too pricey though. Any suggestions?'

The first squeeze? Well, he had to sleep somewhere and it made sense to keep a close eye on him till the situation got clearer. Wield examined this conclusion for self-deceiving edges, but quickly gave up. You didn't devote your life to deceiving others without becoming expert at deceiving yourself.

'You can sleep on my couch tonight,' he had said.

'Can I? Thanks a million,' said the boy with a smile which hovered between gratitude and triumph. 'I promise I'll curl up so small that you'll hardly know I'm there at all.'

But he was there, in the bathroom, splashing and singing like a careless child. Wield was acutely aware of his presence. His existence had been monastic for a long time. There had been another dark-skinned boy, a police cadet, who had ambushed his affections against his will, but nothing had come of it, and the cadet had been posted away. Sharman reminded him of that boy and he knew that, if anything, the danger was even greater now than then. But the danger to *what*? His way of life? What kind of life was it that a simple surge of desire put at risk?

The youth's bag was lying on the floor. More to distract himself than anything else, Wield leaned forward, unzipped it and began to examine the contents. There wasn't much. Some clothes, shoes, a couple of paperbacks and a wallet.

He opened the wallet. It contained about sixty or seventy pounds in fivers. In the other pocket were two pieces of paper. One had some names and telephone numbers scribbled on it. One name leapt out of the page. *Mo.* He made a note of the number and turned his attention to the other piece of paper. This was a timetable for coaches from London to the North. A departure time was underlined and the arrival time in Yorkshire. The latter was about ten minutes before Sharman's call to the Station. The little bastard hadn't hung about. So much for his talk of arriving here by chance!

He heard the water running from the bath. Quickly he returned everything to the bag. He had no doubt that Sharman would emerge all provocatively naked and he rehearsed his own coldly scornful response as he demanded explanations.

The door opened. The boy came into the room, his hair spiky from washing, his slim brown body enveloped in Wield's old towelling robe.

'God, I enjoyed that,' he said. 'Any chance of some cocoa and a choc biscuit?'

He sat on the sofa, curling his feet up beneath him. He looked little more than fourteen and as relaxed and uncalculating as a tired puppy.

Wield tried not to admit to himself he was postponing a confrontation but he knew that it was already postponed. By his old standards this was a mistake. But he had felt all the old parameters of duty and action begin to thaw and resolve the moment Pascoe had said there was a call for Mac Wield.

One word, one phone call. How could something so simple be allowed to change a whole life?

He stood and went to put the kettle on.

CHAPTER 4

'Lexie! Lexie Huby! Hi. It's your cousin, Rod. Remember me?'

'Oh. Hello,' said Lexie.

She wished that Messrs Thackeray et cetera would invest in some lightweight phones. These cumbersome old bakelite things were not made for small hands, nor for heads whose ears and mouth were not a foot apart.

'Hello to you too,' said the voice.

'What do you want?'

'Well, I'm up here again, didn't expect to be so soon after the funeral, but sometimes things work out that way, don't they? I'll tell you all about it when we meet.'

'Meet?'

'Yes. We didn't have much chance to talk after the funeral and I thought, wouldn't it be nice to have lunch and a *tête-à-tête* with my little cousin Lexie.'

'What do you want to talk about?'

'Well, old times, the sort of thing cousins do talk about,' said Lomas, sounding a little hurt.

What old times? wondered Lexie. Their blood relationship was so tenuous as to make the title *cousin* an unwanted courtesy. As for old times, they'd only met on those rare occasions when Mrs Windibanks's hopeful forays north coincided with the Old Mill Inn Hubys' monthly tea visit. Mrs Windibanks had always treated them like the lady of the manor acknowledging the peasants, and Rod ignored the two girls altogether. Prior to the funeral, the last time they'd met had been at Aunt Gwen's sick-bed some three years earlier. The old lady had suffered her first stroke shortly after returning from a trip abroad. Arthur Windibanks had died in a car accident only a fortnight later leaving his widow in dire financial straits, according to rumour.

'Old Windypants was hoping to mend her fortunes with the old girl's death!' John Huby had chortled. 'You should've seen her face when the doctor said she were on the mend!'

Rod Lomas, fresh out of drama school, had been as offhand as ever towards his young 'cousins', but some allowance had to be made for his black tie. Three years later he seemed ready to make amends and Jane, very susceptible to masculine charm, now reckoned he was lovely.

Lexie was not so easily won over, however.

'Hello. You still there?' inquired the voice.

'Yes.'

'Look. Do come and have lunch with me. To be honest, I don't really know another soul in town and you'd be doing me a real favour.'

Three years in a solicitor's office had taught Lexie to distrust openness above all things. But she was curious now and also she could hear her employer's footsteps on the creaky stairs.

'I only get an hour,' she said.

'Monstrous! They give them longer on the Gulag! So, a bar-snack then, rather than a trifling foolish banquet. There's a pub on the corner of Dextergate, the Black Bull, can't be very far from you. Half an hour's time, twelve-thirty?'

'All right,' she said and replaced the receiver as the door opened and Eden Thackeray appeared.

'I don't know why we have courts, Lexie,' he said. 'I could write out the verdicts if you just gave me a list of the magistrates. Have you been kept busy?'

Lexie followed him into his office. It was just what Hollywood required an English solicitor's chambers to be, all oak-dark panelling and wine-dark upholstery, while behind tall cabinets of lozenged glass marched rank upon leathered rank of the army of unalterable law.

'A few phone calls, Mr Eden,' she said. 'I've made a note. One was from a Mr Goodenough who said he was the General Secretary of the People's Animal Welfare Society. He wanted to see you about Aunt Gwen's will. He's travelling up from London tomorrow afternoon, so I made an appointment for him to see you on Friday morning. I hope that's all right.'

'Yes, of course.'

'And there was another one to do with Aunt Gwen's will. A Miss Brodsworth. She said she was something to do with Women For Empire and wondered if there's been any developments.'

'My God. Some people! Vultures. But Lexie, what must you think? I hope this hasn't upset you. I'd quite forgotten you might find yourself dealing with dear Mrs Huby's affairs when I asked you to step in for Miss Dickinson.'

Miss Dickinson, Thackeray's regular secretary, had been rushed off to hospital with appendicitis and to the surprise of most and the chagrin of a few, Lexie had been elevated from copy-typing in the Inquiries office to this most prestigious of jobs in the firm of Messrs Thackeray etcetera.

'No, it didn't upset me,' Lexie said in her small voice. 'Only I couldn't really help Miss Brodsworth as I didn't know what was happening.'

'No. Of course. Most remiss of me. Sit down and let me fill you in.'

The girl perched herself on the secretarial chair, built for and hollowed by much heavier hocks than hers.

'Yes, the thing is, and you must have realized it, that though the world at large, and her family in particular, has lost your dear aunt, or great-aunt I ought to say, as far as the firm of Messrs Thackeray etcetera is concerned, she is still very much in existence. In law, a client is defined by his or her affairs and our duty now is to the estate which is likely to be almost as demanding as Mrs Huby *in propria persona*, so to speak.'

Thackeray enjoyed playing the stage solicitor. It was some compensation for having to put up with this gloomy mausoleum when privately he longed for strip-lights and computer terminals. But he could think of half a dozen very rich clients (Mrs Huby had been among them) who would probably flee indignantly in the face of such desecration.

'So, let me see. Where's the file? Ah, here it is. Naturally I wrote and informed the putative legatees of the terms of Mrs Huby's will. You might care to examine their replies for yourself. First, the People's Animal Welfare Society.'

He handed the girl a sheet of good quality white paper headed by a logo of the initials PAWS formed into an animal footprint and an address in Mabledon Place, London WC1. The letter was word-processed.

> *Dear Mr. Thackeray,*
> *I am writing to acknowledge receipt of your letter in reference to the estate of the late Mrs Gwendoline Huby. I shall be in touch again after consulting the Society's legal advisers.*
> *Yours sincerely*
> *Andrew Goodenough (General Secretary)*

'Next CODRO, which is to say the Combined Operations Dependants' Relief Organization.'

This was rather amateurly typed on pale blue paper heavily embossed with an address in Bournemouth.

> *My dear Mr Thackeray,*
>   *Thank you for the news of Mrs Huby's most generous bequest. I gather from what you say that it is most unlikely that Mrs Huby's son will be able to claim his inheritance but, alas, this will not help us all that much, as, by the very nature of things, the number of those who can claim relief from our Organization will have dwindled almost to non-existence by the year 2015. If, however, it were possible to effect an advance at the present time, however small, it could be put to very good use indeed.*
>   *I await your reply hopefully.*
>   *Yours sincerely,*
>   *(Lady) Paula Webb (Hon. Treasurer)*

'Finally Women For Empire,' said Thackeray.

This was handwritten in spindly writing, strong at first but failing towards the end, on pink writing paper with the address in Gothic script, Maldive Cottage, Ilkley, Yorkshire. Across the head of a sheet a rubber stamp had printed in purple ink *Women For Empire*.

> *Dear Sir,*
>   *I was much distressed to hear of Mrs Huby's death. She was an old and valued member of Women For Empire and I was touched that she should have remembered us in her will. I myself am not in the best of health. Happily I am fortunate enough to have a young and vigorous assistant in the onerous task of running the affairs of Women For Empire. She is Miss Sarah Brodsworth, who has been vested with full authority in this and all other WFE matters. I will pass your letter on to her and doubtless she will get in direct contact with you.*
>   *God save the Queen.*
>   *Sincerely yours,*
>   *Lætitia Falkingham (Founder and Perpetual President WFE)*

'Well, Lexie,' said Thackeray when she finished the last letter. 'What do you think? You have the advantage of having spoken to two of the people concerned. What did you make of them, by the way?'

'Mr Goodenough was Scottish and sounded, well, sort of down-to-earth, businesslike.'

'And Miss Sarah Brodsworth?'

She hesitated, then said, 'Well, she was businesslike too. Youngish but hard, sort of aggressive, but it was just a voice and some people on the telephone...'

'No. I fear you may have heard all too accurately, Lexie,' said Thackeray. 'Silly old women and their unpleasant little organizations can attract some very dubious people when there's money involved. Well, that's the way the world wags, I'm afraid. Question is, what do you think will happen next?'

Lexie said, 'I don't rightly know, Mr Eden.'

'Come now! I have a better opinion of your intelligence. Why do you think I asked you to take Miss Dickinson's place?'

'I'm not sure,' she said ingenuously. 'To tell the truth, when you sent for me, I half thought, what with Great Aunt Gwen dying...'

She let the sentence fade and Thackeray burst out indignantly, 'My God, you didn't imagine I was going to sack you, did you?'

'Well, I thought, maybe, as I only got the job because of Aunt Gwen in the first place...'

A phenomenon often observed by Thackeray in his clients was the greater the guilt, the greater the indignation. It was a reaction he understood now, for there was no denying that without her great-aunt's influence, Lexie Huby would never have done for Messrs Thackeray etcetera. Not that she lacked qualifications, but she was awkward of manner, careless of appearance, spoke what few words she managed to get out with a strong Yorkshire accent, and looked like a twelve-year-old. But when old ladies of great wealth pronounce, old lawyers of good sense take heed, and Lexie had been taken on and hidden away in the nethermost reaches among the storage cabinets and deed boxes so that she would not besmirch the Messrs Thackeray etcetera image.

That had been three years ago. Only a month after she joined the firm, old Mrs Huby had had her first stroke. Had it proved fatal, there was little doubt in Thackeray's mind that after a decent interval, little Lexie might well have been urged to seek a job more suited to her taste and talents.

But the three years that passed had seen a change, not so much in the girl herself who seemed almost indistinguishable from the odd little creature who had first arrived, but in Thackeray's conception of her. Observation and report had slowly convinced him there was genuine intelligence here. Checking back, he had seen that her school references all said she could have stayed on after O-levels, but family pressure had been brought to bear. That awful man Huby! Thackeray shuddered every time he thought of him. It was partly as an anti-Huby gesture, partly because he liked to toss the occasional cat among the complacent office pigeons, but mainly on the basis of true desert that he had elevated this little sparrow to Miss Dickinson's perch.

'Lexie, I won't deny your aunt's influence helped you get the job, but it's your own abilities that will keep you in it,' he said rather tartly. 'Now, what do you think of these letters?'

'Well, they'd all like the money sooner rather than later, but from the sound of the letter and from him coming all this way to see you, this Mr Goodenough at PAWS is the one who'll do something about it.'

'Excellent. Yes, even before he telephoned, I guessed that Mr Andrew Goodenough was going to be the focus of action.'

'You don't seem bothered, Mr Eden,' said Lexie in a puzzled voice.

'Bothered! I'm delighted, Lexie. Merely administering the estate until 2015 would be very dull. Not unprofitable, of course, but dull. But if we have to act on behalf of the estate against an attempt to overturn the will, that could be both lively and extremely profitable. Instant money too, always welcome. So, bring on the lawsuits I say!'

He sat back, pleased at being able to show this naïve young thing what a sharp and worldly fellow he really was.

The naïve young thing, far from looking impressed, was glancing at her watch.

'Am I keeping you from something, Lexie?' he said sharply.

'Oh no. I mean, I'm sorry, Mr Eden, it's just that I've got an appointment in my lunch-hour and it's nearly half past twelve…'

She looked so distressed, his sternness dissolved instantly.

'Then you must run along,' he said.

She left, darting from the room with the swiftness of a wren. An appointment? Hairdresser perhaps, though that close crop of indeterminately brown straight hair didn't look as if it owed much to the coiffeur's art. Dentist, then? Or boyfriend? Alas, least likely of all, he suspected. Poor little Lexie. He could see her growing old in the service of Messrs Thackeray etcetera. He must do what he could for her. Getting her out of the Old Mill Inn and away from the influence of that awful father of hers would be the first step. But how to manage it?

He sat quietly, applying his mind to the task. It was a good mind and it enjoyed the business of manipulating other people's destinies.

He heard the building emptying. His nephew and junior partner, Dunstan Thackeray, stuck his head round the door.

'Coming to the Gents', Uncle Eden?' he asked.

This was not the odd inquiry it sounded. The Gents was the familiar abbreviation of The Borough Club For Professional Gentlemen, the prestigious Victorian institution which had had a Thackeray on its founding committee and of which Eden was the president-elect. As a liberal modernist, he deplored and detested it. As a senior partner in Messrs Thackeray etcetera he had to keep his mouth shut. But he was not in the mood for the usual Gents diet, conversational as well as culinary, of traditional stodge.

'Later. I may be in later,' he said.

He heard his nephew's feet descend the stairs. Then all was silence. He fell into a reverie which a casual observer might have mistaken for a doze.

When he opened his eyes, it took him a few seconds to realize there actually was a casual observer to make the error.

Seated before him where Lexie had perched a little earlier was a man. There was something familiar about him, and not very pleasantly familiar either.

Suddenly it came to him. This was the same sunburnt intruder who had disturbed Gwendoline Huby's funeral.

He jumped up, alarmed.

'Who are you? How did you get in? What the devil do you want?'

The man stared at him as if looking for something in his face.

'You are Eden Thackeray?' he said.

He spoke with a certain hesitancy, like a man reassembling old ideas, old words.

'Yes, I am. And who are you?' repeated Thackeray.

'Who am I?' said the man. 'In my passport and in my life for the past forty years, it says that I am Alessandro Pontelli of Florence. But the truth is that I am Alexander Lomas Huby and I have come to claim my inheritance!'

CHAPTER 5

'What's up with Wield?' said Dalziel.

'I don't know. Why?'

'He's been sort of distant these last few days, like he's got something on his mind. Perhaps he's decided on plastic surgery and can't decide whether to go for the blow-lamp or the road-drill.'

'I can't say I've noticed,' said Pascoe.

'Insensitivity, that's always been your trouble,' said Dalziel. He belched, then raised his voice and cried, 'Hey, Wieldy, bring us another of them pies, will you? And ask Jolly Jack if it's my turn to have the one with the meat in this month.'

No one paid any heed. Dalziel and his CID squad were lunch-time regulars in the Black Bull and familiarity had bred discretion. A minute later Wield returned from the bar with two pints of beer.

'You've not forgot my pie?'

The sergeant put the glasses down and reached into his jacket pocket.

'Christ,' said Dalziel. 'I'm glad I didn't ask for the *lasagna*. Cheers.'

Pascoe sipped his pint with a sigh. It was his second and he'd been promising both himself and Ellie to cut back on the calories for a few days. At least he'd only had one pie.

'What's up with you then, Sergeant? Not having another?' Dalziel had just noticed Wield had not bought himself a drink.

'No, I'll just finish this, then I've got to be off.'

'Off? It's your lunch-hour!' expostulated Dalziel with the same note of exasperation he sounded if any of his flock showed the slightest sign of demur when told they were working till midnight or had to get up at four a.m.

'I've some catching up to do,' said Wield vaguely. 'This shoplifting. And that Kemble business.'

'Anything new there, Wieldy?' asked Pascoe.

'Not much. I've been researching back through the old information sheets. There's this National Front spin-off group, works a lot through university students, bit different from the usual Front lot in that they keep their heads down, infiltrate Conservative student groups, that sort of thing. Not like your usual Front bully-boy who wants the world to admire his jackboots.'

Wield was sounding quite heated for him.

'What makes you think there could be a link here?' asked Pascoe.

'They call themselves White Heat,' said Wield.

'White Heat. That rings a bell,' said Dalziel.

'James Cagney. Top of the world, ma!' said Pascoe.

The other two looked at him blankly, clearly not sharing his passion for old Warner Brothers movies.

'One of the things sprayed on the Kemble was *White Heat Burns Blacks*,' said Wield, glancing at his watch.

He finished the beer, stood up and said, 'Best be off. Cheerio.'

Pascoe watched his departure with a feeling of faint concern. He hadn't been lying when he told Dalziel he had noticed nothing odd in the sergeant's behaviour recently, but now his mind had been steered in the right direction, he realized that there were a number of minor variations from the norm which, crushed together, might make a small oddity. It was annoying that Dalziel should have proved more percipient in this than himself. He wouldn't call Wield a friend, but a bond of respect and also of affection had developed between the men, a closeness signalled perhaps by his growing irritation at Dalziel's 'ugly' jokes.

His mind was diverted from the problem, if problem there was, by the landlord's voice from the bar.

'Sorry, love, but you don't look eighteen to me, and it's more than me licence is worth to sell you alcohol. You can have a fruit juice, but.'

It was, of course, a stage-loudness for their benefit, thought Pascoe. Though indeed Jolly Jack Mahoney, the licensee, might well have objected even without a police presence to serving this customer, a small bespectacled girl who didn't look much above thirteen.

Mahoney leaned over the bar and said in a quieter voice, 'If it's grub you're after, love, go through that door, there's a bit of a dining-room, the girl'll slip you a glass of wine with your meal, no bother. Them gents over there are the police, so you see my trouble.'

The girl did not move except to turn her head so that the owl-eye spectacles ringed Dalziel and Pascoe.

Her voice when she spoke was nervous but determined.

'I thought you boasted at the Licensed Victuallers Association that the police never bothered you as long as the CID could get drinks at all hours, Mr Mahoney.'

The publican's jaw dropped through shock into dismay.

'Hold on, hold on,' he said, glancing anxiously towards Dalziel who was viewing him malevolently. 'You shouldn't say things like that, lass. Do I know you?'

'You know my father, John Huby, I think.'

'Up at the Old Mill Inn? By God, is it little Lexie? Why didn't you say, lass! You must be near on twenty now. I know her, she's near on twenty!'

These last affirmations were directed towards Dalziel who finished his pint, placed the glass on the table and pointed menacingly into it, like Jahweh setting up a widow's cruse.

A young man had come into the bar, of medium height, elegantly coiffured and dressed in a black and yellow striped blazer, cheese-cloth shirt and cream-coloured slacks. His regularly handsome features broke into a gleaming smile as he spotted the girl and bore down on her, arms outstretched.

'Dear Lexie,' he cried. 'I am late. Forgive me. Purge me with a kiss.'

Pascoe was amused to see that the girl ducked at the last second from his questing lips and got him in the eye with her big spectacles. Then the newcomer obtained two glasses of white wine and a plateful of sandwiches from Mahoney and he and the small girl sat down at the far side of the room, still within sight but now out of earshot.

He returned his attention to Dalziel who was saying, 'That Mahoney, I'll need to have a quiet word about going around slandering the police.'

'Now?' said Pascoe.

'Don't be daft! When he's shut and we can get down to some serious drinking.'

And he bellowed with laughter at the sight of the pained expression of Pascoe's face.

At their distant table, Lexie and Rod Lomas heard the laugh, but only Lexie registered the source.

'I really am sorry I'm late,' Lomas was saying. 'But I'm afraid I still tend to think of all urban distances as minute outside of London. To compensate, I tend to treat all country distances as vast. Had we been meeting at your father's pub, say, I dare say I'd have been there an hour ago.'

Lexie did not reply but bit into a sandwich.

Lomas said with a smile, 'You don't say a great deal, do you, dear coz?'

'I were waiting for you to finish putting me at ease,' said Lexie.

'Oh dear,' said Lomas. 'I see I shall have to watch you, little Lexie.'

'I'm not your cousin, and I'm five feet two inches barefoot,' said Lexie.

'Oh dear,' repeated Lomas. 'Are there any other sensitive areas we ought to check out straightaway?'

'Why do you call yourself Lomas?' said Lexie. 'Your name is Windibanks, isn't it?'

He grinned and said, 'There you're wrong. It was changed quite legally by deed poll. Rod Lomas is in fact and law my name.'

'Why'd you change it?'

'As I launched myself on what I hoped would be a meteoric theatrical career, but what now looks like being a long steady haul to the top, it occurred to me that Rodney Windibanks was not a name fit easily into lights. Rod Lomas on the other hand is short, punchy, memorable. Satisfied?'

She continued to chew without replying. Her silence somehow declared its source as disbelief rather than good manners.

'All right,' he said. 'It's a fair cop! Why *Lomas*? It was Mummy's idea. Butter up Auntie Gwen—yes, I know she wasn't my auntie but that's how I thought of her. Mummy made a big deal of it, of course, writing and asking permission to resurrect the family name, promising that I would never bring anything but fame and good report on it. Auntie Gwen replied that I must call myself what I wished. Left to myself, I might have chosen something a little more evocative, like *Garrick* or *Irving*, but Mummy is very strong-willed in the pursuit of fortune. Do I shock you?'

She swallowed, opened the half-eaten sandwich, said disgustedly, 'Brisket. And more gristle than brisket.'

Lomas looked nonplussed for a moment, then he said with an edge of malice. 'Not that it should shock you, of course. You are a fellow-initiate in the great sucking-up-to-auntie club, aren't you? Indeed, almost a founder member, since you joined shortly after birth. Correct me if I'm wrong, but surely Lexie is short for Alexandra, and I doubt if *that* was a simple coincidence!'

Lexie said abruptly, 'What do you want? What are you doing here?'

Lomas looked at her as if considering taking up the challenge. Then he grinned boyishly and said, 'Believe it or not, dear coz, I came back north in response to a cry for help. When I was up for the funeral, I popped into the Kemble to see some old chums. I'm sure a cultured young person like yourself will be aware that the Kemble has as its artistic director Ms Eileen Chung. Chung and I are long acquainted and I know all her ways, which include a rather distorting tendency to socialize or, worse still, feminize all material that she turns her big doe-eyes on. She is not strong enough to resist the demands on the English set-book, however, and next week as you must know her very first production is *Romeo and Juliet*. At Salisbury we did it for art, in Yorkshire they do it for O-level! But disaster struck. Night before last, Chung's Mercutio got beaten up and is *hors de combat*. Desperate for a top-class replacement well-schooled in the part, her thoughts naturally turned to me. By chance I was free. Or rather I was just on the point of signing a big Hollywood contract, but who can resist a friend's cry for help? I dropped everything and came up last night. The show is saved!'

Lexie said, 'I read in the *Post* the chap who get beaten up was black.'

'Indeed yes. A little surprise for the good burghers, a black Mercutio. But Chung says it was not of the essence. She thinks his obvious homosexual passion for Romeo will be quite enough for the city council to bear. But enough of me, fascinating though I am. What of you? How goes the Law?'

'All right,' said Lexie, discarding another sandwich.

'Any news on the will front?' he asked casually.

'How should I know?' she said, alert.

'Well, you *are* acting as old Thackeray's secretary, aren't you?'

'Who told you that?'

'I don't know. Keechie, I suppose.'

He laughed at her surprise.

'Didn't I say? I'm staying out at Troy House. Well, I needed digs. I can only afford the Howard Arms Hotel when Mummy's with me, picking up the tab. Dear Mummy. It doesn't matter how strapped she is for cash, she never settles for less than the best.'

'She's hard up, is she? Your dad didn't leave her anything, then?'

Lomas stiffened.

'Not much,' he said, charm subsumed by some genuine emotion. 'Why do you mention my father?'

'No reason,' said the girl.

He glowered at her, then burst out, 'People said he was a crook, but if he was, he'd have left us stinking rich, wouldn't he?'

She said, 'You were telling me about staying at Troy House.'

Lomas visibly pulled the charm back over him like a bright-patterned slipover.

'So I was,' he said. 'I couldn't afford decent digs let alone the Howard Arms so I thought: What about old Keechie? We'd always got on well, so I gave her a ring. She was delighted. It must be lonely for her with nothing but those animals for company. What a nuisance they are. After the funeral feast, Mummy trod in something quite disgusting in the drive! Keechie, I'm glad to say, runs a rather tighter ship than old Gwen and apart from the odd moggie on my pillow, I've been unmolested. But it is, of course, early days. I only got here yesterday.'

He regarded her speculatively.

'One thing I have realized already is how far it is out of town if you haven't a car. The buses seem to be as rare as virtuous women and go all around the houses, if that's not a contradiction. Keechie tells me you run a car.'

'You've done a bit of talking about me, haven't you?' said Lexie. 'Yes. I've got an old Mini. The Old Mill's out of the way too.'

'Precisely. And rather out of the same way, isn't it? What I mean is, you must pass within a few yards, barely two miles anyway, of Greendale village. Perhaps I could persuade you to make a diversion some morning?'

She said, 'I thought actors slept mornings.'

'Art never sleeps. Are you game?'

'I'll not wait around.'

'I shall be ready and waiting before the bawdy hand of the clock has reached the prick of eight. It's all right. That's not rude, it's Shakespeare. You shall hear for yourself. As reward for your kindness, you shall have a complimentary ticket for our first night next Monday, and an invitation to the party afterwards. Then you can run me home too! Talking of which, how about running me home tonight? I work office hours till we open.'

'I'm not a taxi-service,' said Lexie, standing up. 'Besides, I've got an evening class so I'll not be going straight back. Thanks for the wine. I'd not pay for them sandwiches if I were you. I'd best get back.'

'It's been a pleasure,' said Lomas. 'You won't forget to call?'

'I said so,' replied Lexie. 'Cheerio.'

She left, passing quite close to Pascoe and Dalziel, who was on his fourth pint and third pie. Neither man paid her much attention. She wasn't the kind of woman to catch a man's eye. Indeed, with her close-cropped hair, big spectacles, un-made-up face and big leather handbag slung over her shoulder like a satchel, she looked for all the world like a schoolgirl returning to the classroom.

But Rod Lomas watched her out of sight.

CHAPTER 6

'Maurice? It's Mac. Mac Wield.'

'Good Lord! Mac? Is that really you?'

'Yes, it's me.'

'Well, how've you been? How are you?' With a sudden injection of sharpness. '*Where* are you?'

'It's all right, Maurice. I'm safely up here in Yorkshire.'

I'm sorry, I didn't mean… My dear chap, you'd be more than welcome to come and visit…'

'Except you've got someone staying and you haven't forgotten last time, in Newcastle.'

'Don't be silly. You were upset. Naturally. How do you know I've got someone staying?'

'I rang your flat last night. He answered. I rang off. I didn't want to risk causing embarrassment. Also I wanted a private chat.'

'So you ring me at the office? Not very good police work that, Mac.'

'It's lunch-time. You're by yourself, else you'd not be talking like this,' said Wield confidently.

'True. You just caught me. I was on my way—and I must get back on it pretty soon. Mac, can I ring you this evening? Is it the same number?'

'I'd rather you didn't,' said Wield.

'Oh. Same reason?'

'In a way. I'm ringing from work too,' said Wield.

'My, we are getting bold,' said Maurice Eaton.

Wield heard the savagely scornful irony with sadness, but it stiffened his resolve.

'Mebbe we are,' he said. 'I'll not keep you. There were just a couple of questions I wanted to ask.'

'Really? Don't tell me I'm helping with inquiries at last!'

The voice had changed a lot. It was lighter and slipped more easily into an archness of delivery which Eaton had once been at great pains to avoid.

'You're getting bold too, Maurice,' said Wield.

'Sorry? Don't get you.'

'You used to be so scared of anyone spotting you were gay, you'd even say your prayers in a basso profundo,' said Wield, savage in his turn.

'Have you rung me to quarrel, Mac?' asked Eaton softly.

'No. Not at all. I'm sorry,' said Wield, fearful the connection would be broken before he got answers.

'Very well. Then what *do* you want?'

'Do you know a lad, name of Sharman? Cliff Sharman?'

There was a silence which was in itself an answer, and more than just a simple affirmative.

'What about him?' said Eaton finally.

'He's here.'

'You mean up there, in Yorkshire?'

'That's what *here* means up here.'

'Then my advice to you, Mac, is, get shot of him quick as

you can. He's a poisonous little asp. Put him on his bike and send him on his way.'

'You do know him, then.'

'Yes, of course I do. Or I did. Mac, he's trouble. Believe me, get rid of him.'

'What's he done to you, Maurice? How well did you know him?'

'What? Oh, hardly at all as a matter of fact.'

'He said he lived with you.'

'I took him in as a favour to a friend. Just a few nights. He repaid me by spreading foul gossip about me at my club and then decamping with twenty quid out of my wallet and several knick-knacks I was rather fond of. I almost called the police.'

'He did, Maurice. He did.'

Again there was silence.

'Oh shit, Mac. Has he been bothering you? How the hell...? Oh, I get it! I've got some old stuff tucked away, photos and things, sentimental corner, I call it. The young sod must've come across it when he was ferreting around looking for something to steal.'

Wield let this go for the time being. He could feel a rage deep down inside him but it was like the glow of a forest fire in the next valley, ignorable till the wind changed.

He said, 'What's his background, Maurice?'

'I only know what he's told me and God knows how much credence one should give that. He comes from Dulwich, the seedy end I should imagine. His mother still lives there, I gather, but his father took French leave about three years ago when Cliff was fifteen and he's been out of control ever since bumming around the West End in every sense. This town's full of them.'

'Must break your heart. Work?'

'You're joking! The odd odd job, but nothing more. No, State Benefits and fool's wallets, that's what kept little Cliffy going. Mac, is he causing you real trouble? I mean, not to put too fine a point on it, blackmail? I'm assuming you've still not come out.'

'No, I've not,' said Wield.

'Listen, I'm sure I can get enough on the little shit for you to be able to threaten him back with a good stretch behind bars if he doesn't shut up and go.'

It was a genuine offer of help and it seemed to spring from a real concern. Wield felt himself touched.

'No,' he said, 'That won't be necessary. But thanks anyway.'

Eaton laughed.

'Oh, I'm sorry,' he said. 'Here's me teaching me grandmother to suck eggs! You've probably done courses in fitting people up!'

The momentary softening was past. The wind was blowing hard from that neighbouring valley and suddenly the flames came leaping from treetop to treetop over the crest of the hills.

'Yes,' said Wield harshly. 'I've done courses on memory and deduction as well. And I remember I never had a picture taken of me in any kind of uniform or with any kind of inscription that would show I was a copper. Someone told Sharman that, and told him my rank, and where to find me. And told him what you used to call me. That's what I remember, Maurice. And what I deduce from that is that you had a little giggle one night, lying in your pit with this young lad you took in to oblige a friend. You showed him some old photos and you said, "Can you imagine I once used to fancy *that*! And you'll never guess what he does for a living. He's a copper! Yes, really, he is." Am I right, Maurice? Is that how it was?'

'For God's sake, Mac, take it easy! Look, I can't talk now...'

'What's up, Maurice? Has someone come in? No, you mean to say there's people in this brave new fucking world of yours that you're still lying to?'

'At least there's more than half my life, and that's the most important half, that isn't a lie. Think about that, Mac. Just you bloody well think about it.'

'Maurice...'

But the phone was dead.

Wield replaced his receiver and sat with his head in his hands. He'd handled it badly from any point of view, professional or personal. One of Dalziel's dicta for police and public alike was, if you can't be honest you'd better be fucking clever. Well, he hadn't been clever, and he'd certainly not been honest. He'd not let on that Cliff was staying with him and he'd given the impression that the youth had turned up just yesterday instead of several days ago.

Several days! There he went again. It was a good week since Cliff had moved in. There had been no sexual contact offered or invited, no threats or demands from Cliff, no aggressive cross-questioning from Wield. It was truce, a limbo, the eye of the storm; whatever it was, Wield had discovered in himself a growing fear of disturbing it, and it had taken a conscious act of will for him to ring Maurice. His relief the previous evening when the stranger's voice had given him an excuse to ring off had been great, but it was his awareness of that relief which had sent him impulsively out of the Black Bull today. Had Maurice already left for lunch, he doubted if he would have found the will to try to contact him again.

Well, now he'd done it, and how much further forward was he?

He didn't know. He glanced at his watch. It was surprising how little time had elapsed. He could if he wished get back to the Black Bull in plenty of time for another pint and something to eat. But he didn't wish. Pascoe's merry quips and Dalziel's badinage was the last thing he wanted. Whatever the future held, there was work to be done here and now.

He turned to the files on his desk, a thick one entitled *Shoplifting*, a thin one labelled *Vandalism (Kemble Theatre)*. Their size was relevant to incidence, not to progress. The best he could say was that nothing needful was omitted, nothing superfluous included. He was the best keeper of records, the best drafter of reports in the CID. It occurred to him that if he came out now, either voluntarily or through pressure from Sharman, the best he could hope for would be a sideways shuffle into the dusty solitude of *Records*. He had no illusion about the degree of liberalism informing the upper reaches of the Mid-Yorkshire Force.

Well, perhaps it wouldn't be so bad. Perhaps he only imagined he enjoyed the hustle and bustle, the long hours and continuous pressures of CID work, because they filled a yawning emptiness in his life.

It seemed a reasonable hypothesis and he was a great believer in the rule of reason. But not all the reason in the world could stop him looking at the phone and wishing that it would ring and he would pick it up and hear a voice say, 'Hello, Mac. Cliff here. How're you doing?'

Cliff Sharman dialled. The phone rang eight times before it was answered by a female voice slightly muffled by a half-masticated sandwich.

'*Mid-Yorks Evening Post*, good morning, sorry, afternoon!'

'I'd like to talk to one of your reporters,' said Sharman.

'Anyone in particular, love? Thing is, they're mostly out at lunch.'

'Someone in your investigation department,' said the youth tentatively.

The voice giggled.

'Are you sure it's not the *Washington Post* you're after? Hang on, love. Here's Mr Ruddlesdin.'

He heard her voice call, 'Sammy!' and a man's voice reply distantly, 'Oh hell, Mavis, I'm on me way out!'

A moment later, the same voice said, 'Sam Ruddlesdin here. Can I help you, sir?'

Cliff's resolution was ebbing by the second. He'd thought of trying one of the big nationals, but they all seemed a long way from Yorkshire and also their numbers weren't in the book. He reminded himself that all he was dealing with here was some provincial hayseed.

He said boldly, 'Mebbe I can help you.'

'How so?'

'What's a story about a bent copper worth?'

'Bent? You mean gay! Or crooked?'

'Both,' he extemporized. 'His bosses don't know he's gay, so he's got to be crooked to keep it quiet, know what I mean?'

'Who are his bosses?'

'Well, he's a detective, isn't he?'

'Local?'

'Yeah, that's why I'm ringing you and not one of the big papers, see? So what's it worth?'

'It depends, sir,' said Ruddlesdin. 'What's his rank?'

'Higher than constable and that's all I'm telling you for nothing. Come on, let's talk money!'

'It's a bit hard over the phone, sir. Why don't we meet and chat it over? I didn't quite catch your name…'

'You chat it over with yourself! I'll be in touch again later. Maybe!'

Sharman slammed the receiver down. He was surprised to find he was trembling slightly. He wasn't sure yet how far he intended going with this, but it was Wield's own fault, that was sure. He obviously didn't trust him. He'd been there over a week now, and the ugly bastard hadn't laid a hand on him. He was obviously scared of compromising himself. Stupid sod, as if there wasn't enough on him already to rattle him around the cop-shop like a ping-pong ball. He'd thought of suggesting as much to his face, but then he'd lost his nerve. Direct blackmail wasn't something he'd care to attempt, not with a man like Wield. In any case, he told himself pathetically, all he wanted was a bit of trust, a bit of support, a bit of affection even. He'd not come up here looking for trouble, but if Wield couldn't take him on trust, he'd fucking well have to take him the other way.

He went out of the phone-box and started wandering round the streets as he had done every day since his arrival, scanning the faces that he met in search of the one face that would bring his searching to an end.

Sammy Ruddlesdin drank his lunch in solitude and thought long and hard about the phone call. He had a good nose for news and could sniff out the iron pyrites from the true gold with ninety per cent accuracy.

When the pub closed at 2.30, he went back to the office, arriving simultaneously with the editor.

The editor too respected Sammy's nose, but when he had digested the story he shook his head and said, 'Not our cup of tea, Sammy. I'm not going to risk getting up yon mad bugger Dalziel's hairy nostrils for anything less than a full-scale scandal. He doesn't just look like an elephant, he's got a memory like one, and we've got to live in this town.'

'What if it is a full-scale scandal?'

'Then it's too big for us. That's *Challenger* material. I'll give Ike Ogilby a bell. Anything more comes through, we'll follow it up in conjunction with one of his whizz-kids.'

Ruddlesdin looked disgruntled and the editor laughed.

'Don't look so unhappy, Sammy,' he said. 'It'll probably come to nothing. But if it does, is it worth losing that nice friendly relationship you and that Inspector Pascoe have got just for what sounds like a rather squalid splash?'

Sammy scratched his long nose.

'I suppose not,' he said.

The editor smiled with the complacency of papal infallibility, picked up the phone and said, 'Get me Mr Ogilby in Leeds, love.'

Ruddlesdin went about his business. It was true he did feel rather disgruntled, but he was if nothing else a positive thinker.

The editor was right. Why fall out with the fuzz over something like this? In fact the clever thing to do might be to plant it firmly in the lap of those chancers on the *Challenger* and get himself in credit for a bit of a favour at the same time.

He went out of the building to a pay-phone and dialled a number.

'Inspector Pascoe, please... Sammy Ruddlesdin, *Evening Post*. Hello, Peter. Listen, it's probably nowt but you've done me a few favours in the past, so I thought I'd just let you know. Got this odd phone call...'

CHAPTER 7

Yorkshire is the only English cricket club which still requires its players to be born in county limits. Foreigners, however long domiciled, can never be trusted not to revert to playing the game for pleasure.

A similar high seriousness of approach is required of Yorkshire publicans and John Huby was well qualified to open the batting for any county side of licensed victuallers.

'John, love, it's turned six,' said Ruby Huby.

'Oh aye.'

'Shall I open up? There's a car in the car park.'

'So what? Let the bugger wait!' said Huby, continuing to stack bottles of light ale on his bar shelves.

Ruby Huby looked anxiously out of the window. Happily the newcomer did not seem impatient. He was standing by his car examining with speculative interest the foundations of the restaurant and function room extension which, begun in anticipation of Aunt Gwen's will, looked like being its first casualty.

'Right,' said Huby looking round to make sure everything was as serious and sombre as it should be. 'Let him in. But he'd best not want owt fancy. I'm not in the mood.'

As 'fancy' when John Huby was not in the mood could include any mixture from a gin and tonic to a shandy, the odds on a clash seemed high.

Fortunately the man who entered, in his thirties with a dark beard, a mop of strong crinkly hair and a broad-shouldered athletic-looking torso, had driven far enough to develop a simple thirst.

'What's your pleasure?' asked Huby challengingly.

'Pint of best, please,' said the man in a soft Scottish accent.

Mollified, Huby drew a pint. First of the night, it was rather cloudy. He looked speculatively at the stranger, who looked speculatively back, sighed, drew another, got a clear one at the third time of asking and handed it over.

'Cheers,' said the man.

He drank and looked round the bar. The landlord's ambition for development had clearly not begun here. The furniture and fittings would probably have pleased Betjeman. Even the inevitable fruit machine belonged to a pre-electronic age. There was a deep recessed fireplace which contained real coal piled on real sticks ready for lighting, if and when the landlord decided his customers deserved it. On the brick hearth lay a sleeping Yorkshire terrier. A stout woman of mid to late forties was bustling around the room, laying out ashtrays and a girl in her late teens with a mass of springy blonde curls and an even greater mass of even springier bosom was polishing glasses behind the bar. She caught his eye and smiled invitingly. Pleased at this first sign of welcome, the stranger smiled back.

Huby, intercepting the exchange, snapped, 'Jane, if you've nowt better to do than stand about grinning, bring us some fresh martini up. We'll mebbe be getting a rush of the gentry tonight.'

The stranger put his glass down on the bar.

'Mr John Huby, is it?' he asked.

'That's what it says over the door.'

'My name is Goodenough, Mr Huby. Andrew Goodenough. I am the general secretary of the People's Animal Welfare Society. You may recall that the Society was mentioned in your late aunt's will.'

'Oh aye, I recall that well enough,' said Huby grimly.

'Yes. I fear it must have been something of a disappointment to you.'

'Disappointment, Mr Goodenough? No, I'd not say that,' said Huby lifting up the bar flap and coming to the public side of the bar. 'I'd not say that. It was her brass, to do with as she liked. And she didn't forget me; no, she didn't forget me. And I'll not forget her, you can be sure of that!'

He had walked across to the fireplace, and as he spoke these last words with great vehemence, to Goodenough's horror he raised his right leg and delivered a vicious and powerful kick at the sleeping dog. The force of it drove the animal against the brickwork with a sickening thud.

'For Christ's sake, man!' cried the animal protectionist, then his protest faded as he realized the dog, though now on its back, still retained its sleeping posture.

'Can I introduce you to Gruff-of-sodding-Greendale?' snarled Huby. 'I were going to stick it on the fire at first, but then I thought: No, I'll keep the thing. It'll lie there as a lesson to me not to waste time being friendly to those who don't know the meaning of gratitude or family loyalty. Now, what can I do for you, Mr Goodenough? It's not the welfare of Gruff here that's brought you all this way, is it?'

'Not exactly,' said Goodenough. 'Could we talk in private?'

'Instead of in this crowded bar, you mean? Ruby, you look after things in here when the rush starts, will you? Come through, Mr Goodenough.'

The living quarters behind the bar proved to be distinctly more comfortable than the public area, though the same air of antiquity reigned.

'Been in the family a long time, has it?' said Goodenough.

'Long enough. It were me grandad's to start with.'

'Yes. I was talking to Mrs Windibanks in London and she gave me something of the family history.'

This was enough to shatter any barrier of reticence.

'Old Windypants? What's she know about owt? Nose stuck in the air when it weren't stuck up the old girl's bum! Well, she got as little for her pains as me, so that's some consolation. But you don't want to pay any heed to owt she says about the Hubys. Listen. I'll tell you how it really was.'

He settled down in his chair and Goodenough followed suit, like the unlucky wedding guest. Though, in fact he was not incurious to hear Huby's version of the background to this old business.

The landlord began to speak.

'This place were the cottage belonging to the mill that stood behind it, alongside the river. Well, it's long gone now and it were pretty much a ruin even when my grandad got the cottage. He were just a farm lad, but he had his head screwed on, and he set up an ale house here with his sister to keep house for him. Lomas's were a small brewery then, just starting, and their eldest lad came round to try to get Grandad to sell his beer. Well, Lomas had no luck selling the beer, but Grandad's sister, Dot, took his fancy and off he went with her instead! Grandad weren't best pleased by all accounts, but there was nowt the poor devil could do except get himself married so he'd have someone to help around the place. And this is what he did, and him and grandma had twin sons, John, my dad, and Sam.'

He paused not in anticipation of any challenge to this interesting view of marriage, but to fill and light an ancient and malodorous pipe.

'Come 1914 and they both upped and offed to the war,' he resumed. 'What's more, they both came back unscathed, which was more than most families could claim. Grandma had died early on, and Grandad went too in 1919. The pub was left between 'em, but Uncle Sam had been left all restless by the war, so he took his share in cash and left Dad with the pub. Sam disappeared for a year doing God knows what. Then one day he came back, stony broke. He turned up here, asking my dad for a sub till he got on his feet again. Now Dad were a fair man, but he weren't soft. He'd got married by then and he was just about making ends meet, but only just. So he told his brother he were welcome to his supper and a bed for the night, but after that he'd have to make his own way. That sounds fair enough to me, wouldn't you say? Sam had made his bed and now he had to lie on it.'

Goodenough nodded agreement. The consequences of dispute were not to be lightly provoked. Besides, he had some real sympathy for the viewpoint.

'And what was Sam's response?'

'Well, he were a hard man too,' said Huby, not without admiration. 'He told Dad to shove his supper and wedge the bed in after it, and went right back to town the same night. Next thing Dad heard, Sam had sweet-talked Auntie Dot into making Lomas give him a job as a salesman for the brewery. That did it. Grandad would've turned in his grave. He never made it up with Dot. Always felt she gave herself airs. Well, that's what mixing with them bloody Lomases does to you, I've seen it for myself. Still, Grandad would probably have had a laugh at what happened next.'

'And what was that?' inquired Goodenough, recognizing the straight-man's cue.

'Well, Sam did well at his job, he had the gift of the gab, it seems. And not just for selling ale either. Lomas had a daughter, Gwen. Big plans for her, evidently. He'd made a pile of brass, bought Troy House in Greendale, and was in a fair way to setting himself up as a gentleman though he were no better than my grandad to start with. Gwen was going to marry a real gentleman, that was the idea. Then it happened. Her poor cousin Sam put her in the club!'

Huby chortled at the family memory.

'And that's how Sam came to marry into the Lomases?' said Goodenough.

'Aye, that was it. Lucky for them he did, too! Everyone says Lomas's would've gone under in the depression if it hadn't been for Sam. He kept 'em going and when things got better, he was the boss of the whole shooting match. By the end of the Second War they were booming and they amalgamated with one of the really big firms and went national, though they kept the name. That's what sticks in my throat! All that so-called Lomas money, it's Huby money really. They'd have been in the sodding work-house if it hadn't been for Sam.'

'Didn't he try to put any of it his brother's way, when he was doing so well?'

'Oh aye. He came round once when he were coining it. Offered to make things up. Fancy clothes, fancy car, fancy wife, he had the lot, and Dad was still just keeping things together here. Never had the money, you see. That's what this place needs. Capital. Brass breeds brass, that's the way of it.'

He stared gloomily towards the window where the beginning of the extension stood silent in the evening sunshine.

'And your father's response?'

'What do you think?' snarled Huby. 'He told him to sod off again. What else could he say? Well, that did it!'

'I suppose it would,' said Goodenough. 'Now, about your uncle's son, your cousin, the missing heir...'

'Missing?' exclaimed Huby. 'Bugger's as dead as Gruff-of-sodding-Greendale, and everyone knows it. She knew it too, I reckon, only her conscience wouldn't let her believe it.'

'Conscience?' said Goodenough, puzzled.

'Oh aye. Between her and Sam, the poor devil had a hell of a life. *Her* wanting him to be a proper gentleman, *him* wanting him to be a proper he-man!'

'And what did Alexander want?'

'Just to be a lad, I reckon. I didn't know him well though we were born within a month of each other. He went off to some fancy school, of course, while I just went local, and only when they caught me! But we'd bump into each other in the holidays sometimes and I'd say *how do?* and he'd say *hello*, all very polite, like. Being of an age, we got called up at the same time in 1944. We went off on the same train and did our basic at the same depot, so it were natural we should chum up a bit, being cousins. He asked what I wanted to do. Stay alive, I said. I were good with engines and so on, so I was looking for a berth in the REME and I got it too, ended up a Lance-jack at a depot down near Tunbridge. He sounded dead envious when I told him this. What about you? I said. He was going for an officer, he said. His mother would like that, the uniform and people sirring him and all. And then he thought he might volunteer for training as one of them Commandos. I looked at him as if he were daft. Anyone less like a Commando I couldn't imagine. But he did it, the poor sod. I heard later his dad were chuffed to buggery. My son, the officer, Gwen would say in that hoity voice of hers. My lad, the Commando, Sam would say. Well, between 'em, they did for the poor sod. Me, I never left these shores. Him, he's picked clean on the bed of the Med by now. Sam finally accepted it. She never did. Couldn't. She knew whose fault it was he ended up like he did.'

With this interesting bit of deep analysis, Huby seemed well satisfied. His pipe had gone out and now he relit it.

'But you were reconciled with your uncle's family to some extent,' prompted Goodenough.

Huby laughed and said, 'I thought so. Our dad died in 1958. Uncle Sam came to the funeral. I talked to him man to man. Well, it weren't my quarrel. Me and Ruby got invited to tea a short while after. That were a frosty affair, I tell you. But I said to myself, I can thole frost if it's going to bring brass. I even started selling Lomas ales in the pub. Me dad must've turned in his grave! Then just as I felt I were getting on champion with uncle Sam, what does he do but keel over and die, not a six-month after our dad! Well, her ladyship got the lot, not a penny for any bugger else. But fair do's, I said. It were hers by right. And didn't she get hold of me after the funeral and say it'd been her Sam's particular wish that this new friendliness between our families should continue and she'd like me and Ruby to come to tea? But she'd not changed, not her!'

'What do you mean?' said Goodenough.

'Guilt! That's all it was. Like she knew she'd buggered her lad up, now she must've wondered if she'd helped push Sam into the grave. All right, it sounds daft. But why'd she do it, else? More than five-and-twenty years of having us to tea once a month. For what? I'll tell you for what, from my point of view. Gruff-of-sodding-Greendale, that's what!'

He banged his pipe against the wall so hard he left a mark in the plaster.

Goodenough said, 'I sympathize with you, believe me.'

'Do you now? Well, that's good on you. But you've not come all this say to sympathize, have you? What are you, any road? Some kind of lawyer?'

'To some extent,' smiled Goodenough who, under parental misdirection, had in fact studied law instead of the veterinary science he would have preferred. When the chance had come of a poorly paid organizational job with PAWS, he had leapt at it, and in a dozen years he had helped build it up from a rather ramshackle semi-amateur body to one of the top animal charities. Large legacies like Mrs Huby's were rare, and it was his frustration at the thought of waiting all those years as much as advice from the Society's official legal advisers that had made him choose this course of action.

'Let me explain,' he said. 'We at PAWS are naturally eager to get our share of the estate sooner rather than later. To do this, we'll need to challenge the will in court and get Alexander Huby's unlikely claim put aside. You follow me?'

'You want the brass now,' said Huby. 'I can see that. What's it to do wi' me?'

'To maximize our chances of success we need to keep things simple as possible. One thing is that all three beneficiary organizations must act in concert. I've got CODRO's consent to go ahead in their name and while I'm up here, I intend sounding out these Women For Empire people.

'The second and more important is for the judge to be presented with a clear line of vision. He must be able to see that the only possible hindrance to our collecting the money in 2015 is the return of Alexander Huby, which we will then persuade him is so unlikely as to be negligible.'

Huby had been listening closely.

'What other hindrance could there be?' he asked.

'You!' said Goodenough. 'And Mrs Windibanks. You're the two closest relatives. In fact, I believe you occupy precisely the same relationship with the deceased...'

'What? She told you that, did she? Bloody liar!' cried Huby indignantly. 'The old lass were my auntie. Windypants is nowt but a sort of cousin, well removed!'

'In matters of this kind, it's blood relationships that count,' said Goodenough crisply. 'Mrs Huby was your aunt only by marriage. Mrs Windibanks's father was her cousin on the Lomas side, just as your father was on the Huby side. *That's* the relationship that matters. What I would like from you, Mr Huby, is a waiver, acknowledging that you will not be making any claim on Mrs Huby's estate, now or ever.'

The pipe hit the wall with such force, the bowl cracked wide. But Huby didn't seem to notice.

'Well, bugger me,' he said. 'Is that all? Bugger me!'

'Yes, it isn't really much to ask, is it?' said Goodenough, deliberately misunderstanding. 'I mean, I assume you've already consulted your own solicitor and been advised on the feasibility of contesting the will on your own behalf.'

'That's my business,' growled Huby.

'Of course it is. I do not wish to pry. But if his advice was that it would be such a chancy business that it was hardly worth risking the necessarily large legal costs, and if you have decided to accept this advice, then what do you have to lose by signing the waiver?'

'What do I have to *gain*, that's more to the point,' said Huby cunningly.

'There would possibly be a small compensatory payment for your time and trouble,' said Goodenough.

He was disappointed but not too surprised when instead of asking *How much?* Huby said, 'You say you've spoken to old Windypants?'

'To Mrs Windibanks, yes.'

'What's *she* say?'

'She's mulling it over, but I've no doubt she will make the wise decision.'

'Well, I'll tell you what,' said Huby. 'I learnt early not to jump when lawyers crack the whip. So I think I'll do a bit of mulling too. You've got other business up here, you say? Well, call back in a day or so, and I'll mebbe be better placed to make a decision.'

Goodenough sighed. He'd been hoping that need and greed might have made the man grab at a cash offer, but he judged that to make one now would merely be to weaken his position.

'Very well,' he said, rising. 'Thank you for your hospitality.'

'What? I've given you nowt, have I?' For some reason this seemed to touch his conscience and he added magnanimously, 'Listen, have a glass of beer on your way out, tell Ruby I say it's on the house.'

'Thank you, but the one was enough. I noticed, incidentally, you no longer serve Lomas's?'

'No! I had the bloody stuff taken out right after the funeral,' snarled Huby. 'Can you find your own way? Good night, then.'

After the door closed behind Goodenough, Huby sat in silence for several minutes staring sightlessly into the fireplace. He was roused by his wife saying, 'Phone, John!'

He went through the bar to the pay-phone in the entrance passage. It was a continuous complaint of Jane's that they didn't have a phone of their own, but the more she complained, the more Huby was confirmed in his economic policy.

'Old Mill,' he grunted into the receiver. 'Huby speaking.'

He listened for a while and a slow grin spread across his face.

'I were just thinking about you, Mrs Windibanks,' he said finally. 'Fancy that, eh? You're at the Howard Arms, you say. Well, it's a bit hard for me to get away from the pub tonight... you'll come out? Grand, that'll be grand. Always glad to have a chat with a relative, that's me.'

He put the phone down and laughed out loud. But his amusement died as he tried to refill his pipe and discovered the cracked bowl.

'Bloody hell!' he exclaimed. 'What rotten bugger's done that?'

CHAPTER 8

'Good morning, Lexie.'

'Good morning, Miss Keech.'

Pascoe, as the nearest thing in Mid-Yorkshire to a socio-logical detective, might have read much into this exchange. Miss Keech's connection with the Hubys had started as a fourteen-year-old in 1930 when she had been taken on at Troy House as a nursery maid. By the time young Alexander left for boarding-school some eight years later, she was fully in charge of not only the nursery but most of the household management. Came the war, and young, fit unmarried women were called upon to do more for their country than look after the houses of the rich and, despite Mrs Huby's indignant protests, Miss Keech was sucked into the outside world. Contact was lost, though it was known through her local connections that she had risen to the dizzy heights of being a WRAC driver with two stripes. Then in 1946 she returned to Troy House to convey her sorrow at the sad news of Alexander's loss and there she had stayed ever since, first as housekeeper, gradually as companion, eventually as nurse.

Mrs Gwendoline Huby called her *Keech*. Alexander Huby had called her *Keechie*. John Huby generally called her nothing to her face and 'that cold calculating cow' to her back. It irked him greatly to hear old Windypants using her surname as to the manner born, and even more to hear her poncy son drawling out *Keechie* as if he'd got a silver spoon stuck in his gob!

To the Old Mill girls, she was always *Miss Keech*, which was right and proper, for children should be polite to adults, however undeserving; but Huby did nothing to discourage their private conviction, fostered by the more imaginative and better-read Lexie, that this dark-clad figure was really the Wicked Witch of the West.

'Notice the *Beurre Hardy*, Lexie. In all the years I have been at Troy House, I do not believe I have seen a more bountiful crop.'

Lexie duly noted the pear tree. She did not resent Miss Keech's gubernatorial manner, nor was she offended (as her father claimed to be) by such a pedantic style and affected accent in one of such humble origins. But she hadn't liked Miss Keech from her earliest memories of her, and had been consistent in this dislike as in most things.

The feeling, she suspected, was mutual. Only once had it come near to open declaration. On visiting Sundays, the two girls were normally allowed to escape after tea and play in the garden with Hob, the donkey, and the two goats. On wet days, they would descend into the capacious cellar which was used for storage of old furniture and other junk. Well lit and relatively dry, it provided a marvellous playroom for the children. At one end of it was a small oaken door with a Norman arch which looked as if it should have been in a fairytale castle, and Lexie invented various enthralling tales of what lay beyond for her wide-eyed sister. Then one day as she finished one of her stories, she became aware of Miss Keech standing at the head of the cellar stairs.

'Is Lexie right, Miss Keech?' piped up Jane. 'Is there really a magic garden through that door?'

'Oh no, Jane,' said Keech in a matter-of-fact tone. 'That's where we keep the old bodies of everyone who's died here.'

The effect had been devastating. Jane had fled from the cellar and refused ever to go down there again. On wet Sundays thereafter they had found themselves constrained to sit in the dull drab drawing-room looking at dull drab books. Miss Keech had told Jane not to be silly, but Lexie had detected the edge of malicious satisfaction there and knew it was directed at her. She had boldly demanded the key to the oaken door from Miss Keech, ready to explode her own fairytales in the cause of revealing Miss Keech's lie. The woman had produced it without hesitation, saying, 'Of course you may look inside, Lexie. But you must go by yourself. I have no time for such childishness.'

Again the malice. She had known full well that a small girl of eight, no matter how self-possessed, was not impervious to such imaginative fears.

But Lexie had descended alone. Terror had weakened her skinny legs, but something stronger than terror had urged her on. There was no way she could articulate it, but it had something to do with a sense of what was right.

The door had swung open without even a creak to reveal a smaller inner cellar lined with wine racks, empty since Sam Huby's death. His widow admitted a little sweet sherry in the drawing-room but had no need of wine. As for Lomas's beers on which her fortune rested, she had tasted a light ale once at the age of twenty, and never repeated the disagreeable experience.

Lexie had gone to fetch Jane to show her the truth of the matter, but the words of an adult are stronger than the word of a sister, and Jane had only collapsed in tearful refusal while Miss Keech looked on in silent triumph, knowing she had ruined the cellar for them for ever.

All that had been ages ago, but it had stamped a seal on their relationship. Only once had Lexie had cause to waver in her judgment and that was three years ago when Great Aunt Gwen had had her first stroke. The degree of Miss Keech's distress had amazed everyone. 'Must know she's been left out of the will!' John Huby had posited mockingly. But the woman's concern and agitation and unsparing attendance on her sick employer had impressed most observers deeply, causing even Lexie to admit a slight modification of her judgment.

'Is Mr Lomas, Rod, ready?' she now asked.

'Just completing his breakfast. Have you time for a cup of coffee? Do step inside in any case.'

It was Lexie's first visit to Troy House since the funeral meats. Externally, the square, grey Victorian building was little changed. The well-kept garden with its gloomy shrubberies still had the goats on long tethers at the foot of the lawn while Hob the donkey grazed nearby, indifferent and free.

Inside, however, there were signs of change, subtle but significant. Several of the doors off the large but gloomy entrance hall were closed for a start. In Great Aunt Gwen's time, no door and few windows were ever closed as this interfered with her animals' right to total access to every part of the house. Also the hall itself was surely not quite so gloomy as before. The heavy velvet drapes which, even when drawn open, still inhibited ninety per cent of the light entering via the stained-glass windows on either side of the door, had disappeared, and on the dark green silk wallpaper two lighter rectangles showed where half-length portraits of King Edward and Queen Alexandra had glowered out of gilded frames these past seventy-odd years.

The kitchen had changed too, but not subtly. There were bright new chintzy curtains at the windows, a new sink unit in stainless steel had replaced the ancient deep-crazed pot one, yellow and white vinyl tiles covered the old stone floor and there was a new drop-leaf formica table in bright blue in place of the old solid-state wooden one which had impeded passage for all but the very slimmest.

At this table sat Rod Lomas, drinking coffee and smoking a cigarette.

'Lexie,' he said, 'you must be early.'

'You've got two minutes,' she said.

'Time for another coffee, then,' he replied.

She didn't answer but stared at him with that expression of nervous determination he was beginning to recognize.

'All right,' he said, rising. 'I'll get my jacket.'

He left the room. Miss Keech poured a cup of coffee and handed it to Lexie. The Old Mill Inn girls had always thought of her as old, but today, aged about seventy, she looked somehow younger than Lexie could ever recall. It was perhaps the touch of colour which varied the hitherto unbroken blackness of her clothing; a red silk scarf at her neck, a diamanté brooch at her bosom.

'You've got the kitchen nice,' said Lexie.

'Thank you. It's never too late for change, is it?'

Lexie sipped her coffee and did not reply.

Miss Keech laughed, and this was as surprising as the vinyl tiles and the red scarf.

'You must come again, Lexie, and talk over old times.'

This time Lexie was saved from having to answer by Lomas calling, 'Ready!' from the entrance hall.

'Thank you for the coffee,' was all she said as she left, but Miss Keech only responded to this evasion with that surprising laugh once more.

Outside, Lomas, though not particularly tall, made a great business of folding himself into the Mini.

'This is a most selfish kind of car for you to drive,' he complained. 'Can't you afford something larger?'

'I can't afford this,' said Lexie, accelerating to the forty m.p.h. which both her own caution and the car's limitations dictated was the optimum maximum speed.

'But your mad social life demands that you have wheels,' mocked Lomas.

Lexie replied seriously, 'The buses don't run very late from town. And I like to get across to Leeds quite a lot.'

'What excitements keep you late in town and take you across to licentious Leeds?'

'I like to go to concerts,' said Lexie. 'And they've got the opera at Leeds.'

'Good lord!' said Lomas. 'Of course. The will! Auntie Gwen left you all her operatic records. It struck me as odd when I saw that.'

'Odd to leave them to someone like me?' said Lexie.

'Well, not exactly that...'

'It would seem odd, I suppose,' said Lexie. 'But she knew I liked music. She made Dad send me to piano lessons. Dad thought they were a waste of time, but she said a girl should have music. He didn't argue with her, but he kept on at me about the expense.'

'So you've got more reason to be grateful to Gwen than most of us,' mused Lomas.

'Not really. When Dad said it was a waste of time for me to stay on at school, she backed him up there. Education was for men; girls had to settle for accomplishments like drawing and playing the piano, and then get married and settle down to mothering handsome, talented boys.'

'Do I detect a bitter note?'

'Mebbe. But I was grateful about the lessons, even if I got them for the wrong reasons. And I don't play bad. Great Aunt Gwen liked me to play for her, and sing a bit too. That's how I started with the opera.'

'And you drive all the way to Leeds in this antique just to listen to that caterwauling? You're full of surprises, little Lexie. What about *real* art? The Theatre? Shakespeare!'

'Yes, I quite like it,' she said seriously. 'But music is different, isn't it? I mean, it takes you out of...'

She glanced down at her skinny frame and Lomas felt an upsurge of pity.

'You look jolly nice to me,' he said gallantly.

She looked at him in puzzlement and said, 'Do I?'

'Yes, you do. I'll be proud to have you along as a family claque on my first night next Monday. With Mummy, of course.'

'She's staying that long, is she?'

'You knew she was here?' said Lomas in surprise. 'I didn't know myself till last night.'

'She's been out to the Old Mill to talk to Dad,' said Lexie. 'Jane told me when I got home from my class.'

'Has she now? I've not seen her myself. I just got a message via Keechie inviting me to lunch at the Howard Arms today. She doesn't let grass grow under her feet, does she? And what do you imagine Mummy and your father found to talk about?'

'Don't know. He didn't tell me,' said Lexie, though as Jane had also told her about Andrew Goodenough's visit, she was able to make a guess.

She dropped Lomas outside the theatre. As she got out of the car, he leaned forward and kissed her on the lips. It was done too quickly for her to take evasive action and her small gasp of surprise only rendered the kiss a little less cousinly. She was careful not to crash her gears as she drove away.

In the office, she found Eden Thackeray already at his desk. He had been in a strange, almost distracted mood the previous afternoon but now he seemed back to normal.

'Lexie, my dear. Would you get me the police on the phone? Detective-Superintendent Dalziel.'

A few moments later Lexie heard a voice like a mastiff's roused from slumber growl, 'Dalziel.'

She put her employer on.

'Hello. Eden Thackeray. Listen, I was just wondering if you could spare the time to have lunch with me. Yes, today. I thought the Gents at one.'

'The Gents?' said Dalziel dubiously.

A couple of years earlier he had been persuaded to apply for membership of The Borough Club For Professional Gentlemen, having been a guest several times and expressed appreciation of the solid fare, cheap booze and plentiful snooker tables. To the embarrassment of his sponsors, some member had exercised his right of the anonymous blackball and Dalziel had vowed never to go near the place again unless through a pole-axed door at the head of a vice-squad raid.

'Yes, I know there was that unfortunate business, but the villain responsible will surely be more pained by your presence than your absence.'

It was the right psychological approach.

Dalziel said, 'Right. One o'clock it is.'

Putting the phone down, he demanded of the empty air before him, 'And what does that cunning old sod want?'

The air did not reply.

In the middle of the morning, Andrew Goodenough turned up for his appointment with Eden Thackeray.

When Lexie took in the coffee and biscuits a few minutes later the two men were already down to business.

'I already have CODRO's agreement to proceed in this business and I have made an appointment to see Mrs Falkingham of WFE in Ilkley early this evening when her assistant, Miss Brodsworth, will be present. I don't anticipate any objection there. I've conferred with the two nearest relatives, Mrs Windibanks and Mr John Huby...'

Thackeray coughed discreetly.

'My secretary here is Mr Huby's elder daughter,' he said.

'Oh,' said Goodenough uncertainly. 'How do you do?'

'I'm very well, thanks,' said Lexie. 'Sugar?'

'No.'

After Lexie had left, Thackeray said, 'You may rely on her discretion, I believe. And in any case there can be no clash of interest. I know Huby's solicitor and I do not doubt that his advice has been that to make a claim on his own behalf would be a waste of money. No doubt you will be offering an *ex gratia* compensatory payment...'

He smiled. Goodenough smiled back.

'Negotiations have been opened,' he said. 'They are a matched pair when it comes to bargaining, Windibanks and Huby. I'm only glad they're not working in concert. Still, I don't doubt we will reach an accord. Which leaves only one question to be considered by the learned judge hearing our suit. Is there any mathematically significant possibility of Mrs Huby's son turning up to claim his inheritance? That's what I'm here to ask you, Mr Thackeray. I presume Mrs Huby was assiduous in pursuit of evidence that her son was alive, and no doubt she confided the results of her researches to you.'

'You mean you would like to use Mrs Huby's efforts to prove her son was alive in order to prove he must be dead?' murmured Thackeray. 'Now, *there's* ingenious. Still, for once I see no harm in frankness. Do you know about the advertisement?'

Goodenough shook his head.

'Well, it happened like this. Three years ago, Mrs Huby had a serious stroke. For a while, it was thought she might die, but in fact she made an excellent recovery, in body at least. Mentally, there was a little vagueness, plus, and this was the significant thing, a strong delusion that the stroke had been deliberately provoked by a malicious demon, masquerading as her son!'

'Good God!' exclaimed Goodenough.

'Don't worry,' smiled Thackeray. 'The will had been in existence too long before this for the question of unsound mind to arise. But she was now convinced that the devil in all his black malice was bent on striking her down so that she would remain alive but be incapable of pursuing the search for Alexander. Therefore she devised an advertisement to be placed in the papers in the event of another stroke. I helped her to a form of words I thought likely to provoke fewest fraudulent replies. She'd advertised before, of course, and I dare say spent a pretty penny in buying useless information from mountebanks. This time, respondents were instructed to get in touch with me. The advert gave her name, said that she was seriously ill and not expected to recover, and was placed in all the main Italian papers.'

'Just Italian.'

'Yes. She wanted it worldwide, but I persuaded her to limit it to Italy. That's where her son went missing and that was where she was convinced he'd remained.'

'Did you get any replies to the ad?' asked Goodenough.

'A few. All quite obviously frivolous or fraudulent. Then at her funeral, a man appeared...'

'What kind of man?' demanded Goodenough.

'Sunburnt. Lightweight Italian suit. The same rather square face that John Huby has. He knelt at the graveside and cried out *Mama!* It caused quite a stir, I can assure you.'

'I can imagine,' said Goodenough, enthralled. 'What happened?'

'Nothing. Well, many things, but nothing as far as the mysterious stranger was concerned. He just disappeared in the confusion. No one saw him again and I think we'd all decided he was best forgotten. Until yesterday.'

'Yesterday?'

'That's right,' said Thackeray. 'I found him in this office. He claimed he was Alexander Huby. He didn't stay long. He seemed strangely nervous, or perhaps it wasn't so strange after all. He promised to return with proof positive of his identity. Well, he has not yet reappeared. But the significant thing from your point of view, Mr Goodenough, is that before he left, he had said enough to persuade me that he could present a case to be answered. Impostor he may be, but unprepared he is not, believe me!'

CHAPTER 9

Deputy Chief Constable Neville Watmough sat in the bar of The Borough Club for Professional Gentlemen and sipped his sherry. This of all places in the world was where he felt most at home, and he didn't exclude home. Here he was in the true power centre of the city. Only a few yards away sat Councillor Mottram, local magnate and, more importantly, chairman of the Police Committee who would shortly be interviewing him. He had greeted Mottram warmly, as a fellow clubman, but not over-effusively, and made no effort to join the councillor and the young man who was his guest. Mottram, he hoped, would appreciate this refusal to do anything which might smack of canvassing support.

But that he would receive it, he had no doubt. Was he not, after all, known to the man as a respected fellow member of the Gents, long-time committee man, and soon to be President-elect? He must surely also be regarded as Chief Constable-Elect! Everyone knew that Tommy Winter had been demob happy for nigh on two years and he, Neville Watmough, had been running the show single-handed. He had missed no opportunity of expressing his frank and unqualified belief in police accountability. Liaison with the Police Committee had never been closer and no opportunity had been missed to urge upon its members the high quality of policing in Mid-Yorkshire, its smooth traffic flow, its efficient administration, even its above-average detection rate. If you want to see my memorial, look around you! thought Watmough grandiloquently.

And you need not look too far either. It was one of his most laudatory though least advertised triumphs that when some ill-advised and irresponsible members had proposed Dalziel for the Gents, Watmough had blackballed him without a second thought.

Here perhaps was the last safe place. Here he could sit in peace, contemplating the sunlit heights of a political future as he waited for the guest who was going to help pilot him there.

That guest entered the bar at that moment, a small dark man in his mid-thirties, his every movement eloquent of that restless energy which was his most obvious characteristic.

'Neville! There you are!'

'Ike! Nice to see you again.'

Ike Ogilby, editor of the *Sunday Challenger*, shook Watmough's hand warmly, then gestured to the young man who had followed him rather diffidently into the room.

'Neville, I hope you don't mind, but I brought one of my bright young things to meet you. Henry Vollans, Neville Watmough, Deputy Chief Constable and soon to be Chief, we all hope!'

Casting an anxious look towards the chairman of the Police Committee who happily seemed not to have heard this perhaps over-confident assertion, Watmough shook the young man's hand.

'Let's have a drink,' he said. 'Ike, your usual? Mr Vollans, you'll join us?'

'No, really. I was just going to be in the area seeing a colleague on the *Evening Post* this lunch-time and Mr Ogilby thought I should meet you. I've got to dash now.'

'See you back at the factory, Henry,' said Ogilby.

'Yes, sir. It'll probably be late. I'm going back via Ilkley, remember.'

'Yes, fine. Cheers.'

Vollans left. Watmough ordered Ogilby a Scotch and soda.

'Pleasant young chap,' he said. 'Grooming him for the big time, are we?'

'Not particularly,' smiled Ogilby. 'I just like to put my boys in direct touch with the real power sources wherever I can. Never know when your name might come in useful. He could be parked on a double yellow at this very moment!'

The two men laughed, both of them knew that what they were joking about was a basic truth.

Their liaison went back several years. On an official level it was easy to justify on both sides. The *Challenger* got the news and the Force got the image. Everyone was happy.

But each of the men nursed other, longer-term motives.

For the present, Watmough relied on the paper to give him a good neutral press, giving offence to neither the Arcadian Squirearchy to the North of his area nor to the People's Republic to the South. But once the Chief's job was his, then he wouldn't care who he offended! He intended to become a national figure. Four or five years of pontificating on Law and Order via the media in general and the *Challenger* in particular would see him ready for the next big step—Westminster!

Ogilby didn't much mind how Watmough's career developed. To be going on with, there was a constant stream of inside information which could be more inside still if he made Chief Constable. And if he then ended up in Parliament, well, no journalist ever objected to have a close relationship with an ambitious MP. Even if his dreams came to nothing, Ogilby reckoned there'd still be a nice juicy series of memoirs for the *Challenger* to serialize. *Top Cop Tells All*. Watmough would have been surprised to know how closely documented were all the off-the-record juicy bits imparted to Ogilby over the years, ready as an aide-memoire for his chosen 'ghost'.

Meanwhile they consorted like lovers in a space-capsule, each certain he was on top.

'Good of you to come so far,' said Watmough.

'Not at all. It's only forty minutes and I wanted to pop into the *Post* anyway. Besides, I always enjoy eating here.'

Privately Ogilby regarded the Gents as something Dornford Yates might have invented on a bad day or P G. Wodehouse on a good one, but he lied with the ease of occupational practice.

'Good. Let's go through, shall we? Bring your drink.'

They made their way out of the bar and into the long, rather chilly dining-room which had something of the smell of a school refectory.

Here Watmough halted so suddenly that Ogilby got jammed beside him in the doorway.

'Sorry,' said the DCC in the voice of one who has drunk and seen the spider. 'No, George, could we stay up at this end, please?'

This last was to the catering manager who was trying to usher Watmough to his usual privileged window table, but he had no desire whatsoever to sit there today, for at the next table along slumped the huge bulk of Andrew Dalziel.

He looked up now, saw Watmough and waved the lamb chop he had just impaled on his fork.

'I see the cabaret's arrived,' he said to Eden Thackeray.

Thackeray glanced towards Watmough and nodded his head, perhaps in greeting, perhaps in agreement. He was adept at such ambiguity, and he recognized the dangers of both alliance with and opposition to Dalziel.

The two men had known each other professionally for a long time and though superficially they were poles apart, they had discovered in each other a sound core of realism and common sense.

Dalziel emptied his wine glass, Thackeray emptied the bottle of *Fleurie* into it and waggled it at the caterer, who a moment later advanced with a new one.

'Right,' said Dalziel. 'Now we've established that I'm in profit even if I've got to tell you to sod off, what is it you want?'

'I have a problem,' said Thackeray. 'Does the name Huby mean anything to you? Gwendoline Huby.'

'Let's see,' said Dalziel. 'Weren't she that daft old bird who left her brass to a son who got killed in the war? I read about it in the papers.'

'That's the one. Now, the thing is, yesterday a chap actually turned up at my Chambers claiming to be the man.'

'Oh aye? How much brass is there?'

'Getting on for a million and a half, depending on the market.'

'Jesus!' exclaimed Dalziel. 'With that kind of money I'm surprised you haven't had queues like the January sales.'

'Yes. There have, of course, been several quite obviously crank letters. But the thing about this chap is that at first sight he is extremely plausible. And frankly, Dalziel, I find myself in a quandary as to how to proceed.'

Dalziel regarded him steadily.

'Me too,' he said.

'Really?'

'Aye. Shall I start calling you Thackeray if you call me Dalziel? I don't mind, but it doesn't come easy off my tongue.'

Thackeray looked bewildered, then began to smile.

'Would Eden come any easier, Superintendent?'

'Andy,' said Dalziel. 'Now we've got things on a proper friendly basis, see if you can tell us what you want without going all round the houses.'

'I'm not sure. Let me put it this way. My main concern as Mrs Huby's solicitor and as executor of her will is to see that her wishes are carried out.

'Now, this man turns up and claims to be the heir. I am practically certain that he cannot be the heir, yet he has contrived to sow a seed of doubt. It would be easy for me to say to him, no, go away, you are fraudulent unto such time as you prove you are not. I could pull all obstacles of the law in his way and force him to choose between abandoning his claim or setting out on a long, tedious and extremely expensive path to a very doubtful conclusion.'

'I'm with you,' said Dalziel. 'You don't think that's your job, right?'

'My job is to carry out my client's wishes, and I have serious doubts as to whether that would be the nearest way to doing that.'

'Bugger me,' said Dalziel. 'I never thought I'd hear a lawyer wanting to do what was nearest rather than what was dearest.'

'I am full of surprises. You're probably wondering how you can help me, Dalziel—sorry; Andy.'

'No. I'm wondering how you imagine I can help you,' said Dalziel with the easy confidence of a man who could without embarrassment reject the appeal of a molested maiden if something important, like opening time, diverted his attention. 'And while you're choosing your words, I think I saw there was mum's trifle on the menu. I'm always in a better mood for a slab of mum's trifle.'

Meanwhile at the other table, after some preliminary indecision as to whether he should sit with his face towards Dalziel and be continually reminded of his presence, or with his back towards him and risk being stolen upon unawares, Watmough had compromised with a sideways seat and had soon lulled himself into forgetfulness with that most soothing of music, his own harmonic future.

Ogilby contented himself with reassurance and optimistic agreement throughout the brown windsor and well into the steak and kidney pudding. He felt he'd gone quite far enough when Watmough said, 'Mid-Yorks is a good force and a clean force, and people in the know will give credit where it's due, Ike. I've carried this lot, you know that. Old Tommy Winter's been demob-happy for two years at least.'

'Everyone knows you're a great administrator, Nev,' said Ogilby.

'Not just an administrator,' retorted Watmough. 'Round here they've not forgotten the Pickford case.'

I bet they bloody haven't! thought Ogilby with an inward groan. The Pickford case had been Watmough's finest hour. It had happened a few years earlier when Watmough was Assistant Chief Constable in South Yorkshire. A seven-year-old Wakefield girl, Mary Brook, had gone missing. A friend thought she'd seen her getting into a car which might have been a blue Cortina. Four weeks later her body was found in a shallow grave on the moors. Then another girl, this time from Barnsley, went missing in similar circumstances, and at almost the same time, a third child vanished from the small mining town of Burrthorpe only ten miles away. Watmough took charge of the investigation, holding frequent press conferences in which he talked confidently of the modern age of detection and assured his listeners that the answer was already in the new police computer. It was just a matter of waiting for it to come out.

Not long after, a blue Cortina was discovered in a lonely country lane near Doncaster. In it was Donald Pickford, a sales representative from Huddersfield, asphyxiated by exhaust fumes. He had left a rambling incoherent letter expressing horror at what he had been compelled to do. A search of the area revealed the body of the Barnsley girl a quarter of a mile away. No reference was made to Tracy Pedley, the missing Burrthorpe girl, but there was a clear reference to Mary Brook and to another unsolved child-murder in Mid-Yorkshire some two years before.

Watmough at his final press conference made no bones about claiming to have solved just about every child-molesting case in the county over the past decade. Dalziel was heard to opine that likely Pickford was Jack the Ripper and had murdered the Princes in the Tower too, but his many enemies regarded this as sour grapes. Watmough was meanwhile flourishing a piece of computer printout at reporters and declaring, 'Look, here is the man's name. He knew we were pressing close and took the only way out. This is a triumph for modern detective methods!'

Privately, like many others, Ogilby reckoned that it wasn't difficult after the event to get any bloody name on a printout. But he already had a vested interest in Watmough, and the media as a whole had had their full quota of bungling half-wits for the week, but were a bit short on heroes. So Watmough got the vote and a month later returned triumphantly to Mid-Yorkshire as Deputy Chief Constable.

'You've not got another spectacular murder solution up your sleeve, have you, Nev?' inquired Ogilby, a touch satirically.

'No,' said Watmough, slightly miffed. 'Prevention's better than cure. A good modern force is the best deterrent, and that's what I've created.'

'Indeed yes,' said Ogilby placatingly. 'I know you've been most eloquent in your arguments for policing that reflects the changes in modern society. Talking of which, how do you feel about homosexuals?'

'Generally? Well, what I feel is, a man's entitled to his own beliefs and tastes, as long as they don't involve breaking the law, of course,' said Watmough. 'Personally, I don't much care for poofters, but I would never let that personal distaste prejudice my judgment on a legal matter, of course.'

'Of course not,' said Ogilby.

He paused, quietly savouring the moment, then resumed, 'But what I really meant, Nev, was—how do you feel about homosexual policemen? I only ask because the *Evening Post* got rung up the other day inquiring if they'd care to buy a story, about a gay copper in Mid-Yorkshire CID.'

Watmough's bout of coughing as he choked on his wine drew Dalziel's attention.

'He were weaned too early,' he said in explanation. 'Now, let me get this straight. You want me to help you check out this man's credentials? That's not police work, you know that. Hire a private eye. The estate can bear it.'

'Despite the television, as you well know, the competent and reliable private eye is a rare bird, hard to find outside Southern California, and more likely to be caged or shot at than assisted by the *carabinieri*. I need to check Signor Alessandro Pontelli's background in Florence. I need to know when he left Italy, when he came to this country, where he's staying, who he's seen. I need to compare his physical characteristics with any records that exist of Alexander Lomas. All these things can be done swiftly and easily by the police, whereas a poor solicitor…'

He smiled sadly and topped up Dalziel's *Fleurie*.

'It's the Co-ordinator for Interpol you should've asked for lunch, not me,' said Dalziel. 'My job's investigating crime, not running a where-are-they-now agency.'

'In a sense, this could be classed as a criminal investigation, surely,' murmured Thackeray.

'What sense is that?'

'If this man's making a fraudulent claim, surely that's a crime? Personation, forgery, fraud—all of these must be involved?'

'Mebbe,' said Dalziel. 'I'd need better grounds than you're giving me, though.'

'Yes. I realize that I shouldn't have asked. Still I thought, at a personal level perhaps…but never mind. I hope you've enjoyed your lunch.'

'It were grand. I always like it here,' said Dalziel.

'Time for a game of snooker after coffee, perhaps? Yes, we really need more members of your calibre, Andy.'

'Oh aye? There's at least one bugger doesn't think that!'

He glowered suspiciously towards Watmough.

'What? Oh yes. I assure you, the vast majority of the membership thought that blackballing business was a scandal. But what to do? Rules are rules, even when they're based on a silly and outmoded tradition. Have you ever thought of letting yourself be renominated?'

'I've a hard head,' said Dalziel grimly. 'And it doesn't bother me much if someone uses it once as a coconut-shy. But after that, I've sense enough to keep it down!'

'I appreciate that. But it seems such a shame. Incidentally, we've another rather silly tradition here which allows the President to have in his gift, as it were, a couple of memberships, virtually by invitation. Did you know that?'

'No.'

'Yes, it's so. I'm President-elect, by the way. My term of office starts next month. Andy, I'd be delighted if you'd give serious consideration to accepting my presidential nomination. The way it works is, the new President nominates, the new President-elect seconds, and after that it's a formality, read straight into the minutes. Indeed, it's such a formality the President-elect usually signs the forms at the start of his term with no idea who the President may nominate.'

'You know how to make a man feel wanted,' grunted Dalziel. 'Thanks, but I'll pass.'

'I'm sorry,' said Thackeray, alarmed. 'Good Lord, that did sound gratuitously offensive, didn't it? Unintentional, believe me. No, the point I was about to make is that my President-elect will be your friend Mr Watmough.'

His bland gaze met Dalziel's shrewd stare. After a while both men began to chuckle, then to laugh.

Dalziel raised his glass and through his chortles said, 'Cheers! And here's to Interpol!'

Watmough could see nothing to laugh at and felt his CID Chief's distant amusement as a personal affront.

'Of course,' Ogilby had said, 'It's not the kind of thing a local evening paper would run, but if there's a story there, the *Challenger* couldn't ignore it. I thought it only right to warn you, Nev, in view of our special relationship.'

He watched with hidden amusement as Watmough sipped his wine in an effort to lubricate his urbane chuckle. He's counting how many Sundays he's got to get through between now and the Board! he told himself.

Two, thought Watmough. Two peaceful Sabbaths, ten tranquil bloody days, that was all he asked. It was one thing to point out the smooth perfections of a well-disciplined Force and say modestly, *These are down to me;* quite another to appear as the self-advertised controller of a force split by hints of corruption and rumours of scandal.

He managed his urbane chuckle.

'There are no regulations forbidding the employment of gays as policemen,' he said. 'On the contrary, any attempt to prevent such employment could itself be a contravention of the law under the Sexual Discrimination Act.'

'Of course,' said Ogilby. 'But the implication is that there'd be a story to sell. Gays are open to blackmail, undue influence, that sort of thing. That's why the KGB are so keen to suss 'em out in the British Embassy over there. You can be caught in bed with a girl and laugh it off, but a boy's still something different. Despite Mrs Whitehouse, this is still a Puritan country.'

'You think so, do you?' said Watmough. 'What would you like, mum's trifle or Spotted Dick?'

'I think I'll skip the pudding,' said Ogilby. 'Off the record, I'll keep you posted if anything else comes up, Nev. On the record, I take it you've no idea if there is any truth in this?'

'I'm sure there's none whatsoever,' said Watmough firmly.

But I'll bloody well soon find out, he assured himself. And God help the nasty little pervert if there is!

At the far end of the room, Dalziel was still laughing.

CHAPTER 10

Neville Watmough was not the only one to be served shocks with his luncheon.

When Rod Lomas arrived at the Howard Arms to eat with his mother, he was amazed to find her on a bar stool in company with John Huby.

'Hello, darling,' said Stephanie Windibanks, offering her cheek. 'You know John, of course.'

'Of course. Hello, er, John.'

'How do,' growled Huby. 'You'll want a drink, I expect?'

'That would be kind of you,' said Lomas.

'Half a bitter,' interposed Huby rapidly. 'By God, if I had the nerve to charge these prices, I'd not have been bothered about the old girl's brass!'

As Huby paid for the beer, Lomas glanced interrogatively at his mother, who said brightly, 'Fetch that through into the dining-room with you, dear. John, I must give this child his lunch as I know he only gets the teeniest of breaks. You'll wait here and keep your eyes skinned? Let me know the moment he arrives. 'Bye for now.'

As they made their way to the dining-room, Lomas said, 'Strange bedfellows you're finding these days, Mummy.'

'Don't be vulgar. That approach I reserve for last resorts and large resources. Incidentally, I hope you haven't been having your wicked way with that anorexic child of his?'

'No fear,' grinned Lomas. 'I'm not into pædophilia. She's a strange creature, though. Not half so dumb as you might imagine.'

'That means you're getting nowhere with her and nothing out of her, I suppose. Well, keep at her. I think we're probably in the clear, but it would be useful to have an early warning system in Thackeray's office. Meanwhile, as I anticipated, the charity people are moving. I had a visit yesterday morning from a man called Goodenough who works for the animal welfare lot. He's one of those shrewd Scots terriers who will worry their way through solid rock once they get the smell of money in their nostrils. He's planning to organize a concerted action to overthrow the will as far as the time element goes. But he needs me, and the incredible hulk there, to sign affidavits renouncing any interest in the estate. The point is, we're the nearest relatives, and any action, or even threat of action, on our behalf would take precedence over the action he is proposing to bring. He wants to buy us off. The service here is not what it should be, considering its bloated prices.'

She looked around the crowded dining-room and said, 'God, you can smell the expense accounts, can't you?'

'Not on me you can't, darling,' murmured Lomas. 'Does the expectation of plenty entitle me to order the smoked salmon?'

'Plenty it won't be,' said his mother sharply. 'You'll have the prawn cocktail and be grateful.'

'How much will you screw him for, then?'

'I suggested ten per cent, but he just laughed and offered five hundred in cash. I was greatly offended. I said I was contemplating a legal action on my own behalf. He said perhaps I would like to talk to my legal adviser again. I said I certainly would. We parted.'

'And what did your legal adviser say?'

'Oh, I knew what *he* would say. I'd had Billy Fordham round to dinner a couple of nights earlier.'

'Aha. Free consultation time!'

'There is no such thing as a free consultation,' she said icily. 'Billy said if I had large funds, it might be worthwhile trying to throw the whole thing over on the grounds of Gwen's incompetence, but it was very risky and as I don't have large funds, I'd need to get someone to act for an extremely large percentage, and frankly he himself wouldn't touch it with a bargepole. But he also made the point that Goodenough's advisers must have made, that any action on my—or Huby's—part could drag on for ages, and might, just might, succeed.'

'So it's a real bargaining counter?'

'Indeed. I rang Goodenough back in mid-afternoon and discovered that he'd set off for deepest Yorkshire. I just had time to catch the next train myself. I've come with positively nothing to wear!'

Lomas looked at his mother's immaculate turnout and smiled admiringly.

'But why have you come?' he asked.

'Because I knew he would be seeing that awful man Huby and I was worried in case he settled for a large Scotch and a fiver and ruined the market. I phoned him as soon as I arrived, and sure enough, Goodenough had been round. But I needn't have worried. I'd forgotten how hard-nosed about "brass" they are up here! Huby's low peasant cunning had produced the same answer as my sophisticated intelligence—wait and see. So we've joined forces. A matched pair is always worth far more than merely double a broken set. I invited Huby to consult with me here this morning. Meanwhile I discovered that Goodenough was staying here too, so after we had worked out our strategy, I thought we might as well confront him with it as soon as possible. Frankly, I'd rather do it alone, but Huby doesn't seem to trust me to look after his interests.'

'Oh, I can't imagine why!' cried Lomas. 'You who are so good at looking after other people's interests!'

He saw his mother's expression harden and realized he'd gone too far in his filial mockery. He did not doubt she would soon strike back.

'I've had practice looking after yours,' she said.

'And don't think I don't appreciate it, Mother. I need looking after. Oh, I am Fortune's fool!'

'And that, if I recall aright, is one of Romeo's lines,' said Mrs Windibanks. 'Spoken after you in your minor role are dead and left with nothing to do but snooze in your dressing-room till the curtain-calls, always assuming there are any curtain-calls!'

Lomas shook his head in reluctant admiration.

'Oh, you don't hang about, do you, Mother?' he mocked. 'One, two, and the third in your bosom. Ah!'

He affected to stab himself with a fork and flipped back in his chair, eyes closed. When he opened them he found John Huby and a bearded stranger looking down at him with a waiter bobbing anxiously in the background.

'Rod, stop playing the fool,' ordered Mrs Windibanks. 'Mr Goodenough, may I present my son. Rod, this is Andrew Goodenough from CLAWS.'

'PAWS,' corrected the Scot., 'I'm pleased to meet you, Mr Windibanks.'

'Lomas, actually. Stage name, but I'm used to answering to it now.'

'Indeed. Mrs Windibanks, I didn't expect to find you up here too, but it falls very handy to have you and Mr Huby together. Can we talk for a moment?'

It amused Rod to see Goodenough adroitly remove the initiative from his mother.

But she's a bonny wee counter-puncher, he thought. She'll have another thou out of you for that, Mr Secretary!

'I'm just about to have my lunch,' said Mrs Windibanks. 'Perhaps in the lounge in, say, forty-five minutes?'

'I'd prefer now,' said Goodenough. 'I have a busy afternoon. And I'm driving across to Ilkley later.'

'To see the WFE woman? You have my sympathy. I gather she's as mad as a hatter. But how thorough you are, Mr Goodenough. Never a step forward without making sure your back's well covered.'

'If it's inconvenient, however, I'll get in touch when we're both back in London,' continued Goodenough, as if Mrs Windibanks had never spoken.

'I can't be hanging around here all bloody day,' exclaimed John Huby. 'I've got a pub to look after.'

Carefully Stephanie Windibanks folded her napkin and set it down.

'Very well,' she said. 'Rod, darling, do order and start without me. I shall have a slice of rare beef and a tossed green salad.'

It was more than half an hour before the woman returned with Huby lowering behind her, but no sign of Goodenough. Lomas was drinking his coffee.

'I've left some wine,' he said. 'To toast your triumph or drown your sorrows. Which is it?'

'Both,' she said tersely.

'Nay, lass, but we'll be all right. I must say, you're a dab hand at sorting out these money matters,' said Huby with reluctant admiration.

'That sounds promising,' said Lomas. 'What's the deal?'

'Five hundred advance payment for our waivers,' said Mrs Windibanks.

'What?'

'Each.'

'Even so,' said Lomas. 'It's not much, is it? I mean, I must confess that in anticipation of your success, I rather went to town on the wine, and I decided on the smoked salmon after all.'

'I said advance payment. Against five per cent of the estate at its present value.'

'Each?'

'Each!'

'Good lord. That must come to, let me see, about seventy thousand pounds. Mother, you're a marvel!'

He rose to embrace her. She pushed him back in his seat.

'Sit still till I finish,' she said sharply.

'Oh dear. There's something else.'

'Nowt to worry about as far as I can see,' said Huby uncertainly.

'But how far can you see, John?' snapped Mrs Windibanks.

'Tell me, what is it?' cried Lomas. 'You're worse than Juliet's nurse!'

His mother fixed him with an angry eye.

'It seems,' she said, 'that some lunatic has appeared in Thackeray's office claiming fairly convincingly to be the missing heir, Alexander Lomas Huby.'

'It'll be nowt, you'll see, we'll get him sorted,' said John Huby grimly.

But Rod Lomas subsided in his chair and waved a limp hand at a distant waiter.

'Oh shit,' he said. 'I think we're going to need another bottle.'

CHAPTER 11

'Have I done well? Have I done right?'

So Andrew Goodenough addressed the twin *penates* of his Presbyterian upbringing, canniness and conscience, in search of their approval for the deal he had just struck with the wily Windibanks and the horrible Huby.

Obtaining no firm answer, he pragmatically shelved the questions and concentrated his mind on his immediate mission.

He was driving westwards to see Mrs Lætitia Falkingham, founder and perpetual president of Women For Empire. All he knew of WFE he had picked up from Eden Thackeray, whose old-fashioned liberalism had unlocked his lawyer's discretion.

'Pathetic rather than sinister, but none the less deplorable,' he had categorized them. 'Basically a correspondence circle of colonial windows, nostalgic for ayahs and chota pegs, plus a handful of home-grown fascists like Mrs Huby. Their political platform, if so it could be called, is that Enoch Powell's a little soft on immigration, South Africa is an earthly paradise, and the nice, jolly and exceedingly cheap blacks have been lured off the strait and narrow by nasty communists, which is to say trade-unionists and all points left.'

'Large membership?' Goodenough had asked.

'Rapidly declining and no recruitment,' said Thackeray. 'The nasty right prefers less genteel outlets for its nastinesses. No, until recently I'd have said WFE looked set to die off with Mrs Falkingham.'

'Where would the money have gone, in that case?' wondered Goodenough.

'You mean, could PAWS have got hold of it?' laughed Thackeray. 'I doubt if we shall ever know. It seems that Mrs Falkingham has got herself what sounds like a young and vigorous assistant, name of Brodsworth. Ms Sarah Brodsworth. I fear a new generation of WFE members may be spawned, and they won't be so pathetically ineffectual as the last, not with half a million under their belts.'

Well, that was not his problem, thought Goodenough. If getting PAWS' third of the Huby fortune involved dropping an equal amount into the lap of the loonie Right, that was how it had to be.

A signpost told him he was within a couple of miles of Ilkley. Combining his sole foreknowledge of the place, which was that it had a moor, with what Thackeray had told him, he realized he was expecting Maldive Cottage to be a cross between Wuthering Heights and the Berghof at Berchtesgaden.

The reality was very different.

Ilkley turned out to be a bustling, prosperous and handsome little market town and Maldive Cottage was straight off a biscuit tin lid, with grey Yorkstone walls, red tiles and leaded lights, nestling in an English cottage garden alight with the colours of late summer and early autumn.

He went up the path, raised the lion's head knocker and knocked.

The door opened immediately. A man in his late twenties stood there. He was of medium build with rather short, neatly trimmed fair hair. He wore a well cut grey suit, white shirt and striped tie. He smiled interrogatively, showing strong, even, white teeth. He looked a little like Robert Redford.

'Good day,' said Goodenough. 'Is Mrs Falkingham in?'

'Yes, she is. Would it be Mr Goodenough?'

'That's right.'

'Yes, she mentioned you. Do step in. My name's Vollans, by the way. Henry Vollans.'

Goodenough let himself be ushered into a sitting-room which was as hot as a tropical house at Kew. A huge fire burnt in the open grate and the central heating radiators seemed to be working at full blast too.

'Pretty overpowering, isn't it?' said Vollans, smiling. 'She says that old blood has a high boiling point. She's just gone in search of some photos, by the way.'

'Photos?'

'Yes. I'm afraid it's Memory Lane time. I was just admiring that chap there with the coal scuttle on his head and that started her off.'

The young man gestured at a photograph above the mantelshelf of a man in a white uniform and the feathered head-gear of a Colonial governor.

'Mr Falkingham, is it?' inquired Goodenough.

'So I gathered. Tell me, you're from PAWS, aren't you, come to talk about the will? What are the chances of getting something done about it, do you think?'

Goodenough did not answer immediately but concentrated on finding a spot as equidistant as possible from the Scylla of the roaring fire and the Charybdis of the pulsating radiator.

'Forgive me, Mr Vollans,' he said finally. 'But what is your precise relationship with Mrs Falkingham?'

The young man laughed.

'It's a fair cop,' he said. 'You think I'm after the money! Well, I am in a way. I'm a reporter, *Sunday Challenger*, and I just got here five minutes ago, so my relationship with Mrs Falkingham is about as precise as yours.'

'I see. Then you'll forgive me if I do not discuss my business with you before I've had the chance to discuss it with the lady herself.'

'Fair enough,' said Vollans. 'Have you met this Miss Brodsworth yet? When I rang earlier, I was assured that there would be little purpose in my coming to talk about WFE unless Miss Brodsworth were present.'

'I too,' said Goodenough. 'I was also assured she would be here by now.'

He glanced at his watch, frowning.

'Incidentally, Mr Vollans,' he said. 'I can't quite see what your newspaper's interest might be. Is it the nature of the will, or the nature of the possible beneficiaries that interests you?'

'That's for me to write and you to read,' said Vollans, faintly mocking. 'Ah, here she is.'

The door opened to admit not the little old lady he had somehow imagined but a rather large old lady. Eighty-odd years had certainly ravaged the fabric but not much reduced it.

'Mrs Falkingham, this is Mr Goodenough from PAWS,' said Vollans.

'Mr Goodenough, how nice of you to come. Two visitors in one afternoon. Am I not a lucky old woman? Mr Vollans and I have been having such an interesting talk. I was just telling him how much he reminded me of my husband when he was a young District Officer. It's a shame that fine young men like this should no longer have the chance of a career in the Service, don't you agree, Mr Goodenough?'

'The Service...?'

'The Colonial Service, I mean,' she said sharply. 'I have some few photographs here which may interest you. Ah, happy days, happy days at a God-given task which was never easy but from which we in our generation did not shrink, Mr Goodenough. They have tried other ways since then, and you see where it's got them. Well, well, if they learn from their mistakes, as God grant they may, it's a blessing to know that there are still fine young men like Mr Vollans to take up the burden again. Don't you agree?'

Goodenough avoided Vollans's quizzical eye and made a noncommittal sound, possible only to a man brought up to pronounce *loch* correctly.

'I mentioned on the phone that I wanted to talk about Mrs Huby's will,' he began.

'Yes, yes,' said the old woman. 'Sarah will see to all that when she gets here. Meanwhile, let us look at these photographs, shall we? There's history here, Mr Goodenough. And not just family history. The history of an empire, and of its decline. No, not decline. Decline's too gradual a word. They gave it away in a trice, in the twinkling of an eye, those fools and knaves. Will you print that, Mr Vollans? Does your paper dare to print *that*?'

The journalist was spared answering this fierce question by the sound of a key in the front door.

Mrs Falkingham heard it clearly and a look of pleasure replaced the wrath on her face.

'There she is. Sarah. Miss Brodsworth. My strong right arm. Before she came, I feared Women For Empire might die with me, but now I know it will live on. There must be many like her, young people who still hold to the old values and are full of regret that they were born too late to see the Empire at its greatest and best. But it will come again, I am certain of it. God did not create us and advance us so far in front of our coloured brethren not to intend that we should guide and comfort them to the promised land. It's all in the Bible, of course. I can show you chapter and verse. Sarah, my dear, come in, come in. We have company!'

Sarah Brodsworth was a surprise. Somehow Goodenough had been expecting a young Mrs Falkingham, a sturdy, tweedy, fox-hunting type. What he got was a pocket Venus with honey blonde curls, heavy make-up and a pneumatic bust. She reminded him a little of the girl who'd given him the eye at the Old Mill Inn till Huby intervened the previous evening, but the resemblance did not survive a closer examination. This girl's eyes were not for giving. Pale blue, diamond hard and unblinking, they fixed him with a blank stare which seemed to register, without reacting to, his physical make-up, his motives, his weaknesses and his intentions. In her left hand she carried a black leather briefcase.

'This is Mr Goodenough from the People's Animal Welfare Society,' said the old woman. 'And this is Mr Vollans from...'

Her memory failed her. Vollans said, 'The *Sunday Challenger*. Pleased to meet you, Miss Brodsworth.'

He stepped forward and offered his hand.

The young woman ignored it.

'You want to talk about the Huby will?' she said to Goodenough. 'Let's go next door.'

Her voice was clipped and slightly harsh. He put her age at twenty-four or five, her physical age, that was. In other ways he felt she was much older than anyone else in the room.

'I wonder if you could spare me a few moments,' said Vollans.

'I see you have your albums,' said the girl in a softer tone to the old woman. 'I'm sure Mr Vollans is eager to see your photographs. This way, Mr Goodenough.'

She led him from the lounge into a dining-room, closing the door firmly behind her. It was still very warm in here but at least there was no open fire.

She sat down in the carver chair at the head of a lovely old mahogany table, placed her briefcase on the table slightly to one side, and motioned him to the chair opposite her. After he had seated himself, she inclined her head gently towards him like an old-fashioned teacher giving a child the signal to commence its lesson.

Deciding to play her at her own game, this was more or less what he began to do. In a dry, legal tone he recited the details of the will and his own reaction to date and proposals for the future.

When he had finished he looked at her expectantly, then inclined his own head in an imitation of her gesture.

Something which with a little more warmth might have been a smile touched her lips, then she said, 'You say that if the suit fails, PAWS will bear the total expense, but if it succeeds, the expenses will be shared between the three beneficiary organizations?'

'That would seem equitable,' he said. 'I appreciate your group and CODRO possibly do not have large reserves to draw on.'

She frowned and said, 'What are these expenses likely to be?'

'Legal, mainly, and therefore difficult to estimate in advance. And any expenses incurred by me in pursuance of this matter.'

'Hotel bills, you mean?' she said with a hint of a sneer.

'Those, certainly,' he said, unruffled. 'And other things. I keep a running account. You might care to see it to date.'

He handed her a sheet of paper.

She examined it, still frowning.

'These payments to these two, Huby and Windibanks. What are they for?'

'Their agreement not to pursue any claim of their own as relatives.'

'Have they any claim in law?'

'Only if the will were entirely overthrown on the ground of the testator's mental incompetence. As Mrs Huby made the will some years ago and lived thereafter with noone questioning her competence, at least not openly, this seems unlikely.'

'Then these seem large sums to pay people to give up something they don't possess,' she said coldly.

'I said *unlikely* not *impossible*. The law cannot be forecast, Miss Brodsworth. In any case, they possess the right to challenge the will. *That* is what they are giving up. In a democracy, a right is not something which should be undervalued.'

Am I defending my own judgment or Thackeray's liberal values? he wondered ironically as he heard his words come out more sharply than he intended. But the woman only returned the paper to him indifferently.

'In that case, I agree. What do I do now?'

'I understand you have full executive authority in regard to WFE.'

'That's right.'

He hesitated and she opened her briefcase, took out a cardboard wallet, removed from it a sheet of paper and handed it to him.

'Signed, sealed and witnessed, Mr Goodenough,' she said. 'May we proceed?'

He read the sheet and passed it back.

'That seems in order. Would you now read this?'

From his own case he took a typed sheet of paper and handed it to her. It must have felt like this, he thought with an uncharacteristic flight of fancy, sitting in that railway carriage at Compiègne in 1918. Or did he mean 1940?

He said, 'It's simply a statement of WFE's agreement to common action on the lines I have outlined. You might like to show it to WFE's legal adviser before signing.'

She read through it swiftly.

'No. I'll sign.'

'Before you do,' he said. 'There is one other thing. I learned this morning that a man has come forward claiming to be Alexander Huby, the missing heir. Investigation of his claim will certainly delay our suit and, of course, if he establishes that claim, our suit becomes redundant.'

She fixed those cold blue eyes on him and said, 'This claimant; I presume he is fraudulent?'

'That's for the law to say, Miss Brodsworth.'

'The law again!'

Her red lips twitched in that cold mockery of a smile once more, and she signed the agreement.

That was the conclusion of their business. She made no sign of wishing to offer him any hospitality and he fastened his brief-case, eager to be on his way out of this house.

The door opened and Vollans stepped in.

'Sorry to interrupt, but the old lady seems to have fallen asleep. In mid-sentence more or less. Is that all right?'

'Yes. She does it all the time. I'll come through now. We've finished here.'

'Really. Perhaps I could have a few moments of your time, then.'

'If you wish,' she said indifferently.

'Have you been with WFE long, Miss Brodsworth?' asked Vollans.

'Not long.'

'How did you make the connection? Forgive me for asking, but it's just that I got an impression that it was an organization for, how shall I put it? ladies of a certain age?'

'I was a student in Bradford,' said Sarah Brodsworth. 'I heard about WFE from some friends in a group I belonged to. It sounded interesting. I contacted Mrs Falkingham. She invited me to call. We got on well. I suggested that perhaps I could help get the WFE message across to a younger age group. She was delighted.'

'I see,' said Vollans. 'And what would you say this message was, Miss Brodsworth?'

The girl did not reply at once but glanced towards Goodenough, who had made an unnecessarily complicated busi-ness of fastening his briefcase as his curiosity to eavesdrop on the journalist's interview overcame his eagerness to leave.

Now he nodded and made for the door. But before he reached it she spoke, very gently.

'What I think Mrs Falkingham and her friends have been trying to say for a long time in their rather muted way, Mr Vollans, is that this great country of ours is ready for a good cleansing. Yes, that's about it, I believe. A good cleansing. That sums it up, I believe.'

The young woman went through into the lounge.

Goodenough and Vollans exchanged glances.

'If you're not too busy, perhaps we could have a chat too, Mr Goodenough,' said the reporter.

'Why not?' said Goodenough, suddenly not taken by the prospect of an evening in his own company.

'There's a pub on the corner of the main road. Shall we say half an hour? I don't get the impression of being very welcome here.'

'All right.'

Goodenough glanced into the lounge before he left.

The old woman was still asleep. In repose she looked deflated. You could almost feel sorry for her. Brodsworth sat quietly opposite her. She didn't acknowledge Goodenough's appearance.

He wondered what account her 'good cleansing' would take of the old and helpless and stupid.

Then he went out in the fresh air and bright sunshine.

CHAPTER 12

The man who claimed to be Alexander Lomas Huby moved in the bed and the woman by his side thought: Christ! the bastard's coming up for the third time! But she'd been paid generously for the whole night and like a good professional began to arrange her limbs for the onslaught.

Instead the man rolled out of the bed and began to get dressed. Immediately her suspicions were roused. They had settled a price for the whole night, but he'd only paid half in advance.

'Where're you going.' she demanded.

'I have an appointment,' he said. 'I will be back.' He spoke excellent English but with an intonation which suggested it was not his main language.

'Bit late for an appointment, isn't it?' she said. 'Must be nearly midnight.'

He pulled his shirt round his body. A fillet of scar-tissue punctuated with small dimples ran diagonally across his right ribcage and round into the small of his back. She'd run her hands along it and commented, 'National Health appendix, was it love?' but he hadn't joined in her laugh.

'How do I know you'll be back?' she asked.

She didn't think of him as dangerous. Some men gave off a feeling of menace, of a personality delicately balanced, and she'd got no such vibrations here. But you never could tell and her hand under the pillow was gripping the heavy cosh she kept tucked between the mattress and the bedhead. She bought herself a measure of protection against general hassle by fucking that long gangling community copper every Tuesday, but that meant nothing here and now. A girl had to look out for herself.

He was fully dressed now and came to the bedside. Her muscles tensed. She should have got out of bed as soon as he did. On her feet she might have a chance. Recumbent, even with the cosh, she was almost completely vulnerable. He reached out a hand. She prepared to scream and strike.

He caressed her shoulders and said, 'Don't worry. You will get your money. See, I leave my grip in your care. I will be back in one hour, two perhaps. Then we will ride the dolphin again.'

She rose as soon as she heard the door close and went to the window. She saw him under the streetlamp below, getting into the old green Escort he had brought her home in from the pub. She watched it move away down the quiet street, flashing to turn left at the junction with the main road.

She bent down and pulled his grip from under the bed. The zip fastened with a lock. It would probably be easy to force it with a knife, but it wasn't worth it, not when he was coming back.

There was a noise in the bedroom and Wield was instantly awake. He reached out and snapped the bedside light on. The boy was standing in the door. He was completely naked and the soft light gave his skin the glow of dark-gold honey.

'What do you want?' asked the sergeant with a thickness in his voice he tried to disguise as sleep.

'I couldn't sleep,' said Cliff sullenly.

'I could,' said Wield. 'Make yourself some cocoa.'

'You know what? This is fucking stupid,' said the boy.

'You're right. Close the door as you leave.'

'For Christ's sake, Mac, what's the matter with you? I've been sleeping on that sodding couch for a fortnight now!'

Wield pushed himself upright.

'What are you trying to say, lad. *See anything you fancy, big boy?* is that it?'

'Well, don't you? I'm young, I've got needs too. You've let me stay here, we seem to get on pretty well. You can't blame me if I wonder where it's all leading.'

Wield ran his fingers through his thick crinkly hair.

'Me too,' he said wearily.

He should have given him his marching orders as soon as he'd talked to Maurice. He should have put the fear of God into him, then slipped him some spending money and his ticket back to London. It wasn't a permanent solution but at least it would have bought time. Time to make decisions in his own way, under his own control, with no external pressure. It was a matter of dignity.

And then he thought: *Dignity? Crap!* It was just another excuse to do nothing, to continue in this dull limbo which he had chosen to inhabit for God knows how many years. He recalled again that first moment when he had heard Cliff's voice on the telephone, the sense of shock and of threat; had there not also been a tremor of delight at what was perhaps the first intimation of liberation?

He looked at the young body and yearned for it. *See anything you fancy?* He had parodied the gay come-on savagely but the answer was *yes, oh yes*!

And why not? What would be changed if he pushed back the sheets and held out his arms.

'What's your hang-up anyway, Mac? Scared of AIDS, is it? Or are you saving yourself for the Chief Constable?'

The lad had blown it. Like an inexperienced interrogator, he had pressed hard when all that was required was silence. Wield let the detumescent anger sweep over him.

'Listen, you little bastard,' he said with measured savagery. 'I know all about you and your nasty little mind. You're a thief and a liar and you probably fancy your hand at blackmail too. And don't look all falsely accused and innocent, I'm used to that kind of ham acting, remember? Did you imagine I wouldn't check up on you? I know what you got up to in London, sonny. And all that crap about hitch-hiking and just happening to get dropped here! You bought a bus ticket, son. This was your destination, and I was your mark.'

'That's what you think, is it?' cried Sharman. 'That's what you think?'

'No. That's what I know,' said Wield wearily.

'Then fuck you, Sergeant. Fuck you!'

He turned and rushed out of the bedroom, slamming the door behind him.

Wield listened for a while. Then he put out the light and pulled the sheet up over his chin. But it was a long time before he could get to sleep.

Neville Watmough lay awake beside his wife who was also awake because her husband's wakefulness was never a restful thing. On the other hand, to ask him *why* he was awake would merely be to invite the answer that he wasn't till she had woken him with her wittering.

It is not an easy thing to be married to an ambitious man. His mind is a turbulent sea of plans and projects, of policy and strategy, of deep thought and high aspiration. So Mrs Watmough told herself, trying as usual to bury her chronic irritation in her chronic humility and get back to sleep.

Meanwhile Watmough's ferret-like mind pursued the bobtail thoughts which had been scuttling around his head ever since his lunch with Ogilby.

Who was the poofter in CID?

He had headed back to his office and dug out the files. Like many another middle-aged, provincial, professional man who has picked up enough modern jargon to get by pretty well in the here-and-now, his intellectual and moral roots were firmly anchored in that stratum of history where eighteenth-century evangelicism had fossilized into Victorian respectability. Some truths seemed immutable. One was that a homosexual would most likely be a young bachelor of artistic temperament who frequented unisex hair salons and wore very pungent aftershave. Unable to find many on the CID strength who fitted this profile, he sought further guidance in the big bookcase behind his desk which contained, besides the conventional official tomes, the literary relics of several of his predecessors, preserved because he felt that the crowded bookshelves added a certain *ton* to the *ambience* of his office.

As half remembered, there was a volume there on *Sexual Deviancy*. He opened it and began to read. To his horror, instead of narrowing things down, it opened up new and dreadful vistas. Oscar Wilde, he discovered with amazement, had been a respectable married man with two children.

This meant the bastard he was looking for was as likely to be married as not!

Nor, it appeared, was it something you grew out of. So it could be a man of some seniority, with a wife. This widened the field considerably. Of course, no woman would knowingly put up with such a husband. Mrs Wilde had sought a divorce when the truth emerged. So it could be a senior CID officer whose wife had divorced him with some acrimony...

Dalziel!

Oh, please God, if I must be given this burden to bear, let it be Dalziel!

Alas for Watmough, he was not a man blessed with a high, creative imagination. He could manage to conjure up various future triumphs in his career such as turning down the Commissionership because he had been offered a safe Parliamentary seat, or accepting an invitation to be the SDP Home Secretary in a coalition government, but his fancy balked at dressing Dalziel in a frilly blouse with a green carnation behind his ear.

But Pascoe now. That was quite different. Married with child, yes, but that was, according to his recent reading, a matter almost of confirmatory evidence. He dressed smartly but often in that casual linen-safari-jacket kind of way which Watmough had always found irritating and now found suspicious. Interested in books, plays, music; university educated and, through his wife, preserving links with the academic world; and wasn't there sometimes just the discreetest whiff of lily-of-the-valley or some such stuff wafting off him as he passed by?

It all fitted perfectly; or rather, he could see no evidence to the contrary. It did not occur to him to wonder what evidence to the contrary might look like, though, in fairness, having had much to do with anonymous phone calls during his career, it did occur that it would probably all turn out to be nothing in the end.

So long as it didn't turn out to be something in the next few days!

Meanwhile he'd keep a close eye on Detective-Inspector Pascoe. There was something about the way he laughed. And didn't he walk funny...?

So Deputy Chief Constable Watmough let his restless mind worry him into wakefulness. And other players in this as yet uncertain drama woke and watched who would rather have slept and forgotten. Peter Pascoe nursed his restless daughter and told her the story of his life. Ruby Huby turned in bed and did not find her husband, but never doubted that he sat below in the darkened bar, soothing his chronic anxieties with a rich-fumed pipe. Sarah Brodsworth strained her eyes in the darkness and saw again the inquisitive, doubting face of Henry Vollans and heard his probing questions and knew he was an obstacle to be over-come, or removed. Rod Lomas too watched and waited and felt himself grow angrier with each minute of waiting and watching. Miss Keech heard noises, Andrew Goodenough heard an outra-geous proposal, Eileen Chung heard an obscene phone call, Stephanie Windibanks heard heavy breathing, Lexie Huby heard a motor-car, and Superintendent Dalziel heard the late, late film.

It was, as most nights are, a night more full of fear than hope, of doubt than certainty, of pain than comfort. Mothers and fathers worried about their children; husbands and wives worried about each other; and sons and daughters worried about them-selves. But not all and not equally, for children are unfathomable, unforecastable, in their treatment of parents. It is not always hatred that makes a daughter long to leave her family.

And it is not always love that brings a son back home.

CHAPTER 13

Dennis Seymour had mixed feelings about Operation Shoplift. It was (a) very boring and (b) very unsuccessful, which was to say that while he was yawning in one place, the thieves always seemed to be thieving in another.

But it did give him a legitimate excuse to spend part of the day in the city centre's largest store, Starbuck's, where he took his refreshment in the restaurant at one of the tables serviced by Bernadette McCrystal.

'You're never here again!' she said. 'The old dragon follows me around with a calculator. She's sure I'm slipping you freebies.'

'What? And me saving the store thousands with me dangerous undercover work,' said Seymour, parodying her Irish lilt.

She laughed as she walked away, an infectious trill which made her other regular customers smile. Seymour felt a little jealous of them but not much. He and Bernadette had been seeing each other regularly since they met the previous year and though so far she had resisted all his attempts to get her into his bed, he was almost certain she felt as strongly about him as he did about her. She loved dancing—*real dancing*, as she called it, *none of your heathen shaking*—and he had discovered something almost sexual in that formal and public coordination of two bodies, which, plus a great deal of heavy petting, not to mention a lot of hot squash and cold showers, had kept his frustration within tolerable bounds to date.

She returned a few minutes later with a plateful of lamb chops, roast potatoes and steamed cabbage.

'I don't like cabbage,' he protested. 'I wanted peas.'

'There's another chop under it,' she whispered. 'You can't hide a chop under peas now, can you?'

Seymour shook his mop of carrot-bright hair which promised a good account of itself when his genes finally mixed with those producing the subtler, richer redness of the girl's.

'You're a natural criminal,' he said. 'I'm glad Sergeant Wield's calling this farce off after today.'

'Today, is it? So I'll have to find someone else to steal for?'

'You'd better not,' he said. 'Incidentally, the old girl's really glowering. Shouldn't you be off to fetch me that glass of beer I ordered and you've forgotten.'

But Bernadette seemed to have lost interest in their exchange of badinage and found it in something over his head and behind him. Starbuck's restaurant occupied nearly half of the second floor and was divided off from the shopping area by a glass wall which permitted the passage of light but not of cooking smells. This wall was hung with a variety of ornamental plants, mostly of the trailing variety, producing an effect which Seymour had likened to an unkempt fish-tank. In the best police tradition he always chose to sit with his back to this wall and his face to the main body of the restaurant.

'What's up?' he said. 'Have you spotted Tarzan swinging about one of those creepers?'

'No,' she said. 'This is your last day, is it? Will you get a bonus for catching somebody at it?'

'Sergeant Wield might smile, but I probably wouldn't notice,' he said. 'Why?'

'There's a young fellow through there, stuffing things into his bag like there's no tomorrow,' said Bernadette.

Startled, Seymour turned and peered through the greenery. Immediately behind him was the section of the store devoted to leather goods—wallets, purses, ornamental knick-knacks, that sort of thing—and there, sure enough, was a young man in a blue and yellow check shirt, jeans and trainers, examining items in a critical way, returning some of them to the shelf, and thrusting those which passed his scrutiny into a large plastic carrier bag over his left arm.

'Perhaps he's got a lot of birthdays this month,' said Bernadette.

'Mebbe.'

As they watched, the man set off at a brisk pace across the floor, passing two cash-and-wrap points without a glance and making towards the lifts.

'Sorry about the chop, love,' said Seymour. 'I'll pick you up tonight, usual time. 'Bye.'

Bernadette watched him go. He moved well for a big man. His dancing had improved a hundredfold since she took him under her wing. Not that he'd ever be Fred Astaire, but he would do very well for her if it wasn't that her heart sank lower than a peat bog every time she thought of telling them back home that she was wanting to marry a Protestant English policeman.

She sighed, picked up the chops and returned to the kitchen. The old dragon blocked her way.

'Well?' she said.

'He's run off without paying,' said Bernadette. 'Shall I go and call a policeman?'

Peter Pascoe was leaving his office at what he thought of as a mental tiptoe. This meant that to the casual gaze his body gave the impression of a detective-inspector whose week's work had finished at one o'clock on Saturday and who was on his way home to spend the rest of the weekend relaxing in the bosom of his family. But his soul, or whatever that part of being is which contains our individual essence, was not striding out confidently. It was sneaking out furtively with many a backward glance, hearing a voice in every wind, and the voice was Dalziel's.

The fat man's timing was usually deadly. There would be a matter of unpostponable import to discuss; the Black Bull would be the place to discuss it; and the weekend which should have started with a light lunch with Ellie and Rosie about one-thirty would instead kick off with a beery row about three.

Pascoe had just made it to the bottom of the stairs. The door to the car park and freedom was in view. Then the voice spoke.

'Any chance of a quick word?'

He turned his head reluctantly, summoning up his nerve this time for the great refusal. Then relief washed over him like rain in a heat wave. It was only Wield.

'Yes, sure, if you can walk and talk,' he said, resuming his progress into the car park.

Wield followed. His craggy features showed as little of his inner turmoil as Pascoe's had shown of his inner stealth. He had woken up that morning to find that Cliff had already breakfasted and gone out. As the day wore on, he had found himself beset by a need repressed for years, the need to talk about himself, not necessarily in a soul-searching, dial-Samaritans kind of way, but with an openness which a lifetime of disguise made difficult. But to whom? And the election had fallen on Pascoe, colleague, superior, and if not precisely a friend, at least the nearest thing to one he had in the 'normal' world.

'I thought, mebbe a quick…not the Black Bull…if you've got the time…it's personal…'

Oh shit! thought Pascoe. One half of his mind was doubting if Ellie would be much impressed by the fact that it was Wield not Dalziel and some pub other than the Black Bull which made him late for his lunch. And the other half was trying to cope with the horrid suspicion that the rock-like Wield was about to turn to shifting sand. Wield with personal problems? It was a contradiction in terms! Jesus wept, the man had no right to be anything but a Victorian Gothic tower of strength!

Surprised and ashamed at the depth of his instinctive resentment, Pascoe said, 'I can't manage too long...'

But he was saved from further ungraciousness by another voice calling his name.

Once again it wasn't Dalziel but Sergeant Broomfield, maker of illicit books and one of the central pivots of uniformed life in the Station.

'Sorry to butt in, but I just wondered, that car in the corner, is it something to do with your lads?'

Pascoe looked. The car in question was a battered green Escort, parked tight against the wall in the most unpopular corner of the yard where a branch of the large chestnut tree on the neighbouring premises shed its stickiness, and gave the birds a good perch from which to shed theirs, on whatever stood below.

'Not that I know of. Why?'

'Just wondered. It was there first thing, that's all.'

The two men stood and regarded the vehicle, thoughts of terrorist car bombs unspoken in their minds.

'Let's take a look,' said Pascoe.

Glancing apologetically at Wield, he headed for the Escort with Broomfield reluctantly in pursuit.

He didn't touch the car but peered in from a couple of feet. The windows were so begrimed as to make it very difficult to see much more than the steering-wheel.

A car swung into the yard and its horn blasted, making Pascoe and Broomfield jump nervously. Pascoe looked round and glimpsed Seymour's grinning face.

'Silly bastard,' he muttered and returned his attention to the Escort.

'What do you think, sir?' said Broomfield.

What Pascoe thought was if he didn't do something now, he'd have to hang around while somebody was fetched who would do something and that might take hours.

He took a deep breath, reached forward to the handle of the passenger door and tried to open it. It seemed to be jammed rather than locked. He gave a sudden violent tug and it flew open.

'Oh Jesus!' said Broomfield. 'They've started a delivery service.'

It was a comment to treasure later, but not then.

Pascoe was too busy being amazed as he looked down at the body which slowly slid out of the car door.

It was a man and he was certainly dead; no living eyes could stare so sightlessly or living limbs be locked in so cramped a pose.

He peered closer. There was blood on the man's shirt, though from what kind of wound he could not see.

'Don't touch anything,' he said to Broomfield with what he hoped was unnecessary pedantry. 'Sergeant Wield.'

To his surprise, the discovery of the body seemed to have startled Wield even more than the two closer men. His rugged features had gone quite pale and there was a smear of perspiration on his lips.

What's up with the bloody man? wondered Pascoe.

'Come on, Wieldy,' he urged. 'Bang goes Saturday, eh?'

But the sergeant did not answer. His eyes were still fixed on the entrance to the Station through which he had just seen Detective-Constable Seymour, after giving him a triumphant thumbs-up sign, escort Cliff Sharman.

THIRD ACT

VOICES FROM THE GALLERY

Whatever in those climes he found
Irregular in sight or sound
Did to his mind impart
A kindred impulse, seem'd allied
To his own powers, and justified
The workings of his heart.

Wordsworth: *Ruth*

CHAPTER 1

'Bear hence this body, and attend our will;
Mercy but murders, pardoning those that kill.'

The applause was on the polite side of enthusiastic. Ellie Pascoe kept her clapping going a couple of beats after most people and several bars after her husband.

In the interval she said, 'You're not enjoying it?'

'Well,' he said, 'It's OK for Shakespeare, but *West Side Story* it's not!'

'Peter, stop being flip. You're just determined not to be impressed by anything Chung does, aren't you?'

'On the contrary, I quite approve the slant Big Eileen's giving the text. I feared something much more fearsomely feminist! But two kids being mucked about by the oldies is more or less what Shakespeare was on about, wasn't it? Though probably he didn't envisage Capulet and his wife looking quite so like Maggie and Dennis or the Prince so like Ronnie Reagan! But the production's a bit ponderous, isn't it? Perhaps it'll get better now that Mercutio's out of it. The only bit of life in him was when he died and I reckon that that was because it came so natural.'

'Peter,' said Ellie warningly. 'I hope *you're* not going to be the life and soul of the party afterwards.'

'What? And risk Big Eileen's karate chop? You must be joking!'

The second half was in Pascoe's judgment a great improvement, though the tragic momentum was momentarily checked in the scene in which Romeo purchases poison from the apothecary.

The latter, bent and quavering to start with, seemed to lose his way after his opening line, 'Who calls so loud?' Prompted, he spoke the next couple of lines in a much stronger voice and was immediately detectable as the actor who had played Mercutio. In the uppermost tier where the school parties were concentrated a piercing young voice said, 'Please, sir, I thought he were dead!'

It took a little while to repair the damage caused by the outburst of laughter, but the Gothic glooms of the closing scenes finally cast their pall and Pascoe was able to match Ellie clap for clap as the company took their calls.

Pascoe had never been to a backstage party, but he had watched many a Hollywood musical and was not surprised to be disappointed. The atmosphere though far from restrained was even further from riotous. No champagne corks popped, though Sainsbury's hock flowed like Sainsbury's hock. Jeans and T-shirts had it over evening gowns and tiaras. And the only truly Hollywood touches came from the mayor's wife, who looked like Margaret Dumont and wore a rope of imitation pearls as big as her husband's mayoral chain; and from the chairman of the Council's Library and Arts Committee who, tuxedo'd, cigarred, and pop-eyed, was behaving like Zero Mostel in little-old-lady land.

But now came a third authenticating detail, this time sonic.

A voice cried, 'Chung, darling! We thought it was marvelous! So touching! So true!'

Pascoe turned to applaud the satirist who was producing this ghastly gush and was horrified to find himself listening to Ellie.

'Cut the crap, honey. We nearly bombed. If any of this council lot could tell shit from Shakespeare, they'd cut us off at the subsidy tomorrow.'

Switching his gaze and his applause to the speaker of this good plain sense, he found himself looking up at Big Eileen herself. Television had certainly not exaggerated her length. What it had failed to convey, however, was her extraordinary beauty.

'I don't think you've met my husband,' said Ellie.

'Chung, this is Peter. Peter, Chung.'

'Chung, *hello*,' said Pascoe, grinning inanely.

'You're the cop, honey? I'd not have known.'

'They train us in make-up,' he said. 'I'm really a sniffer dog.' He sniffed doggily. Ellie looked pained. Chung looked alarmed.

'None of my jokers are smoking shit, are they? I warned them, not while the councillors are reassuring themselves how clever they've been with their money.'

'I'm not sure about the mayor, but I think everyone else is clean,' said Pascoe.

'Chung! Miss Chung! Hold it.'

A flash bulb flashed. When he stopped being dazzled, Pascoe recognized the long lugubrious features of Sammy Ruddlesdin from the *Evening Post*.

'That'll be nice,' said Ruddlesdin. 'Beauty and the Beast. Chung, any words for the Press? The popular press, I mean. I know there's a *Guardian* intellectual out there somewhere but he's almost pissed on the free plonk already. We're your channel to the real public. This is my colleague, Henry Vollans, by the way. *Sunday Challenger*. The Voice of the North.'

'Hi!' said Chung to the young man with Ruddlesdin. 'Anyone ever tell you you look like Robert Redford?'

Pascoe felt a pang of something like jealousy.

Ruddlesdin said, 'Night off, Pete? I'd have thought the mighty Buddha would have had you all working full time in the temple tonight, waiting for the call.'

'After losing my weekend, I told him that if I missed this lot, Ellie would personally shoot either me or him, not necessarily in that order.'

'Have there been many calls? Come on, we have cooperated, haven't we?'

The *Evening Post* had printed a photograph of the dead man in the Escort that day after the weekend had brought the police no nearer an identification. Cause of death had been established as haemorrhaging of the aorta caused by a single bullet from a 9 mm handgun, possibly an old Luger.

Pascoe hesitated. Before he left the office, there had only been one call of any weight and that had been from Eden Thackeray, insisting on talking to Dalziel, who had relayed the news with a surprising lack of surprise.

'Says he's certain the man is an Italian called Alessandro Pontelli who turned up at his office claiming to be Alexander Huby, the lost heir in that daft will that were in the papers the other week. I'm just off to take him round to the mortuary.'

He had looked at Pascoe speculatively, then growled, 'All right. Don't grit your teeth like that. I'm not going to stop you getting your dose of culture.'

'Nothing positive, Sammy,' he said to Ruddlesdin.

'But something, eh?'

'Something, maybe. I'll let you know when it's positive. No, that's it. I'm here to enjoy myself, so no more pumping!'

'Wouldn't dream of it. As long as you don't try to pump *me* about our fairy phone calls,' said Ruddlesdin provocatively.

'There've been more?'

'One. Saturday morning. It was directed to Robert Redford there in Leeds. Like I told you, the chief reckons it's *Challenger* stuff if it's anything. I gather it was much the same as before. No names, talked about money, then said he'd be in touch again maybe, and cut off.'

'And that's all?'

'Yes, Peter, that's all. And don't go asking young Vollans about it either. Remember you're not supposed to know owt. I don't want it generally known I'm a grass! Though...'

'Yes?'

'Well, Henry came across last week to sniff around. His editor, Ike Ogilby, was in town too, lunching at the Gents with—guess who? Mr Wonderful himself, your beloved DCC. So perhaps the grass grows taller than you think.'

'Sammy!' It was Chung. 'I was just telling your friend here that I've got a bottle set aside in my office for the gentlemen of the Press, but you can come too. Half an hour's time, shall we say? Round up the other piss-artists for me, would you, honey? Now I've got to socialize!'

Ruddlesdin and Vollans moved away, and Chung began to say something to Ellie, but before she'd got more than a couple of words out, she was interrupted by a newcomer whom Pascoe recognized as Mercutio and the apothecary compressed into one palely handsome young face that looked familiar beyond the context of the play.

'Chung, I'm sorry. I was awful,' he said bluntly.

'You'll get no argument from me, honey,' said Chung.

There was a hard edge to her voice. Words too can deliver a karate chop, thought Pascoe. Oh beautiful tyrant! Fiend angelical! He sighed lustfully and converted it into a cough.

'Pete! Ell! I'm being a bad hostess. Meet Rod Lomas. Ell and Pete Pascoe.'

'Hello,' said Ellie. 'We were just saying how much we enjoyed the play, weren't we, Peter?'

'Oh yes. It was so touching, so true,' said Pascoe.

'Well, don't scrape around for nice things to say about me,' said Lomas with a wan smile.

'You died well,' said Pascoe judiciously.

'Oh yes. I did that all right.'

'Rod.'

It was a little voice and to find its source, Pascoe had to lower his gaze from Chung's Himalayan splendours to the drab foothills where a small girl stood. A fanzine? Pascoe wondered. She looked familiar. Then he took in Lomas and the child as a pair and recalled the Black Bull. It didn't make her look older.

'Lexie. I'm sorry. I forgot. Have you got a drink?'

'Not when I'm driving,' she answered, shaking her head so firmly she almost dislodged her huge round spectacles.

'I won't ask if you enjoyed the show,' said Lomas.

'It was all right. I don't go to plays much,' she added, glancing apologetically up at Chung.

'Lexie prefers opera,' said Lomas, rather defensively.

'Oh?' said Chung. 'It's the elitist, escapist, and totally unreal that turns you on, is it, hon?'

She *does* pick on people not her own size! There's hope for me yet, thought Pascoe admiringly.

'It's not all like that,' said the girl. 'Some of it's quite real; well, at least as real as waking up in a tomb and finding your dead lover beside you.'

Chung looked taken aback, like a giraffe threatened by a mouse. Then she laughed heartily and said, 'Who's your friend, Rod?'

'Sorry. This is my cousin, sort of. Lexie Huby. Lexie, Chung. I've forgotten your names already. Can hardly remember my part today. Sorry.'

'Pascoe. Ell and Pete,' said Pascoe, thinking that *Huby* also meant something. Of course, the Italian who might be their corpse. It was a Mrs Huby's will he'd been trying to claim on, wasn't it?

Then his mind was diverted by Ellie saying, 'Hello, Lexie. How are you?'

'Fine thanks, Mrs Pascoe,' said the girl.

'Hey, listen,' said Chung. 'I must go and be nice to the mayor and his wife. With those things round their necks, they look like they could both have slipped anchor and be on the point of drifting out to sea. Pete, honey, I'm thinking of doing something on the fuzz once I've lulled the council into a false sense of security. Maybe we could talk some time to make sure I get it right. OK?'

'Oh yes, indeed,' said Pascoe. 'OK. Right on.'

'Great. I'll be in touch. Ell, Lex, see you.'

She glided away, tall and graceful as a swan through ducklings, towards the mayor.

Rod Lomas said, 'Fuzz?'

'That's right,' said Pascoe. I'm your friendly neighbourhood bobby.'

He was used to being a conversational hiccough but this was more like a hiatus hernia.

Lomas tried to speak, coughed and finally got out, 'Yes, well, nice to meet you. Lexie, that lift... I'm a bit knackered.'

'I'm ready,' said the girl. ' 'Bye. 'Bye, Mrs Pascoe.'

' 'Bye, Lexie,' said Ellie.

'Ciao, Rod, Lex,' Pascoe called after them. 'Odd little thing. How do you know her?'

'Oh, I've met her at meetings,' said Ellie vaguely. 'That's what meetings are for.'

'You don't mean she's a WRAG activist?'

'Why shouldn't she be?' demanded Ellie. 'Though she's not, actually. It's appeal work mainly. She delivers pamphlets, goes out collecting for Oxfam, Save the Children, that sort of thing. Quiet but willing.'

'That's how I like 'em,' said Pascoe wistfully. 'Well, Ell. What's next on the programme? Hurry on down to Sardi's and wait for the first reviews?'

'Shut up, creep,' said Ellie. 'What happened to all that Big Eileen satirical stuff?'

'I told you, I was afraid of her.'

'You fancied her, you mean! One smile and you were grovelling at her feet.'

'That's all I could reach,' said Pascoe.

'Bastard!'

'So true,' said Pascoe. 'So very, very touching and so very, very true!'

CHAPTER 2

It was a week of that motley September weather, uncertain as April's but much more troubling to the human spirit, when days swing between noons of high summer and frosty midnights, and the shades of municipal trees, heavy and still on sunlit pavements, start to shift and squirm beneath a fragmented moon.

Cliff Sharman appeared in court on Tuesday morning. He had spent three nights in police custody, as the only address he would give was his grandmother's flat in East Dulwich, and he hadn't lived there on any regular basis for at least three years. Questioned, he said he was hitch-hiking round the country and had been living rough. Seymour didn't believe him. He didn't have the look or the smell of rough living. But it didn't seem a point worth labouring with rubber truncheons.

Wield had moved into another stage of his long limbo, no longer waiting for something to happen, for it *had* happened, but now waiting for a voice—Cliff's? Watmough's? Even his own?—to speak the cue for the next scene in this black comedy.

At last he felt he really understood this term. Black comedy was when a man stood naked and helpless under a spotlight and felt rather than heard the surrounding darkness crackle with malicious laughter.

He knew he should have spoken immediately Seymour brought the boy in, but he had waited instead for the boy to speak. He knew now that he had always waited for others to speak. Waiting was his forte. There was nothing anyone could teach him about waiting.

Seymour, young, ambitious and not insensitive, was hurt by Wield's lack of interest in his collar.

'I know he's probably just a one-offer. I mean, he was going at it so cack-handed, anyone could've spotted him...'

'You didn't,' interrupted Bernadette.

'I've not got eyes in the back of my head!'

'Nor in the front, or is it some fancy step you're after showing off by getting us out here among the tables?'

'Sorry,' said Seymour, steering her back towards the dance-floor proper. 'What I mean is, OK, he's probably not one of the gang we're after, they'd not employ anyone so useless. All the same, he was a collar, *my* collar, something to show for a week's work. And Wield didn't even give him a second glance, left me to question him all by himself.'

'Oh you poor boy,' mocked Bernadette. 'Reverse! Reverse! It's dancing we're at, not a route march!'

Standing in the witness-box giving evidence, Seymour observed that Wield had at least condescended to turn up in court, standing at the back, near the door, inscrutable as something carved on a totem pole with a tomahawk.

Sharman pleaded guilty, claiming a sudden impulse, wholly unprecedented, wholly regretted.

Seymour confirmed that nothing was known, the clerk muttered at the magistrate, the Bench conferred. Finally they delivered their judgment, which was that this first offence merited the leniency of a fine, and that, while they had no authority to ride the defendant out of town on a rail, they strongly recommended that he return to London as soon as possible.

When Seymour glanced to the back of the court, he saw that Wield had already left.

Sod him! he thought. It's one to me on my record sheet, no matter what that miserable bugger thinks!

The Pontelli murder investigation was still very much in the information-collecting stage. Eden Thackeray's identification had been firm and the body, having been taken to pieces for the benefit of pathology, was now reassembled for the benefit of whoever might appear to mourn and bury it. The fatal bullet had been definitely identified as a Luger Pistole 08 which, though it had clearly done damage enough, had not done as much damage as it might, leading the ballistics expert to surmise that the cartridge was perhaps rather ancient and had not been kept in prime condition. 'Weapons like the P 08 were popular war souvenirs, from both wars in fact, and this might well be one of the original rounds some idiot brought back with it,' he posited.

The pathologist's report included the possibly helpful findings that the deceased had had sexual intercourse a few hours before death, that the shot had not been immediately fatal and the deceased probably lived for at least thirty minutes after the shooting, that he was a man of about sixty in good general health, that he had at some time, at least twenty-five years previously, received serious gunshot wounds in the chest and abdomen probably, by the line of puncture scars, from an automatic weapon, and that he had a small but distinctive birth mark on his left buttock in shape not unlike a maple leaf.

To this, Superintendent Dalziel was able to add that Alessandro Pontelli had entered the country on a flight from Pisa on August 28th, that he was a resident of Florence, where he was well known in the tourist industry as a freelance courier and accommodation agent. The speed with which Dalziel produced this information was impressive to those who knew nothing of the unofficial official inquiries he had put in train at Thackeray's behest the previous Friday afternoon.

But this initial momentum was not maintained and by the end of Tuesday, they were no further forward in discovering where Pontelli had been, or what he had been up to, during his sojourn in England. The car, which proved to be beyond all reach of an MOT test certificate, was traced to its last official owner, a Huddersfield schoolteacher, who had traded it in as deposit on a second-hand Cortina eighteen months before. No doubt a long pursuit through trade-ins, scrap merchants and car-auctions would eventually lead to Pontelli coughing up a hundred quid, but meanwhile the CID cast around for closer, warmer trails.

Help when it came sprang from uniformed branch, which was not all that unusual. But the shape it took was far from common.

Police Constable Hector was hard to miss but easy to mistake. Shambling splay-footed along the pavement, his eighty inches reduced to a nearer seventy by curvature of the spine and a fifty per cent retraction of the head between the spiky shoulder-blades, he looked not so much like the law in motion as a reluctant party-goer cheated by a fancy-dress costumier.

Tonight, however, there was a jauntiness in his step and a light in his eyes which might easily have passed for intelligence. His features too were deceptive, being set in that expression of painful devotion seen on the saints of the Florentine masters, while his lips moved constantly as though in silent prayer. He was in fact counting the numbers of a terrace of once proud but long shabby Victorian houses, a task requiring all his concentration as some had fallen off and he was walking down the odd side, going from big to little.

Finally he reached No. 23, climbed the four steps with scarcely a stumble, entered a long narrow hallway which smelt of Eastern spices and Western detritus, and started up the stairs.

On the second landing he paused, got his bearings and knocked on one of the three doors. When no one answered, he opened it cautiously and found himself looking at a lavatory. Selecting one of the other doors, he knocked again. It was opened immediately by a woman in a dressing-gown.

'Is it Tuesday already?' she said without enthusiasm.

She turned back into the room. He followed, closing the door carefully behind him and sliding home the bolts. By the time he had finished, the woman had removed her dressing-gown and was lying on top of the rumpled bed, stark naked, her legs splayed. Hector undressed as rapidly as fumbling fingers and a reluctance to take his eyes off the unmoving form on the bed would allow. Ready at last, he advanced eagerly.

'Are you not taking your hat off?' asked the woman.

'What? Oh aye.'

Removing his helmet, he fell upon her recumbent body like a starving man upon a steaming platter. Two minutes later he rolled off, replete.

'You don't muck about much, do you?' said the woman.

'Don't I?' said Hector, who couldn't imagine what 'mucking about' would entail.

'Not much,' said the woman beginning to get dressed.

It was three months since Hector had appeared at her door, introducing himself as the new community policeman. She had thought he was a funny-looking bugger then, but had offered him the same arrangement she'd had with his predecessor, and it had worked out well enough, no hassle for her and a weekly bang for him.

There were, however, threats more perilous than officialdom and she reckoned she was earning protection there too. Mind you, as in this case the threat seemed to have been quite literally destroyed, she might do better to keep quiet. But whoever had done the destroying was still out there somewhere, and she'd come to the conclusion that the sooner she shared what little she knew with the law, the less chance there was of anyone wanting to make sure she kept it to herself.

She picked up a copy of Monday's *Post*.

'Here,' she said. 'This picture of that chap they found dead outside the cop-shop at the weekend.'

The location of the body had caused much simple mirth locally.

'Oh aye,' said Hector, struggling to master the mechanism of his zip. 'Foreigner.'

This, uttered as if in total explanation of the killing, was the sum total of what Hector had picked up about the case from station gossip.

'Foreigner, were he? Well, foreign or not, I reckon he were here on Friday night.'

'Here?' said Hector incredulously.

'Aye, that's what I said,' replied the woman, offended at this implied doubt of her veracity. 'He left his bag.'

Hector paused in the contorted position of one who found it difficult to think and fasten his fly at the same time.

'But what were he doing here?' he asked finally.

'Doing? What do you think he were doing?' said the woman impatiently. 'Same as you, you daft bugger.'

'Same as me?' he said, amazed. 'You mean you let someone else do it too?'

And the two of them regarded each other from twin but unbridgeable peaks of incomprehension, their faces lit by a wild surmise.

CHAPTER 3

'Monica Mathews,' said Pascoe. 'One conviction for soliciting, fined fifty pounds. When Hector took over that beat from Lewis a few months back, Lewis left him a list of useful addresses. When he knocked on Monica's door, she automatically offered him the same deal she'd had with Lewis. Our Hector just thought she was bowled over by his natural charm. He's all shook up to find out the truth.'

Dalziel shook his head in disbelief.

'That Lewis, happily retired, is he?'

'With his wife and three kids and part-time security job at the Co-op.'

'I'll give him Co-op if ever I run into him,' said Dalziel grimly.

'You can hardly blame him for Hector,' said Pascoe.

'I can blame him for dipping his wick in police time,' said Dalziel. 'Anyway, what've we got?'

'Well, it's definitely our man. She remembers the scar on his body. She picked him up in the Volunteer about nine o'clock.

They had a drink and talked terms. He wanted to know how much for the whole night. She got the impression he wanted somewhere to doss with no questions asked, and he wasn't averse to having a jump thrown in. Two, in fact. He managed two and promised a third when he got back.'

'He was taking a risk leaving his gear in her tender care when he went out, wasn't he?'

'Not really. The grip was well locked. Also he still owed the second instalment and the grip was security against his return. At the same time, if he found she'd been fiddling with it, she could probably have whistled for her money.'

'Any useful pillow talk?'

'Not really. He was very businesslike in advance. During, he just grunted. Afterwards he said nothing till he announced he had an appointment and would be back in one or two hours at the most. She watched him drive away. He went up to the end of Brook Street and turned left on to the main road. She said she got the impression he knew his way around.'

'Oh aye. Is that significant?'

'I don't know, sir. But if you keep on that road it takes you north along here—' he was pointing at a map of their area on the wall—'and you'd pass the road end into Greendale *here*, and a few miles further on, if you fork left, you come to the Old Mill Inn.'

'So?'

'Well, two Huby connections. Troy House in Greendale, and the Huby pub. And it was the Huby will that brought him here, wasn't it?'

'So that's where you'd look for a motive?' said Dalziel. 'You're a great one for a motive, Peter, even if it does sometimes take you round your backside to pick your nose. Me, I start with a body and work backward to find out where it's been and who with. But you go ahead and try it your way. Talk to 'em at Troy House and this pub. See if there's owt there for us.'

'Right, sir,' said Pascoe, a little cautiously in face of this sudden approval of his admittedly vague line of thought. 'You think there might be a connection?'

'Mebbe. More to the point, I've got a report here which says PC Hewlett was driving his patrol car back towards town along that road about one o'clock on Saturday morning. He got stuck behind a green Escort on the bendy stretch between Greendale road end and Stanton Hill.'

'Did he get the number?'

'No. The idle bugger was on his way to sign off and all he was interested in was getting by and back here as quickly as possible. I doubt if he'd have paid much heed if there'd been a masked man with a tommy-gun on the roof. He got by it and recalls it kept behind him for a long way after that.'

'You mean, that's how Pontelli got here? Followed Hewlett?'

'Why not? Foreigner with a bullet in him, needs help, sees a cop-car. Why not follow?'

'Why not blow his horn?' objected Pascoe.

'You've not read the car report very closely, lad,' said Dalziel triumphantly. 'Horn didn't work. It's a wonder anything did. Any road, he sees Hewlett distantly turning into our yard and follows suit. Comes to a stop in the corner. Can't get out of his door because he's tight against the wall. Slides over to try the passenger door. It's jammed. Gets down on the floor to try to push it open, passes out and bleeds to death. Is his grip still with Forensic?'

'Yes, but I doubt if they'll get much more from it.'

The grip had contained little of interest except some Italian clothes and an Italian passport. Pontelli clearly travelled light.

'He must have stayed somewhere while he's been in England,' continued Pascoe. 'He can't have dossed down with pros every night.'

'Don't see why not,' said Dalziel. 'Randy buggers, them wops. One thing, Peter. If you reckon this has got something to do with this Huby will, you'd best make up your mind if Pontelli got killed because he was a fraud or because he was genuine.'

'Yes,' said. Pascoe. 'I thought I'd have a word with Thackeray, if you don't mind.'

'Why should I mind?'

'Well, I know you're friends…'

'Are we? News to me! You talk to whoever you like, lad. By the way, where's Wield? I've not seen him this morning.'

'No. He rang in sick. He's been looking really peaky these past few days. We could do with him, though. It leaves us short-handed.'

'Sick?' said Dalziel unsympathetically. 'What's the bugger got? Some wasting disease? Mebbe he'll come back handsome! Well, if you're short-handed, Peter, no use sitting on your arse all day, is it? Get to work, lad, get to work!'

'He's on the phone,' said Lexie Huby. 'He shouldn't be long.'

'Thanks,' said Pascoe. 'We've met, haven't we? After the play the other night.'

He smiled winningly as he spoke. There were those who thought he had a very winning smile, but this little girl obviously listed him among her losers. She returned his smile with a gaze of owlish indifference through her huge spectacles and began to type.

Suit yourself, thought Pascoe morosely. He shouldn't feel too hard done to. If she looked about twelve to him, he probably looked about seventy to her. *Looked?* Some days he felt it! It wouldn't be long till the male menopause started squeezing his scrotum. The sensible approach was a philosophical jocularity. Middle age is when you start fancying your friend's daughters; old age is when they look too antique. That was the right note to hit. But sod philosophy! He'd tried it already, but Chief Inspectorship kept on breaking in. He ought to be a DCI by now. His whizz-kid curve demanded it. Much longer and he'd be bottom-side of a normal plodding career parabola. What was holding things up? Was it incipient paranoia, or had the DCC really been looking at him rather strangely of late? He'd passed Watmough in the corridor only this morning and the man had actually sniffed in a very marked fashion. Could it be BO? He resolved to give himself a really good squirt with that body lotion spray Ellie's mother had given him at Christmas before he next encountered Watmough.

'Mr Pascoe. Mr Thackeray's ready now.'

From the girl's tone, she had clearly already addressed him once. Bloody hell, she must be thinking the poor old sod's brain is falling apart.

He stood up and the movement shook the bits of his brain back together again.

'Huby,' he said. 'Your name's Huby.'

'Yes, I know.'

'And the actor you're friendly with is called Lomas?'

'Yes.'

'My secretary is the late Mrs Huby's grand-niece, Inspector. Mr Lomas is the son of Mrs Huby's cousin once removed, Mrs Stephanie Windibanks. I did explain all these connections to Superintendent Dalziel.'

Who left me to muddle along by myself! thought Pascoe as he went to meet Eden Thackeray who was standing in the doorway of his office.

'You'll have to explain it all to me again,' said Pascoe.

It took more than thirty minutes. Thackeray was determined he was not going to have to repeat himself a third time.

When he had finished, Pascoe said, 'You knew Mrs Huby very well, I suppose, Mr. Thackeray.'

'I was her solicitor for fifteen years, Mr Pascoe. Before that, my father acted for her. When he died and I became senior partner, Mrs Huby's affairs were part of my inheritance. But I would not say I knew her well. It took her several years to come to regard me as much more than a usurping office boy.'

Pascoe smiled and said, 'What kind of woman was she?'

Thackeray looked thoughtful and said, 'Between ourselves?'

Pascoe nodded and made a big business of putting away his notebook.

'Between ourselves, she was a pretty awful kind of woman,' said Thackeray. 'Overbearing, rude, opinionated and snobbish. She could also be charming, entertaining and considerate, but only on feast days or to members of the Royal Family. Her pretensions to culture started and finished with a passion for Grand Opera. She was politically naïve, which is a polite way of saying she was a natural fascist. She found it hard to forgive the Tories for conniving at the giving away of India and she sat glued to her television set during the Falklands crisis in the firm belief that after the task force had mopped up the Argies, it would carry on its cleansing crusade wherever frogs, wogs or reds pretended to rule the waves. She treated her animals better than her relatives and she squandered what little she did have of unselfish, altruistic human affection on one crazy obsession which ruined her own life, soiled the lives of others, and brought us all to this present unhappy situation.'

'You should have been a barrister,' said Pascoe. 'That was a pretty powerful speech for the prosecution. It's this obsession of hers I'm interested in. Was it based purely on a mother's intuition or did she actually educe evidence that her son might in fact have survived? What, in other words, are the facts?'

'I can be of very little help to you there, Inspector,' said Thackeray. 'I gathered from remarks she let slip from time to time that she never gave up the active investigation of her son's disappearance, but our firm was only peripherally involved. Perhaps this was because her investigations had to be clandestine while her husband was alive, and she found it hard to get out of the habit. Or perhaps it was because she recognized my own strong scepticism and my father's before me.'

'Her husband didn't share her hope, then?'

'No, indeed. He bore with her, and perhaps even had a faint glimmer himself, till the war was over and the POW camps had all been accounted for. Then, so my father told me, he gave commands that his son was not to be mentioned except as dead. He had a memorial tablet put up in St Wilfrid's at Greendale and a service was held. Mrs Huby was too ill to attend.'

'But she paid heed to his wishes? He must have been a pretty strong-willed fellow too,' said Pascoe.

'It was a battle of giants,' said Thackeray, 'He was a truly hard man, Sam Huby. But she had the one weapon most ladies keep up their sleeves to administer the *coup de grâce*.'

'What's that?'

'Longevity, Inspector. Look around you. The graves are full of men, and the cruise-liners full of widows.'

Pascoe laughed out loud.

'You know how to keep a chap cheerful,' he said. 'You said just now your firm had little to do with Mrs Huby's actual researches, but you must have drawn up the will?'

'Indeed yes. Many years ago.'

'Did you approve of the will?'

'That is not a proper question,' said Thackeray. 'So this is not a proper answer. No, I did not. I pressed for such modification as I could, but she was adamant about the main clause and I saw no reason to lose the firm a profitable account.'

'No question of balance-of-the-mind-disturbed?'

'Not when she made her will, certainly.'

'But later, you think there was?' pressed Pascoe catching a lawyer's quibble.

'In the past three years, perhaps. She had a stroke, you know. She was seriously ill for a little while, but made a remarkable recovery, except that now she spoke quite openly of a psychic conspiracy to keep her son from her. Who the conspirators were was never quite clear, but according to the old girl they'd sent a black demon as a pretended emissary from her son but she had seen through the deception and dismissed him. Don't ask me how, but the victory, as she called it, reaffirmed her confidence that Alexander was alive. But, fearful of being incapacitated again, she framed an advertisement to be placed in the Italian papers saying she was seriously ill and inviting anyone with information to contact me. This advertisement I caused to be placed in the Italian press two months ago when she had her second stroke. When Pontelli approached me, he produced a copy of the advertisement from *La Nazione*.'

'I see. Were there any other responses to the advert?' inquired Pascoe.

'Naturally. We are talking about human beings, Inspector. In both our trades we know that rogues abound. Mainly they consisted of people who wrote claiming to have information about the whereabouts of Alex and offering to sell it.'

'What did you do with them?'

'I replied with a photograph asking if they were certain the mature man they knew and the young man on the photo could be the same person.'

'I should have thought they'd have all passed that test,' laughed Pascoe.

'Indeed they did. One hundred per cent positive identification. Happily the photograph I sent them was a snapshot of myself aged twenty and looking as unlike Alex Huby as you can imagine!'

'Clever,' said Pascoe sincerely. 'But Pontelli, I gather, was convincing.'

'Oh yes. He didn't write, of course. Just turned up to discover, he claimed, that he was too late and his mother was dead. Hence his dramatic appearance at the funeral.'

'Not so convincing now we know he had been in the country for a week beforehand,' said Pascoe.

'He admitted that, said he had vacillated, uncertain how best to proceed. He claimed to have rung up Troy House to ask after his mother's health on three occasions and on the last was told she was dead. Miss Keech confirms there were calls of inquiry from people she did not always identify.'

'And Pontelli was persuasive?'

'Oh yes. He had certainly done his homework. Date of birth, details of family, schooling, Troy House—he trotted out enough to give me pause, but when I started asking about his reasons for staying away all these years, he grew agitated, tapped his head, said something about long-suffering and a time of healing, and left very abruptly, saying he would be in touch again soon.'

'Leaving you half convinced?' asked Pascoe.

'Oh no. It takes more than that even to half-convince a lawyer!'

The phone rang. Lexie Huby told Thackeray there was a call for Pascoe. He took it at the solicitor's desk while the other man courteously pretended to be examining the view from the window.

It was Dalziel.

'Peter, that picture of Pontelli's been run in some of the other papers in the *Challenger* group and we've had a call from Leeds. Owner of the Highmore Hotel says he reckons our boy was there for two weeks registered as Mr A. Ponting of London. Did a bunk last Friday, they reckon, with a fortnight's bill outstanding. I've cleared it locally for you to drive over there and chat to this fellow, name of Balder. OK?'

'I suppose so, but I want to go out to Troy House, and then to the Old Mill...'

'Get 'em on the way back, you've got all day,' growled Dalziel. 'You're not the only one who's busy, you know. I've got landed with a Rotary lunch. Them things go on most of the afternoon. Then it'll be back to the grindstone. I've found out that this PAWS fellow, Goodenough, and the Windibanks woman are still staying at the Howard Arms. Interesting they should still be hanging around, isn't it? I thought I'd better stroll round and have a chat.'

And I bet it just happens to coincide with licensing hours! thought Pascoe viciously.

He said, 'I'd better take some prints in the hotel room just to be one hundred per cent sure. Could you ask Seymour to get a box of tricks and meet me back at the station? In fact, he can drive me. My own car's knocking a bit and I don't want to risk getting stuck in the Leeds rush.'

'Seymour? I suppose you can have him,' grumbled Dalziel. 'It's a bloody nuisance yon bugger Wield skiving off.'

'Wield. Oh yes. Glad you mentioned him,' said Pascoe provocatively. 'Thought I'd drop in on my way home tonight, see how he is. Want to go halves on a bunch of grapes?'

'Bunch of bananas more likely!' said Dalziel. 'Tell him the organ grinder would like his monkey back! Cheers!'

The phone slammed down. Pascoe carefully replaced his receiver and greeted Thackeray with the sunny smile of a man who is ashamed of his own murderous thoughts.

'Incidentally,' he said. 'What sort of records did Mrs Huby keep of her search for her son?'

'I've really no idea,' said Thackeray. 'It was a very personal thing for her. I believe there's a filing cabinet in the study at Troy House full of her private stuff. All her business and financial papers were kept here or at her accountant's, of course. Normally the next of kin would sort out the personal things, but in this case...well, I suppose it will fall to me as executor in the end.'

'Yes. Perhaps I could collect them for you, save you the bother of a trip...' murmured Pascoe. 'I'd like to look myself.'

'But don't want to bother with a warrant,' suggested Thackeray. 'Of course. I'll tell Miss Keech you're coming, shall I? What time?'

'Oh, it'll be four, four-thirty, I should think. Thank you, Mr Thackeray. Good day.'

As he left he tried the winning smile on the little secretary again but the big spectacles merely flashed light at him, then darkened as she bowed her head once more to the typewriter.

(HAPTER 4

By his own not unreasonable standards, Dalziel was right in his suspicions of Wield. Not that the fat superintendent was unwilling to admit that there might be conditions of the heart more painful than angina, but unless they were treatable under the NHS, he wasn't about to accept them as excuses for absence.

The sergeant had returned to his flat the previous evening uncertain of what he might find. Most probable seemed that Cliff Sharman would have preceded him to collect his belongings and continue on his way. He felt both disappointment and relief to discover the boy's bag where it had been since the previous Saturday.

He was still unable to work out precisely what the youth was playing at. Why for instance had he kept quiet about his connection with Wield when he was brought into the Station? The obvious, if not the only answer, was that the last thing a potential blackmailer wants is to bring things out in the open. Also, the boy's silence had invited his own, and thus deepened his complicity.

He sat with these and other equally cynical thoughts till close to midnight when he heard a key turn in the lock. He held his breath. The lounge door slowly opened. The single table lamp threw the boy's face into strange relief.

'Hello, Mac,' said Sharman.

Wield did not reply.

'I left my things.'

'They're where you left them.'

'Yeah. I'll get 'em and be on my way.'

'You'll have a bit of a wait for your bus!' said Wield savagely.

'Bus?'

'Yes. All that crap about hitch-hiking and turning up here by chance! With a timetable in your wallet!'

'You went through my wallet?' said the youth in apparently genuine surprise. 'Christ, I should've known you would! That's what you're trained to, isn't it, being a pig.'

'Don't knock it, son,' said Wield. 'After all, that's what brought you here in the first place, wasn't it?'

'To stay with a pig?'

'To see what you could squeeze out of me. I've had a word with Maurice, lad. I know all about you, believe me.'

'You two speaking again, are you? Nice to think I've brought you together,' said Sharman with a not very convincing sneer. 'What'd he have to say?'

'What do you think? A glowing testimonial?'

'No. But if he told you I came up here just because of you, he's a bloody liar! I mean, think about it, Mac! I'm going to take off into the sticks to try to put the black on a gay cop just on the basis of what Mo lets slip in bed? I mean, shit, the kind of pigs I know in the Met would have had me picked up at Heathrow with an arseful of junk if they got half a sniff I was a threat to them! No one told me it'd be any different up here in the paddy-fields.'

'You rang me all the same,' said Wield, rendered almost defensive by the force of this argument.

'I felt lost,' said Sharman. 'I mean, here I was, not knowing anyone. For all I knew, they still tarred and feathered gays up here. I needed a friendly native and you were the nearest possibility.'

It was almost convincing, except that Wield was acutely aware of his readiness to be convinced and this made him reinforce his scepticism.

'Very touching,' he said. 'So what *did* bring you up to sunny Yorkshire? A message from Mo, was it?'

'Listen,' said Sharman. 'It wasn't Mo that mentioned this place first, it was *me*. That's what set him on telling about you. It was me who started it, not the other way round, OK?'

'Oh aye? And what the hell did you have to say about Yorkshire?' sneered Wield.

The boy hesitated a moment, then took a deep breath and began.

'Mo had been asking me about my family. I don't think he was really interested. You know the way you chatter on when you're...well, you know. Anyway, I told him I lived down in Dulwich with my gran. My mum died a few years back, and Gran brought me up. Dad paid the bills, well, he paid what he could, and he'd come and stay with us as often as he could, but he worked a lot up west, in clubs and hotels, and he had to live in, so he couldn't get down to Dulwich as often as he'd have liked. Then about three years ago, he went off. Well, he did sometimes. I got a card from him. He always sent me a card if he went off anywhere, so I'd know not to expect him in the next week or so, then he'd send another saying when be was going to be back. Only this time there wasn't another card, just the first one. And that one came from here. This town. That's what I told Mo; that's when he said he used to live here and started telling me about you. Well, he wasn't really interested in what I was saying, was he? Why should he be? So I shut up and let him tell me these funny stories about him screwing around with a copper.'

Wield ignored the pain in his heart and said coldly, 'So, you decided to come up here and look for your dad? After three years? Is that it?'

'Yeah, that's it!' said the boy defiantly.

'This postcard, you've still got it?'

'I did have it,' said the youth, looking distressed. 'But I must've left it at Mo's when I came away.'

'Very careless. But then you are careless, aren't you? Careless with other people's possessions as well as your own.'

'What's that mean?'

'Maurice says you robbed him,' said Wield.

'He's a lying cunt! I didn't take nothing that wasn't owing me!'

'Owing you. For what?'

'We'd been sharing expenses, that sort of thing. When we split up, I was owed.'

'Bollocks,' said Wield. 'Let's have the truth, lad.'

'We had a row,' said Sharman sullenly. 'I brought someone back to the flat. I thought Mo was away for the night but he came back unexpected. He was very nasty and he chucked me out. I went back for my stuff next day when he was at work and, like I say, I just took what was owing me.'

'And you decided to come up here and look for your dear old dad after three years?' mocked Wield.

'That's right!' exploded Sharman. 'That's what I decided. I'd thought of it before, but I'd never done anything about it. Don't you ever put things off and keep putting them off?'

Oh yes, thought Wield. I do. I do.

He said, 'And what did you expect to do when you got here? Just walk around till you bumped into this father of yours?'

'Why the fuck not?' cried Sharman. 'I didn't think it'd be quite as big as this, and I thought he might sort of stick out.'

'Stick out?'

'Yeah, stick out. He's black, you see. I mean, not like me, but really black, and I thought...'

'You thought it was all sort of little villages up here where the kids'd follow a black man round the streets, staring at him like he'd dropped out of the moon?'

'No, don't be stupid,' said the youth unconvincingly.

'And what have you done to find him?' said Wield, still unpersuaded by any of this.

'What the fuck could I do? Ask a policeman?'

'Why not? First thing you did was telephone one.'

The boy suddenly grinned.

'It's daft, but I never thought of it that way,' he said. 'No, I've tried ringing round the Sharmans in the phone book in case there were any relatives. I think he came from up north originally. But no luck. So then I thought I'd advertise.'

'Advertise?'

'Yeah. Get my name in the paper. I thought he might see it if he was still up here.'

Wield's eyes widened in disbelief.

'You trying to tell me that's why you got arrested for shoplifting?' He recalled Seymour's description of Sharman stuffing goods into his pockets like he was picking brambles.

'That, and...'

'And *what*? Come on, tell me. It's at least half a second since I heard something incredible.'

This sparked off the boy's anger once more.

'Because of you!' he yelled. 'Because of what you said the night before. You made it clear you thought I was only out for what I could get, so I thought I'd show you...'

'Show me what?' demanded Wield. 'Show me up, you mean?'

'I don't know,' said Sharman, subsiding. 'I was all mixed up about you and Dad and everything. I don't know what...anyway, I didn't show you up, did I? I had the chance but I kept schtumm, didn't I?'

He stood before Wield, part defiant, part scared.

Wield could not feel his own emotional state was any clearer. How much of this was truth, how much lies? And how much an inseparable mix of the two?

He said, 'I had every chance to say something too.'

'Don't be bloody stupid,' said the boy in genuine surprise. 'Why the hell should you have said anything? You had everything to lose, nothing to gain.'

Then after a pause he added slyly, 'I bet you were shitting yourself, though.'

Wield nodded slowly.

'That's one way of putting it, I suppose,' he said.

The boy relaxed.

'Well,' he said. 'I suppose I'd better get my gear together.'

It was a toe in the water rather than a statement of intent.

'It's late,' said Wield. 'It's very late.'

❊ ❊ ❊

In the early hours, Wield awoke. He lay very still, fearful of disturbing the slim, warm frame beside him in his narrow bed. But it was an unnecessary effort.

Sharman said, 'You awake, Mac?'

'Yes.'

'There's something I should tell you.'

'Oh aye?'

'I did think of trying to make something out of it, you being gay, I mean.'

'Is that right? Blackmail, you mean?'

'Well, no. I didn't think you were the blackmail type.'

'Scared you, did I?'

'Too bloody true! No, I thought I might make a few quid from the papers, though. I thought it'd make a good story.'

'And?'

'I rang one up. The local one.'

'The *Post*? Not their cup of tea, I shouldn't have thought.'

'No. They put me on to the other lot, the *Sunday Challenger* next time.'

'Next time? You rang twice?'

'Yes. I'm sorry. It was after we'd had that row. I didn't know what I was doing. That's when I ended up nicking stuff from that shop.'

'So you talked to the *Challenger*.'

'Yeah. Some guy called Vollans. He wanted to meet and talk about money and things. But I wouldn't. And I didn't mention any names or anything, though he kept on asking.'

Wield smiled secretly at the way in which humble confession was changing to a display of virtue.

'You're sure?' he growled.

'Yes. Honest, Mac. I wouldn't... I just rang off. I'm sorry. I wanted you to know.'

'Well, now I know,' said Wield. 'Let's get some sleep.'

A silence followed but not the silence of repose.

'Mac.'

'What?'

'It must be great being...well, *older*,' said Sharman wistfully. 'I mean, old enough not to be worrying about what's best to do, and how to do it, all the time.'

'Oh aye,' said Wield. 'You're probably right. It must be great.'

CHAPTER 5

The Highmore Hotel had started as a boarding-house in a quiet suburban street. Slowly it had started feeding on the houses on either side of it in the once stately Edwardian terrace. By the time the other inhabitants of the street were alerted to the danger, it was too late. Suddenly almost overnight the woodwork of the 'hotel' was painted a piccalilli yellow and the whole world could see that the monster was out of control. Now began the downward spiral of private householders rushing to sell their properties and by their own haste and numbers creating the falling market they feared.

A pub on the corner of the street had previously spilled its hungry customers towards the distant main road and its chippies. Now, with heavy traffic towards the Highmore and the neighbourhood's ever-growing number of multiple occupancies, a Tandoori takeaway plus a chip-bar cum video-rental completed the street's decline from upward-aspiring Edwardian to dingy 'eighties commercial.

Mr Balder was in fact a very hairy man who made it quite clear that it was no mere knee-jerk sense of civic duty that had made him ring the police but a passionately held belief in the right of landlords to get what was coming to them.

'Fortnight's rent for his room he owes me,' he averred. 'Fortnight's! What that idiot cashier of mine was thinking of! I'll kill her, I'll kill her!'

The idiot cashier turned out to be Mrs Balder who had clearly found Mr Ponting a very attractive and persuasive guest.

While Seymour was lifting prints from the room, Pascoe got the story, such as it was, of Pontelli's stay. A quiet man, kept himself to himself, implied he was a commercial working for some small London firm starting a selling operation in the North. No visitors. A couple of phone calls out from the hotel pay-phone, but none in till the previous Friday, when there'd been three or four in the afternoon and then a man had called in person at night asking for Mr Ponting.

Age? Hard to say. Youngish; well, twenties, thirties, that sort of thing, or well-preserved forty. He was well wrapped up. No, it wasn't a cold night, was it? But there had been a threat of rain after a fine day. Hair, lightish brownish. Height mediumish. Accent, not Yorkshire. Southern maybe. Or posh Scottish.

Pascoe gave up. Seymour appeared with several sets of prints. Balder, who evidently felt they should have gone through the dead man's pockets and extracted the money for his hotel bill, let his impatience show, and Pascoe coldly wondered how long it was since the fire department had examined his property or the local police his register.

They headed back to town, Pascoe feeling a curious sense of homecoming as they left the Leeds boundary and crossed into Mid-Yorkshire territory.

Christ, I really must be getting old! he mused. Next thing, I'll be nostalgic for Dalziel.

Back at the Station, they checked the prints and found one set from the Highmore room which matched the dead man's. Dalziel was not yet back from his Rotary lunch, so Pascoe sketched out a report, dropped it on the fat man's desk, and set out with Seymour to Troy House.

'Funny business, this,' observed the young constable as they once more left the town.

'In what way?' said Pascoe encouragingly. He had moderately high hopes of Seymour.

'Well, this chap Pontelli says he's really Huby who was supposed to be killed in the war. And he ends up dead from an old bullet fired by an old German pistol.'

Pascoe sighed and said, 'That's it, is it? Better stick to the *paso doble* if that's your best shot at detective work.'

Seymour looked and felt hurt at this unkindness. Since his translation from disco to ballroom under the guiding hand of Bernadette McCrystal, he had grown used to cracks about sequins on his socks and yards of tulle, but Pascoe rarely joined in this lumbering jocularity. Seymour had a forgiving nature, however, and as they drove up to Troy House, he said, 'Look! They've got horses.'

'Donkeys,' said Pascoe. 'And that donkey with the horns is a goat.'

Well, pardon me for breathing, thought Seymour.

The door opened before Pascoe could ring.

'Mr Pascoe?' said the woman who stood in the threshold. 'Mr Thackeray said you would be coming.'

'Miss Keech, I presume. This is Detective-Constable Seymour.'

Miss Keech extended her hand to Pascoe, nodded at Seymour and led them into the house.

She was more *grande dame* than housekeeper, or perhaps it was much the same thing, thought Pascoe, whose acquaintance with both types was cinematic. She walked rather stiffly, body erect, head high. She had strong grey hair, elegantly coiffured, and was dressed in a long dark burgundy shirt and a blue silk blouse. A faint effluvium of cat or dog laced the air of the entrance hall but was completely absent from the large drawing-room into which they processed.

'Please be seated. Would you care for some tea?'

The trolley was ready and the steam issuing from the teapot spout showed that it was already massing. She must have been watching from the window.

'Thank you,' said Pascoe. 'It's a lovely house.'

'You think so?' said Miss Keech, pouring the tea. 'I've always found it rather barn-like. But it's been my home now for many years and doubtless will be till I die, so I shouldn't complain. Buttered scones?'

Pascoe shook his head but Seymour fell to with a will.

'Yes,' said Pascoe. 'I gather that under the terms of your late employer's will, you are to remain in charge here.'

'Unless, of course, her son reappears and wishes to make other arrangements,' said Miss Keech pedantically.

'You don't feel this is likely? I mean, you didn't share Mrs Huby's faith in her son's survival.'

'Mrs Huby was my employer, Inspector. I started as her nursery maid and I ended as her companion. As a maid, I learnt to be obedient. As a companion, I learnt to be discreet.'

'But as a friend...'

'I was never a friend. You don't pay friends,' she said sharply.

Pascoe drank his tea and took stock. This was not what he had expected. The rich, snobbish, racist Gwendoline Huby sounded to have been a formidable woman. He had not expected her companion to be other than meek and self-effacing.

He probed further.

'You mean Mrs Huby was sensitive to the...er...social gap, between you?'

'Mrs Huby was sensitive to the social gap between her and half her relatives,' snapped Miss Keech. 'Starting at her husband.

I'm sorry. I shouldn't have said that. It was not a snobbish thing, you understand. More an aspect of her faith in an orderly universe.'

'The rich man in his castle, the poor man...'

'Yes, precisely. She saw no reason to quarrel with the world as God had created it.'

'Including white supremacy, I gather,' said Pascoe, recalling the legacy to Women For Empire.

'She was not political in the strict sense,' defended Miss Keech, perhaps guilty at her posthumous disloyalty. 'She sincerely believed that if God put the black people in backward countries and the whites in civilized countries, that was part of his plan.'

'But the supposed death of her son wasn't?'

'No. She persuaded herself not. What I don't think she could bear was the sense of responsibility...'

'I'm sorry? From the sound of her, she'd have found someone else to blame surely?'

'Oh yes. She and Mr Huby certainly blamed each other. *She* was so proud that he got a commission and everyone could see that he was a gentleman. *He* was so pleased when he went to do commando training and everyone could see he was a real man. *She* thought he courted danger to please his father, and *he* thought she'd made him soft. But inside, I think they both blamed themselves. Parents do, don't they? Even the most selfish and self-centered. In the dark of the night, all alone, it's hard to hide from the truth, isn't it? Mr Huby I think learned to bear it. She never did, and that's why she couldn't let him be dead.'

Seymour had his notebook balanced on his knee but he clearly saw no need to divert his hands from the buttery scones to record any of these psychological insights.

'You've obviously thought deeply about this, Miss Keech,' said Pascoe.

'Not really,' she denied, suddenly all brisk and housekeeperish. 'Now, I presume you've come to see me about this man. The one whose photograph appeared in the *Evening Post*.'

'Why should you think that?' wondered Pascoe.

'Because Mr Thackeray told me,' she said with a show of exasperation.

Pascoe smiled, produced a copy of the photograph and handed it over.

'Do you recognize him, Miss Keech?'

'I would say, without being absolutely sure, that he was the man who interrupted Mrs Huby's funeral at the graveside. I expect Mr Thackeray described the incident?'

'Yes, he did,' said Pascoe. 'That was the only time you saw him?'

'It was.'

'Mr Thackeray felt there was what he called a Huby look about his features. Would you agree?'

'To some extent,' she said. 'A certain coarseness of feature, perhaps, not unlike John Huby, the publican. But nothing of the Lomases, that's for sure.'

'We're trying to trace his movements on Friday night. You weren't disturbed at all, were you? Unexplained phone calls? Or noises outside?'

'A prowler, you mean? No, Mr Pascoe. And surrounded as I am by livestock, I think I would have been well warned.'

'Possibly. Oh, by the way, Mr Thackeray asked me to pick up some papers for him,' said Pascoe. 'Mrs Huby's records of her researches or some such thing.'

'Yes, he said so. If you would care to follow me, I'll show you where they are.'

She rose and the two men followed, Seymour with a regretful back glance at the cream cake which his determined onslaught on the scones had so far prevented him from sampling. They went down the long hallway and entered a booklined room which was like a Disney design for the Athenæum in that all the deep leather-bound chairs were occupied by sleeping animals. A huge black labrador stretched along a Chesterfield opened one sagacious eye, owned an inmate, and went back to sleep without disturbing the small tabby kitten snoring between his shoulder-blades.

'Here's where she kept her personal papers,' said Miss Keech, pointing to a two-drawered filing cabinet resting on a table in one corner. 'I have the key somewhere.'

Pascoe said, 'I don't think you'll need a key, Miss Keech.'

Reaching forward one finger, he pulled open the top drawer.

'Dear me,' said the woman. 'I'm sure it was locked.'

'Indeed, it probably was,' said Pascoe.

It was an old cabinet with a simple lock. A thin knife inserted between the drawer and the frame could easily push the catch aside. A couple of scratches on the edge of the drawer convinced Pascoe this was what had happened.

He said, 'When did you last look in here, Miss Keech?'

'To my knowledge, it's only been opened once since Mrs Huby's death. Mr Thackeray's clerk came to collect any financial papers relating to the estate and he wanted to see what was in here. I opened it for him, he glanced through, said there didn't seem to be anything there for the accountant, and I locked it up again.'

'I see. Seymour, still got that printing kit in the car? Good. Dust around here, will you? But wipe your fingers first. You're like an EEC butter mountain. Miss Keech, you don't have a photograph of Mrs Huby's son I could see, do you?'

'Of course, Inspector. This way.'

She led him out of the study and up the stairs.

Oh God, thought Pascoe. She's going to open up one of those rooms they have in the old movies. It'll be just like he left it all those years ago. Toys and books and teenage decoration; slippers by the bed and coverlet turned down; the only doubt is whether it will be kept scrupulously clean or thick with dust and draped with cobwebs!

So vivid was his mental picture that the reality was almost disappointing. The unlocked door opened on a smallish bedroom perfectly clean and tidy, with its sash window raised to admit a fresh-ening draught of bright air. A faintly pathetic touch was provided by a pair of neatly folded pyjamas on the quilted counterpane. Pascoe regarded these while Miss Keech approached an old-fashioned mahogany wardrobe. It said much for the self-conditioning of his gothic anticipation that it took a good thirty seconds for him to start wondering why these putative relics of 1944 should bear a modern brand label with a European size and the interesting information that the material was 65% polyester and 35% cotton.

He turned to discover Miss Keech mounting a chair to reach a pair of old suitcases on top of the wardrobe.

'Here,' he said. 'Let me.'

'It's the bottom one,' she said.

The top one appeared to be empty. More interestingly, it had a modern Alitalia flight label stuck to it.

Pascoe said casually, 'Miss Keech, has anyone been using this room?'

'Why yes, of course. But don't worry, he won't mind. He's such a nice boy.'

'Boy?'

Pascoe recollected the dead man. It had been a long time since he was a boy!

'Who is *he?*' he asked.

'I'm sorry. Didn't I say? It's Mr Lomas. Rodney Lomas. He's appearing at the Kemble, you know, in *Romeo and Juliet*. He wanted me to go to the first night, but I don't go out much in the evenings. To be honest, I don't much care for Shakespeare either, and there was a good thriller I wanted to see on the television.'

'Yes, I know. *The Killers,*' said Pascoe sadly. 'So Mr Lomas is staying here, is he? I didn't know that. That means you needn't have relied on the animals to protect you from a prowler on Friday night. You had a young fit man to take care of you.'

'Oh no,' she said, as if put out by the implication that she needed taking care of. 'Rod wasn't here on Friday.'

'You mean, he didn't move in till later?' said Pascoe, recalling seeing the young man in the Black Bull on—when was it?—Thursday lunch-time.

'No. He came last Wednesday. But he rang me up on Friday night to say he was spending the night with a friend.'

'Locally, would that be?' inquired Pascoe casually.

'He didn't say, but in Leeds I presumed. The silly boy ran out of change and had to reverse the charge, and the operator said Leeds.'

Pascoe digested this as he opened the old case.

'Why did you put Mr Lomas in this room, Miss Keech?' he wondered.

'Why? Well, simply because it was the only bedroom in the house which has been kept cleaned and aired and fit for instant occupation. He arrived unexpectedly and I saw no reason not to use it.'

'Surely Mrs Huby's old room…' murmured Pascoe.

'I have moved in there myself, Mr Pascoe,' she said briskly. 'My own bedroom I now use as a dressing-room. I am not a senti-mentalist, nor do I believe in ghosts. The old clothes belonging to both Mrs Huby and her son I have cleared out and donated to the WVS for charitable distribution. Some photographs and other memorabilia which were kept in this room I put into that case.'

It was a collection pathetic in every sense. Christening mug, baby bootees, school reports, a school cap, examination certifi-cates—all the mileposts of childhood were here. Also there were photographs, framed, loose and in an album, plus several card-board cylinders containing yards of schoolboys in tiers outside a grey castellated building. Here it was then, a record for all who cared to view it, of the progress of Alexander Lomas Huby from the comfort of the cradle to the edge of the grave.

Such was Pascoe's grim thought as he looked at the last of the photographs which showed a young man in a subaltern's dress uniform, smiling, half-embarrassed, at the camera.

There was an echo of someone there.

Suddenly he caught it clear. The little girl in Thackeray's office; something about the eyes and the shape of the head; but above all the same quality of uncertain reserve.

But there was no way of translating these young features into that waxen mask lying in the mortuary.

'I'll hang on to this photograph if I may,' said Pascoe. 'Shall we go down?'

Seymour had finished his dusting and had found a couple of good prints on the cabinet where a man might rest his left hand while sliding a knife into the gap with his right.

'Miss Keech, would you mind letting my constable take your prints just for elimination purposes?' inquired Pascoe.

'My fingerprints? How exciting. I've seen them do it on the television. Would you like to come through to the drawing-room, young man? We'll be more comfortable there.'

She looked sternly at the animals who had clearly decided the newcomers were harmless and continued to sleep soundly in their chairs.

'And Seymour,' Pascoe added softly as Miss Keech left the room, 'pop upstairs afterwards, second bedroom on the left, dust around in there. Don't leave any traces, though.'

'Right on,' said Seymour ethnically.

Alone, Pascoe started to examine the contents of the filing cabinet. There were a number of cardboard wallets each marked with a year starting at 1959, and three older-looking undated wallets. Pascoe started with these and found, as he had guessed, the record of Alexander Huby's death, starting with the telegram which regretted that he was reported missing in action.

Slowly he pieced the story together. Early in 1944 Huby had joined his unit in Palermo, Sicily. The Allies were making slow progress north against heavy German resistance on the mainland, but by May, the enemy were falling back from the Gustav Line, south of Rome, to the Gothic Line from Pisa to Rimini.

Huby was put in charge of a four-man team whose job it was to land on the Tuscan coast north of Leghorn, make contact with local partisans, send back surveillance reports on German troop movement, and be picked up five days later. A corvette dropped them in heavy seas at the appointed time and that was the last that was seen of them.

There was no radio contact, they failed to make their pick-up rendezvous, and a leaking and capsized dinghy of the type used in the operation was spotted floating in the sea some thirty miles away.

Lack of any report of contact from the partisans, or of prisoners being taken from the Red Cross, made it almost certain that the five men had died before reaching the shore. Huby's CO wrote consolingly if conventionally, and as far as the army was concerned, that was that.

Pascoe looked at the silver-framed photograph he had placed before him. The young soldier smiled uncertainly back. Anything less like the deadly commando of Pascoe's boyhood comics was hard to imagine. Perhaps—in fact, certainly—appearances deceived. He must have volunteered for the job, met the selection criteria, and passed the doubtless extremely rugged training course.

'Here's looking at you, kid,' said Pascoe.

Next followed correspondence between Mrs Huby and the War Office, the Red Cross, the War Graves Commission, the American Occupation Authority in western Italy, her local Member of Parliament, and a host of other individuals and bodies whom the desperate woman saw as straws to grab at. It was repetitiously pathetic on her side, politely formal on theirs.

Pascoe skipped on through the files, came across a reference to 'the enclosed photograph', tracked back a couple of bundles and came across the original.It was from a 1945 *Picture Post* and showed Allied troops driving through the city of Florence to the ecstatic greeting of its citizens. Among the crowd lining the pavement, someone (Mrs Huby presumably) had ringed a single face. It was ill-defined and slightly out of focus; a man, pensive and watchful rather than joyously enthusiastic, though this might have been an effect of light, shadow and distance rather than a reflection of his feelings; a face which in shape and proportions bore some resemblance to the face in the silver frame and in which love and loss could very easily trace the exact lineaments of Alexander Lomas Huby.

There were letters to the editor of *Picture Post* and, once discovered, to the photographer who supplied the picture. There were letters to the authorities, military and civil, in Florence. And finally, in 1946 there were letters to the main newspapers in Italy instructing them to place the enclosed advertisement in their personal columns in both Italian and English. It was a simple appeal for Alexander Huby or anyone knowing his where-abouts to get in touch with his mother at Troy House, Greendale, Mid-Yorkshire, UK. There was a reward.

Here the early files ended. Pascoe could have guessed what had happened even without Eden Thackeray's confirming testimony. By 1946 Sam Huby's little store of hope was utterly depleted. His son was dead. His wife's desperate belief he toler-ated till she placed these advertisements. Doubtless the promise of reward had brought replies, most of them blatantly fraudu-lent—probably *all* of them, in his eyes. Enough was enough. He had said *No more!* And his will had been strong enough to hold sway, or at least drive her underground, for the next thirteen years till his death.

Once Sam Huby was safely interred, the old obsession so long repressed burst out with renewed vigour. This was where the regular yearly files began. The spate of letters recommenced, coupled now with personal visits both to the relevant offices in London and to Italy. Investigation agencies, both English and Italian, were employed. Pascoe read a selection of their reports which appeared scrupulous in their detailed nil-returns and ultimately in their blunt assertion that they doubted if they could hope to achieve anything in this matter.

The woman's dogged refusal to accept the obvious was both heroic and lunatic. The *Picture Post* photograph apart, there was not in forty years a single scrap of anything resembling evidence that her son had survived, unless you counted (as she did) reports from assorted 'sensitives' that they could find no trace of him 'on the other side' but that they had strong visions of someone very like him working in an olive grove, or that their divining pendulums always swung violently across the map of Europe towards Tuscany.

There was a tapping at the door. Pascoe put the papers he was studying back in the file and called, 'Come in!'

Miss Keech appeared with a tray newly replenished with tea and toasted muffins. Pascoe wanted neither but, guessing that Seymour had devised the task as a means of keeping the woman out of his hair while he worked upstairs, he thanked her kindly and did not demur when she offered to pour his tea and butter his muffin.

As he chewed at the luscious dough, he said butterily, 'Did you assist Mrs Huby in her investigations, Miss Keech?'

'Directly, only by typing and ordering her correspondence,' she replied. 'Indirectly, by remaining here and taking care of the animals while she was pursuing her researches elsewhere.'

'She seems to have spent a lot of time and presumably money on this.'

'I assumed so. The money, I mean. I have never had, or desired to have anything to do with Mrs Huby's accounts,' she said rather tartly. 'Time I know about. She spent a regular period in London and abroad each year until she had her first stroke. This was immediately after returning from a visit to Italy and thereafter she no longer went abroad. She did not trust foreign medicine. She was obsessed by the fear of finding herself in a hospital run by Catholic nuns with black doctors.'

Pascoe smiled and said, 'Yes, Mr Thackeray told me about this fear of black men. Something about black devils masquerading as Alexander. It must have been hard for you to cope with. You nursed her, I believe.'

Her face went still and pale as if at an unpleasant memory and suddenly she looked very old indeed.

'It was not always easy,' she said with little inflection. 'Will you give me a receipt for whatever you take, Inspector?'

'Of course,' he said, a little surprised.

'You see, I am after all only a custodian and in the end accountable,' she said.

Seymour entered as Pascoe was writing the receipt. His eyes lit up at the sight of the muffins and he seized one avidly.

As they left the house, Pascoe glanced at his watch and said. 'We should get to the Old Mill Inn just at opening time, Seymour. Shall I ring ahead and tell them to start buttering the teacakes?'

'No, this'll do me till my supper,' grinned Seymour, licking his fingers.

'I hope you haven't got your prints all over the car,' said Pascoe. 'And talking of prints, any luck?'

'A bit,' said Seymour. 'There were a few of Miss Keech's prints on the cabinet, but a lot that weren't. And at a casual glance, these look to me just the same as the ones all over that room upstairs.'

'You reckon so? I wonder. Do ghosts leave prints, Seymour?'

'Why not?' said the redhead cheerfully. 'All them chilly fingers running up and down your spine!'

Pascoe groaned quietly and said, 'Just drive me to the Old Mill Inn.'

CHAPTER 6

'Shall we go up to my room, Superintendent?' asked Andrew Goodenough.

Dalziel looked up at him in mild surprise.

'Got some etchings up there you want to show me?' he inquired.

'No. I just thought it would be more private.'

Dalziel glanced round the bar of the Howard Arms Hotel, taking in the plush carpet, the plusher upholstery, the rows of gleaming bottles.

He sank into one of the chairs. It was as comfortable as it looked.

'Nay, this'll do me, Mr Goodenough,' he said. 'If you feel an urge to confess to anything a bit embarrassing, I'll ask them to turn the Muzak up. We'll just look like a couple of businessmen having a chat.'

Goodenough said, 'In that case, perhaps you'll join me in a drink? For the sake of verisimilitude, I mean.'

'Whisky,' said Dalziel. 'Thanks.'

He noted with approval that the Scot brought doubles.

'Now, how can I help you?' said Goodenough.

'You can tell me what you're doing here, Mr Goodenough,' said Dalziel.

'You must know that or you wouldn't be wanting to talk to me,' said Goodenough.

'No. I know why you came up here in the first place. Eden Thackeray's explained all that. But he also thought you'd have gone back south by now, and at Reception they told me that in fact you were due to check out on Saturday, then you extended your stay. Why was that?'

'My business proved more complicated than I foresaw,' said Goodenough evenly.

'Oh aye?'

'I'm sure Mr Thackeray has filled you in on the details. I had people to see about pursuing my organization's claim to a share in Mr Huby's estate.'

'These people being...?'

'Mr Thackeray himself, naturally. Mr John Huby of the Old Mill Inn...'

'Why'd you want to see him?' asked Dalziel.

'To obtain a waiver to any claims he might possibly make against the will.'

'Did he have a claim?'

'He might imagine so. The point is, he along with Mrs Stephanie Windibanks, that's the other nearest relative, could cause considerable delay if they pressed their case either separately or in unison. Also it strengthens our hand if we can say in court that no other challenges to the will are likely to be forthcoming.'

'So they've got nuisance value?'

'That's about the strength of it.'

'This Windibanks, you'll have seen her as well as Huby.'

'Yes. I saw her first in London, then again when I came up here. She's staying at this hotel, in fact.'

'Is that so?' said Dalziel, who knew very well it was so, and also that Mrs Windibanks too had extended her stay.

'Did they both agree to this waiver, then?'

'Yes, as a matter of fact, they did.'

'How much?'

'I'm sorry?'

'How much did it cost you?'

'Superintendent, I shouldn't like you to think...'

Dalziel interrupted him by lifting his now empty glass into the air and shouting at the barman. 'Two more of the same, sunshine!'

The barman thought of ignoring him, thought better of it, and turned to his optic.

It seemed a good example to follow.

'Five hundred,' Goodenough said. 'They each get five hundred now.'

'That sounds cheap,' said Dalziel. 'For a merry London widow and a Yorkshire publican. You said *now?*'

'That's up front. If we break the will and get immediate payment they each get five percent of the estate's current value.'

'Which is?'

'Million and a quarter to a million and a half.'

Dalziel computed.

'Jesus,' he said. 'That's a hell of a lot of nuisance!'

'It'll be worth it if we get the money. And if we don't, they don't,' said Goodenough.

'What're your chances?'

'Fair, I'd say.'

'Fairer now that Alessandro Pontelli's out of the way, I dare say. You didn't try to get him out of the way by any chance, did you, Mr Goodenough?'

A silence fell between the two men which not the Muzak, nor the chink of glasses or the tinkle of small talk, nor the more distant susurration of a large hotel at the start of a busy evening could render less silent.

'I'm not sure I understand your question,' said Goodenough finally.

'Well, it's simple enough,' said Dalziel innocently. 'You've just been telling me how much you're willing to shell out to buy off Mr Huby and Mrs Windibanks because of their nuisance value. Anyone claiming to be the actual heir would have the biggest nuisance value of all, I'd say. So I just wondered if, after Mr Thackeray told you this Pontelli fellow had been to see him, you might have tried to buy him off too. That's all. Perfectly natural, I'd say.'

'Yes, it might have been,' said Goodenough. 'Except I'd have had to know where to find him, wouldn't I?'

'That's right. I'd not thought of that,' said Dalziel ingenuously. 'It must be age creeping up. Where were you on Friday night, by the way?'

'Night. You mean evening?'

'Aye, well. Start there.'

'Well, I was across in Ilkley early on...'

'Ilkley. Now there's a thing. What were you doing there?'

'I went to see Mrs. Lætitia Falkingham, the founder and president of Women For Empire which you will recall is the third beneficiary under Mrs Huby's will. I wanted to get her organization's accord in my plans for contesting the will.'

'And did Mrs Falkingham play ball?'

'Indirectly. Mrs Falkingham is old and frail and has handed over the reins of WFE to a young woman called Brodsworth who has full legal and executive authority.'

'Sounds important if you put it like that. What's it mean?'

'Nothing at the moment. WFE consists almost entirely, I suspect, of a very small, extremely geriatric membership. It has small funds and less influence. In short, it seems set to die with Mrs Falkingham.'

'Except...?'

'Except that Miss Brodsworth and her friends seem determined to keep the organization going.'

'Friends? What friends?'

'I find it hard to believe that a woman like this Miss Brodsworth would be content to channel her political energies and beliefs through an organization like WFE.'

'You sniffed an ulterior motive?'

'Very strongly. But she seemed to be legally empowered to act on behalf of WFE, so I got her signature on a document empowering PAWS to initiate proceedings on behalf of all three secondary beneficiaries.'

'You don't look to me like a man of quick judgments, Mr Goodenough,' said Dalziel.

'Thank you. I'm not. That's partly the reason I stayed on up here over the weekend. I know Eden Thackeray wasn't happy about the Brodsworth woman either and I wanted to be sure that I understood the extent of her executive power.'

'Because you were worried about the money falling into the wrong hands, or because you were bothered in case her signature mightn't be valid?'

Goodenough frowned.

'I see you're a cynic, Mr Dalziel,' he said. 'But I admit my motives were mixed.'

'And Eden Thackeray?'

'Confirmed that if the money dropped into WFE's hands tomorrow, there's very little to prevent Miss Brodsworth presenting it to the National Front or worse...'

'You think she would? But you've got no evidence?'

'Not yet. There was a journalist at Maldive Cottage too, however, and he's obviously interested in the woman.'

'A journalist?'

'Yes. From the *Sunday Challenger*, I think he said. Not a paper I know. Henry Vollans is the reporter's name.'

Dalziel nodded. Pascoe had told him about meeting Vollans at the Kemble party and learning from Sammy Ruddlesdin that he'd be following up the gay cop story, if story there were. It had put him in mind of seeing Watmough and Ike Ogilby having lunch at the Gents.

'So you finished your business at Ilkley. What next? Didn't go into Leeds by any chance?'

'As a matter of fact I did,' said Goodenough. 'Any reason why I shouldn't?'

Dalziel was slightly nonplussed. He'd been trying to fit Goodenough into the frame as the man calling at the Highmore Hotel in search of Pontelli, and would have preferred evasiveness.

'What took you there?'

'I had a drink with this reporter, Vollans, after I'd seen Mrs Falkingham. We got talking. By the time we'd finished it was too late to get back to the Howard Arms for dinner and he recommended a Chinese restaurant in Leeds. I'm rather partial to Chinese food...'

'Oh aye? So, yellow press followed by yellow nosh. I shouldn't have thought you'd have had much time for tabloid journalism, Mr Goodenough.'

'I like good publicity for PAWS whatever its source. Also I got the impression that Vollans also sniffed something not quite right about this Brodsworth creature, and I respect the power of the Press to ferret out things the individual citizen can't hope to discover.'

'Like the police,' said Dalziel. 'Did you do a deal, then?'

'We established a climate of mutual dorsal confrication,' said Goodenough.

Clever bugger, thought Dalziel malevolently. I shall have you!

Courteously he inquired, 'What time did you get back on Friday night, Mr Goodenough?'

'Oh, latish. Eleven o'clock, something like that.'

'Straight to bed?'

'Yes, that's right.'

'They don't remember you coming in at the desk,' said Dalziel gently.

'Don't they? Now, now I recall, there was no one in Reception so I just helped myself to my key.'

'Oh aye? Poor service for a posh place like this.'

'It happens in the best hotels, Mr Dalziel.'

'Does it? I wouldn't know.'

Dalziel belched gently and raised his left leg to scratch his under thigh.

'Superintendent Dalziel? I thought it must be you from the description they gave me at Reception. I got your message. Mr Goodenough, how nice to see you again. Vincent, darling, my usual.'

Stephanie Windibanks sank into a chair between the two men. Elegant in a salmon pink blouse and a tartan pleated skirt, she crossed legs whose flesh was still firm enough to give a sensuous tautness to silk stockings, patted her expensively coiffured hair and smiled brilliantly at Dalziel to show perfect white teeth.

'Mrs Windibanks?' said the fat man, slowly eyeing her up and down.

'That's right. Was it something particular you were looking for, Superintendent, or are you just taking a general view with the idea of making an offer?'

'Nay, the coach-work is grand, but I'd need an expert to look at the engine,' said Dalziel.

The woman's smile froze for a second, then she let out a trill of laughter. The barman set a tall, well fruited drink before her and she picked it up and made a mock-toasting gesture towards Dalziel.

'Why I ever left the North, I cannot imagine.'

'I sometimes wonder the same,' said Goodenough.

Dalziel said, 'I was just asking Mr Goodenough here where he was on Friday night. What about you, Mrs Windibanks?'

'Where was I, you mean? Oh, here and there. I had a meal in the restaurant, a couple of drinks in the bar, took a stroll to get some air, went to bed, watched some telly, read a book. That would just about fill the evening in, wouldn't you think?'

'You didn't answer the telephone,' said Dalziel.

'I'm sorry?'

'There were a couple of calls for you late on. The switchboard got no reply from your room.'

'Perhaps I was in the bath.'

'Long bath,' said Dalziel.

The woman sipped her drink, then turned her brilliant smile on the other man.

She said, 'Mr Goodenough, perhaps you can tell me what this is all about.'

'I think,' said Goodenough slowly, his dry Scots accent giving his words a measured forensic weight, 'I think it's about whether I, in order to improve the chances of PAWS inheriting half a million pounds, or you, Mrs Windibanks, in order to improve your chances of gaining seventy-five thousand pounds, would brutally do to death one of our fellow human beings.'

The woman said, 'My God! You're joking, of course?'

But her eyes were narrow with calculation rather than wide with shock.

She went on. 'Has he actually spelt this out, Mr Goodenough?'

Dalziel said, 'Thinking of a lawyer, are you, Mrs Windibanks? Quite right. I admire someone with a sharp eye for a quick profit. But you'll not get rich chasing after poor bobbies with defamation suits, isn't that right, Mr Goodenough? Or have you forgot all your law?'

'You seem to know a good deal about me,' said the Scot.

'I've just started,' said Dalziel. 'I like to know about people. About you. About Mrs Windibanks here. About Pontelli or Huby or whoever he was.'

'That'll be hard to prove now one way or another,' said Goodenough.

'Oh, there's always science,' said Dalziel with the Archimedean certainty of one who found it hard to understand why electricity didn't leak from light sockets with no bulbs in them.

Mrs Windibanks, who had been sitting listening to this exchange with an air of weary superiority suddenly said, 'Hang on a sec. Perhaps I can help.'

The two men looked at her with a shared surprise.

'How's that?' said Dalziel.

'This body you've got, could I see it?'

'For identification, you mean? I doubt that'd help very much, luv,' said Dalziel. 'Forty years changes faces a lot. I mean, you saw this man at the funeral and you didn't think, here's Alexander back to claim his cash, did you?'

Mrs Windibanks smiled.

'True,' she said. 'But I wasn't thinking of his face. You see, Superintendent, I've just remembered. When I was a little girl, I used to go to Troy House with my parents and when poor Alexander was at home, he used to be given the task of looking after me. Neither of us enjoyed it much. He was ten years older than I was, you see...'

She paused as though daring a challenge. Five years older, guessed Dalziel, six at the most!

'The one thing I did enjoy was when he took me down to the river. He used to go in swimming. I just paddled in the shallows. The thing was, he used to swim in the buff. That school he went to was one of those places where the boys all used to swim nude in the school pool, a considerable perk for some of the staff, I dare say. Well, who am I to blame them? I used to enjoy watching Alex, believe me. He didn't consider me as female—I was a child relative and a bloody nuisance—so he was completely uninhibited. Alas, I spoilt it all one day, though.'

She sipped her drink and looked at them coquettishly over the foliage.

Dalziel said, 'You stripped off.'

'You're spoiling my story!' she protested. 'Yes, I decided that paddling was dull, so while he was floating around, I took off all my clothes and started to wade in. I was just beginning to develop then, you know, enough to be visibly different.'

Dalziel did a quick calculation. The lad must have been seventeen at most. He went in the army at eighteen. So take her alleged ten from his estimated seventeen and you got a most unlikely seven!

'You must have been an early developer, luv,' he said with a broad wink.

'Thank you,' she said as though he'd paid her a compliment. 'As soon as he saw me, everything changed. From being a naked shepherd lad bathing in the spring, he became a blushing, stuttering schoolboy who was so embarrassed he almost drowned! He couldn't get dressed quickly enough. It was my first, but not, alas, my last disappointment. We went bathing together no more.'

'Very touching,' said Dalziel. 'But what's your point, luv?'

'My point is he had a mark, a sort of mole on his left buttock, like a little leaf. I thought that was what it was, first time I saw it, that he'd sat on the grass and it had stuck. But when it didn't wash off, I realized it was part of him. There you are, Mr Dalziel. If your poor corpse has got that mark in his skin, then I would say yes, indeed, this man could be Alexander Huby!'

CHAPTER 7

Gruff-of-sodding-Greendale soared through the air, hit the wall with a dusty thump, and crashed to the flagged floor.

John Huby, the climax of his tale of woe achieved, now returned the centre of the stage to a dumbfounded Pascoe with an angry glance.

Seymour picked up the recumbent animal and said with relief, 'It's stuffed.'

The couple of early regulars who were standing at the bar guffawed appreciatively.

Pascoe said, 'I'll have that drink now, if you don't mind.'

'Aye. Well, come through to the kitchen then, out of the way of flapping lugs.'

With a sour glare at the two customers to make sure they didn't miss his point, John Huby led the way into the private quarters behind the bar. As Pascoe followed he glanced at Seymour and with a flicker of his eyes gave him the probably not unwelcome command to chat up the blonde who was polishing glasses against her straining, plunging blouse.

'I see you're extending, Mr Huby,' said Pascoe. 'Business must be good.'

'You think so? Then you don't know much about it, do you?'

'No, not really, but I thought...'

'I'm extending to *make* business good,' said Huby. 'If it *were* good, I'd not be bothered, would I?'

Pascoe tried to work out if this interesting economic theory were Keynesian or Friedmannite, gave up and said, 'It must be costing a packet.'

'What if it is? What's that to you?'

'Nothing, it's nothing,' Pascoe assured him.

'As long as that's understood,' said the man. 'Ruby!'

A larger, older version of the girl behind the bar appeared.

'Fetch us a couple of beers, will you?' said Huby.

'Halves?'

The man looked at Pascoe. It was a moment of significant assessment, he guessed.

'Pints,' said Huby.

The woman disappeared.

'Your wife?' suggested Pascoe.

'Aye.'

Ruby Huby. Pascoe savoured the name. Ruby Huby.

He said, 'I'm sorry about your disappointment, Mr Huby. But, as I said to you before, what I'm here about is this man who was murdered, the man, we believe, who interrupted your aunt's funeral and claimed to be your missing cousin.'

'He didn't do that,' objected Huby. 'Not at the funeral.'

'I believe he said, *Mama*,' Pascoe pointed out.

'Our Lexie and Jane, they've got a stack of old dolls that say *mama*,' retorted Huby scornfully.

'The implication was clear enough, I should have thought,' murmured Pascoe.

Huby glowered at him with the expression of a man who was regretting having said 'Pints'.

Somewhere a telephone shrilled.

'He certainly claimed to be Alexander Huby in the presence of Eden Thackeray,' said Pascoe.

'Him? What's he know? Bugger all. He didn't even know Alex when he were a lad.'

'But you did, of course?'

'Aye. Not well. He were off at that fancy bloody school most of time, but I knew him. I knew him well enough to be able to say if some bugger turning up after all these years were him or not.'

'And what was your considered verdict?' said Pascoe, certain of his answer.

Mrs Huby came in with two pints on a tray.

'You're wanted on phone,' she said to her husband.

'Who is it? Tell 'em to ring back. I'm busy.'

'It's that woman,' she said. 'Says it's important.'

Grumbling, Huby rose and left the room.

'Cheers,' said Pascoe sipping one of the pints. 'Good ale, this. Is that your daughter behind the bar, Mrs Huby?'

'Aye. That's our Jane.'

'Yes. I've met your other daughter, Lexie, isn't it? She works at Mr Thackeray's.'

'That's right.'

'Bright girl,' said Pascoe fulsomely. 'You must be proud of her.'

'Oh yes,' said the woman, with sudden enthusiasm. 'She were always clever, our Lexie. She could've stayed on at school and done her Highers, you know. Teachers wanted her to. But John said no. It'd be wasted on a girl.'

'Do you think it would've been?' asked Pascoe.

The woman sat down suddenly. She must've been good-looking in her prime and it wasn't long past. Pascoe guessed she was a good ten years younger than her husband.

'Times have changed,' she said. 'Especially in the town. I'm glad she got a job there. She's a good help in the pub and everyone likes her. But it isn't for Lexie, I could always tell that.'

Pascoe tried to tune into the little girl being useful and popular in the public bar and failed to get a picture.

He persisted, 'But do *you* think she should've stayed on and done her A-levels, Mrs Huby?'

'Not just A-levels,' said the woman. 'College. They reckoned she could've gone to college. Not just nights, like she does now. But proper college.'

'She goes to night classes, does she? What in?' wondered Pascoe.

'At the Institute. Something to help in her job, I think,' said the woman, whose pride clearly did not extend to the particular. 'And she drives her own car, you know. And listens to that fancy music. I wish she could get herself a nice boy, though. But she doesn't seem much interested.'

The door opened and Huby returned. His wife stood up, nodded pleasantly at Pascoe and left.

'Nice woman,' said Pascoe.

Huby regarded him with deep suspicion.

'You've not come here to pass compliments at my wife,' he said, making it sound like technical rape. 'I thought you wanted to ask me about this Italian fellow.'

'That's right. But not much point really as you only glimpsed him the once,' said Pascoe negligently.

'Who said I only saw him the once?' demanded Huby. 'That were you, not me!'

'You mean you saw him again?' asked Pascoe, amazed at the admission rather than the fact.

'Aye, did I. He came here last Friday.'

'Friday night, you mean?'

'No, I bloody well don't! If you want to answer the questions as well as ask 'em, why don't you sod off and talk to yourself!'

It occurred to Pascoe to wonder if some distant consan-guinity existed between the Hubys and the Dalziels.

'Tell me about it,' he said politely.

'It were Friday afternoon. I'd been in town. I got back here just on closing time and he were sitting out there in the bar, by the window. Not that I paid any heed at first. I didn't really notice him till Ruby called time. Well, after a while most of the buggers moved off, but he sat fast. I were helping clear up and I went over to him and said, time to trot, sunshine, or some such thing. He didn't budge, but just looked up at me and said, *Hello, John.*'

'And did you recognize him?' asked Pascoe.

'I saw he were the fellow who'd caused the fuss at the funeral,' said Huby.

'I see. Go on.'

'I said, what's your game then? He said, I'm your cousin Alex. Do you not remember me? I said, I remember you made a farce out of my auntie's funeral. He said, I didn't mean it, but I had to pay my respects to Mama. I said Mama be damned! I'm not standing here listening to this twaddle! I said, if you're my cousin, then I'm Lord Lucan, and I told him if he wanted to bother old Thackeray or hang around Troy House, that were his business. Happen he'd not be out of place there, I said, as Keech'd already got one third-rate actor staying with her. But if I caught him hanging round the Old Mill again, I'd give him a good kicking. He didn't like the sound of that much, so he up and left.'

'You know how to make your guests feel welcome, Mr Huby,' murmured Pascoe.

To his surprise the man looked rather shamefaced.

'Well, I did go over the top a bit, I suppose, but me rag had been up ever since I heard about him calling on old Thackeray...'

'And how did you hear that?' asked Pascoe, annoyed with himself for not having picked up the reference first time.

'I'd been in town that day seeing Goodenough, the animals fellow. He told me.'

'Goodenough?' Pascoe recalled Dalziel's mention of the PAWS man. 'What were you talking to him about, may I ask?'

'You can ask,' rasped Huby. 'But it'll still be none of your sodding business!'

Suddenly Pascoe had had enough of Yorkshire moeurs.

'Listen, Huby,' he rasped. 'You'd best get it into your head that I'm not one of your bloody customers to be pushed around. This is a murder inquiry and if I don't get answers here, I'll get 'em down town at the Station. Right?'

'Keep your hair on,' said the publican. 'If you must know, we were talking about the will. What else? This Goodenough fellow don't want to wait till next bloody century for his money, so he's going to court. Only, he wants to be sure me and old Windypants aren't going to make a fuss...'

'Windypants?'

'Aunt Gwen's cousin on the Lomas side. Windibanks is her name from that crooked husband of hers, but she were Stephanie Lomas when she were a lass.'

Pascoe noted but resisted the tempting side-track of 'crooked husband' and pressed straight on.

'So Goodenough was buying you off?' he said. 'I hope you didn't come cheap.'

'Cheap enough unless he wins the case,' grunted Huby. 'Then we get a bit more. But I'll believe that when it happens.'

'A percentage is it? I see. Then you'd not be all that happy to see someone turning up and claiming he was your dead cousin so he could sweep the pool?'

'Just hold your horses!' said Huby. 'All right, I weren't best pleased when I saw this bugger sitting in my pub. And mebbe I were a bit sharper than I should've been. But if any bugger goes around saying I'd kill someone for a bit of brass, I'll knock his bloody head off!'

This seemed a curious way for a man to deny his potential for violence, and it was followed up by a piece of reasoned argument perhaps even more curious from such a source.

'Any road,' said Huby, 'if he were a fraud, the law'd never give him the money, and if he were genuine, it were his to have anyway.'

'If he were genuine?' said Pascoe. 'I thought you were absolutely certain he was an impostor?'

'Nay, that was you again, answering your own questions,' said Huby. 'I thought that at first, fair enough. And second time we met, I weren't in the mood to look favourably at him. But thinking about it later, I got to wondering if mebbe I'd been too hasty. Mebbe I should've given him a hearing at least. He went meek as a lamb when I told him to get out, and that was just like Alexander. Never a lad to stand up to rough handling.'

Pascoe digested this.

'You're talking about the boy you remember,' he said.

'But that boy became an officer, he did commando training. If Pontelli was by some remote chance your cousin, he'd been shot up pretty badly, and he'd made a life for himself in a strange country and cut himself off from everything familiar and comfortable back here. That sounds pretty tough to me.'

'Mebbe,' said Huby. 'Except mebbe it were easier to stay away than come home. Mebbe he found himself out of the war and didn't fancy getting back into it. What was to come back to in Greendale, any road? They pushed him round, his mam and dad, and it didn't help that they pushed in opposite directions. No, happen he got a bang on the head, and when he started recalling his happy childhood days, he thought he'd be better off staying put where he was.'

Pascoe was taken aback by this analysis. Not that he doubted Huby's intelligence, but to date his impression had been that the man only regarded other people as potential obstacles to be walked through.

'It's a pity you didn't take this sympathetic view while you had the chance,' said Pascoe. 'You might have been able to ask some useful questions.'

'Aye, you're right,' said Huby. 'But I weren't to know silly bugger were about to get himself killed, were I?'

Pascoe glanced at his watch and groaned inwardly. Another late return to the steadily hardening bosom of his family.

'Can I use your phone?' he asked.

'All we've got's the pay-phone near the front door,' said Huby. 'Use it as much as you like, long as you keep feeding it money.'

'Thanks,' said Pascoe, rising.

As he reached the door, Huby said, 'Hang on. There were one thing. I recall some mention of a birthmark or summat young Alex had. On his bum, so it would only be referred to all delicate like, the Lomases being so genteel.'

'A birthmark. On his bum, you say!' said Pascoe, keeping his face blank.

'Aye. Not that I ever saw it myself, we weren't that close. Perhaps me dad mentioned it, I don't know. A sort of mole, or something. Shaped like a leaf. Aye, he'd still have that there, wouldn't he, Mr Inspector?'

Business looked fairly good as Pascoe made his way through the now crowded bar. It was a fine warm evening, of course, good drinking weather.

Seymour was leaning on the bar, engaged in what seemed like a very humorous conversation with Jane Huby. He caught Pascoe's eye and Pascoe signalled two minutes as he passed. The phone was on the wall quite near the entrance and as he reached it, the door opened to admit the slight figure of Lexie Huby.

She stopped short when she saw him.

'Hello,' he said.

'Hello. There's nothing wrong, is there?'

'What am I doing here, you mean?' he laughed. 'No. Just routine, as we say. I'm just going to ring my wife to tell her I'm late, which is what she knows already.'

This bit of domestic tittle-tattle seemed to reassure the girl and she managed a smile.

'Just back from work?' he asked. 'They must put you through it at Thackeray's!'

'No. I had to go to the library to pick up some books I'd ordered.'

He'd noticed she was carrying a battered old briefcase which looked packed to bursting point. Pascoe had a picture of this quiet little girl curling up in her room with a stack of highly coloured extremely romantic historical novels, bodice-rippers even, shutting out the noise and bustle and masculine heartiness of the pub below. But her mother said she was useful and popular! Well, what were mothers for if not to be partial on their children's behalf?

He smiled and said, 'Well, nice to see you again,' and picked up the phone. The door opened again to admit a large rubicund man who looked like a children's book illustration of a farmer, an impression confirmed by a pair of well-manured Wellingtons.

'Ee, Lexie, luv, is that you?' he said with evident delight. 'I hoped we might be in luck tonight.'

'I'm just back from work, Mr Earnshaw,' said the girl. 'I've not had me tea yet and I'll be busy later on.'

'Date, is it?' said the farmer.

'Yes, that's right.'

'Well, I'm glad you've found yourself a young man at last,' said Earnshaw with that hearty insensitivity which is the hallmark of the northern rustic. 'But surely you could spare us a couple of minutes? I'll tell that miserable old dad of thine I'm off to the Crown else!'

The girl, who had been standing with her hand on the handle of the door marked *Private* which presumably led directly into the Huby's living quarters, glanced at Pascoe who had been eavesdropping unashamedly. He grinned and shrugged slightly in what was intended as a gesture of young person's solidarity but which quite clearly came across as old person's patronization.

'All right,' the girl said, dropping her briefcase with a dusty thud. 'A couple of minutes won't harm.'

Earnshaw ushered her into the bar and Pascoe, irritated once more at the ageing process the girl seemed to provoke in him, completed his dialling.

As expected, Ellie was not pleased. Her displeasure prompted him to lie when she asked where he was ringing from. *A kiosk in the middle of nowhere* seemed less provocative than a pub. Unfortunately just then the bar room door opened letting out the sound of animated chatter, clinking glasses and, most damning of all, the merry tumult of an old piano on which *Happy Days Are Here Again* was being played with great vigour.

'And that's a passing hurdy-gurdy man, I suppose?' said Ellie icily. 'How long do you expect to be?'

He said, 'I've got to get back to town and collect my car. Oh, and I really ought to look in and say hello to Wieldy. He's off sick. I won't stay long, especially if he looks infectious.'

He would have postponed the visit altogether, except that he remembered guiltily his efforts to choke Wield off on Saturday when he'd been so keen for a private chat. The opportunity to talk hadn't arisen since and he felt somehow he'd let the man down.

'Be back by eight, or you'll find your dinner coming to meet you,' ordered Ellie. 'Ciao!'

Pascoe opened the bar door to summon Seymour but the redhead was not inclined to have his eye caught. Interestingly, it wasn't the busty blonde who was holding his attention but the piano-player in the corner who also made a verbal summons impossible. Irritated, Pascoe went across the room and grasped Seymour's elbow.

'Sorry, sir. Didn't see you were ready. Hey, but she can really swing that old Joanna, can't she? You'd not think she'd have the strength to hit the keys like she does.'

Pascoe looked to see who the object of this encomium was. There on the piano stool, doll-like in stature but electric with pent-up energy in every curve of her slight body, Lexie Huby was launching herself into the grand climax of what had turned into something like symphonic variations on *Happy Days Are Here Again*. With a series of accelerating arpeggios she brought these musical pyrotechnics to an end and the red-faced farmer led the rest of the listeners in enthusiastic applause.

'More, more!' he cried as the girl, slightly flushed with either exertion or pleasure, made to rise from the stool.

She shook her head, caught Pascoe's eye, hesitated, and sat down again. Her fingers moved, the music started again; Pascoe recognized the tune instantly. It was *The Bold Gendarmes*.

'Let's go,' he said to Seymour.

As he opened the front door of the pub, he noticed the girl's case still lying by the *Private* door. Ignoring Seymour's curious gaze, he stooped and opened it.

He would have been disappointed now to find it full of bodice-rippers, but he whistled in surprise when he found himself looking at *Milton's God* by William Empson, *The King's War* by C. V. Wedgwood and *The English Legal System* by R. J. Walker.

'Anything up?' asked Seymour.

'No,' said Pascoe, refastening the case. 'Just a simple lesson in not judging the goods by the packaging, my boy. You'd do well to remember it.'

'You mean the little lass playing the piano?' said Seymour astutely. 'I see what you mean, sir. On the other hand, that was her sister I was talking to behind the bar, and did you see the packaging there!'

'You lecherous young sod,' said Pascoe. 'And you almost an engaged man! Mind you, it could all be done with fibre glass and Bostik, couldn't it?'

'Mebbe. But it'd be fun finding out,' said Seymour dreamily. 'It'd be fun finding out.'

CHAPTER 8

It had been a strange day for Wield. Guilt and happiness had boxed for possession of his mind. During the morning, happiness had established a points lead. Cliff had been content to sit around the flat, drinking coffee, listening to a pop channel on the radio, chatting about nothing in particular. Wield had sat and watched and listened and understood his loneliness in recent years, and felt it as a personal reproach.

Guilt began to fight back in the afternoon as the boy grew restless and sullen and said he was tired of being cooped up, and couldn't they go out? Wield said that he'd rung in sick, something he'd only done a couple of times ever and never when it wasn't true, and he couldn't go wandering off. Someone might ring, or he might be seen. But there was no reason why Cliff shouldn't go out if he wanted to.

To his disappointment the boy accepted with alacrity, and for an hour or more it was Wield's turn to feel restless, but when Sharman returned about five o'clock, he was so lively and affectionate that the sergeant's insurgent misgivings were soon soothed away. They ended up in bed again. At half past six the youth rose and said he would sort out their evening meal. This evidently involved another trip out of the flat as Wield heard the door open and shut. He lay for another quarter of an hour, then got up himself and decided to have a bath.

He'd been in it long enough to start worrying once again when there was the sound of the flat door and shortly afterwards, Sharman's voice calling that dinner would be on the table in five minutes, so would he get a move on?

Wield took his time, discovering in himself a reluctance to be bossed around in his own apartment. When he entered the living-room wrapped in the towelling robe which Cliff had borrowed on his first night here, he saw the table set with a Chinese takeaway feast. It was not food he cared for very much, but he forced an appreciative smile. There was, however, in the air a smell additional to the rich odours of oil and spices and soy sauce. He looked at the boy, sitting crosslegged on the floor with an easy grace and an expression of fatuous self-congratulation. He was smoking and it wasn't tobacco.

Before Wield could speak, the doorbell rang.

He answered it without considering possible consequences as it delayed the saying of whatever he was going to say to Sharman.

'Sick call,' said Pascoe. 'Oh hell, have I got you out of bed?'

This seemed the obvious interpretation of the robe. Then through the open door of the living-room he glimpsed the food-laden table.

'Oh good. You're eating anyway,' he said. 'How goes it?'

'I'm fine,' said Wield. 'Thanks. I'll be back tomorrow.'

Pascoe, all primed with reasons for not coming in and sitting down, was curiously put out by the lack of any attempt to urge him to do so. He felt a childish compulsion to delay his departure with uncharacteristic gabble.

'Great,' he said. 'That'll be great. We're up to our necks as usual. This Italian corpse is turning out to be really interesting. And if that's not enough, Mr Watmough has finally flipped. Watch your aftershave when you come back! He's decided we're all Gay Gordons in CID and he's determined to sniff us out!'

He sniffed stagily in demonstration.

And again, not at all stagily.

Wield said, 'What do you mean?'

'Nothing. Some nonsense of the DCC's. You know how they get these ideas and with the selection board coming up, he's terrified in case anything happens to rock his boat. Look Wieldy, I'll not keep you from your dinner. It smells very...exotic. So take care. See you in the morning, I hope.'

Pascoe left, running down the stairs. His mind was running too. With Wield in his bathrobe, who was responsible for the presumably takeaway Chinese feast?

And for how long had marijuana been an ingredient of Chinese cuisine?

He shook the questions out of his head and concentrated on getting across his own threshold before his pork chop came out to meet him.

Wield re-entered his living-room.

'One of your mates?' inquired Cliff. 'Why'd you not invite him in?'

Wield stepped forward, tore the joint out of his fingers and hurled it into the fireplace. He'd seen Pascoe's expression and was suddenly filled with fear for the future.

'You don't smoke shit here,' he said.

'No? Why the hell not? Afraid of being raided, are you?'

Wield ignored this.

'Last night,' he said. 'You said something about trying to turn me into a news story.'

'Did I? Bad news, from the way you're acting now,' said the boy negligently.

'Tell me again, what exactly did you say when you rang the paper?'

'Why? What's so important? Last night you said it didn't matter. What's changed?'

Nothing. Except that in Pascoe's heedless quip about Gay Gordons he'd seen how what he felt as potentially tragic would be trivialized in the macho world of the police force. If Pascoe thought gay cops were comic, how would a monster like Dalziel respond? And why was the DCC interested?

He was feeling the onset of panic, and knowing it didn't help control it. Once, with Maurice's strength allied to his own, it had seemed possible to face, and outface, the world. But the moment had passed, and Maurice's strength had proved delusory, and this child before him did not even offer the illusion of strong support.

'Tell me again,' he urged. 'I need to know.'

'Why? Why do you need to know? Don't you trust me?' demanded Sharman, beginning to grow angry.

Wield drew in a deep breath. He didn't want another row. Or perhaps he did.

He said quietly, 'I just need to know. There's evidently been something said down at the station, and I'd like to be quite sure what it is, that's all.'

'Oh, is that all?' mimicked the boy. 'So you can make up your mind how to play it, is that it? So you can decide whether to go on being a fucking hypocrite all your life? I'll tell you what your trouble is, shall I, Mac? You've lived so long with straight pigs that you've started to think like them. You actually believe they're right and there really is something nasty and funny about gays. You know you can't help being one, but you wish you could, like a man who's got piles can't help it, but wishes he hadn't.'

The youth paused as if afraid of Wield's reaction to what he'd said. Perhaps if Wield had kept quiet too there might have been a chance of truce, a fragile calm settling into a firmer peace.

But too much control for too long takes its toll of a man as much as any other excess.

'So that's my trouble, is it?' said Wield with soft savagery. 'And what's *your* trouble then, Cliff? Mebbe it's what I thought from the start. Mebbe you're nothing more than a nasty little crook who came up here to put the black on me, then got scared. Mebbe all that stuff about your long lost dad is a load of crap. Mebbe Maurice got you right when he said you were a thief and a tart...'

The boy jumped up, his face working with rage and pain.

'All right!' he screamed. 'And Mo was right about you too! He said you were a bloody loonie who wanted everything his way, no one else's! He said you were fucking pathetic and you are! Look at yourself, Mac. You're dead, did you know that? From the neck up and down. Dead. What do you know?—I've screwed with a dead pig! They should stick you on a platter with an orange in your mouth!'

He stopped, appalled at where his rage had taken him.

'You'd better go,' said Wield. 'Quickly.'

'What? No charges, no threats?' said Sharman with a poor effort at jauntiness.

'You're a liar, a cheat, a thief. What should I threaten you with? Just get out of my sight.'

Cliff Sharman went to the door, glanced back once, and said something inaudible, and left.

Wield stood quite still by the table looking down at the array of congealing dishes. There was a voice high in his skull screaming at him to drag the tablecloth off and bring the feast crashing to the floor. He ignored it. Control was everything. He took three deep breaths, letting the steady surf-like rhythms of his breathing drown out that strident, insistent voice.

He paused.

Silence.

Then the voice screamed again with an intensity that vibrated the whole arch of his skull and he seized the cloth and with one spasmodic pull he hurled the Chinese feast across the room to trickle down the opposing wall like blood and guts from a belly wound.

He went through to the bedroom and stared at himself in the mirror, aghast. Once he had hated the way he looked. Then for many years, the years of control and disguise, he had thought of his face as a blessing, a mask ready made for a man who thought he needed a mask.

Now he hated it once more.

He threw aside his bathrobe, dragged on his clothes and minutes later went out in the cidrous gold of the autumn evening.

A farm labourer found Cliff Sharman's body early the next morning. It lay in a shallow grave no deeper than the scrape of a hare's form, beneath an old hedge of blackthorn and hawthorn and alder, bound round with ivy and jewelled with pearly dog-rose. Some hand, either of the killer or the night wind, had strewn the childishly young face with the first dead leaves of the season, but when the labourer's fingers brushed them aside, the bright colours seemed to remain to stain the bruised and torn features. More terrible still was the gaudy T-shirt across which ran the unmistakable tread of the tyre which had crushed the boy's chest.

From a high tree the voice of a telltale blackbird sang out its bubbly warning. The labourer rose and looked where best to go for help. Over the hedge about a quarter of a mile distant, he could see a roof and chimneys sailing ship–like through the morning mist.

Pushing his way through the hedgerow, the man began to trot at a steady pace towards Troy House.

FIRST ACT

VOICES FROM A FAR COUNTRY

Then come home, my children, the sun is gone down,
And the dews of night arise;
Your spring and your day are wasted in play,
And your winter and night disguise.

Blake: *Nurse's Song*

CHAPTER 1

It was mid-morning when Dalziel paid his first visit to Troy House.

He was admitted by a young man in shirtsleeves who identified himself as Rod Lomas and pre-empted Dalziel's self-introduction as he led him in to the drawing-room.

'You've heard of me, then?' said Dalziel.

'Not to know you argues oneself unknown,' said Lomas.

Dalziel digested this, then broke wind gently.

'Sorry,' he said. 'Miss Keech at home?'

'Yes, but she's unwell, I'm afraid. This business has come as a tremendous shock to her.'

'Which business?'

'*This* business,' said Lomas, looking at him as if doubtful of his sanity. 'This murder on our doorstep.'

Dalziel walked to the window and peered in the general direction of the quarter-mile distant hedgerow beneath which Sharman's body had been found.

'If that's your doorstep,' he said, 'there's a donkey crapping on your hall carpet.'

'Yes. Look, Superintendent, this is the countryside and Troy House is pretty isolated, so the thought of a killer wandering around loose is surely quite enough to upset most old ladies, wouldn't you say?'

'Likely you're right. Did you hear owt last night?'

'I've already made a statement,' said Lomas impatiently. 'I heard nothing, saw nothing. Do I have to go through all this again?'

'For someone who makes his living going through the same old stuff night after night, you're making a lot of fuss about saying summat twice,' observed Dalziel.

'All right,' sighed Lomas. 'Catechize me if you must.'

'Why? Is there summat you want to get off your chest?'

'But just a second ago...'

'Grasshopper mind, that's me. Let's go up and see the old lady.'

'Really, no,' said Lomas. 'I've had the doctor to her and he says she ought to rest.'

But he was talking to Dalziel's broad back as it vanished through the door. Moving with surprising speed and not-so-surprising instinct, the fat man was already tapping on Miss Keech's bedroom door by the time Lomas caught up with him.

'Come in,' called a slightly quavery voice.

Dalziel opened the door.

'Morning, ma'am,' he said to the old lady in the huge bed. 'Sorry to disturb you.'

He recalled Pascoe's description of the woman as lively and bright for her years and saw indeed that the morning's events must have been a shock. The face that turned towards him was pale, the features pinched sharp as though by a killing frost.

Lomas behind him whispered, 'For heaven's sake, Superintendent!'

'I'll not be long.'

'But she doesn't know anything!'

'About the body, you mean? Mebbe not. But it's not that body I wanted to ask about. Miss Keech, you were Alexander Huby's nurse when you first came to Troy House, weren't you?'

He advanced to the bedside as he spoke.

'Indeed I was. Nursery maid to be exact.'

Ill she might be, but there was still an alert gleam in her eyes.

'Did the boy have any distinguishing marks that you recall? Birth marks, scars, that sort of thing?'

'No. None,' she said without hesitation.

'To be more precise, did he have a mark on his right buttock, a sort of mole shaped a bit like a maple leaf?'

'No,' she said very clearly. 'He did not.'

'Thank you, Miss Keech. I hope you get well soon.'

He gravely touched a phantom forelock and left.

'Is that it?' inquired Lomas as they descended the stairs.

'Still wanting to unburden yourself?' said Dalziel.

'No!'

'Well, that's it for me. I'm off back to town. Some of us work for a living.'

'All of us!' said Lomas looking at his watch. 'I've skipped this morning's rehearsal, but Chung will kill me if I don't make it this afternoon. Oh, Mrs Brooks, there you are!'

A woman had come through the front door, middle-aged, headscarfed, gat-toothed and squint-eyed.

'Mrs Brooks cleans for Miss Keech,' explained Lomas. 'She said she'd come back and stay with her this afternoon so I can get about my business. Many thanks, Mrs Brooks.'

'My pleasure, love,' said the woman, observing Dalziel keenly with her fixed eye. 'He the police? I thought so. I'll see if she'll try a boiled egg for dinner. Here, I wouldn't like to have the feeding of *him!*'

With a stomach-churning sweep of the left eye and a rising trill of laughter, she went up the stairs.

'Excuse me,' said Loams, 'it occurs to me, if you're going into town…'

'You'd like a lift? Can't shake you off, can I, lad? You're like one of them gropies.'

'I think—I *hope*—that possibly you mean groupie,' said Lomas. 'And the lift?'

'As long as you don't start reciting and frighten me driver,' said Dalziel. 'Come on, then! I'll not hang about.'

'Why is it that up here no one can offer you a lift without saying that?' wondered Lomas as he went rushing off in search of his velvet jacket.

Back at the station, Dalziel found Pascoe and Seymour shuffling sheaves of paper like a pair of nervous fan-dancers.

'Are you going to swallow these after you've read them?' asked Dalziel. 'Where's Wield? He can rhyme things off like he's got a real mind when the fancy takes him.'

'Still ill,' said Pascoe. 'Or perhaps,' correcting himself pedantically, 'ill again. He showed his face, said he was OK, then off he went again.'

'That's right,' chimed in Seymour. 'I was bringing him up to date with what's going off, and he just keeled over. I wanted to call the doctor, but he wouldn't have it.'

'We'll have to make do with paper, then,' grunted Dalziel. 'Come on up to my room, Peter, and just bring what you think's necessary.'

In Dalziel's room, the fat man poured himself a slug of malt so pale it might pass for water to the uncritical eye.

'Start,' he said.

Pascoe began.

'I've been talking to Florence, sir,' he said.

'Oh aye? And what did she have to say?'

Dalziel never let the popular prejudice against the obvious interfere with his jokes. He was, however, slightly puzzled when Pascoe laughed appreciatively before going on, 'Alessandro Pontelli, born Palermo, Sicily 1923, wounded while serving with partisans, hospitalized by Americans near Siena, continued in Tuscany after the war acting as interpreter and courier, first for military authorities, then as things got back to normal for the tourist trade. No criminal record, unmarried, no known family. Flew out of Pisa airport four days before the funeral. At this end we have the immigration record at Gatwick. After that, nothing.'

'And before that, not bloody much,' grumbled Dalziel with the sour complacency of one who hadn't expected anything more from foreigners.

'We've not got much more on our true-blue British boy,' protested Pascoe.

'Bugger looked half brown to me,' said Dalziel. 'But give.'

'Sharman, Clifford, age nineteen, born Dulwich, London, address given to court was Flat 29, Leacock Court, East Dulwich, occupied by his grandmother, Mrs Miriam Hornsby, but he hasn't lived there for more than three years. Various other addresses for social security claims, but nothing permanent or significant. Only previous was that shoplifting fine last week.'

'What was he doing up here anyway?' wondered Dalziel. 'It's a long way to come just to shoplift.'

'God knows. He told Seymour he was just hiking around, living rough. Interesting, Seymour says he didn't believe him. He didn't smell right—or ripe. We've got the p.m. report already. Mr Longbottom was working late—or early—and still in the cutting mood. Cause of death was confirmed as having his chest crushed by being run over after he'd been beaten up. Oh, by the way, Longbottom says the body looked pretty well scrubbed. Also underwear was clean, apart from soiling caused at time of death, so it sounds as if Seymour could have been right.'

'So where was he staying?'

'Don't know, but we'll soon find out,' said Pascoe confidently. 'Best leads seem to be that his last meal was a toasted cheese sandwich not long before death, he'd recently had anal intercourse, and he was carrying five grammes of pot in a small plastic bag from a local supermarket, so presumably he brought it up here.'

'They're selling it in supermarkets now, are they?'

Again Pascoe laughed so appreciatively that all Dalziel's defence mechanisms went on red alert.

'Might as well,' the Inspector said. 'It's not difficult to get hold of, but it does cost. Could be that Sharman was flogging his ring to pay for the pot and his boyfriend decided to give him a punching rather than pay up and went too far.'

'Bloody sight too far,' grunted Dalziel. 'Was he on the game, do you reckon?'

Pascoe shrugged.

'Hard to say, but perhaps his grandmother, that's Mrs Hornsby, can tell us more. She's arriving at two by the way, sir. I've given instructions for her to be taken straight up to see you as I thought you'd like a chat before you took her to the mortuary...'

'Whoa!' shouted Dalziel. 'So that's why it's been laugh-along-with-the-Super time! No sale! Being nice to grieving grannies isn't my speciality; that's what we employ smarmy sods with degrees for!'

'I'm extremely busy with the Pontelli inquiry, sir. I've got Seymour sorting through the contents of Mrs Huby's cabinet, and I've still got to see Lomas about why he broke into it.'

'He's lunching in the Kemble bar,' interposed Dalziel. 'I brought him in with me. Funny young sod, isn't he? Fancies himself. And not the only one round here. You reckon you're on to something with these papers, then?'

'Not really,' admitted Pascoe. 'They're just a rather pathetic record of an obsession. Seymour claims to see a bit of a gap a few years back, but as it coincides with the time the old girl had her first stroke, there would be, wouldn't there?'

'But you'll still waste time chasing after Lomas?' said Dalziel satirically. 'You still really believe you'll find a motive in this Huby will business, do you?'

'I'm sure there's something there,' said Pascoe. 'I ran everything through CPC...'

'Oh God. I knew the mighty Wurlitzer would be in on the act!' growled Dalziel, who regarded the Central Police Computer with a luddite hatred.

'...and I came up with a few things. John Huby's bad temper doesn't just confine itself to kicking stuffed dogs. He has a record for brawling as a young man and more recently he got fined for using excessive violence in ejecting an unwanted customer.'

'Some bleeding heart on the Bench, I dare say,' grunted Dalziel.

'No. It was hang 'em, flog 'em, castrate 'em, Mrs Jones JP. Even she thought that throwing the customer through the windscreen of his own car was excessive. Nothing on the other Hubys. Rod Lomas, assorted motoring offences and one possession charge. Hash. They found it on him at Heathrow. He managed to persuade them it was for his own use, not for re-sale. Nothing on his mother except...'

'Yes?'

'Well, her husband was the Arthur Windibanks who was involved in the big holiday homes scandal in the 'seventies. He got out of it by running his car off the Autostrada. There was a convenient fire at the Company's London office, all papers burnt, so there was no way of tying her in, but I gather it was a narrow squeak.'

'Aye, she's a cool one,' admitted Dalziel. 'I went down to the morgue with her yesterday afternoon to look at Pontelli's bum.

That's it, she said. *I'd recognize it anywhere.* Never cracked her face! Incidentally, Miss Keech says that no such blemish existed on young Alexander's lily-white body. With Huby that makes two for, one against. Who's lying?'

Pascoe frowned and said, 'Why should Keech lie?'

'At the moment she's got a sinecure for life, which mightn't be all that long from the look of her this morning. Mebbe she's afraid that if Pontelli does turn out to be the lost lad, she'd be out in the cold.'

'That'd mean she was pretty quick-thinking when you asked her the question this morning.'

'You said you thought she was pretty sharp.'

'She wasn't ill in bed when I saw her. All right, let's put it the other way. Why should the others lie?'

'How about, they're the heirs if Pontelli is Huby and dies intestate?' said Dalziel cunningly.

Pascoe shook his head, 'I don't think so. They're equal closest relations of the old lady, that's true, but it's different with Alexander. John Huby's a full cousin, Windibanks is something removed.'

'You're sure?' said Dalziel distrustingly. 'Better check it out with Thackeray. One thing I'm sure of, lying or not, that Windibanks woman wouldn't have opened her mouth without good cause.'

'No. I wonder...' Pascoe postponed his idea until he could test it and returned to the main track once more.

'I also ran Goodenough,' he said. 'He's down as a suspected sympathizer with some of the more extreme animal protection groups. Nothing concrete, but his views have got him into hot water with the ruling council at PAWS.'

'Scraping the barrel, aren't you, Peter?' said Dalziel.

'Extremism tends to overflow,' said Pascoe. 'Some more scrapings. WFE are on a Special Branch list of right-wing fellow traveller groups.'

This had surprised him. It had also occurred to him to wonder if the list which WRAG had got and which he'd been so satirical about might not also have emanated from Special Branch. Perhaps there was a mole, perhaps there was a controlled leak, or perhaps some leftie hacker was into the police computer.

It was a packet of microchips he was not about to open.

'And...?' said Dalziel.

'Nothing on Mrs Falkingham except a lot of memsahib background. And on Miss Sarah Brodsworth, nothing whatsoever at all.'

'You make that sound like a triumph, lad,' growled Dalziel.

'Well, it could be. I ran the White Heat lot Wield was on about. He was right. Infiltration's their game. Getting into the system—schools, local Tory parties, voluntary agencies. They like the odd outburst, such as this anti-Chung campaign, just to keep up their status in the wider spectrum of right-wing extremism. But generally it's heads down, let's work from within. So someone like Brodsworth could very well be a plant, slipped into WFE at the first sniff of money, and left to take root till the cash comes through.'

'And they'd kill Pontelli to get him out of the way, you think? What a mind you've got, lad!'

'Worth checking, though?'

'Aye. Check away. Listen, Goodenough said he met that journalist, Vollans, at Mrs Falkingham's place. He seems to be sniffing around this Brodsworth woman's background too. Might be worth seeing if he's come up with anything. These newspaper ferrets aren't bound down by rules and regulations like us. Also they can afford bigger bribes. HALLO!'

The bellow was directed into the telephone which he had snatched up at first ping.

'Yes? Who? What? What...what? Oh, *Watmough*! DCC... yes, sir, I know you're the DCC. What can I do for you, sir? Well, I'm right busy just now...all right, sir, soon as I can, sir.'

He replaced the receiver.

'Rover the Wonder Dog,' he said. 'Now what's he want? I wonder...'

He picked up the receiver, jiggled the rest, then said, 'Hello, Herbert, DS Dalziel here. How's your missus? Grand! Look, I'm just checking on a call for the DCC, just a matter of timing, it'd be this morning about...aye, that's the one. Grand. Thanks a lot.'

He replaced the receiver, grinning ferociously.

'Rover had a whistle from the *Challenger* about half an hour ago,' he said. 'I reckon it's find-the-fairy time. It's his interview next Wednesday and he'll be crapping himself in case something comes up to upset the applecart. All right, Peter, I can see you're eager to be off. I'll grapple with Grannie when she turns up, but I'll not forget you owe me one. Meanwhile, I'd best not keep laughing boy waiting else his tiny mind'll forget what he wants to see me about!'

CHAPTER 2

Neville Watmough banged the receiver down, not displeased that the fat superintendent had already contrived to anger him. A good head of fury was the best preparation he knew for an interview with Dalziel.

So far it hadn't been a happy morning. The news of Sharman's murder had caused deep personal distress. The selection committee weren't going to be impressed by two unsolved killings on his patch at the same time. He had worked out a strategy which would involve discovering from Dalziel where the greatest progress had been made, then taking over the investigation himself with a public statement including a modest passing reference to the Pickford case.

Then Ike Ogilby had rung.

'Just to keep you in the picture, Nev,' he said. 'This chap rang again last evening. Same business. Henry Vollans, that's the young chap you met at the Gents, set up a meeting with him for first thing this morning, but he didn't turn up. Must've got cold feet, but he's obviously working up to it. Or maybe he got a better offer.'

'Offer?'

'Oh yes. Money was mentioned. He said he could tell us things which would tear Mid-Yorkshire CID apart, but he wanted to be well paid. Well, maybe he's just trying it on, Nev, but I promised I'd keep you in the picture.'

'Bastard!' said Watmough as he put the receiver down. 'Thanks for nothing!'

He had no doubt that if Ogilby had got a story and it was a good one, he'd have planned to run it with little reference to himself. This way, the smart bastard was able to put Watmough under an obligation without really doing anything.

It was time that he, Neville Watmough, took control of the situation and became once more master of his own fate.

There was a gentle tap on the door.

'Enter,' he called.

Another tap. Again he called, 'Enter!' but all he got was another tap.

Sighing, he rose and opened the door. Dalziel stood there, smiling nervously in a grotesque parody of the naughty schoolboy summoned to see the headmaster.

'For Christ's sake, come in and sit down!' snarled Watmough.

Dalziel advanced and sat. The chair creaked like an old ship in high seas. Watmough sought for the best approach and opted for man-of-the-world directness.

'OK, Andy,' he said crisply. 'It's been brought to my notice there may be a practising homosexual in the CID. I want to know who it is.'

Dalziel looked unhappy rather than shocked. He glanced around the room, then leaned forward across the desk and said confidentially. 'You really want to find out, do you, Neville?'

Watmough found himself drawn forward irresistibly until their heads were almost meeting.

'Yes, I do, Andy,' he said.

'Then give us a kiss and I'll tell you!'

Dalziel rocked back in his chair, roaring with laughter. Watmough remained leaning forward, every muscle spanned to breaking-point, knowing that the slightest relaxation might send him hurtling across the desk to strangle the fat man.

Dalziel's laughter finally subsided, then faded away completely.

'Here,' he said. 'You're not serious, are you?'

'Deadly serious,' said Watmough, slowly straightening up.

'Well, bugger me. What do you want me to do?'

'Track him down. Surely I don't need to spell out the implications?'

Dalziel said, 'I think that mebbe you do, sir.'

'Very well. Perhaps you're right. I'd like us both to be quite clear what's involved. If there is a gay in CID and you don't know about him, Andy, presumably he reckons it's best that you remain ignorant. Now in my book, that makes him a security risk, right off. Gays, by the very nature of their needs, can find themselves moving in pretty shady areas. Even those who are most open can find themselves mixed up with some pretty dicey characters. As for the ones who try to keep up the pretence of being straight, they are natural blackmail victims. You follow me?'

Dalziel said, puzzled, 'What would you threaten a gay cop with?'

'Exposure, of course. It would ruin his career.'

'Being gay would?'

'Not having admitted it might,' said Watmough confidently.

'But if he *did* admit it, would that ruin his career too?'

Watmough turned aside from this line of argument.

'It's not just the job, though it would make things hellish difficult. A gay is susceptible in so many ways. Suppose he's married and his wife and family don't know...'

'A *married* gay?' said Dalziel.

'Oh yes,' said Watmough, safe with the support of *Sexual Deviancy* on the shelf behind his head. 'Didn't you know that Oscar Wilde, for instance, was married with two children?'

'No. I didn't know that,' said Dalziel. 'Would that be Chief Inspector Wilde at Scarborough?'

Watmough said in the very quiet voice of a man who knows there is nothing on his diapason between softness and uncontrolled explosion, 'Just do as I ask, Mr Dalziel. Just do as I ask.'

'Of course, sir,' said Dalziel formally. 'But just so I know for sure what that is, could you mebbe put it down on paper?'

Watmough regarded him speculatively for a moment, then he smiled. Dalziel thought he was being clever asking for a written instruction, but written instructions worked both ways.

He pulled an internal memo pad towards him, inserted a carbon and began to write rapidly.

To: Detective-Superintendent Dalziel A.

Further to our discussion of today's date concerning allegations of sexual deviancy against an unnamed CID officer, you are instructed to investigate same allegation and report with all reasonable speed.

He read it through. It was direct without being over-detailed; firm evidence, if the worst happened and there was any kind of scandal, that he had been on top of his job. Dalziel, he was pretty certain, would do nothing. Well, that was his lookout. It would be *his* failure, either through negligence, incompetence, or a cover-up!

He signed the memorandum and passed it over.

'I think that ends all ambiguity,' he said.

Dalziel read the sheet of paper carefully, folded it once and put it in his wallet.

'Thank you, sir,' he said. 'I'm not sure, though, how I should go about this. I'd be grateful for any ideas.'

Watmough smiled. He knew that Dalziel distrusted above all things psychiatrists, particularly when they affected to be helping in police affairs.

'Why not have a word with that chap Pottle from the Central's psychiatric unit? He's helped us in the past. Maybe he can give you a few pointers what to look for.'

Dalziel considered, then grunted noncommittally. He did not look happy. It was rare to have the fat man at a disadvantage and Watmough decided to ride his luck.

'Now, Andy,' he said. 'Back to real policing. I'd like a full rundown on progress in these murder investigations. Two in less than a week. It's not good, not good at all.'

He made it sound like Dalziel's personal fault and to his delight the Superintendent rose to the bait.

'That's nowt to do with me,' he growled. 'The buggers don't consult us when they're going to do a killing, do they?'

'No, Andy,' said Watmough silkily. 'They don't. But the Police Committee consults us when they want to know what we're doing about it. People get worried, Andy. The public voice. We must liaise closely with them. Public relations is the name of the game nowadays. You'll have studied my directives on this matter?'

'Oh aye,' said Dalziel unconvincingly.

'Good. Then you'll know that information and consultation are what the Committee require and what it's our duty to give them. I can't perform my part in that duty unless you consult and inform me too, Andy. You'd do well to remember that.'

'Consult and inform,' repeated Dalziel as if committing two important phrases in some strange language to heart.

'That's it. All right. What's the latest on your investigations? How can I help, Andy. That's all I want to know. How can I help?'

(HAPTER 3

OPEN ALL HOURS! announced the placard. *TRY A BIT OF CULTURE WITH YOUR BAR-SNACK!*

Pascoe recalled Chung on local radio declaring her hatred of theatres that were locked and barred most of the time.

'The Kemble belongs to the people, honey,' she'd told the bemused interviewer. 'I don't want to run a place that's barred and bolted like Fort Knox most of the time, with actors slipping in through a side door like bishops visiting a brothel. You can't sell culture if there's no one minding the store!'

Culture today seemed to consist of a pair of adenoidal folk singers in the foyer who were bewailing the miseries of the weaver's life. Perhaps, as the weaver in question seemed to be a Lancastrian, this catalogue of woes was aimed at raising Yorkist spirits.

On achieving the bar, Pascoe was gratified to be received like a Butcher of Broadway.

'Pete, *honey*!' cried Chung, heading towards him with lesser beings bobbing in her wake like the Blefuscudian navy behind

Gulliver. 'I was just talking about you. Could you lay your hands on a dozen riot shields? We're thinking of making our police thing a musical and I can just see this chorus line doing a great rhythmic number with stomping boots and truncheons rattling on the shields.'

Seymour dropped back in alarm. Inspectors with degrees might be able to survive this kind of thing on their files, but not constables with ambition. Chung, sensitive to stage movement, lowered her voice and said, 'Shit, listen to my big mouth. Pete, honey, I don't mean to be embarrassing, I just come out that way sometimes. Forgive me?'

She had lowered her face with her voice so that her breath zephyr'd sweetly on his cheek.

Pascoe said, 'Some shall be pardon'd and some punished. State the alternatives preferred.'

Chung laughed like Kipling's temple bells.

'Is your visit social or are you raiding the joint?' she asked.

'I wanted a word with Mercutio.'

'Rod? He's over there in the corner with his cousin.'

She gave an actress inflection to the last word which puzzled Pascoe till he caught sight of Lomas in a distant corner of the long bar, seated next to Lexie Huby, their heads so close together they were almost touching. Could there be something going on there? The idea surprised him. There seemed little love lost between the Hubys and the Lomases in general, and these two in particular didn't look cut out to be Romeo and Juliet.

He excused himself from Chung and went to join the couple. When they spotted his approach they stopped talking. He stood over them.

'Mr Lomas, Miss Huby,' he said.

'It was Rod and Lex last time. This must be official,' said Lomas.

'Can we speak privately, Mr Lomas?'

'Won't this do?'

It was true that the noise level of the bar, as conversation within vied with music without, made eavesdropping unlikely.

He looked at the girl.

She said, 'I'll go.'

'No need,' said Pascoe. 'My constable will buy you a drink at the bar, Seymour.'

The girl rose and went barwards with the slightly bewildered detective.

Pascoe slipped into the vacated chair and said, 'Just a couple of questions, Mr Lomas. First, why did you break into the filing cabinet?'

'What? I didn't! That's absurd!' he protested, emoting surprise and shock in a sub-Stanislavskian style.

'Missed your line,' reproved Pascoe. 'First comes, *what filing cabinet*? After I've told you, *then* comes the indignation.'

'You're quite a clown,' said Lomas thickly.

'Thank you. Look, there are fingerprints outside and inside. They match those on the tumbler by your bed...'

Pascoe was lying about the internal prints. There had been a confusion of overlaps, nothing positive.

'You've been poking around my bedroom!' said Lomas, genuinely indignant this time.

'No,' said Pascoe gently. 'We had a look in the late Alexander Huby's bedroom, with Miss Keech's permission. But we're wandering. To return to the cabinet...'

Lomas thought a moment, then gave a frank, open, rather rueful smile.

'Yes, all right, I did look in the cabinet. But I didn't break in. The lock had been forced already. I was just poking around.'

'With what end in view?'

'Nothing, really. No, that's silly. Look, to tell the truth, I just had this daft idea there might be another will, one that old Thackeray didn't know about. Well, it was a possibility, wasn't it?

I couldn't really believe the old girl kept on believing her precious boy was still alive right up to the end.'

'I see,' said Pascoe. 'What you hoped for, I presume, was a will leaving everything to the family?'

'I was born on St Jude's day,' said Lomas. 'Only congenital optimists become actors.'

'And did you find anything?'

'Nothing. Just a lot of stuff confirming dear old Gwen was dotty.'

'Hardly worth forcing a lock for, then.'

'Listen. It could have been anyone. Why pick on me?'

'Hardly *anyone*. There's just you and Miss Keech. And she had a key.'

'Other people come to the house, you know.'

'For instance.'

Lomas glanced towards the bar rather furtively and lowered his voice.

'What about John Huby, Lexie's father? He came round a couple of days ago to see Keechie. He was asking questions about wills and letters and things. Yes, it could've been him. He's a wild sod, that one. It's hard to believe little Lexie's his daughter.'

Pascoe made a note.

'Now tell me about your visit to Italy,' he said.

Lomas frowned, then let it dissolve into his frank, open smile.

'You saw the labels on my suitcase,' he said. 'Clever old detective, you! Yes, I was in Italy in the summer. I'd run around like a mad thing looking for work after the Salisbury Festival. Finally I said, for turning away, let summer bear it out, and accepted Mummy's offer to sub me abroad.'

'Your first visit to Italy, was it?'

'No. I've been several times.'

'Where do you go?'

Pascoe's pen was poised.

'Here and there.'

'Tuscany?'

'Yes, I've spent a lot of time in Tuscany. Look, what's all this about?'

'Did you ever come across Alessandro Pontelli?'

Lomas didn't pretend not to know the name.

'You mean the dead chap, the one who turned up at the funeral? What the hell are you trying to say, Inspector?'

Pascoe said gently, 'I'm just asking a simple question, Mr Lomas.'

'Then the simple answer is no.'

'That's fine. Do you still smoke marijuana, by the way?'

Lomas shook his head in slow amazement.

'By God, once you've got a record, you've really got a record! Do you really expect me to answer that?'

'Why not? You admitted smoking it in court. All I'm asking is if you've given up the habit.'

'But why? What's it to do with anything?'

'Nothing that I know of. The boy who got killed near Troy House last night, he had some marijuana in his possession.'

'You're scraping the barrel, aren't you?' said Lomas, unconsciously echoing Dalziel's accusation.

'Very probably.'

He became aware of someone at his shoulder. He looked up but not very far. It was Lexie Huby.

'Rod, I've got to get back. Mr Eden's working through the lunch-hour and he's got a load of typing for me.'

'OK,' said Lomas. 'But you'll call in at Troy House tonight to check on Keechie? Mrs Brooks is very good, but she's got her own family to look after.'

'Yes, of course I will. My class finishes at eight.'

'If you hang on a sec, Miss Huby, I'll walk back with you,' said Pascoe, trying his winning smile again. 'I need to see Mr Thackeray. Oh, by the way, Mr Lomas, this friend you stayed with last Friday night. Did he live in Leeds by any chance?'

It was an often productive technique, the sudden probing question just when the suspect thought it was all over. This time too it looked set to enjoy success.

Lomas actually twitched and when he opened his mouth it was only to let out a dry nervous cough.

'You were in Leeds, weren't you?' said Pascoe pleasantly.

'Of course he was,' said Lexie Huby in a tone of exasperation.

Pascoe looked at her in surprise.

'He was at the opera with me. *Madam Butterfly.*'

'Was he?' said Pascoe.

He turned back to Lomas. All signs of discomfiture had vanished. He smiled at Pascoe and said, 'She's determined to convert me from the straight theatre.'

'You rang Miss Keech. Said you wouldn't be returning to Troy House because you were staying with a friend.'

'And so I did,' grinned Lomas lecherously. 'So I did.'

'I've got to go,' said Lexie Huby. She leaned forward and pecked Lomas on the cheek. Pascoe recalled the eye-poking evasion with which she had greeted the actor's attempt at an embrace only a week before. The girl turned away and made for the exit.

Pascoe said, 'We'll talk again soon, Mr Lomas,' and went after her.

The girl moved so quickly that he didn't catch up till they were outside the theatre.

'Hold on!' he said. 'It must be a good job for you to be so keen to get back to it.'

'It's all right.'

He digested this, then said, 'But not so good as being a solicitor?'

'You looked in my briefcase,' she said.

This omission of a couple of steps in the reasoning process was impressive. Or perhaps he'd just forgotten to fasten it up.

'What're you doing? A-levels followed by SFE? Or do you want to do a degree?'

'Whatever I can manage,' she said indifferently.

'Mr Thackeray must be pleased.'

It took him a couple of paces to interpret the silence.

'He doesn't know? But why? Surely there would be...'

'I don't need favours.'

'Favours? Everyone's entitled to an education.'

'Entitled?' She didn't raise her little voice, but she was speaking with greater vehemence than he had known in their brief acquaintance. 'Kids are entitled to what adults let 'em get. And adults are entitled to what they can afford.'

'And that's it? You're over eighteen. You're adult. What can you afford?'

Suddenly, transformingly, she grinned.

'Not much. Choosing for myself mebbe. If I'm lucky.'

They were at the office building. Pascoe glanced back. Seymour was tracking a few yards behind like a Royal body-guard. Pascoe mouthed 'Car' at him and the redhead nodded and turned away.

As they clambered the creaking old wooden stairway, he said, 'You'd rather I didn't mention your course to Mr Thackeray?'

She shrugged her narrow shoulders indifferently.

'You'll likely do what suits you best,' she said. 'I'll see if Mr Eden's by himself.'

Thackeray did not look too pleased at being interrupted. His desk was littered with papers and his jacket hung over the back of his chair. But he rose punctiliously and began to put it on as Pascoe entered at Lexie's behest.

'Forgive me,' he said. 'So busy. Some new development?'

'Not really,' said Pascoe. 'I gather Mr Dalziel's told you about Mrs Windibanks's possible identification of Pontelli as Alexander Lomas.'

'Yes. He rang last night. Extraordinary, quite extraordinary.'

'Isn't it? And Mr John Huby confirms it. On the other hand, Miss Keech denies any knowledge of such a mark. But what I really want to get clear is, if Pontelli is Huby, where does that leave us in law?'

'Oh dear,' said Thackeray. 'Let me see, let me see. The situation still retains a certain ambiguity, I fear. At first sight it would seem that with Alexander Huby still being alive after his mother's death and having made a verbal claim to his inheritance in this very office, then the Huby estate should be treated as *his* estate.'

'I see. Now as I understand it, under the rules of intestacy, this would elevate John Huby of the Old Mill Inn to his main heir?'

'His only heir. But you're forgetting something, Mr Pascoe. Alexander Huby, if so he be, has been living in Italy for forty years. He may be married with a large family. He may have made a will of his own leaving everything to his local football team!'

Pascoe shook his head.

'He's not married as far as the Italian authorities know. And there are no obvious next of kin. In any case, if there were, they would be the real Pontellis, wouldn't they, if he *was* Huby and if there *was* a real Pontelli. I don't know about a will.'

'And I don't know about Italian intestacy laws, assuming his Italian citizenship is genuine,' resumed Thackeray. 'But sticking to what we do know and to English law, the real difficulty still remains with Mrs Huby's will. It states that PAWS, CODRO and WFE cannot get the money until 2015 unless her son's death is proven beyond all possible doubt before that time. I confess it was I who cajoled her into adding that rider, though I wanted "reasonable" not "possible". But she was on to me, I'm afraid. The thing is, if Pontelli is proven to be Alexander, then it might be argued that under the terms of the will, his death has simply been proven beyond all possible doubt, and the charities get the estate immediately.'

'But that's absurd! I mean, he's the heir.'

'But did he make proper legal claim to the estate before he died?'

'Is that necessary?'

'Not usually, of course. But it would be interesting to argue that Mrs Huby's sole intention was that her son should be able to enjoy the benefits of her estate while he lived, not that these benefits should be distributed haphazardly around Italy, always supposing that Pontelli has a family there.'

Pascoe left, feeling little the better for his visit.

Seymour was waiting for him, parked recklessly on a double yellow.

'Where to sir?' he asked.

'The Old Mill Inn,' said Pascoe. 'We may get a bite to eat there if you hurry.'

He wished he hadn't said this. Not even a detailed account of their several other purposes in visiting John Huby could distract the redhead from what he saw as the main one and the need for speed to achieve it. But despite his desperate driving, it looked at first as if Seymour was to be disappointed.

'Food!' said John Huby as though it were a four-letter word. 'We do sandwiches, but they finished half an hour back.'

'I'll make some more, Dad,' offered Jane Huby, fluttering long eyelashes at Seymour who responded with a smacking of lips which had more to do with lust than hunger.

Huby growled a reluctant assent and the girl went off, swinging her haunch provocatively. Seymour sighed deeply. Pascoe paid for their drinks, but decided to postpone his talk with the landlord. The bar was pretty crowded and rustic drinkers were clearly as sensitive to the approach of last orders as Faustus was to his last midnight. Huby and his wife were fully occupied.

Seymour noticed this too and murmured, 'I'm going for a run-off, sir. I noticed as we came in there was a door marked *Private* just beyond the Gents. Worth a quick poke around while everyone's nice and busy here, do you think?'

'You mean, illegal entry without a warrant in case you might come across something removed from Gwen Huby's filing cabinet? Or something suggesting collusion with Mrs Windibanks? Or anything else linking Huby to either of these murders?' said Pascoe. 'I find that quite outrageous. If I thought that was your intention, I'd forbid you to move.'

'Yes, sir,' said Seymour. 'Shall I go and have my pee?'

'Don't get lost,' said Pascoe.

Seymour grinned and left.

A voice said, 'Inspector Pascoe, isn't it?'

He turned to find the young blond-haired reporter, Henry Vollans, at his elbow.

'We met at the Kemble party,' Vollans said.

'I remember. What are you doing here? You're a good way off Leeds.'

'I had to come across this way this morning first thing for an appointment, only the fellow didn't turn up,' said Vollans. 'Fortunately there were one or two other things to follow up.'

'At the Old Mill Inn?'

'Why not? You're here!' said Vollans slyly.

'Even policemen need refreshment. As a matter of interest, your name was mentioned to me earlier this morning.'

The young reporter looked threatened for a moment, then quickly recovered.

'Complimentarily, I hope?'

'I gather you were at Maldive Cottage in Ilkley when Mr Goodenough of PAWS called the other day.'

'Right.'

'Do you mind telling me what took you there?'

Vollans hesitated, then said, 'Sammy Ruddlesdin speaks very highly of you, Mr Pascoe.'

'That's nice.'

'He reckons you're the kind of chap who strikes a fair bargain, not like some who'll take everything, then renege on the giving.'

'Sammy says that? I'll remind him next time he starts moaning at me about non-cooperation! What were you doing there, Mr Vollans?'

'Sniffing at the edge of a story,' said Vollans. 'Mrs Falkingham's an old correspondent of the *Challenger's* so when we noticed WFE might be in line for a big hand-out, we thought we'd take a look. Mrs Huby's will of itself was worth a mention, but like my editor says, there's usually a cuter angle if you care to crawl around it.'

'And was there? A cuter angle, I mean?'

'Well, Mr Goodenough turning up while I was there, that was a bit of luck. Opens up the story a bit.'

'And Mrs Falkingham's assistant, Miss Brodsworth, was she able to open it up any more?'

Vollans gave his Redford grin.

'Not half as much as something else I heard this morning.'

'Yes?'

'I heard a rumour that there's a body in the mortuary which some people reckon might belong to the missing heir.'

Pascoe digested this. They'd kept the Huby connection as quiet as possible, but there were too many people who knew something about it for total leak-proofing.

He said, 'You're not the *Challenger's* crime reporter, are you? I've met him, fat man called Boyle.'

'No, but I'm here and he's not. Mind you, he will be soon, I expect, meanwhile I thought I might do myself a bit of good.'

'And that's why you're out at the Old Mill Inn?'

'Just looking the family over, checking out angles.'

'You haven't spoken to them yet?'

'Not yet.'

Pascoe smiled to himself at the thought of the young man's still-to-come first encounter with John Huby.

He said, 'Getting back to Sarah Brodsworth...'

'Yes.'

'Mr Goodenough gave the impression you might be checking on *her* background.'

'Did he now?'

'Was he right?'

'Was Sammy Ruddlesdin right?' grinned the reporter.

Pascoe was beginning to find the grin rather irritating.

'Tell you what I can do,' he said. 'I'm not in a position to confirm or deny rumours, you must see that. But I could, if you like, introduce you to John Huby and pave the way as best I can to an interview.'

It was an offer so ludicrous that only inexperience would even consider it, let alone accept it.

'All right,' said Vollans. 'Yes, I did try to check out Sarah Brodsworth. WFE as far as I can make out is a gang of mouldy-oldies, relicts of the Raj, and I couldn't see where she fitted in as an individual. But if she's a member of a group, then there's some very good security. In fact, I can find precious little about her as a member of the human race!'

'When you say group, you mean right-wing group, and she could be a plant, after the money?'

'That's what I wondered. Right wing, left wing, what's it matter? The money's the thing. What about you, Inspector? You got anything on her?'

'Not yet.'

He saw that the rush at the bar was over. Huby glanced around and looked as if he might be about to retreat to the living quarters. There was no sign of Seymour yet.

'Take a seat,' said Pascoe to Vollans. 'I want a word with Mr Huby before I introduce you. A seat out of earshot, I mean.'

Grinning again, Vollans rose from his bar-stool and withdrew to a table.

'Mr Huby,' called Pascoe. 'Could you spare a moment?'

'I might've known you buggers'd not be here for the beer alone,' said Huby.

'It's very good beer,' complimented Pascoe. 'I gather you visited Troy House the other day.'

'Any reason I shouldn't?'

'None whatsoever. I just wondered what the purpose of your visit was.'

'If you've been talking to that cow Keech, likely you'll know already.'

'She said something about you being interested in papers or letters or anything post-dating Mrs Huby's will.'

'That's right.'

'What precisely were you...?'

'Owt that'd prove that bloody will's a load of cobblers! You don't have to be Sherlock bloody Holmes to ravel that out, do you, Mr bloody Inspector? I wanted to have a good look around, that was all.'

'Did Miss Keech object?'

'No. She were as nice as ninepence. Why shouldn't she be, but? She's come out of it all right, set up for life. Me, what've I got but a back-yard full of building bricks I've not paid for!'

'And did you find anything?'

'Not a bloody sausage.'

'Not even in the filing cabinet?'

'Not even there.'

'You did look in the filing cabinet?'

'Yeah, why not? Here, what's that old bitch been saying?'

'Nothing, nothing,' assured Pascoe. 'I just wondered how you got in to the cabinet if it was locked.'

Huby thrust his face close to Pascoe's.

'With a key, lad. With a bloody key! Keech unlocked it for me and stood over me while I went through it, and if she tells you owt different, she's a bloody liar!'

Huby's harangue had drawn the attention of several customers who clearly considered the landlord's ill-tempered outbursts as a free cabaret act.

Pascoe said gently, 'She didn't say anything different, because she wasn't asked. What she does say, however, is that to the best of her knowledge, Alexander Huby had no birthmark on his buttock.'

'Does she?' said Huby indifferently. 'That's not what I heard, but she ought to know, I suppose.'

Out of the corner of his eye, Pascoe saw that Seymour had returned and sat down at a table near the window.

'Yes, I suppose she ought. By the way, that young blond fellow by the fireplace is a reporter for the Sunday *Challenger*. He'd like a word if you have a moment. Seems a nice young chap.'

Huby looked suspiciously towards Vollans, then came round the bar and made towards him. Pascoe downed his beer. Seymour's was still untouched on the counter. He offered his own glass to Mrs Huby and asked for a refill.

As he paid, he said casually, 'Last night, you remember Mrs Windibanks rang while I was talking to your husband. She didn't say if she was still in town or not, did she?'

It was a flimsy subterfuge but enough for the open honest landlady who replied, 'No, she didn't mention where she was ringing from.'

Pascoe said, 'Well, it doesn't matter,' picked up Seymour's beer and took it to him at his table.

Jane arrived simultaneously with the sandwiches.

'I've done you some crumbly cheese and some nice chicken breast with a bit of my own spicy chutney,' she breathed into Seymour's ear as she leaned against him to place the plates on the table.

Pascoe was surprised to note that the DC's response was on the chilly side of lukewarm. He was also surprised to observe simultaneously that Huby had gone over to Henry Vollans and, far from offering him the anticipated verbal violence, seemed to be chatting almost amicably and was now actually sitting down.

Doubtless he was telling him the story of the will and poor old Gruff-of-Greendale, residing in his everlasting sleep by the fireplace, was soon going to be launched into space once more.

'What's up with you?' he said to Seymour as Jane retreated, looking rather piqued. 'Gone off busty blondes, have we?'

Seymour replied by taking a sandwich and biting it viciously.

'You were a long time gone,' said Pascoe. 'Find anything interesting?'

'Nothing helpful. I went all over and couldn't spot anything to do with the case.'

There was more to come, Pascoe guessed.

'But…?' he probed.

Suddenly it came out.

'I got upstairs in her bedroom,' said the redhead with all the indignant pain of disenchanted idolatry. 'Didn't expect to find anything there, but I like to be thorough. I was poking around some bookshelves and there they were!'

'What for God's sake?'

'A blonde wig and a bloody great pair of falsies! You can't trust anything these days!'

Pascoe tried to look sympathetic but a grin tugged at his mouth and finally he laughed so heartily he almost choked on his sandwich.

John Huby in close conference with Henry Vollans was distracted by the sound.

Glaring balefully in Pascoe's direction he said, 'Listen to that! You'd think that people came in here to bloody well enjoy themselves!'

CHAPTER 4

Mrs Miriam Hornsby was sixty-ish, stout, and wore enough make-up to keep the Kemble going for a fortnight. She moved in an aureole of roseate fragrance through which on every breath came a waft of what Dalziel's specialized nose identified as barley wine.

'Have you eaten, love?' he asked solicitously.

'Yes, thank you. There was a buffet on the train,' she replied in what to his ear was merely a London accent with a slight overlay of refinement to match the solemnity of the occasion.

None of these observations of voice, scent or appetite was a put-down in Dalziel's mind. Where there was leisure for refreshment there could still be time for grief; indeed, the barley wine smell tended to predispose him in her favour; he had once enjoyed a robustly meaningless relationship with a well-made lady who favoured strong ales.

'Well, let's get it over with,' he said, intuitively adopting the hearty no-nonsense approach he sensed best suited her emotional make-up.

At the mortuary she clung tightly to his arm in preference to the proffered support of WPC Aster who was chaperoning them, and as she looked down at the still, dark features of the young man whom death seemed to have shrunk back to childhood, he felt the full weight of her distress.

'Is this your grandson, Cliff Sharman?' asked Dalziel formally. She nodded.

'You have to say it, love,' he instructed her.

'Yes, that's him, that's Cliff,' she whispered. Tears came with the words and ran glistening spoors across her powdery cheeks.

As they came out of the chilly steel box of the actual mortuary into the plastic anonymity of the vestibule, Dalziel was surprised to see Sergeant Wield standing there.

'Hello,' he said. 'You better?'

'I'd like a word,' said Wield.

'Aye. Let's get Mrs Hornsby here a cup of tea, shall we? No, better still, let's get out of here!'

He led the way out. Two hundred yards away was a pub, the Green Tree, not named after any visible vegetation. It was just past closing time and the landlord was ushering the last customers into the afternoon air prior to locking up.

'Hello, Steve,' said Dalziel, who knew half the town publicans by name and the rest by reputation. 'We'll just sit quiet a few moments in your snug. You might fetch us a couple of barley wines in one glass and I'll have a Scotch, and you'd better have one too, Sergeant, you don't look too clever to me. Oh, and an orange juice for the young lady here. Uniformed officers shouldn't be seen drinking on duty!'

The landlord sighed but did not demur. Mrs Hornsby, who had been weeping steadily all the way from the mortuary, glimpsed herself in the bar mirror and headed for the Ladies followed by WPC Aster.

'What're you doing at the mortuary, Sergeant?' inquired Dalziel.

Wield said, 'I'd been to see the body.'

'Sharman's? Oh aye. Didn't know that Mr Pascoe had put you on this case. In fact, I'm sure he said you'd gone off sick.'

'I knew him,' said Wield dully. 'I came in this morning and Seymour started telling me about this body they'd found. I wasn't paying much attention till he said it were the same lad he'd arrested for shoplifting last week.'

He fell silent. Dalziel said, 'Is that what you mean when you say you knew him.'

'No. I knew him before that. He was...a friend. I couldn't believe what Seymour told me at first. But I looked in the book and there it was. Cliff Sharman. I had to get out of the Station. I've just been walking around all day. I didn't have much idea where I was, what I was doing. Then I found myself here. I had to see him. Mebbe it was mistaken identity. Mebbe it was...'

His voice faltered. Dalziel asked unnecessarily. 'Was it him, your mate?'

'Oh yes,' said Wield. 'Oh yes. I came out and I saw your car drawing up. So I waited.'

'You were going to come and see me anyway, likely?' suggested Dalziel, half helpful, half sarcastic.

'I don't know,' said Wield indifferently. 'I came out. There you were.'

Before Dalziel could say anything further, the door opened and Mrs Hornsby appeared, repaired.

'Sit quiet and say nowt,' said Dalziel. 'We'll talk later. Here, luv, sup this. It'll make you feel better.'

Gratefully the woman downed half her drink.

'I knew it'd end badly,' she said suddenly, the layer of refinement washed out of her voice. 'But never in my wildest dreams did I think that it'd end like this.'

'What do you mean, end badly?' asked Dalziel.

She drank again and said, 'Cliff was always wild. Like Dick, his father. I never liked him from the day Joanie took up with him, but there's no telling children, is there? It wasn't just his colour, though that didn't help. I've got nothing against 'em personally, you understand, but it makes things that bit harder, bound to, isn't it?'

'Colour? Your son-in-law was...?'

'Black, wasn't he? Not jet black, but dark brown, a lot darker than Cliff. That was one blessing when Cliff came along, he was just sort of heavy tanned, you know, could pass for an Eyetie or one of them Maltesers, well, you've seen him for yourself. But Dick, he was black outside and he could be black inside too...'

She paused as if uneasy at the histrionic hyperbole of her assertion, then nodded as if to confirm that she meant it.

'Black...' prompted Dalziel.

'Not all the time, I mean, he could be a bundle of laughs and he knew how to spend and enjoy himself, Joanie would never have fancied him else, stands to reason, don't it? But he was always on the lookout for people putting him down, bit of a chip on his shoulder, know what I mean?'

'About his colour?'

'Well, that, yes. But other things too. He was brought up in a home, Nottingham or somewhere like that. When he was beered up and the black mood was on him he'd talk about it sometimes. He reckoned his mam was white, or mebbe it was his dad that was white, and he'd been dumped there because he was black, something like that. Well, anyway, they seemed to get along all right, him and Joanie, and Cliff came along, accident that was, I reckon Joanie would've had an abortion but Dick wouldn't wear it. So they muddled on. He was away from home a lot, and that probably helped things. He worked up West, in hotels and places, porter, doorman, barman sometimes, so he often lived in, it was handier. Joanie went her own way, but discreetly, like. Then one night, it's about ten years back now but I remember it like yesterday, this friend she was out with had one too many and there was an accident on the bypass and...'

The tears were ready to fall again, but this time with the aid of a pocket mirror and a paper handkerchief she managed to stem them at source.

'Well, it shook Dick, I'll say that for him. Really broke him up for a bit. He stayed on at their flat a while with Cliff—the boy was about nine at the time. Then one day he came to see me and said, could I help? The Council was giving him a bad time about the boy, saying Dick couldn't look after him properly. Well, it was hard, especially with Dick's kind of job. But he was adamant, he'd not have the lad taken into care. He'd been dumped in a home himself, and it wasn't going to happen to his son. You had to admire him for that, didn't you? And the boy was my grandson. So what could I do? I was working full-time at the dry-cleaners just then, but Dick said full-time was no good, would I go part-time and he'd make up the money. I had my doubts, but I said, all right, and give Dick his due, the money wasn't regular, but it nearly always turned up eventually, and a bit over too when he was flush. Plus he paid for all the boy's clothes and so on. I'd no complaints.'

'And did Dick actually live with you?' asked Dalziel, recognizing that there were no short cuts on a marathon.

'Some of the time. But like I said, he worked away a lot. He was restless, didn't like getting into a rut. Also I reckon he often got into a bit of bother and had to move on. But it was nearly always in London and he'd nearly always ring once a week, or send a postcard. And it was rare for more than three or four weeks to pass without him putting in an appearance. He'd spoil the boy rotten then, though I noticed if he was back for more than a couple of days, it wasn't long before he was putting Cliff in his place.'

'You got on well with the boy yourself?' Dalziel asked.

'Well enough,' she said after a hesitation. 'Till he started at the secondary, anyway. I'll make no bones, by the time he reached his teens, he was too much for me to handle. He was in with a bad set, but I expect their mums said that about their lads too. There was bother with the Old Bill too, nothing serious, but enough to make me worry. I soon made up my mind. When he was sixteen and out of school, that was it. He could sling his hook and live permanent with his dad. I liked him well enough, you understand, but it was all getting too much for me. I wasn't as young as I had been, and I wanted a bit of peace and quiet.'

'Nonsense,' said Dalziel gallantly. 'I bet there's life in them old bones yet.'

'You got something in mind?' she said, looking at him assessingly.

Dalziel grinned and said, 'We'll see. What happened to Dick?'

'Three years ago he went off again. He was working up West and we were expecting him at the weekend, but he rang up to say he wouldn't be coming as he was going away for a bit. I said, is it a job? and he laughed, not a real laugh but sort of meaningful, and said, no, it was family business. And that was that. To cut a long story short, we never saw him again. Cliff got a postcard a couple of days later and after that, nothing. Cliff got really upset as more and more time went by, but what was there to do? I rang your lot and all they said was sorry, there was no law against a man going away and not coming back. So I had to make do with that.'

'And Cliff?'

'He stopped talking about it, eventually, but I don't think he stopped thinking about it. Not that we ever discussed it. He left school and he didn't get any work, well, I know it's hard to get these days, but he didn't even look, did he? He just started going up West and only coming back when he felt like it. I don't know what he was doing up there, and I don't want to know, but he was never short of money so far as I could see. In the end we had a row and he walked out with all his things and I never saw him again.'

'When was that, Mrs Hornsby?'

'Two years ago. At least. I told him I never wanted to set eyes on him again and I wish I hadn't, leastways not like this.'

She began to cry again, beyond the staunching of tissue, and Dalziel pulled a huge khaki handkerchief out of his pocket and passed it across to her.

'That'll do for now, luv,' he said. 'We've got you booked into a nice hotel. Why don't you go along there now with the lass here and have a nice lie-down. We'll mebbe chat again later, and have a couple of beers too, eh?'

The prospect seemed to please. The woman began to gather herself and her accoutrements together.

'This postcard Cliff got. Where was it from, do you remember?'

It was Wield who spoke.

'I'm not sure,' Mrs Hornsby said. 'North. It could've been Yorkshire. Yes, I think the picture said Yorkshire.'

She smiled at Wield as though pleased that he had broken his silence, but he had resumed his previous distancing, with-drawn expression.

The landlord unlocked the door to let the woman out, then paused and looked hopefully towards the men.

Dalziel pointed at his glass and raised two fingers in a gesture mathematical rather than derisory.

'And now, sunshine,' he said to Wield. 'Let's you and me have a little talk.'

Wield did not speak till the whiskies arrived and even then he delayed till the landlord had retreated out of earshot.

Then he put the glass to his lips and knocked the smooth spirit back in one swallow. Dalziel's face across the table looked about as sympathetic as a prison wall. But it was not sympathy he wanted, Wield reminded himself. It was the right to be himself. He thought of the effect saying this was likely to produce on Dalziel and felt his courage ebb. He had to admit it—the man terrified him! Here before him in awful visible form, was embodied all the mockery, scorn and scatological abuse which he had always feared from the police hierarchy. At least, to start with Dalziel was to start with the worst.

He drew a deep breath and said, 'I want to tell you. I'm a homosexual.'

'Oh aye,' said Dalziel. 'You've not just found out, have you?'

'No,' said Wield, taken aback. 'I've always known.'

'That's all right, then,' said Dalziel equably. 'I'd have been worried else that I'd not mentioned it to you.'

I'm not hearing him right, thought Wield, now utterly bewildered. Or mebbe he didn't hear me right!

'I'm gay,' he said desperately. 'I'm a queer.'

'You can be a bloody freemason for all I care,' said Dalziel, 'but it's not going to help with your promotion, if that's what you're after!'

It took Wield a full thirty seconds to begin to assimilate this. 'You knew?' he said disbelievingly. 'How? How long? Who else?'

'Ah well, you see, they're not all clever cunts like me,' said Dalziel modestly. 'Listen, Wieldy, what are you telling me? You're a queer? Well, I've known that almost as long as you've been in CID. But it's not interfered with your work, no more anyway than Mr Pascoe having a row with his missus, or Seymour not getting it away with that Irish bint. Only time I was worried was when you went all dewy-eyed when young Constable Singh got himself hurt, so I saw to it he got posted out of harm's way!'

'You bastard!' said Wield, slowly beginning to grow angry. 'Who the hell do you think you are? What am I supposed to be? Grateful?'

'You can be whatever you fucking well like, Sergeant,' said Dalziel. 'Except mebbe insubordinate. Listen, lad, I'll spell it out. What you are is your business except when it touches your job and then it's mine. All I want to hear from you now is if, and how, your relationship with this boy, Sharman, has touched your job. So talk!'

There didn't seem to be anything else to do.

Wield went through the whole thing from the very start, omitting nothing, adding nothing.

Dalziel nodded admiringly when he finished.

'By God, Sergeant, you're the best maker of reports I've ever come across. What's that fancy word Mr Pascoe used about them? Pellucid! That's what they are, pellucid. Just so we know where we are, why don't you tell me what you've done that's illegal in all this?'

Wield said, after a little thought, 'I've withheld information. I've broken police regulations. And I've acted in a manner unbecoming and unprofessional.'

'That's about the strength of it,' agreed Dalziel. 'We'll sort that out just now. Let's concentrate on the boy first of all. You were fond of him?'

'I was growing fond of him,' said Wield in a low voice. 'I found him very attractive. He was young, vital, and I don't know, brave in a kind of way. At least he had the courage to be what he was. He thought I was pretty contemptible, I think. I knew he was all kinds of other less attractive things too. I wasn't blind. When he walked out I thought: That's it. There's pain here, yes, but I'm well out of it. Pain I can bear. It'll fade. I'll survive. Then I found out he was dead...'

His voice, growing steadily lower, faded into inaudibility.

'Easy, lad,' said Dalziel. 'Listen, it might help to know that on the basis of what you've said and something that the DCC told me earlier today, I reckon young Master Cliff went straight from your flat to telephone the *Challenger* and make an appointment to blow the gaff on you this morning.'

Slowly Wield shook his head.

'No,' he said bitterly. 'That doesn't help at all.'

'Sorry I spoke, then,' said Dalziel. 'All right, sunshine, you sit here and feel sorry for yourself while I make a couple of phone calls.'

He went through the bar to the telephone and got through to the station. First he asked for Watmough. The DCC did not seem happy to hear his voice nor did what Dalziel had to say much increase his store of felicity.

'This murdered man is possibly the same person who has been ringing the *Challenger*, you think?'

'Seems likely.'

'Has anything emerged about the precise details of his allegations?' asked Watmough cautiously.

'As far as I can make out, he said nowt and he's left nowt in writing,' said Dalziel disingenuously. 'What I wanted to find out is who was the reporter he was supposed to be meeting, but didn't? I'll need to talk to him.'

'Vollans. Henry Vollans,' said Watmough. Dalziel could almost hear his mind clicking like an abacus as he calculated possible advantages and disadvantages. 'Yes, you must talk to him, I see that. But discreetly, Andy, I'll have a word with Ike Ogilby too. There must be no rushing to judgment on this one, you understand?'

'Aye,' said Dalziel. 'Can you put me back to the exchange?'

Here he asked for Pascoe's extension and found that the Inspector had just got in. Through the open door of the snug he could see that Wield had risen to his feet.

He said urgently, 'Listen, Peter, there's a reporter on the *Challenger* I want a word with, name of Vollans. Can you get hold of him somehow.'

'Henry Vollans? I was just talking to him at the Old Mill Inn half an hour ago,' said Pascoe. 'Yes, I'll get him. What's all this about?'

'Sorry. Got to go. See you in, say, half an hour.'

He dropped the receiver on to the rest and went out to meet Wield who was walking slowly towards the exit.

'All ready then?' he said heartily. 'Good. Let's drop in at your place and have a poke around.'

Wield's craggy features went stiff.

'Poke around? You don't think I had something to do with killing him, do you?'

Dalziel thrust his face close to the sergeant's.

'Listen, lad. I could get you remanded in custody for a week pending inquiries on what you've just told me, you must know that.'

'Yes, but...'

'No buts! I could. And I might yet if the fancy takes me. You've done one clever thing in all this business, and that's talking to me. Now do another and shut up except when I ask questions. Here's a question. Sharman according to the p.m. report had had it up the bum some time in the twelve hours before he was killed. Would that have been you?'

'Yes.'

'Later you had a row and he walked out?'

'Yes.'

'You can start chucking in the odd *sir* if you like,' said Dalziel kindly.

'Yes, sir.'

'And he didn't come back to your flat?'

'No, sir.'

'Then his gear must still be at your place, mustn't it? So let's go there and start poking around.'

CHAPTER 5

Henry Vollans had left the Old Mill Inn with a sense of great relief. Not even the attentions of the attractively upholstered daughter of the house, offered (though he did not know it) on the rebound from the suddenly disenchanted Seymour, could compensate for the aggressive tedium of John Huby's conversation. Vollans was happy to put the man out of his mind and turn his thoughts once more to the enigmatic Sarah Brodsworth. Pascoe clearly thought she was a plant from some organization, after the Huby money. But if so, which? He suspected Pascoe knew more about her than he was saying whereas he himself knew rather less.

But he had a few not inconsiderable advantages over Pascoe. For one thing, he was young and looked like Robert Redford. Should Sarah Brodsworth herself remain resistant to his charms, then he would have to turn them even more strongly on the old girl. It might mean several more hours of colonial reminiscence but somewhere in there he would learn everything about Brodsworth that the ancient biddy could tell him.

So immersed was he in his plans that he hardly noticed the police car till he almost hit it.

Oh shit! he said to himself, thinking of all the reasons why they might be stopping him, which included though it did not end at his recent consumption of three pints of the Old Mill Inn's excellent bitter.

'Mr Vollans, is it?' said the uniformed officer stooping to the open window.

'Yes.'

'Superintendent Dalziel would like a word with you in town, if you don't mind, sir.'

It didn't feel like an arrest, but you never knew with the police. Nor was his mind set at rest when he met Pascoe at the Station.

'What's it all about?' he asked.

'I don't know,' said Pascoe honestly. 'Depends what you've been up to.'

He was given a cup of truly terrible coffee, and it had grown cold and he was growing hot by the time Dalziel's imminence was felt.

Pascoe met the Superintendent at the door.

'Later,' said the fat man. 'I'd like a word alone with our friend here.'

Friend came out like a threat. Vollans postponed his indignation like a man on the *Titanic* postponing his letter to the manufacturers. Slamming the door behind his inspector, Dalziel said without preamble, 'Someone rang you last night to arrange a meeting to sell you a story about a queer cop, right? What time did he ring?'

'I'm not sure exactly. Some time after seven. Our exchange will know.'

'He asked for you personally?'

'Yes. We'd spoken before.'

'About the same matter?'

'That's right.'

'Did he give you a name?'

'No. No names.'

'But it was the same voice.'

'Oh yes. Definitely.'

'What did he say?'

Vollans thought, then replied, 'He said he wanted to meet to talk money. He was ready to spill everything he knew, but he wanted cash in hand. I said, all right, let's meet. You name the time and place.'

'And did he?'

'Yes. He said eight-thirty this morning in the railway station buffet.'

'And you were there?'

'Yes. And an early rising I had of it too. All for nothing. He didn't show.'

'How do you know?'

'Sorry?'

'If you'd not met him before, how do you know he wasn't there?'

'Well, put like that, I don't. He was supposed to approach me. I told him what I looked like and what I'd be wearing and that I'd carry a copy of the *Challenger*. That'd be the clincher. I mean, there aren't many people carrying Sunday papers in the middle of the week!'

'No? There's a lot of mean buggers in this town,' said Dalziel.

Though delivered with the utmost seriousness, this observation somehow rang an end-of-round bell and for the first time since Dalziel's entry, Vollans did not feel immediately threatened.

He said, 'What's this all about?'

Before Dalziel could reply, there was a peremptory knock and Neville Watmough entered.

'Mr Vollans,' he said. 'Hello again.'

'You two know each other?' said Dalziel. 'That's cosy.'

'Hello, sir,' said Vollans.

'It's good of you to help like this,' pursued Watmough. 'Routine inquiries, simple elimination. I've just been talking to Mr Ogilby and I mentioned how helpful you were being and assured him he could expect a reciprocal degree of cooperation from us. You might like to give him a ring when Mr Dalziel's finished with you.'

'I'm finished,' said Dalziel, scratching his right buttock and producing a sound which made chalk on a blackboard sound like Menuhin on a Strad.

Vollans found himself being ushered out of the door. Watmough remained on the inside.

'What's he say?'

'Not much,' said Dalziel, varying the note by dragging his nails diagonally across the weave of his tight blue serge. 'Our would-be tipster arranged a meet and didn't show. No more than that.'

'So there's no evidence to show that the murdered man and the tipster were definitely the same?'

'Nothing I'd like to see in print, sir,' Dalziel said ambiguously. 'No names, no pack drill, if you follow me.'

Watmough regarded him distrustfully but this was nothing new.

He said, 'I insist on...' then changed his mind.

He tried again. 'Andy, you're a very experienced officer...'

'And you can rest assured I'll use my experience in the best interests of all of us, sir,' said Dalziel fulsomely.

Watmough decided that no words were good words and opened the door to reveal Pascoe standing there, a look of puzzlement on his thin, nearly handsome face. He stood aside to let Watmough pass but Dalziel spoke again before the move was completed.

'So it's my understanding, sir, that in the Sharman case, you want nothing said or published which might reflect on the good name of the Force without your personal authority.'

Watmough took a deep breath, said 'Yes,' looked as if he instantly regretted it, but before he could add anything further Dalziel had drawn Pascoe into the room and closed the door firmly on the DCC.

'Please,' said Pascoe plaintively. 'Is anyone going to tell me what's going on?'

'Take a chair,' said Dalziel. 'Are you sitting comfortably? Then I'll begin.'

After he had finished, there was silence in the room. Even Dalziel's scratchy serenade was allowed to fade away as he observed the younger man's reaction with interest.

At last he spoke.

'Wield's queer?' he said incredulously. 'Bugger me.'

'Best be careful what you say,' said Dalziel and roared with laughter.

Pascoe looked at him with undisguised distaste and Dalziel stopped laughing and said with a sigh, 'All right. What's up?'

'Nothing. I just don't think it's a laughing matter, that's all.'

'What do you think it is, then? A hanging matter?'

Pascoe flushed and said angrily, 'That's not what I meant at all and you know it. I reckon I'm a damn sight more...'

His voice tailed away as he saw the fat man's sly amusement.

'Liberal, is that the word? Some of your best mates are gay? Well, here's another to join the merry throng!'

Pascoe took a deep breath and said, 'All right. Sorry. Let's start again, sir. You go easy on the jokes and I'll go easy on the righteousness.'

'Sounds fair,' said Dalziel. 'So what's the problem?'

'Well, Wieldy himself, for a start. And Watmough. You've seen his reaction to the thought of a homosexual copper.'

'He's not happy,' admitted Dalziel. 'He wishes I'd just kept quiet about all this.'

'Yes. Well, why didn't you, sir?' asked Pascoe flatly. 'I assume that Sergeant Wield isn't connected with the murder, so why risk dragging him into it at all?'

Dalziel shook his head in only partly mock-amazement.

'This matriculation you need to get into university,' he said, 'does it involve drilling holes in your skull or something? What makes you assume Wield's not connected with the murder?'

'I know him!' exploded Pascoe, then, his voice modulating into a minor key, 'I thought I knew him.'

'Right,' said Dalziel. 'You *thought*. Well, as it happens I don't think he topped our boy either. But Wield's connected all right and that's a fact.'

'I see. And you don't want to risk your career by being connected with a cover-up?' said Pascoe scornfully.

'Fuck me pink!' exclaimed Dalziel. 'Cover-up? What's so scary about a cover-up? I've done enough covering up in my time to fill in Wharfedale! But why should I do the dirty work when there's others as'll do it for me?'

'Meaning?'

'You've forgotten what Tick-Tock, the Talking Clock, said just now already? Christ almighty, Peter, I'd best write it down and get you to sign it! Listen, lad, Watmough doesn't want to know about Wield, doesn't want to know about *anything*, not till the Selection Committee meets.'

'And afterwards?'

'Too late. He'll be personally in charge of the cover-up by then. Last thing he'll want the new Chief Constable to know is how he's been bending the rules.'

'What if he *is* the new Chief?' objected Pascoe.

Dalziel began to laugh. Pascoe didn't join in.

'And Wield? What about him?' he said.

'Sick again,' said Dalziel. 'Till I tell him he's better. He's ploughed himself a deep furrow. Much more and he'll be buried.'

'But you said he wasn't mixed up in this!'

'Not in the murder, not directly. But he's mixed up all right, in every other sense. The boy told him he'd come up here to look for his dad who went missing three years back. They had a row. Wield told him he didn't believe him and that he reckoned he was just a nasty little crook who'd stopped off in Yorkshire to put the black on him.'

'Well, all the other evidence confirms that.'

'Mebbe. But his dad did go missing three years back. His grandma confirms it and says the boy was very upset.'

'But is there any link with Yorkshire?'

'The grandmother knew none. Said she thought he was brought up in a kid's home in Nottingham. I'd like you to check that out, Peter, see if there's anything for us there.'

'Why? Do you believe this story about looking for his dad too?'

'Mebbe. Sharman told Wield he came to Yorkshire because his last contact with his father was a postcard from up here. He also said he'd mislaid the card, so there wasn't any hard evidence to stop Wield blowing his top. The boy's gear, what little there is, got left at Wield's flat. I've had a look through it. Nothing of interest except this. I found it tucked away in the middle of a thick paperback.'

He handed over a postcard. It was addressed to Cliff Sharman in Dulwich. The postmark was illegible except for the year which said 1982.

The message read: *Dear Cliff, sorry about the weekend but I'll be back soon as I've got my business sorted. Take care. Dad.*

Pascoe turned the card over. The photograph was a view of a large Victorian building with a tall central clock-tower.

He didn't need to read the inscription. By stepping to the window, he could glimpse a distant side-view of the same clock-tower on the old town hall.

'So the lad was telling the truth, at least in part,' he said. 'Wield's seen this?'

'Yes,' said Dalziel.

'And you left him alone!'

'He wanted to be alone,' said Dalziel. 'Don't worry. He'll not harm himself.'

'How can you be sure?' demanded Pascoe.

'Because I know the man! Oh aye, so did you; and better, you thought? Well, lad, there's one difference. I've known for years he were bent, so perhaps I'm better qualified to comment now. He'll not harm himself. I gave him fair warning.'

'Warning? What's that mean?'

'I told him if he killed himself, I'd have him drummed out of the Force,' said Dalziel seriously.

Pascoe shook his head in incredulous bewilderment.

'And what did he say to that?' he asked.

'Oh, he perked up a lot,' said Dalziel cheerfully. 'He asked me why I didn't go off and fuck myself. What's that you're thinking, lad? Seconded? Well, I never mind a vote of confidence. But one thing—don't go running round to Wield's place tonight to say you're sorry for not sussing out his guilty secret. Last thing he needs is a lachrymose liberal. That's a good word, eh? I got it off *Top of the Form* on the wireless! So, keep your nose out till tomorrow at least.'

The fat man grinned maliciously.

'Any road, I reckon I've got enough work lined up for you, Peter, to keep you busy till nigh on midnight!'

CHAPTER 6

Lexie Huby's class finished at eight and she was driving up to Troy House by half past. It was a fine night, but moonless and with enough wind to set the trees trembling and shake out the odd dead leaf. The house was in darkness and the slight figure paused for a while by her car before slamming the door and shutting off the courtesy light which was the only illumination.

As she headed for the front porch, she heard a noise in the garden. She stopped and turned. There was movement there, in the shadows by the shrubbery, a menacing presence, now still, now beginning to advance.

Lexie said calmly, 'Hob? Is that you?'

And a moment later smiled as her deduction was confirmed and the old donkey's ears broke the dim skyline above the shrubs.

Next moment a hand descended on her shoulder and she spun round, shrieking.

'Sorry, miss, it's only me!'

It was Constable Jennison, the Greendale policeman, his square face rhomboid with concern.

'Didn't mean to scare you, but I've been told off to keep a weather eye open round Troy House and when I saw the car, I thought I'd better take a look. It's Miss Lexie, isn't it? Mrs Brooks said you was expected. She went off about an hour ago, said the old lady was sleeping sound.'

Lexie, recovered and reassured, said, 'That's good. Will you have a cup of tea?'

'No, thanks. Got to get on down to the Greendale Inn. Big darts match tonight, first round of the cup.'

'And you're expecting bother?'

'No way,' he said. 'I'm playing! Good night now. I'll check back later.'

Lexie let herself into the house with Lomas's key. There was a note to her from Mrs Brooks in the kitchen saying the doctor had called again and Miss Keech had taken some nourishment and gone to sleep. The doctor was arranging for a nurse the following day. A postscript added that all the animals had been fed despite anything they might say to the contrary.

Lexie smiled as she read the note. She knew Mrs Brooks and guessed that Jennison's absence from his darts match had been as much to check on her arrival at the cleaner's request as to check the security of the house at Dalziel's.

She went upstairs to the big bedroom, once Great Aunt Gwen's, now Miss Keech's. It was strange. It was easy to imagine in the semi-darkness that it was still her aunt lying there, though she and Miss Keech bore no great physical resemblance.

As she turned to leave, a quavery voice said, 'Who's there?'

'It's only me, Miss Keech,' she said advancing. 'Lexie.'

She switched on the bedside lamp to give confirmation.

'Oh, Lexie,' said the old woman. 'Little Lexie. What's the time?'

Lexie told her.

'It's good of you to come to see me. Everyone's very good when you're ill, aren't they? Likes and dislikes, they all get forgotten.'

Lexie didn't know how to answer this.

She said, 'Would you like a hot drink?'

'No, thank you. A little tonic wine would be nice.'

Lexie poured her a glass from the bottle on the bedside table. It was mildly alcoholic but she assumed the doctor would have removed it if he felt it was likely to be harmful. Then she helped Miss Keech to sit up, arranging her pillows as a back rest. Her body felt frail and skeletal and she smelt of lavender and old age.

She sipped the wine thirstily, but not indecorously, her little finger crooked in that much parodied signal of refinement.

'More?' said Lexie.

'No, thank you, dear.'

She put the glass down.

'Do you want to sleep now? Or listen to the radio perhaps?'

Miss Keech smiled like marsh-light on a dark pool.

'You've never liked me much, have you, Lexie?' she said.

Lexie considered her reply.

'No. Not much,' she said finally.

Miss Keech laughed silently.

'You were always such a blunt little thing. No. That's wrong. You were always a timid, quiet, rather frightened little girl, but once you set your mind on something, that was it.'

'Was it?'

'Oh yes. I remember when we put you and Jane on Hob. And Hob brayed at Jane and that was enough. She'd never go near him again. You fell off at least a dozen times, but it didn't matter. You had to be lifted up again. And then when you changed your name! We all went on calling you Alexandra for a while. It was hard to break old habits. But you broke it all right. We could call you Alexandra till the cows came home and you'd carry on like someone stone deaf. It was because of Mrs Huby's son, wasn't it?'

Again Lexie considered before answering.

'Yes,' she said. 'I never thought much of it, my name being so like his, till one Sunday I said I couldn't come here to tea, I had too much homework, and Dad lost his temper. He said, Did I imagine he came here to enjoy himself, and the only reason he put up with it was because of securing his family's future, and Aunt Gwen would be right offended if I didn't go as I was the only one she really thought anything of because of the music, and because I had the same name as her missing son. It had never struck me before. That was why I'd been christened Alexandra, not because it was a name Mam and Dad liked and wanted to call me, but in order to butter up Aunt Gwen. So I changed it. Jane had always called me Lexie from a little girl. That was my *own* name, no one else's.'

Miss Keech nodded sleepily.

'Yes, that's you, Lexie...your own name...your own person... it must be a gift...like grace...a precious, precious...'

Her eyes closed, forcing out of each a tear which might have been just an old woman's rheum, yet they gleamed as bright as a young woman's grief.

And she slept.

Others talked and listened, waking and sleeping, that night too. Rosie Pascoe, content to have summoned her father by her cries on his late return home, let his flow of meaningless words lull her back to sleep.

'I don't get it, kid,' he said to her. 'Sergeant Wield, that's the one who's so ugly, *you* fall about laughing every time you see him, he's turned out to be gay. Perhaps it was people like you laughing that did it. Jocund company turns you gay, doesn't it? That's a sort of intellectual joke. Ellie, that's your mother, remember, the one with the short hair, she says that's my trouble. She says she's always known Wield was gay, and Fat Andy says he's always known too. But me, I'm supposed to be a bit afraid of feelings, I've got an intellectual censor, that's what your mother says. It's what keeps me sane in the fuzz, but it cuts off part of me too. Is she right, do you think? Has part of me been cut off? What's that you say? Forget the fruit-cake analysis and how am I getting on with the Pontelli murder? It's slow, kid, but I'm getting there. I think I know what's happening, only I can't really believe it. Story of my life, kid. Story of my life!'

Sergeant Wield had opened the door of his flat to a long insistent ring earlier that evening. He had been certain it was Pascoe. Instead the doorway was filled with Dalziel.

'Peter'll come and see you tomorrow,' said Dalziel, casually thought-reading. 'I told him to go straight home. He's so full of guilt at not being any use to you, he'd probably offer you his bum in atonement if he came tonight, and that'd do none of you any good.'

Wield considered punching Dalziel on the nose, but found himself smiling wanly instead. The fat man was right. The last thing he needed was a guilty shoulder to cry on.

'You'd best come in,' he said. 'Only I've finished the whisky.'

Silently Dalziel produced a bottle of Glen Grant out of an inside pocket. He unscrewed the top and threw it away.

'You got some big glasses?' he said.

Sarah Brodsworth was asleep and in her sleep she dreamt of Henry Vollans. The reporter's face, too lupine now for Robert Redford, thrust itself eagerly at her, snapping and snarling questions and driving her back into a darkness filled with voices. Simplest would be to turn and run away and leave him sniffing fruitlessly at the space where she had been. But that would be an unforgivable weakness, and it wasn't weakness that had brought her to where she was. Her task was to get her hands on the Huby money if and when it came to WFE, and waking or sleeping she wasn't about to let anybody, journalist, policeman or *anybody*, interfere. But she would need to be vigilant, waking or sleeping. There was a noise. Someone opening a door. Faint footsteps. Shallow breathing. Was she sleeping or waking now? She did not know.

It was ten to midnight when Rod Lomas got back to Troy House. He found Lexie in the lounge asleep on a huge sofa beneath a patchwork quilt of cats and dogs who, barred from entry under Keech's strict regime, had not missed this chance of celebrating their Paradise regained.

Lomas stooped and brushed the girl's forehead with his lips. Her eyes opened and blinked myopically. He picked up her spectacles from beneath a labrador's protective paw and dropped them on to her nose.

'Hi,' he said.

'Hello,' she said, struggling upright. 'What time is it?'

He told her.

'Sorry I'm so late. Only we had some trouble at the theatre. Someone let off a smoke bomb in the first act. The place had to be cleared. Chung insisted on starting right at the beginning again when we got things sorted, so even though we all spoke at twice our normal speed, we ran very late!'

'Who did it? Kids?'

'Well, the place was full of school parties. But someone had been at work with a spray can in the foyer. Nasty racist stuff, mainly about Chung. So if it's children, you can put me down for the W. C. Fields' Fan Club. I would have rung, but I was worried in case you'd gone home and I'd just wake Keechie. How is she?'

Lexie struggled to her feet, disturbing a cry of cats, and went with the accuracy of childish memory to the sideboard where the drinks were kept. Under Keech's rule, there was Scotch as well as sweet sherry.

'I'm not sure,' she said, pouring a stiff one. 'She seems strong enough in herself but she was rambling on very strangely till she fell asleep.'

'What about?'

'Just rambling,' said Lexie vaguely, handing him the drink. 'It may be some drug the doctor's given her. Mrs Brooks left a note saying a nurse would be coming in the morning.'

'Thank God for that,' said Lomas wearily. 'I only hope she doesn't wake up in the night.'

He sipped his drink and regarded the girl speculatively. 'I don't suppose there's any chance, just in case, that you could stay...' he said.

'To take care of Miss Keech, you mean?'

'Oh yes. Purely honourable motives,' he assured her. 'And I'd like a chance to talk to you.'

'Why?'

'Why what?'

'Why are your motives honourable?' It was, like most of her questions, not ironical but single-dimensional, direct.

He considered, then grinned.

'Fail-safe,' he said. 'Then if my physical weakness or your mortal strength prevails, I can always claim that's what I intended anyway. What do you say, Lexie? Seriously, on your terms. Can you give the Old Mill a ring?'

'I've done it already,' said Lexie. 'For Miss Keech's sake, not yours.'

'That's great,' said Lomas. 'Where will you sleep?'

Lexie took a long look at him.

'Anywhere,' she said, 'as long as it's not full of cats and labradors.'

'I know just the place,' said Lomas.

It was the corny, the obvious thing to say. But it was not what he had intended to say. There were things to talk about, things to sort out. He had no interest at all in this anorexic child's skinny body. He could not, did not want to imagine what it would be like, what her reaction would be to his masculine size and hardness. But it was too late. The offer had come, had been accepted. He followed her out of the room and up the stairs, pausing by Keechie's door in hope of hearing her saving bell. But all that came was the gentle snoring of peaceful sleep.

It was a sleep that remained peaceful, which was fortunate for Miss Keech as there were moments when it would have taken a very strong hand and a very large bell to attract the attention of her putative nurses.

'By Christ, but I enjoyed that!' said Lomas.

'No need to sound so surprised,' said Lexie.

'I'm sorry! I didn't mean…no, what I meant was…'

'Try the truth.'

'Well, the truth is, I thought it might be like being in bed with a boy,' confessed Lomas, wrapping his arms and legs round her narrow little body in way of illustration.

'And was it?'

'If it was, bring on the boys!' laughed Lomas. 'Also…'

'Yes?'

'I thought it'd be your first time.'

'Nearly right,' said Lexie. 'Third.'

'You're very exact.'

'I did it first during my O-levels,' said Lexie. 'Everyone talked about it and I knew some girls who really had done it, and I thought I ought to give it a go.'

'Jesus. I've heard of an inquiring mind, but this is ridiculous. How was it?'

'Painful. Cold. Uncomfortable. The lad said he'd done it before, but I'm not sure. And we were outside, on the edge of the playing fields, and it had been raining.'

'But you tried again?'

'Oh, yes. Everyone said it always hurt first time off and you didn't start enjoying it till second time.'

'Were they right?'

'It were better,' conceded Lexie. 'But not enough to give me a taste.'

'And the third time?'

'I'm not sure yet. Mebbe I'll be able to tell you after the fourth.'

'You'll have to hang around for that,' he said. 'Lexie...'

'Yes.'

He knew what he wanted to ask her, and he guessed she knew too. But he couldn't ask without himself answering questions, and there were things in his life he suddenly did not want this girl mixed up with.

He heard himself saying, 'Lexie, do you love your parents?'

That took her by surprise.

She said, 'Love,' as though trying a new taste.

'That's what I said. The other things—gratitude, obedience, dependency and so on—they don't matter, they're for anyone. Parents need love, don't they, otherwise, who'd bother?'

'They fuck you up, your mam and dad. They may not mean to, but they do,' said Lexie.

'Good Lord.'

'Larkin,' she said.

'I know.'

'But you're surprised. Because I've heard of Larkin or because I said fuck?'

'I'm, sorry,' he said. 'Old habits. You can't expect me to stop patronizing you just because of one good screw, can you?'

'Two had better do it,' she said. 'But you're right in a way. I'd never heard of Larkin till some lad in the fourth form found this poem with the word fuck in it. It were funny. I could hear it, and worse, any time I wanted in the playground or back home at the pub. But seeing it printed there in a book of poems was still a shock. 'Specially when it said those things about my mam and dad.'

'Not about *your* mum and dad, surely. It's a little more generalized than that.'

'There's no such thing as generalized when you're a lass of fourteen and you've just started having periods. Not when most of the other girls in your class and even your little sister had started a lot sooner. I used to lie, not to be different. I tried asking Mam but she said I should be grateful and not to bother her. No, everything anyone said or did or wrote was about me. Earthquakes in China were about me! Any road, what about you? Do you love your mam?'

'Old Windypants?' he said with a laugh. 'Yes, I think so. It's always been an artificial relationship in the best sense. A thing of delicate artifice. Up until three years ago I was the marvellous boy of infinite promise. Then Daddy died and soon after I became just another resting actor. Mummy did some quick re-writing, I tell you. Now we're both word perfect in an intimate two-hander in which I don't remind her she's old enough to be my mother and she doesn't remind me that I'm old enough to be earning my own living. Well, not too often anyway.'

'You *are* earning your own living.'

'My own survival, you mean. Chung got me right in the doubling-up part she got me to do. It's not big bold fast-talking Mercutio you're in bed with but the apothecary. *Who calls so loud?* And Romeo replying, *Come hither, man. I see that thou art poor.*'

'The trouble with actors,' said Lexie slowly, 'is acting. What was your dad like?'

'Oh, my astute little Lexie! He was the last of the actor-managers. People think I get it from Mummy, but hers is a thin, brittle, strictly non-transferable talent. Pa was different. He moved from role to role with infinite ease. People said he was a con artist, but he conned himself as much as anyone. He believed totally in every role he played and that's the secret of great acting. It was pure accident that he drifted into finance rather than the theatre. Do you know, he couldn't bear to buy things in a sale? Show him a fur coat marked down from four thousand to two and he'd turn his back in disgust. One simply did not buy such things. But show him the same thing at its full price and he would talk it down fifty per cent in as many minutes.'

He paused. For once, Lexie guessed, he was using his own talents to conceal rather than project emotion.

'You miss him,' said Lexie flatly.

'Oh yes, I miss him. Mum's great, we get on fine—most of the time! But Dad was something else.'

'Yes. I'm beginning to see how things must have worked out.'

'What things, Lexie?' asked Lomas.

'Things,' she said.

He looked at her with an expression of bafflement.

'I'm not sure...' he began.

'What?'

'Of *anything*! What am I doing here?'

'That's a bit rude.'

'No. I mean... Lexie, why did you tell that policeman I was at the opera with you on Friday? And imply that we spent the night together?'

'You've taken long enough to ask,' she said. 'And what is it you're asking? Why I did it? Or why I thought it needed to be done?'

'Oh Lexie, you have been too long already with lawyers! Why you thought it needed to be done, then.'

'Well,' said the girl slowly, 'I guessed why the police were asking. I heard a conversation at work...what I mean is, I eaves-dropped on the telephone...I knew that this man, Pontelli, had been staying in Leeds and that a man had turned up there late on Friday looking for him.'

'And what makes you think that has anything to do with me?' wondered Lomas, searching through his drama college ragbag of faces for honest bewilderment.

She regarded him with the courteous blankness of an unimpressed producer and he knew he was not going to get the part.

'It seemed likely,' she said, 'as it was you that put Pontelli up to claiming he was Alexander in the first place, wasn't it?'

He shook his head not in denial but like a boxer who has just taken a sharp hook. Then he slipped out of the bed and stood looking down at her in a pose which could easily have passed for menacing.

'Oh Lexie,' he said, 'Oh, little, little Lexie!'

CHAPTER 7

It took Rod Lomas a turn round the room and a cigarette and a half to bring him to the talking point.

He didn't deny her accusation then, but demanded, 'How did you know?'

'I was at the funeral,' she said. 'I saw everyone's face when Pontelli showed up. Shock, bewilderment, outrage, that's what I saw. Except on yours.'

'And on mine?'

'Amusement. You were enjoying it.'

'My warped sense of humour, perhaps.'

'Mebbe. But I saw your first night too. You were awful.'

'Gee, thanks.'

'I'd looked for you in your dressing-room before I went on stage to the party. There was a copy of the *Evening Post* there. It had Pontelli's picture in it. I reckoned you must've seen it not long before you went on and that was the first you knew he was dead.'

'At least you don't think I killed him, then!' he said with a slight sneer.

'I'd not have done it if I'd thought that,' she said calmly.

What 'it' referred to wasn't altogether clear. He felt himself in her control and some rubbery imp of resentful ego still twisted in his gut. She was sitting up against the bed-head, naked, her knees drawn up under her chin, watching him. Her steady gaze and her unself-consciousness suddenly made him aware of his own nakedness and he instinctively dropped his cigaretteless hand to his crotch. A small smile sent the imp bounding again.

'You look like an Oxfam poster!' he mocked.

The gibe was surprisingly productive.

'I don't think that's funny,' she snapped.

'Oh. Sensitive about our body, are we?'

'I'm sensitive about the bodies I see on Oxfam posters,' she said.

It was a rebuke which threatened to bring the imp bounding forth once more, then suddenly it was gone.

'I'm sorry,' he said. 'I didn't mean anything. I was just putting off talking.'

'Don't,' she advised.

'It's a long story,' he warned.

'Come back to bed and tell it.'

It wasn't after all too long a story that Rod Lomas told Lexie Huby as they lay side by side in the narrow bed that had once belonged to the lost boy who bore both their names. But it was complicated, not simply in its narrative strands but in the threads of guilt and doubt and pride which were twisted into its telling.

'It was my father's idea,' began Lomas. 'I know he's been dead for three years, but something like this doesn't just spring up overnight. Not that I knew anything about it while he was alive.

He didn't believe in letting even his dearest and nearest see all his sleight of hand! God, he could have run the world if he'd thought it worth his while!'

Lexie said, 'I don't imagine you think he killed himself, then?'

'Christ, no!' said Lomas angrily. 'All that crap about running his car off the road because his company was collapsing was just gutter press garbage. He beat Micawber for optimism!'

'But the company was in trouble.'

'Yes. Well, he always sailed close to the wind. But as long as he could talk and had a bit of working capital, he would have been OK. No, the company collapsed because he died, not the other way round.'

'And the working capital?'

'Oh yes. He had that too. Well, thirty thousand quid's worth of it. Peanuts of course in terms of the whole operation, but enough to wave in the right faces.'

'You're very precise about the figure.'

'I can be. It's what he got from Aunt Gwen.'

Now Lexie showed surprise.

'Auntie Gwen loaned him money?'

'No way!' he laughed. 'There's no one meaner than the rich, Lexie, you'll find that out. No, Daddy knew better than to come cap in hand begging. Instead he offered to do her a favour. I imagine he told her that what she needed to lure Alexander out of hiding was a proper Italian address. He probably argued that while the lost lad might be reluctant to return to England, and be a bit shy even of writing, or calling at posh hotels, an Italian address could do the trick. During her Italian visit that year, I've no doubt he bumped into her by accident and mentioned that he just happened to have this superb villa in Tuscany, the Villa Boethius, on his books, forty thou for a quick sale, splendid investment, all that. She saw it, liked it, knocked him down the twenty-five per cent he'd allowed for, and bought it.'

'That doesn't sound like Aunt Gwen, acting on impulse.'

'No impulse. The completion date was set for a week after her return and she left a post-dated cheque with Daddy's lawyer in Florence. Plenty of time for old Eden Thackeray to pull her and her money out of the deal if he didn't like it. But don't you remember, she got back here and her first night home she had a stroke. Mummy was full of tremulous anticipation, but alas, the old girl recovered. And then a couple of weeks later, Daddy had his accident.'

He fell silent, and Lexie wound her thin arms around him till he started again.

'Then the vultures descended. Everything went, the Fraud Squad were sniffing around with their nasty insinuations, creditors were watching Mummy like a rare comet. They'd have had her gold fillings if she'd slept with her mouth open! Mummy knew about the villa deal, though she hadn't been in Florence when it went through, but any hopes she had that Gwen's thirty thou might be stashed away safe were soon shattered. It was in a nice little account in Zürich, but the Fraud Squad and the creditors between them sniffed it out. Don't believe what you read about Swiss Banks. Millions they may hang on to, smaller sums they hand to the first cop who asks nicely.'

'But the villa. There was nothing in the probate accounts about a villa.'

'Don't be impatient. A couple of months passed. One night the telephone rang. It was a call from Italy, a man who said he'd acted as Daddy's agent on several occasions and he now had an Italian family who were interested in renting the Villa Boethius the following spring. He was sorry to trouble Mummy who must still be mourning her great loss, but if he could be of assistance, etcetera, etcetera. Well, Mummy and I just looked at each other with the dawning of faint hope. Daddy had not left us well provided for. Any source of income, however small, was not to be sneezed at. The creditors were still keeping a weather eye on Mummy, so we split forces. I took a train to Florence and Mummy took one to Yorkshire. We spoke on the phone two days later to exchange information. Hers was excellent. It was quite clear that though Gwen was recovering her health steadily, she had no recollection of buying the Villa Boethuis.'

'But someone had to know? What about Keech?'

'No way. Auntie Gwen treated her like any good-living Yorkshire lady treats the help—called her a treasure and counted the spoons whenever she'd cleared the table.'

'But a draft for thirty thousand…'

'A drop in a pretty large ocean. Also, it would be made out to some very drab-sounding company, not to Daddy personally. There's no evidence that Gwen ever noticed. No, there seemed no reason not to carry on as if the villa were Mummy's by right of inheritance. There's been a steady trickle of rental payments into an account in Dublin ever since.'

'It's fraud,' said Lexie.

'It's a very small fraud.'

'Then it'll be a very small jail sentence. You must have been dead worried when Aunt Gwen died, though.'

'You can say that again. We thought: Any minute now something's going to turn up. And there wasn't much we could do… Jesus Christ!'

A small but extremely hard fist had cracked into his ribs.

'That's what made you contact your "dear cousin", wasn't it? To see if you could pick up anything about the estate from Thackeray's! Likely she'll be too thick to notice she's being pumped.'

'I think you've punctured a lung! Yes, that was about the strength of it, I'm afraid. But I soon realized my error.'

'You'd better not forget.'

'No. I'd better not.'

'You've still not mentioned Pontelli.'

'Yes, I have.'

'When? I didn't hear you...oh.'

'Sharp little Lexie! Yes, you can imagine my surprise when I discovered the astonishing coincidence that Alessandro Pontelli, my father's agent in Florence, should happen to be Aunt Gwen's long-lost son. Can't you?'

'Oh yes. I can imagine!'

'You have an ill-divining soul! Well, here's the truth. This chap Pontelli, well, he knew there was something odd going on about the villa, but I reckon he was used to that, working for Dad. But something about him struck me as soon as we met. The way he moved, the set of his jaw. It took me a little while to pin it down. In fact it wasn't till he brought up the subject himself that it hit me. It was your father he reminded me of. He looked like a Huby!'

'But why should *he* bring the subject up?' asked Lexie.

'Because Dad had obviously noticed the resemblance too! You really had to know Dad to understand what this would mean. He had a truly creative imagination. Something like this would be a seed dropped into fertile earth. Mummy's a very sharp cookie, thinks on her feet, is good in a tight situation, but when it comes to true inventiveness and the long-term view she is nowhere. Her mind works in sharp focus snapshots, Daddy's worked in five-reeler cinemascope!'

'So this was *his* idea?'

'His alone. Mummy knew nothing of it. All her eggs were in one basket, the will. Daddy knew much more about the oddities of the human mind and half-guessed that Gwen's obsession might survive beyond her grave. But even without this suspicion, the sheer magnificent effrontery of the scheme would have fired his imagination.'

'The scheme being to pass Pontelli off as Alexander Huby?'

'That's it! For over a year before his death he had been gathering information about the lost lad and coaching Pontelli in the role.'

Lomas freely admitted now that he was unable to recall whether it was his or Pontelli's idea to revive the scheme.

'Possibly he manipulated me, but I wasn't averse to the manipulation. I don't know, it seemed somehow like a sort of memorial to my father. Also, it had something of the unreal/real nature of the theatre. There was no point in trying anything while Gwen was alive. I mean, suppose Mummy was right and a great chunk of the money was coming her way anyway? But there was no harm in being ready. I gave Pontelli the full benefit of my dramatic expertise plus all the family and geographical background I could recall. He'd been badly shot up in the war, so we were able to work his scars into a lovely scenario of heroic action, near death, long amnesia, psychotic guilt. It seemed like a game in a way. I suppose really I was on Mummy's side and I thought the cash would be hers anyway. When Gwen took ill in August, I was in Italy. I told Pontelli I had to fly back. He didn't say anything, but a week later, he turned up in London. I was down there, as it happened, while Mummy was up here doing her tending-the-sick bit. I told Pontelli to sod off back to Florence. Then the phone rang and Mummy told me Gwen was dead.'

'Your mother didn't know about Pontelli.'

'No. It seemed better. Dad hadn't told her, so I could see no reason to. Well, I came hot foot to Yorkshire for the funeral. Pontelli was not to be shaken off by this time, but I made him stay in Leeds well away from the action till I saw how things were going. Then the news about the will broke, by courtesy of old Thackeray, and suddenly the game began to be for real. How to develop it, I wasn't sure, but it seemed to me to be a good idea to set everyone's mind moving in a certain direction as soon as possible. And I'm afraid I couldn't resist the sheer dramatic impact of having Pontelli pop up at the graveside. All he was meant to be was the mysterious stranger, grieving in the background. It was his own mad Latin idea to go over the top with *Mama*! But, by God, the result was splendid, wasn't it!'

'There were people there who genuinely cared for the old lady,' said Lexie quietly.

'Not you, surely!'

'No, not me. I won't say that. But there were others. And for all her faults, she didn't deserve to go out in farce.'

Lomas pushed himself up on his elbow to study her face in the dim light from the false dawn outside the window.

'You can be quite frightening when you're stern, you know,' he said. 'I'm sorry. You're right. It wasn't decent, was it? But as I am sure you know, that's not what I'm being defensively frivolous about. A bit of comic indecorum never hurt anybody. It's Pontelli's murder that breaks me up. If it wasn't for me, he wouldn't have been here, would he? I feel responsible, and I always flee to farce in times of guilt.'

'But you're not responsible, are you?'

'You beginning to have doubts?'

'What happened?' Lexie said inexorably.

Lomas sighed and said, 'Mummy went wild. After the initial shock, she soon put two and two together. I'd have had to tell her anyway. She'd never met Pontelli but she knew the name well enough. After the funeral she played hell with me. I got mad too and told her she hadn't been so clever either, the way the will had turned out. She said that what should be worrying us to start with was whether old Thackeray as executor was going to track down the Villa Boethius. If he did, then there were going to be all kinds of questions to answer, and the clear link between Pontelli and the villa would plunge us really deep in the mire. I must admit I'd never thought of that. So I went after Pontelli and told him to cool it till we saw how things were developing. Ten days went by without the Fraud Squad banging at Mummy's door. We were in an agony of suspense, to coin a phrase. Then Chung's Mercutio got beaten up and by one of those coincidences too daring for drama I got invited back here to take the part, and Mummy said, why not contact Keechie and ask if you can stay at Troy House?'

'I wondered about that,' said Lexie. 'It's out of the way, inconvenient, and must be a real damper on your love-life.'

'I'm managing very nicely, I think,' said Lomas. 'Anyway, I didn't hang about. My first night here I got into Aunt Gwen's filing cabinet and there among all her bits of paper concerned with the search for Alex, I found her record of the villa purchase. Of course, that's where she would keep it, you see, because that's why she bought it!'

'You stole it.'

'I put it in a safer place,' said Lomas.

'And you activated Pontelli again straightaway,' she said accusingly.

'No! We'd been in touch, naturally. He had been griping on about hanging around doing nothing. And he was short of cash. We subbed him, of course, well, Mummy did; but we were still very uncertain of our long-term plans for him.'

'Don't make it sound like a moral problem,' said Lexie. 'You mean, you didn't know whether to settle for the villa and whatever your mother might get out of the estate via Goodenough and the PAWS suit, or risk going for something much bigger.'

'Christ, I hope you never become a judge!' said Lomas. 'All right, that's about the strength of it. But what we didn't reckon on was Pontelli taking independent action. I think he just got fed up with waiting and decided that the best way forward was to start the ball rolling himself. And that's what he did, the very same day—in fact, as far as I can gather, the very same time—as I was trying to squeeze information out of your stony heart in the Black Bull.'

'So you knew nothing about him going to see Mr Eden?'

'Nothing, I swear it! Nor about him going to see your father. I think he was just putting himself on show, testing the water so he could judge how safe it was to jump in. Very likely he'd decided that the quickest way to make a profit was to create a certain nuisance value so that the estate might buy him off.'

'Work independently of you and your mother, you mean?'

'Why not? He knew we could hardly blow the gaff on him once he was out in the open. I found out what was happening from Mummy at lunch-time on Friday. I was furious! I tried ringing him at the hotel he was staying at in Leeds, but there was no reply from his room. Mummy told me to get myself across there that evening and make sure I saw him and found out what the hell he was playing at. I went by train. I didn't want to show myself at the hotel, so I rang again from a call-box just round the corner. He still wasn't in. It wasn't much of an hotel and I knew I'd be pretty conspicuous hanging around inside, so I spent the evening wandering between a pub and a café on the other side of the road, ringing from time to time in case I'd missed him. Finally I got so desperate I went in and asked for him and made them go up to his room and check he was definitely out. I think they were getting suspicious he'd done a bunk by this time. I'd turned my collar up and put on a phoney accent just to be on the safe side. I didn't know the safe side of what, of course. Finally I headed back to the station. I paused en route to ring Mummy at the Howard Arms to give her a lack-of-progress report, but she wasn't answering either. To cap it all, I got back to the station just in time to see the last train disappearing! So I had to ring Keechie to tell her I wouldn't be back that night as I was staying with a friend.'

'Did you reverse the charges?'

'Yes, as a matter fact—I'd used all my change on the other calls. Why?'

'That's how the police would know you were in Leeds. Keech must've told them.'

'Why shouldn't she? She'd no idea I'd want her to keep it quiet. Anyway, that was it. I dossed down in the waiting-room till the first morning train. I rang the hotel once again on Saturday. By this time they knew he'd done a bunk and were eager for any help I could give them. I rang off, said a little prayer that he'd run all the way back to Florence and forgot all about him till I glanced at the *Evening Post* just before I was due to go on on Monday night, and there he was. I nearly missed my entrance.'

'That's why I knew you didn't kill him.'

'I can't see that fellow Pascoe being so easily convinced. And as for that other tub of lard, the very thought of him makes me shudder—Lexie, what am I going to do?'

'Finish your story first,' she said mildly. 'Save your big remorse scene till you've told me who it was cooked up the idea of proving that Pontelli really was Huby now that he's too dead to question.'

'What? No, that wasn't me, honestly. It was Mummy. I told you she thinks on her feet. I didn't know why she suddenly wanted to know if Pontelli had any distinguishing marks. That was last night, just before she met with Dalziel. I told her-Pontelli and me had gone through the whole thing, about scars, birthmarks, that sort of thing. It wasn't till later I was able to work it out for myself.'

'You surprise me,' said Lexie. 'You being a Lomas and all!'

'Don't you get all high and mighty!' said Lomas, raising his voice defensively. 'If Pontelli was proved to be Alexander, that makes your father the heir. It was pointless Mummy lying unless she could rely on him, wasn't it? I just hope she can trust him for her share, if they get away with it.'

'Not much chance of that,' said Lexie ambiguously. 'And there's no need to shout. I just wanted to know.'

'So now you know! Oh Lexie, I'm sorry. It's all getting too complicated for me. Come between us, good Benvolio; my wits faint. Oh Lexie, what am I to do?'

'Come here,' she said softly. 'You know what to do.'

'What? No, I meant…'

'Oh, methinks I feel some rousing motions in you that do dispose to something extraordinary my thoughts! You're not the only one who can quote, you see.'

'Full of surprises, Lexie. Mind you I think you're wrong. All otherwise to me my thoughts portend—*Christ*! What was *that* for?'

'It's not gentlemanly to cap a lady's quote,' said Lexie. 'And in any case, you were wrong. See?'

CHAPTER 8

It occurred to Peter Pascoe not for the first time that Dalziel might be going mad.

After a morning spent on the telephone to the Florentine police, the Nottinghamshire Social Services and the Ministry of Defence, he was taken aback when Dalziel's only response after a scowlingly cursory examination of his careful notes was, 'That's a lot of phoning, lad. In peak time, too. Cost a pretty penny.'

'Yes, but...'

'No buts. Think on, Peter. We're answerable for every penny we spend. It's public money. The Council likes to know what we're spending it on, and they've got a right to know too. You'll have read the DCC's directive CK stroke NW stroke 743 on Consultation and Information *re* the Police Committee?'

'Well, I expect I glanced at it,' said Pascoe.

'*Glanced!* You'll get nowhere by *glancing*, lad. A long hard look at things, that's the only way to profit. Get that, will you? It'll likely be a transfer charge from New Zealand for you!'

Pascoe picked up the phone and listened.

'No sir,' he said. 'It's for you. Dr Pottle from the Central's Psychiatric Unit.'

Reassuring himself that even if his diagnosis was accurate, at least Dalziel seemed to be seeking professional help, Pascoe left. The fat man now had a long conversation with Pottle who was rather puzzled by this degree of courteous interest from a man whose previous opinion of CID use of psycho-assistance was politely embodied in his overheard comment, 'Them buggers are like weather-forecasters; if the pavement's wet, they can work out it's been raining—just!'

Pottle disposed of with worryingly fulsome thanks, Dalziel read through his notes, grinned like a fox who sees a way into the chicken coop, then turned his attention once more to Pascoe's notes. Shaking his head, he began to make some phone calls of his own.

Wield was drinking his tenth cup of coffee of the day when his doorbell rang.

'Can I come in?' said Pascoe.

'Why not? Like a coffee?'

'If it's no bother.'

'None. I've had a pot boiling since I woke up. I got pissed last night with Mr Dalziel, did he tell you?'

'No,' said Pascoe.

'I needed the coffee first thing to bring me back to life. I've been supping it ever since to stop me going back on the Scotch. Mebbe I shouldn't bother. What do you think?'

The man's voice sounded level and matter-of-fact. His face was as unreadable as ever. But Pascoe felt the tension in him like a fish-taken line.

'Wieldy, I'm sorry,' he said helplessly.

'Sorry? What for?'

'For...' Pascoe took a deep breath. 'For thinking I was a friend but not knowing anything about you. For not noticing that you had troubles. For brushing you off when you wanted to talk. And for the boy. I don't know what he meant to you, but I'm sorry for his death and the manner of it.'

The dark, ugly face of the sergeant regarded him with a frowning intensity.

'Dalziel knew about me,' he said.

Pascoe took this as a reproach and held his hand out to the flame like a good martyr.

'Ellie too,' he said. 'Seems I'm the only short-sighted, insensitive sod in town. I'm sorry.'

'Good thing I was able to fool someone,' said Wield unexpectedly. 'Even if it was only a short-sighted insensitive sod.'

Suddenly there were tears stinging at Pascoe's eyes. He took out his handkerchief and blew his nose violently.

Wield said, 'Coffee's not that bad, is it?'

'No,' said Pascoe. 'The coffee's fine. It's just guilt, I suppose. I could never take guilt. And I've not had a good morning.'

'Oh aye? What's been going off, then?'

Pascoe said vaguely. 'Oh, this and that. Look, Wieldy, what are you going to do?'

'What do you mean?'

'I mean, all this must've shaken you up. I'd hate to think you were going to do something daft.'

'Like resigning, you mean? If Mr Watmough gets Tommy Winter's job and finds out what's been going on, I reckon I'll be saved the bother.'

'It's not a disciplinary matter!' declared Pascoe indignantly.

'Being gay? No, it's not. But shacking up with a known criminal, and concealing the relationship when one of my own lads arrests him, that is, wouldn't you say? No, at the very least, Watmough'll have me shunted off out of harm's way, and I didn't join the Force to sit in one box putting filing-cards in another.'

This was one marked change in the man. He'd spoken more in the short time since Pascoe's arrival than he normally managed in half a day.

Pascoe said. 'Perhaps Watmough won't get the job.'

'Mebbe not. The Super doesn't reckon his chances.'

'No,' said Pascoe doubtfully. He was recalling Dalziel's sudden onset of interest in the Deputy Chief Constable's internal directives. The fat man was a pragmatic. Could this mean that despite all his outer confidence in Watmough's failure, secretly he was preparing himself against the man's success?

'Any road, whatever happens, who cares? A man's got to be mad to stay in a job where the public hates you and Maggie Thatcher loves you,' said Wield. 'You didn't answer my question: What went off this morning to upset you? Something to do with the lad's murder, was it?'

His voice was steady.

Pascoe said, 'Just filling in the background, Wieldy. I'm not sure we ought to be talking about it.'

'Frightened I'm going to ride off into town with my six-guns blazing?'

'No. But perhaps *you* are.'

Pascoe's eyes were fixed on the coffee-spoon in Wield's right hand and the sergeant realized with a shock that he'd bent it double with pressure from his thumb.

'Uri Geller,' he said, straightening it out. 'I stop clocks too. With a face like mine, it's not hard.'

This was the first time Pascoe could recall hearing Wield refer to his unlovely features. Somehow it made up his mind for him and quickly he brought the sergeant up to date on the limited progress so far.

Wield seemed back in full control.

'Still nowt from his dad, then? I'd have thought the bits in the papers would have flushed him out, if nothing else did. Mebbe he'll show up for the funeral.'

'Funeral?'

'Aye. He's going to be buried up here. His grandmother agrees. Couple of days' time.'

Curious, thought Pascoe, the two murder cases colliding in his mind. One funeral where a missing son, perhaps, turns up to mourn a dead mother, now another where a missing father may turn up to mourn a dead son.

'Something bothers me,' said Wield.

'What's that?'

'Why'd Cliff say the station buffet for his meet?'

'Why not?'

'Well, he'd not been anywhere near the railway station, to my knowledge. He came by bus. That's where I met him first, in the bus station café.'

'Charley's place?'

'That's right. Going back there I could understand. But switching to the railway buffet...'

'Perhaps he thought Vollans was coming through by train from Leeds.'

'And was he?'

'No,' said Pascoe. 'I saw him at the Old Mill Inn later. He had a car. All right, perhaps there was someone else getting off, or getting on a train, is that what you're saying?'

'I don't know. Mebbe.'

'I'll check the trains arriving and leaving around the time he set up the meeting,' said Pascoe. 'I don't see it as particularly significant, I must say, but if there's anything there, we'll find it.'

'Will you? Well, mebbe you will,' said Wield. 'Another cup of coffee?'

'No, thanks,' said Pascoe. 'I've got to be off. Something I need to check on out of town. Anyway, one dose of this witch's brew's enough for any sane man!'

He spoke unthinkingly.

'Yes,' said Wield. 'I can't spend the rest of my life drinking cups of coffee, can I?'

'Peter...' His voice did not rise; in fact, it seemed to tremble like the G-string on a fiddle with the vibrations of despair... 'you'll find out what happened, won't you? I've got to know before...before I can work out what's going to happen to me.'

'Oh shit,' said Pascoe helplessly. 'I'll try, Wieldy. I promise, I'll try.'

Ten minutes later he was breaking the speed limit on the road south to Nottinghamshire.

It hadn't taken too long to discover that a child named Richard Sharman had been in a Nottingham Children's Home from 1947 to 1962. All other information on the child was confidential, he was assured. Unimpressed, Pascoe had sought the right Open Sesame, guessed it wouldn't be the thunder of a murder inquiry, and tried instead the still, sad music of humanity by talking of a dead boy and a lost father who needed to be told of his grief.

It worked, but no treasure was revealed, just the information that Sharman had been an awkward, unfosterable child, that his mother had visited him rarely, and there was no address for her, and that his father had been killed in the war. There was a copy of the child's birth certificate. He had been born on November 29th, 1944 at Maidstone, Kent, and his father was Sergeant Richard Alan Sharman of the Royal Signals.

Delving into Army Records was like excavating in the Valley of Kings—sometimes you struck treasure, but often the tomb was empty. Lieutenant Alexander Lomas Huby, for instance, despite (or perhaps because of) his mother's refusal to accept his death, had left minimal traces of his passing, including a medical record so sketchy as to be little help in confirming his sex let alone charting the contours of his left buttock. Sergeant Sharman was there in detail, however. Born 1917 in Nottingham, blue-eyed, fair-haired, white-skinned, he was measured and weighed to his last inch and final ounce. But the really interesting snippet was that his presumably black widow was still in receipt of her army pension which was sent to the Avalon Retirement Home on the outskirts of Nottingham.

At this point, a phone call to the local police asking that someone visit the old woman would have sufficed. After all, it was most unlikely that she could give any information about her son which would have any bearing on the death of her grandson. But something had stopped him from doing the logical thing. Perhaps the memory of Ellie's recent gibes about his intellectual censor rankled. Perhaps Dalziel's apparent indifference to all his researches was also a provocation. But most certainly, his unassuaged guilt feeling about Wield made it essential for him to follow up even the slenderest lead on this case personally and to hell with logic and rules! Ninety minutes later he was being guided through the bright corridors of the Avalon Home by a nurse clad in a nylon overall which in a twilit lake might have passed for white samite.

'How old is she?' asked Pascoe.

'Early seventies. Not so old by today's standards, but after sixty it's a lottery, isn't it? Some stay young to the end, some seem to *want* to be old. With Mrs Sharman I get the impression it's been her life's ambition since her twenties.'

The nurse spoke cheerfully rather than sourly. Middle-aged herself, she looked as if it was her ambition to stay young as long as possible.

Pascoe said, 'How long's she been in the Home?'

'Best part of six years. She obviously wasn't going to rest till she got someone else doing all the work for her! Hello, dear. Here's a gentleman caller for you!'

Mrs Sharman was frail, toothless, swathed in uncomfortable layers of clothing topped with a plaid dressing-gown, and she carried a blackwood knobkerrie with which she supported her weight in motion and her assertions in repose. She gripped it menacingly as he took a seat before her.

'Hello, Mrs Sharman,' said Pascoe.

'What do you want?' she demanded.

It was a good question.

'Just to chat,' he said, giving her what Ellie called his little-boy-lost smile.

'I'm seventy-nine,' proclaimed the old woman with a sudden thrust of her knobkerrie towards his crotch.

Alarmed, he pushed back his chair a couple of feet. Behind Mrs Sharman the nurse mouthed, 'Seventy-three.'

'And I've still got my own teeth,' continued the old woman, baring empty gums. 'Only, I've forgotten where I put 'em!'

This was evidently a favourite joke. She laughed so heartily at it that her screeches set up a sympathetic skirling around the conservatory in which they sat, and out beyond into the garden, as though bagpipe should call to bagpipe from lofty mountain to lowly glen in some serial pibroch.

Pascoe joined in the laughter, out of politeness and also because it delayed a moment of some delicacy. He had examined the old woman closely in the past few minutes and there was no way that her visible skin, tanned though it was by age and weather, could be anything but white. He was no expert on the vagaries of miscegenation, but he recalled the old music hall joke about the Chinese girl who presented her husband with a European baby and was told that two Wongs do not make a white.

Cliff Sharman's father, the woman's son, had been described as unequivocally black. Ergo, Sergeant Sharman was not the father. The poor devil had given his all for democracy before he could learn of his wife's exertions in the same field. On the other hand, the woman still had to face the raised eyebrows and sharp intakes of breath when she returned to Nottingham with a black baby. Could there have been enough pressure and prejudice for her to commit the child to a home? Easily! he answered himself. 1945 might have seen Britain ready at last for the political assertion that Jack was as good as his master, but it was still light years away from any meaningful acknowledgement that Black Jack was as good as White Jack.

He said gently, 'Mrs Sharman, I hope you don't mind, but I'd like to talk to you about your husband, Sergeant Sharman.'

'What about him?' demanded Mrs Sharman with sudden suspicion. 'He's dead.'

'Yes, of course, he is,' said Pascoe reassuringly.

'What do you want to talk about him for? I can't even remember what he looked like.'

Her face screwed up into a grimace which he feared was the harbinger of grief.

He said huskily, 'I don't want to upset you...'

'Upset me? Only thing'd upset me was if you told me that the bastard wasn't dead after all and they wanted me pension back!'

She put her wizened hand to her lips in a stagey gesture of amazement that she had let this sentiment slip out, but Pascoe doubted if there was much accidental in it.

He reminded himself that she was old and infirm and that shortly he would be telling her that her grandson was dead. He reminded himself too that she had once been young and fair and turned the heads of men—well, two at least, Sergeant Sharman and the unknown black who had fathered her son. But he found it hard to get through the dislike to the compassion.

'No, he's dead, all right,' he said. 'It's really your son I wanted to talk about...'

'My son?' She sat up straight, knobkerrie raised with far from accidental menace. 'What son? I've got no son!'

This was worse than he had imagined. The poor little bastard had been put out of her mind as well as her life.

The nurse was looking at him, her eyebrows raised in puzzlement as if to say, are you sure you've got this right?

He resolved to cut through the miasma once and for all.

He said formally, 'Mrs Sharman, the records show that you gave birth to a son in November 1944. A certificate to this effect exists in the registrar's office at Maidstone in Kent, and though it may be inaccurate in naming Sergeant Sharman as the father...'

The stick came down with a thud, narrowly missing his left foot, but it was a gesture of triumph, not aggression.

'It's the black bastard you're talking about, isn't it?' she cried. 'It's not me you want, sonny, it's *her*! She was never his wife. Thought she was, but she had a shock coming to her, just like he'd have had a shock if he'd come back alive and seen what she wanted to pass off as his baby! Oh, you should've seen her face! Thought she'd be getting the pension at least, she did! Came to see the family, they never liked me, sweet-talked them round, Richie's true love and all that baloney even if they weren't really married, but they wanted to see the baby, didn't they? Richie's child, their grandson, and she had to show it. Tried hard enough not to, but you can't keep a baby hid forever. They're often dark to start with, she said. It's the blood being near the surface or some such thing. Oh, it was the blood all right! Three months on and it was black as night, and they wasn't having that, not being chapel and all.'

She was getting so excited that Pascoe became alarmed that she was about to have a fit. Then he focused on her coldly gleeful eyes and ceased to be alarmed.

Leaning forward, he said quietly but distinctly into her left ear, 'Shut up.'

'Mr Pascoe!' protested the nurse, rising.

He ignored her.

'I just want the bare story, Mrs Sharman,' he said. 'Save the entertainment for your friends. Just give me the history. If you can't, I've no doubt there are others who will.'

This threat was enough. Better to be a simple broadcasting machine than to be switched off altogether.

The story was old as time and sad as old bones.

A hasty wartime marriage followed by instant separation and, Pascoe guessed, on the woman's part almost as instant infidelity. Returning from North Africa in 1943, Sharman had found a situation which had prompted him to seek an instant legal separation and institute divorce proceedings. A decree *nisi* had been granted but before it could be made absolute, news of Sharman's death in action had come. Shortly afterwards the woman claiming, and probably believing, herself to be Sharman's wife had contacted the family, who were obliged to tell her that their son's earlier marriage had not been legally dissolved and therefore all pension rights devolved on the first wife. Whatever sympathy and financial help might have been offered to the second quickly vanished with the realization that the child she had borne could not be Sharman's.

'So what became of her?' asked Pascoe.

'How should I know?' said the old woman indifferently. 'Her kind usually do all right, don't they?'

Pascoe rose slowly. Possibly, indeed probably, there was some saving grace in this rag-bag of antique malice, but for once he could not find in himself the energy to seek it out. Was he at last entering the third condition of the human soul? Optimism; pessimism; cynicism.

'Welcome aboard,' he could hear Dalziel saying. 'Quarters are comfy, victuals not bad, and the company's grand!'

Feeling empty, he thanked the nurse and left.

CHAPTER 9

Stephanie Windibanks was a swift, efficient packer. Her husband had once remarked on this unshared talent and she had replied tartly that it came easily when you were married to a man who made a habit of staying at hotels he couldn't afford. Arthur had laughed. There were few things that failed to amuse him. Triumph or disaster were received with equal amusement, and another grand plan.

Suddenly she found there were tears in her eyes at the memory.

There was a knock at the door.

'Come in,' she called, stooping over her case.

The door opened, footsteps sounded heavily behind her and a voice boomed, 'Going off somewhere, luv?'

'Superintendent Dalziel,' she said. 'I thought you were the porter.'

'Knock knock knock,' said Dalziel. 'Nice room. They do you well here.'

'What do you want, Superintendent?'

'Just confirmation,' said Dalziel.

'Then I suggest you see a bishop,' retorted the woman smartly.

'Sorry?' said Dalziel who believed in sinking smart-alecs in explanation. 'Bishop? Is that the manager? You mean, he could help?'

'Help with what?' said Mrs Windibanks, too nimble to be pinned down to explanation of her repartee.

'I don't know. Mebbe he saw you.'

'Saw me doing what?'

'Going into Mr Goodenough's room last Friday night.'

'*What?*'

'Shall I ask him?'

'You may do what you want, Mr Dalziel,' said the woman. 'I meanwhile will get myself back to civilization as soon as may be possible.'

'That's why I'm here,' said Dalziel. 'To help. See, the thing is, if I can be sure of where you were last Friday night when you say you were in your room but weren't answering the telephone, then I'll not be worried if you shove off, will I? And if it turns out you were in Goodenough's room, that kills two birds with one stone, doesn't it?'

She stood in front of him and regarded him unblinkingly.

'You've spoken to Mr Goodenough, have you?'

'Oh no,' said Dalziel, shocked. 'I mean, chivalry apart, a Scottish Presbyterian with a wife and two children's not going to admit he let himself be screwed by a woman nearly twenty years older than him, is he? Well, not right off anyway.'

She glared at him with a cold fury which touched him only as light frost touches a polar bear. Finally she thawed into a smile and then dissolved into laughter.

'I'll treasure these memories, Mr Dalziel,' she said. 'Whenever I feel that London's a noisy, nasty place, I'll think of you. All right, yes, I did wander along to Mr Goodenough's room that night. There were one or two points of our agreement I wanted to get clear in my mind. We had a talk and a drink, nothing more.'

'Well, I'm glad that's sorted,' said Dalziel genially. 'So it's back to London, is it?'

'That's right.'

'Then mebbe a holiday? A few days in the sun?'

'Perhaps. Why do you ask?'

'No reason. I just wondered if mebbe you were planning a trip to Tuscany, a little sojourn in the Villa Boethius perhaps.'

There was a rap at the door and a voice called, 'Porter, madame.'

'Go away,' said Stephanie Windibanks, her gaze fixed speculatively on Dalziel. 'I'll let you know when I need you.'

'I could have had her, I reckon,' said Dalziel complacently. 'She just about spelled it out.'

'But you didn't?' said Pascoe.

'What do you take me for, lad?' said the fat man, indignantly. 'Do you think I'd screw up a case just to screw up a woman?'

'No, but it'd not surprise me to find you'd managed to have your cake and halfpenny,' retorted Pascoe, who was still smarting under Dalziel's smug reproaches about the inadequacy of his telephone calls to Florence.

'You missed the point, lad,' the fat man had said. 'All you were interested in was, could Pontelli be Alexander Huby? Well, mebbe not *all*, but mainly. I asked 'em to go back a bit, find out who he worked for, what he was doing. All that stuff about background, date of birth, family, and so on that you were interested in, that was getting you nowhere. I got a list of properties and agencies. And then I got them to look up the official records of each one till I heard a name that clicked. It's connections that matter in this business, lad. Only connect, then you've got 'em by the short and hairies!'

'And who do we have in that interesting grip?' inquired Pascoe.

'Windibanks and her precious son,' said Dalziel gleefully.

'On what charge?'

'Fraud, theft, how should I know? I just catch the buggers,' protested Dalziel. 'She's been getting rental from a property that's not hers these past three years, that's something. And it's as plain as the nose on your face that they put Pontelli up to claiming he was Huby.'

'That'll be hard to prove with Pontelli dead,' said Pascoe.

'At least I'll give 'em a nasty time proving they had nowt to do with killing him! Now, what've you been up to in Nottingham?'

Pascoe told him and finished by saying, 'But I expect I didn't ask the right questions there either!'

Dalziel looked at him narrowly.

'Peter,' he said carefully, 'at that college of yours, did they never teach you, when a man's too old to learn, he's likely too bloody old to promote?'

Pascoe actually felt himself blushing. Petulance was not large among his vices.

'Sorry,' he said. 'What should I have asked?'

'How the, fuck do I know?' replied Dalziel. 'Connections, lad. You just keep on asking everyone everything till you make a connection. You think Sharman's dad's important?'

'No, well, maybe. I don't know. It may turn out it's like what you said about Pontelli being Huby, irrelevant to the main line, but I can't see any other direction just now.'

'Then let's chase along this one with all possible speed!' proclaimed Dalziel, reaching for his telephone.

'What about the expense?' said Pascoe slyly.

'Expense? What're you on about, lad? These buggers out there are paying for protection, and we'd come cheap at twice the price!'

He dialled. After two rings a bright young voice said, 'New Scotland Yard, can I help you?'

'Commander Sanderson, please. Detective-Superintendent Dalziel, Mid-Yorkshire here.'

A few moments later a voice growled, 'Sanderson here.'

'Sandy!' said Dalziel. 'Andy Dalziel. That's right. I knew you'd be glad to hear from me. What I like is a man who doesn't need to be reminded when he owes a favour. Now here's what else I'd like…'

❖ ❖ ❖

Stephanie Windibanks rang her son at the Kemble and within seconds of the phone being put down, Rod Lomas was ringing Lexie Huby at Messrs Thackeray etcetera.

'Lexie; Rod. Listen, I've just had Mummy on to me. That fat copper's been round. He knows about the Villa Boethius.'

Lexie did not respond to his agitation.

'Well, they were bound to find out, weren't they?'

'Were they? Oh God, what'll happen now?'

'I've been checking on that,' said Lexie. 'Nothing much, as far as I can see. The villa will go into Aunt Gwen's estate, of course. As for the rent, say nothing. If they make a fuss, say there was a verbal agreement and let them prove different.'

'Should we offer to pay back the money?'

'In law, that's almost as good as a confession,' said Lexie.

'And what about Pontelli?'

'Deny everything. He's dead. He won't contradict you.'

'But the connection's so obvious…'

'It always was,' said Lexie sharply. 'You should have thought of that when you started this business. If the worst gets to the worst, you can always blame your dad.'

'Lexie!'

'Why not. (A) he's dead as well, and (b) it's true.'

There was a silence.

'You're taking this very coolly,' said Lomas. 'What if they question you again about Friday night?'

'I'll stick to my story,' said Lexie. 'You and I were at the opera. Only, I've got a season ticket, so you'd better have had a return, in the gallery. All right?'

'Oh, Lexie.'

'Rod, are you all right?' There was concern in her voice contrasting with her previous brusque matter-of-factness.

'Oh yes. Ask for me tomorrow and you may well find me a grave man, but I reckon I'll get through the night. With help. You'll be there when I get back again, won't you?'

'Yes, I've got a class first, but I'll be there to relieve the nurse, like I promised.'

'Don't let me down, Lexie, I'm relying on you.'

'I won't,' said Lexie.

Eden Thackeray came into the room as she replaced the receiver.

'Anything important?' he asked.

'It was personal,' said Lexie. 'Sorry.'

'That's all right. Lexie, I think it's about time we had a little chat about your future, don't you?'

'Yes, Mr Eden,' said Lexie Huby.

Henry Vollans arrived at Maldive Cottage shortly after six o'clock that evening. Mrs Falkingham greeted him with delight.

'How nice to see you again, Mr Vollans,' she said.

'Henry,' he replied, smiling Redfordly. 'Is Miss Brodsworth here?'

'Ah, I might have known it wasn't an old woman you'd come to see,' said Mrs Falkingham knowingly. 'She's in the office, tidying up some papers. You *will* take tea?'

'Thank you...'

In the tiny box-room which a card table bearing an ancient typewriter and a cupboard containing files and stationery elevated to the status of office, Sarah Brodsworth was sorting out the week's mail.

She looked at him with that hard unblinking gaze which gave the lie to her sensuous curves and blonde curls.

'It's you,' she said without enthusiasm.

'You don't sound pleased.'

'I wasn't pleased not to see you when I expected to,' she said. 'Why should I be pleased to see you now?'

'I'm sorry about that. But in my line of work, if something comes up, you've got to drop everything and follow it. If there'd been any way to let you know, I'd have done it. I did leave a message at the restaurant. But I really am sorry. Did you have to come far?'

He spoke casually. When she didn't reply, he grinned and said, 'My, you are a cagey one! Real woman of mystery! You must be a member of the royal family at the very least.'

'I'm just particular on who I get familiar with,' said Sarah Brodsworth. 'Especially journalists.'

'Why so?'

'You put a story before everything. I saw that last week.'

'Not quite everything,' said Vollans softly.

'No?'

'No. I'm not sure, but we may have more in common than you think.'

'That's a good line, Mr Vollans.'

'Henry.'

'Mr Vollans.'

'What about a meal tonight?'

She shook her head.

'No, thanks.'

'Why not? You agreed last time I asked.'

'And got stood up. I don't make the same mistake twice.'

'No?'

Mrs Falkingham's voice quavered distantly, 'Tea's ready.'

Neither of the young people moved.

'What are you really doing here, Miss Brodsworth?' wondered Vollans.

'You think there's a story in it?' she mocked.

'Maybe.'

'But would you print it?'

'Maybe. I'd need a taster before I could give you a firm opinion.'

She regarded him thoughtfully.

'Suppose I were to tell you that it's my intention before I'm finished to see that WFE carries out its original function.'

'Which is?'

'To establish a proper relationship between whites and blacks.'

'By what means?'

Miss Brodsworth smiled, showing even white teeth.

'Ends justify means, I thought all journalists understood that, Mr Vollans.'

'Tea!' called Mrs Falkingham, her quaver imperious now.

'I'll fetch it in here, shall I?' said Vollans. 'It'd be a shame to interrupt our little chat just when it's going so interesting.'

❊ ❊ ❊

Wield went into the bus station café and felt a disjunctive shock as Charley greeted him with a cheery good-evening just as if the world hadn't turned upside down in the last few days.

He said, 'Hello, Charley. All right?'

'Grand, thanks. You're looking well, Mr Wield.'

'Am I?'

He sipped the cup of coffee which had been drawn as soon as he was spotted. He said, 'Remember I was in the week before last? Chatted to a lad in the back room?'

'Oh aye. Darkie, wasn't he? Well, nicely toasted, any road.'

'That's him,' said Wield. 'You ever see him around again?'

Charley thought visibly, then said, 'Yes, come to think of it, I did. Couple of nights ago, it'd be. He had a Coke and a cheese toastie, I remember. Sat by the door there. Yes, that'd be Wednesday. Or was it Tuesday? No, it was definitely Wednesday.'

'Was he by himself?'

'Yeah, far as I recall.'

'What time was it?'

'Latish. Nine, nine-thirty. We shut at ten. He was gone before then, though.'

'Did you see him go?'

'Yes, I did, now you mention it. Hold on. I think he went off with someone. Leastways someone came in, but didn't sit down and next thing, the darkie got up and left.'

Suddenly Charley's face went pink with surmise. 'Here, has this got owt to do with that killing I read about? He were a dark lad, weren't he? Is this what it's all about.'

'Mebbe,' said Wield. There had been no photograph in the papers. Cliff's grandmother hadn't brought one and the injuries to his face had made a death-mask picture difficult. It was a pity. A photograph would probably have jogged Charley's memory twenty-four hours earlier.

On the other hand, perhaps it wasn't a pity at all.

Wield said, 'This person who went out with the boy, Charley, I want you to tell me everything you remember. *Everything.*'

Dalziel was working late. Or rather he was sitting in his office with a large glass of single malt waiting for the phone to ring. He knew Sandy Sanderson of old. As soon as the sod got the info Dalziel had requested, he'd ring back and take great delight in having Dalziel dragged back from whatever he was doing in order to receive it, with the justification, 'You said it was urgent, sunshine.'

Dalziel savoured his drink and thought with some satisfaction: I'll be ready for you, you bugger! Then he thought with less satisfaction that he hadn't really got anything he would have objected to being dragged back from. Pascoe moaned about having his home life disrupted. Young sod didn't know how lucky he was to have something to moan about. Mind you, domestic distractions could take the sharpness off a man's work. He'd now retraced all of Pascoe's phone calls—Florence, Army Records, Nottingham—and asked other questions with other emphasis. The answers he'd got had filled him with self-congratulatory delight. Now he just needed Sanderson to set the seal on them.

The phone rang.

He snatched it up.

A hoarse, muffled voice said, 'I know someone who's a member of a group called White Heat. Interested?'

'I could be,' said Dalziel.

'Then listen.'

He listened, opened his mouth to ask questions, heard the click of a receiver being replaced.

He thought for a moment, drank some more whisky, then began dialling.

'Ellie, luv,' he said heartily. 'Not interrupting your supper, am I? I am? Well, try not to think of it as interruption. Try to think that really I'm liberating you from the drudgery of dull domestic routine.'

Grinning, he held the phone away from his ear till the cry of the liberated woman had faded to a bearable level.

'Nice of you to say them things,' he said. 'I really appreciate it. Now, is the lad there?'

The lad was clearly hovering. Dalziel spoke to him for a couple of minutes.

'I'd sort it myself,' he concluded, 'only I'm working late here and waiting for a call from London. Sorry to break up your night, but I think it's worth looking at right away. You'll clear it with the locals first, though? Don't want any diplomatic incidents. And go careful, Peter. It's an anonymous tip, that's all. I don't want to see your name all over the headlines!'

He put the phone down. He felt a glow of satisfaction which was not altogether due to the ounce of Scotch he now sank. It was nice to push something Pascoe's way. If it came to owt, it'd mebbe make up for this other business, if that came to owt as well.

Half an hour later the phone rang again.

'You still there?' said Commander Sanderson incredulously.

'Never like to go to bed without some good news,' said Dalziel cheerfully. 'I hope you've got some for me.'

'How the hell should I know?' growled the Commander. 'It's just names and dates to me. But here it is for what it's worth.'

When he'd finished he said, 'That's it. Now can you go to bed?'

'I don't know about that,' said Dalziel. 'Thanks a lot, Sandy. But I may stay up just a little longer.'

CHAPTER 10

It was half past eight when Lexie turned up at Troy House to find the nurse waiting impatiently in the hall.

'You said eight o'clock,' she said accusingly.

'Sorry,' said Lexie. 'Is she all right?'

'Yes, fine, I'll be back in the morning.'

Lexie closed but didn't lock the door behind her and then went up the stairs. As she moved silently into Miss Keech's room, the sick woman's voice called, 'Lexie? Is that you?'

'Yes, Miss Keech,' said Lexie, approaching the bed, dimly lit by a small table lamp.

'Has that woman gone?'

'The nurse? Yes.'

'Calls herself a nurse, does she? She couldn't nurse a head-cold.'

Miss Keech spoke vigorously, but it was not a reassuring vigour. Her cheeks were hectic and there was a glimmer of perspiration along her upper lip. Most striking of all, the veneer of pedantic correctness was being eroded from her speech and the rhythms and accents of her village childhood were reasserting themselves.

Lexie said, 'I think mebbe you ought to get some sleep now.'

'Sleep? I'll soon have more sleep than I know what to do with. I hate sleep! Old people's sleep is full of dreams, Lexie. Like a child's. Except that if a child's dreams are bad, she wakes and cries a little, maybe, then shakes them off in the joy of being alive; and if they're good she wakes and bears their joy around with her all the livelong day. But when you're old, the bad is what stays with you, and all the good does is remind you of what is lost beyond all hope of retrieval. Sit and talk with me, Lexie.'

It was an undeniable plea.

Lexie sat on the hard upright chair at the bedside and said, 'All right. I'll sit with you for a while.'

'That's good of you,' said Miss Keech, half sneering. 'I know you don't like my company much. Why is that, Lexie? I asked you last night and you wouldn't answer. Why don't you like me?'

Lexie said, 'You don't want to talk about things like that, Miss Keech.'

'You mean *you* don't!' exclaimed the old woman. 'Come on! I've a right to know!'

'All right,' said Lexie calmly. 'If you must. To start with, Dad used to say things about you. When you're little, you take notice of what your mam and dad say. If they say Conservative's grand and Labour's bad, that's what you think. If they say black's white and white's black, that's what you think.'

'What kind of things did he say?'

'He said that you were stuck-up without cause. That it were bad enough putting up with Aunt Gwen's airs and graces but at least she had the brass to support them. Whereas you were just a jumped-up skivvy from a family of nobodies and ne'er-do-wells.'

Miss Keech nodded vigourously.

'Yes, yes. He were quite right, of course. Farm labourers up the Dale, that was my family; four brothers all older than me, and our dad, always the last to be hired, always the first to be fired, those were the Keeches right enough. Yes. And I came here at thirteen and I *was* a skivvy, that's true. And I could hardly read or write and I had an accent so broad, it made your dad sound like the Prince of Wales!'

This was a new Miss Keech to Lexie and she watched and listened with growing concern. Age, she felt, should be immutable. Being young was problematical enough without the fixed stars shifting in their crystal sphere. Unless she was careful, the old Keech, the Wicked Witch of the West, with her sharp nose and black clothes, was going to assume a human form, though whether she'd like the new any more than the old was doubtful.

Miss Keech was still talking.

'But you didn't depend on your father for your views forever, Lexie. You're far too independent for that. Yet you still went on disliking me.'

'Not really. It became a habit. I only saw you once a month usually. You were always the same. So there was no reason for me to change. You were the adult. You should have done the changing then.'

'I tried to be friendly,' Keech protested. 'I wanted you children to call me Auntie Ella, remember? But you wouldn't.'

'You should've refused to answer to anything else,' said Lexie.

'Like you when you stopped being Alexandra? Oh, there was a difference, Lexie. All that would have happened with me was you'd not have spoken to me at all. I'd no illusions, Lexie, allow me that at least.'

'Miss Keech, I think you ought to rest...'

'No! Pour me a glass of my tonic, there's a love.'

Lexie looked doubtfully at the bottle. It was almost empty. She said, 'Does the doctor say...'

'Damn the doctor!'

Lexie shrugged and filled a glass. The old woman drank it greedily.

'That's better. You're a good girl, Lexie. Strange but good. Did you go home last night?'

'No. I stayed here.'

'Here? You didn't let him touch you, did you? He's a nice boy, Rod, but they're all the same when it's dark. All grey in the dark, aren't they?'

This seemed to amuse her disproportionately and she laughed till she coughed, and had to finish her wine. This seemed to quieten her, and she closed her eyes, and after a while looked to have fallen asleep. But when Lexie rose quietly to go, a thin hand reached out and seized her wrist.

'Don't leave me, not in the dark, there are devils in the dark.'

With a suddenness that made Lexie startle, she sat bolt upright.

'That's what nearly killed the old girl, you know. A devil in the dark. That's what she used to say, remember?'

This she cried out loudly, and then settled back against her pillow and said, 'Stay with me, stay with me.'

'Yes, I will.'

'No, you'll go soon as I close my eyes! I know you will...'

Her face became cunning and she said slyly, 'I'll tell you something if you'll stay.'

'I said I'll stay, Miss Keech. Try to rest.'

The woman's mood changed direction once more.

'You're a good girl, I've always known it. You won't leave me alone, I've been alone too much, I've lived alone...'

'No. You've lived with Great Aunt Gwen...'

'That was like being alone!' she cried. 'A loonie and a ghost, they're no company! But I won't die alone, I won't, I won't!'

Lexie was growing increasingly alarmed. In an effort to divert the old woman she said, 'You were going to tell me something interesting.'

For a second there was blankness, then the sly smile returned.

'Interesting? No; more than interesting. Something strange and terrible and sad...oh Lexie...'

She trembled on the edge of tears, then went very still as if in the effort of containing them.

'Come close, Lexie,' she whispered. 'I don't want *her* to hear... Come close...'

It was more than an hour before one of the silences which punctuated the sick woman's ramblings stretched far enough for Lexie to relax her strained hearing and bring her mind to bear on what she had heard.

Downstairs the phone rang.

At the first note, Miss Keech sat upright.

Oh, *damn*! thought Lexie.

She opened her mouth to offer reassurance, but before she could speak, the woman said briskly, 'Of course, you and Jane may play down there as much as you like, Lexie. And of course you may have the key to the door. But remember what I told you, Lexie.'

She smiled; a curve of the lips as jolly as a sickle moon on a stormy night. Then her eyes focused at a point near the door with an intensity which made Lexie want to turn and look too. The old woman shook her head as though in denial, then her eyes closed and she sank back down into her pillow.

The phone was still ringing.

Swiftly Lexie descended into the hall and picked up the receiver.

'Lexie, it's Rod.'

'Hello.'

'Everything all right?'

She hesitated enough before replying to be noticeable by a man less absorbed in his own cares.

'Fine,' she said. 'And how are you? You still sound worried.'

'I should be. Pascoe was here before the play tonight, rabbiting on about Pontelli. It didn't do my performance much good, I tell you. Has he tried to see you at all?'

'Not that I know of.'

'Good. I just thought he might try something clever like saying I'd caved in, so I thought I'd better ring to say I've stuck to the story. Anyway, enough of selfish me. How's Keechie?'

'She's been a bit incoherent, almost non-stop rambling. Mainly about Gwen and black devils. All kinds of odd stuff. She kept on getting to a certain point, then breaking off. I got the impression that...'

'What?'

'Nothing, I'll tell you when I see you. Will you be long?'

At last her unease got through to Lomas.

He said, 'Look, I've got to hang on for the curtain-calls. After my showing tonight, I daren't get Chung's back up! But I won't wait for that bloody bus. I'll grab a taxi again and blow the expense.'

'It'll cost a fortune.'

'Worth it. Lexie, I think I love you.'

'Yes,' said Lexie quietly and put down the receiver.

She stood in the hall for a while. This was the first declaration of love any man had made to her, but it did not occupy her mind for long. There would be another time to contemplate that in. Meanwhile there were other kinds of love to ponder here and now.

Above nothing stirred.

She went through into the kitchen. Its new brightness was a comfort and she told herself she had come through here to make herself a coffee and sit quietly and wait for Rod.

Something moved behind her and she spun round to see the door slowly opening. Before she could cry out, she saw what it was, and a muted sob of relief, like a soft cough in a concert hall, was all she released as Bob, the big black labrador, paddled into the room.

But the stimulus was enough. Fear had never frozen her but always spurred her to action. It was a version she guessed of her father's bloody-minded stubbornness in the face of opposition. Now she went to the keyboard on the wall above the refrigerator. The key she wanted wasn't there. With a sigh, she went back upstairs into Miss Keech's room and gently removed the bunch of keys from the dressing-table top. The woman did not move or open her eyes, but Lexie had a sense of mocking observation.

Downstairs again, she checked the keys. They duplicated those on the keyboard in the kitchen with a single exception. Both copies of the key Lexie was looking for were on Miss Keech's personal ring.

As she descended into the cellar, she recalled that Sunday afternoon more than ten years earlier when she had come with simulated boldness down these same steps, determined to disperse the aura of horror Miss Keech had wantonly conjured up in this place. She knew now of course what she had not known then, that truth is not always triumphant over dark imaginings, that an idea, however outrageous, can often be stronger than a fact, however firm. Jane had never played in the cellar again and even her own penetration of the empty inner chamber had not restored the old innocence to the outer room.

The dumped furniture looked much the same. She let her mind drift into the pleasant margins of nostalgia for a moment. That sofa had been an elfin ship; that tallboy had been a tyrant's tower... But rapidly she steered herself back from such weakening distractions. Against the door of the small wine-cellar stood an old linen chest. Packed full of God knew what, it felt heavy and immovable to the thrust of her skinny arms. But when she looked more closely, she discovered some pieces of wood wedged underneath and once she removed these, the chest slid easily aside on silent castors.

And now the door.

The key slipped into the keyhole with no difficulty. Deftly she turned it in the oiled wards and pushed the door open with a quiet ease more sinister by far than any Gothic screeching. The light from the main cellar seemed to trickle in like water, slowly filling the inner chamber so that there was no sudden shock, only a gradual awareness of horror, the more intense because her mind further delayed it with the assurance that what she saw must exist only in her fevered imaginings.

The wine-racks had been pulled together to form a bier (*Lomas's bitter bier*, her mind punned desperately in another effort to distance the horror) and on it lay, head turned towards her so that absent eyes seemed to watch her entrance from empty sockets, a body.

Fear urged her backwards to escape it; fear of fear urged her forwards to examine it. For once in her short life she was uncertain which impulse would win. Then both died and in the same instant were reincarnated, as she heard behind her careful footsteps descending the cellar stairs.

CHAPTER 11

The girl on the switchboard at the *Challenger* offices insisted on seeing Pascoe's warrant card.

Satisfied, she said, 'He's popular with you lot tonight, isn't he? Hang on, I'll just jot down his address.'

'Popular? Why do you say that?'

'Well, there was the other chap, wasn't there?'

'Which other chap? What did he look like?'

The girl laughed.

'He was no beauty, I can tell you that! I could hardly believe it when he said he was a copper. That's why I asked to see his card and, fair do's, I thought I'd better see yours too. A sergeant he was. Field or something like that.'

Postponing his contemplation of the implied proposition that beauty was a prerequisite of the police, Pascoe took the address and hurried away. What the hell was Wield doing here? he asked himself. The only answers he could give were not reassuring and he drove through the Friday night busy streets of

Leeds at a speed which won him no friends. Twice he lost his way in a maze of suburban terraces before he pulled up outside the tall narrow house he was looking for.

There was a list of names by the door, most of them illegible. He didn't waste time. The door was open and he went straight in, planning to knock and inquire at the first door he came to, but this proved unnecessary. From the floor above he heard a muffled cry and a thud. Up to the landing. A door stood ajar. He pushed it fully open and went in.

'Jesus Christ!' said Pascoe.

On the floor lay Henry Vollans. He was wearing nothing but a bathrobe open wide to reveal his naked body. Between his splayed legs stood Sergeant Wield and for a second Pascoe thought he was interrupting some homosexual love-play. Then he saw the length of shining metal in Wield's upraised hand and the expression of sheer terror on Vollans's face and decided that this went beyond the bounds of nice, straightforward sado-masochism.

'Wield!' he said. 'For God's sake!'

The sergeant turned on him with a snarl, as if prepared to treat him as an aggressor. Then he recognized the newcomer and the out-thrust blade, which Pascoe now saw was some kind of bayonet, was lowered.

'What are you doing here?' demanded Pascoe.

'Same as you, I hope,' said Wield.

The reporter, seizing the chance offered by this distraction, scrabbled his way across the floor and pulled himself up on a sofa, covering his body with the robe.

Pascoe, lowering his voice, said, 'Dalziel got a phone call saying Vollans was a member of that White Heat group and suggesting we ask where he was on Wednesday night.'

'He was just about to tell me that,' said Wield, turning back to the terrified reporter.

Pascoe seized the sergeant's arm.

'For fuck's sake, Wieldy, put that thing down. Where'd you get it anyway?'

'One of our friend's little war souvenirs,' said Wield. 'Take a look in that cupboard.'

Pascoe looked and turned away, sickened. He led the sergeant to the doorway out of earshot of the man on the couch.

'OK, Wieldy,' he murmured. 'So he admires Hitler and loves the Ku Klux Klan, but that doesn't make him a killer.'

'He lied about his appointment with Cliff,' said Wield. 'I knew there was something wrong. Why the railway buffet? The bus station café would be the obvious place to come to his mind. And why first thing in the morning? What was he going to do that night? Come back to my place where he'd left all his stuff? No. I reckoned he'd be in such a rage that he'd want to get back at me straightaway.'

'Mebbe. But...'

'I talked to Charley. He remembers Cliff being there that night. And he remembers he went out with a young fair-haired chap. I thought of Vollans. I couldn't see what it meant, but I thought it'd be worthwhile having a little chat.'

'Some chat!'

'He tried to give me the runaround. I'd come too far to be turned off with a smooth answer, so I belted him in the gut and had a look around. When I opened that cupboard, I had a good idea I was in the right spot.'

There was a movement by the sofa. Vollans was on his feet. He was clearly regaining control of himself though he still looked more like a frightened fox than Robert Redford.

'You can't do this,' he said in a high voice. 'I'm Press. This'll be all over the front page of every paper in the country!'

Pascoe ignored him.

'What's he said to you, Wieldy?' he asked quietly.

'Nothing yet. You came in just when it were getting interesting.'

'All right. Now I'll handle it, understand?'

The sergeant obviously understood, but equally obviously didn't agree.

Pascoe sighed and stepped towards Vollans.

'Henry Vollans,' he said. 'First let me caution you that anything you say will be taken down and may be used in evidence. Next I'd be grateful if you would get dressed and accompany me to the nearest police station for further interrogation. Oh, and can you give me your car keys, please, as your vehicle will be required for forensic examination?'

'I don't have to do any of this,' protested the reporter. 'I want to ring my office. I want to contact a solicitor.'

'Mr Vollans, that's your right,' said Pascoe. 'But I'm in a bit of a hurry, so in that case, I'll leave Sergeant Wield here to bring you in when you're ready, shall I?'

The sergeant stepped forward. He was still holding the bayonet.

'Don't leave me with that lunatic!' screamed Vollans. 'I'll come! I'll come!'

(HAPTER 12

Lexie Huby stood very still.

Miss Keech had sunk exhausted on to the lower cellar step, but there still looked strength enough in those gnarled and speckled fingers to raise the long-barrelled pistol which rested on her knees.

'It was his, you know. Sam Huby's. Your father's uncle. He brought it back from the war. The First War. He kept it for security. And when he died, she kept it. I knew it was there, of course, in the bedside drawer. But I didn't think it would fire. I certainly never thought she would fire it. But she did. Just the once.'

'She? Great Aunt Gwen?'

Miss Keech looked at her as if surprised to find her there. Then that sly smile which Lexie had noticed earlier crept across her lips.

'I told you, didn't I? Lexie, I said, if you open that door you must bear the consequences. But you never took any notice of me from a little girl. None at all!'

'Tell me what happened, Miss Keech,' said Lexie peremptorily.

Perhaps it was the tone of voice, echoing Great Aunt Gwen's when she addressed her underlings, that did the trick. Suddenly the old Keech was back, in voice at least, matter of fact, neutral of tone.

'All right. We'd just got back from Italy, well, from London really. We broke our journey in London. Perhaps he followed us? Yes, I'm pretty certain that must be it. Our first night back. We were both very tired, but a noise awoke me. One of the animals, I thought. They were such a nuisance, but she insisted they had the run of the place. Anyway, something made me get up. I went out of my room. Her door was ajar. The glow from her nightlight spilled out on to the landing. I could hear her voice speaking. I went a couple of steps towards it when I heard another voice, a man's voice saying, *Mother?* I froze. Mrs Huby said, *Who's there? Closer! Closer! Let me see!* And then she shrieked, and the gun went off and this figure came reeling out and down the stairs, staggering like my dad used to on a Saturday night when he came home drunk.

'I rushed in. She was sitting up in bed, the gun—*this* gun—still smoking in her hand. She said, "It was a devil, a devil pretending to be my son!" Then her mouth went all twisted and she stiffened in the bed and no more words would come. I didn't know what to do so I rushed downstairs to the telephone to call for help. And he was still there, lying in the hallway face down! I almost fainted, but he wasn't moving, he was so, so still. I had to get by him to reach the phone. I put the light on and stopped down to look and see if he was dead or just unconscious. And then I recognized him. All those years, and I could still recognize him!'

Lexie cast a horrified glance over her shoulder.

'You mean it really was him? Alexander, her son, come home?'

Now Miss Keech laughed with a mad heartiness.

'You stupid girl!' she said. 'How could we ever, ever have thought you were clever? Oh yes, the son had come home all right. But not to *her*, not to that mad old woman. It was *my* son who'd come, Lexie, *my* son!'

It was only now that Lexie began to be seriously worried for her life. A delusion as strong as this was capable of taking off in any direction.

She said brightly, 'So Alexander was really your son? I never knew that.'

Miss Keech looked at her in amazement.

'Is something wrong with you, girl? Are all the Hubys mad? It was Richard, my own son, lying there. He'd got into the wrong room, poor lad. Though what I'd have done with him if he'd come to me, I don't know. You know what old Gwendoline was like about blacks. That's why I gave him up in the first place. One of the reasons, anyway. You've no idea what people were like. Not being married was bad enough, but *black*! You'd think I'd bedded down with a gorilla or something. I couldn't see an end to it, no money, no job. What could I do? And then I went to see her and chatted her up about Alex, and how marvellous the spoilt little brat had been, and how I was sure he were alive somewhere, and she took me on. But one sniff of my little black bastard and I'd have been out! I went to see him. I always meant one day…at least I thought perhaps one day…but he grew so surly, always on about coming home with me, or not speaking at all…it seemed best in the long run not to upset him by…'

As her speech grew more rambling, the old Yorkshire rhythms and idiom were surfacing again. Distantly Lexie thought she heard the front doorbell ring. She took a step forward. The gun shifted as Miss Keech seemed to jerk back to awareness. Perhaps it was an accidental movement, but Lexie did not feel like finding out.

'You never told him you worked here, then?' she said.

'Of course not. I didn't dare risk it. Then I stopped going and we lost contact. All those years. All her fault! And now he'd come back and she'd shot him! No, I suppose fair's fair. She'd had a shock. A black man in her room. She always thought their one aim was to rape white women. And calling her "mother" too! So I won't think too badly of her, may she rot in hell! To tell the truth, I didn't know what I felt either. It were such a shock. All I knew was, it'd be best if no one knew about him. It was so complicated, you see. If she lived, then she'd surely put me out when she found out about Richard. And if she died, God knows what they might have said about me bringing my black son here to kill her. I'd put up with her all those years. I was nearly seventy. I deserved to have some peace to look forward to at the end of my life!

'So I dragged him down here into the cellar. It was just a temporary thing till I saw how the land lay. I could always say he must have stumbled down here himself and I'd not found him for a day or two.

'Well, she didn't die. She started to get better, only she thought it was all some kind of visitation. The black devil come to persuade her Alexander was dead! I nursed her well, no one can deny that. And I moved Richard's body back there. I laid him all out decent and said a prayer and burnt a candle. I'm not a religious woman, so I don't reckon you need church and vicar to lie peaceful. You can put me in there with him when I go, and see if I care!'

She spoke defiantly. Lexie thought of the years of self-justification behind that defiance and tried to find some sympathy for the woman, but it was hard. She had never liked her. Now she was beginning to understand why.

The doorbell was still ringing.

She said, 'What about Pontelli, the Italian? Did he come here too?'

'Oh yes,' said Miss Keech, bird-like alertness suddenly back in her mad, bright eyes. 'He came. I found him skulking around.

I had the gun. He said at first he wanted to see Rod and I said Rod wasn't here. He said he knew he was here, then he started calling me Keechie and asking if I didn't know who he was. I said no I didn't and he said he was Alexander. I laughed and said, no he wasn't, Alexander was long, long dead and he was a fraud and I'd make sure everybody knew it. Then he got angry and said when he came into his inheritance, the first thing he'd do was make sure I was thrown out of Troy House. He came towards me and the gun went off.'

She looked at the weapon as if noticing it for the first time.

'I didn't mean to fire it. He turned and ran away. I laughed. I thought he'd been frightened by the noise. I didn't know the gun had hurt him till later when I read about it. It didn't bother me. If he'd died here, I'd have put him in the wine cellar with Richard. Two sons in the same spot. They'd have been company!'

'You think he might really have been Mrs Huby's son?'

'He was someone's son,' said Miss Keech with that now very irritating slyness.

The bell had stopped ringing. Whoever it was must have gone away. Lexie said briskly, 'I think you really ought to get back to bed, Miss Keech. You're not terribly well, you know.'

'Aren't I? Why? What's up with me?' she snapped suspiciously.

'You're just tired, I think. It's all been very hard on you. And that other body being found across the field must have been the last straw.'

She spoke with pseudo-sympathy, introducing the subject of Sharman's death in an effort to divert the old woman's attention from Pontelli and this staring skeleton she claimed was her son. But she realized instantly it was an even stranger path she had diverted on to as hot tears began to stream down Miss Keech's face.

'He came to the house, the man who found him, and asked to use the phone. Then the police came and I was so worried in case it had something to do with…with the other. But everyone was so polite and they just wanted to use the phone and I made them tea and everything was all right till the young man with the red hair came to the house. I heard him on the phone. I heard him say he'd recognized the dead man and it was the dark boy who'd been arrested for shoplifting and his name was Cliff Sharman. I knew at once it had to be my grandson. I didn't know I'd got a grandson till that moment, and all at once I knew, and I knew that he was lying dead in a ditch within sight of Troy House…his father dead inside and him dead outside… I knew…'

The thin body beneath the long cotton nightdress was racked with sobs and now at last Lexie felt that surge of true sympathy which she'd hitherto sought in vain.

'Miss Keech,' she said. 'I'm sorry.'

And moved forward to offer this old, cold woman who had felt the full savagery of time's revenges the comfort of her young arms.

Perhaps Miss Keech misinterpreted the gesture. Or perhaps she found the thought of close physical contact repugnant. She jerked backwards, trying to stand upright, and the gun went off.

Lexie staggered backwards, shrieked and fell. The cellar was full of smoke and the ricocheting echoes of the explosion. Cutting through them came a voice crying her name. Two figures appeared at the head of the stairs. The foremost, young, slim and athletic, bounded down, not pausing by the old woman, and knelt by the fallen girl.

'Oh Lexie,' said Rod Lomas in a tone of despair far beyond his acting abilities, 'lie still, oh, Lexie, don't worry, we'll get a doctor in no time.'

'Never bother with a doctor,' said Lexie Huby sitting upright. 'Fetch a cobbler. It's these bloody high heels I put on so I'd look a bit taller for you!'

The second newcomer, fat and breathless, stooped beside Miss Keech and removed the gun from her unresisting fingers.

'You all right, luv?' he asked. 'We'll have you back in bed in a jiffy.'

He then continued down the steps, nodded at Lexie in passing, saying cheerfully, 'Evening, luv,' and went to the door of the wine-cellar.

'Richard Sharman, I presume,' he said in a tone of some satisfaction. 'That's what I like, a good neat finish.'

And turning, Dalziel smiled like some benevolent Christmas spirit on the recumbent girl, the distraught young man and the slack and broken sick old woman.

CHAPTER 13

It was the day of Neville Watmough's interview, the day of Cliff Sharman's funeral.

Watmough woke with that sense of divine inevitability which comes to most men but rarely, and then usually in little unimportant things. But today it was not just a matter of knowing the putt was going in the hole or the dart in the treble twenty. Today his life's work was truly to begin, and he was ready for it.

He woke early, not because of nervousness but because his whole body felt electric with energy. As he shaved he checked over the reasons for his confidence and found nothing wanting. He was the right man with the right record in the right place at the right time. The gods were with him. They had even made Dalziel, that normally unjust impediment, an instrument of their plan. The solving of both of CID's current murder cases at the weekend couldn't have fallen better. There had been a moment of doubt as to how Ike Ogilby would take the news of the arrest of one of his own reporters, but he needn't have worried. This had been a scoop beyond an editor's dreams, to have the killer on your own staff safe beyond reach of the inducements and insider-stories of your rivals! There had been another bad moment when Vollans had seemed set to recant his confession, claiming it had been extracted under duress, something about Sergeant Wield and a bayonet. But the café proprietor had identified him, Forensic had discovered spots of blood of the right group both in his car and on the tyres, and Vollans, after talking with his solicitor, had shifted his ground and was now angling for a manslaughter deal.

His story was that he had picked up Cliff Sharman as arranged and gone for a drive with him. Sharman had tried to sell him various stories about police corruption and drug-trafficking in Yorkshire, but close questioning hadn't revealed any firm evidence, so Vollans had said there was no deal. At this point Sharman, who was clearly high on something, had grown abusive. He had demanded money, Vollans had tried to eject him from the car, they had struggled.

'I knocked him down, got in the car and started to drive away. But suddenly he was there again, trying to scramble on the bonnet. Next thing he slipped and was under the wheel. When I saw he was dead, I panicked and hid him in the ditch. In case it ever came out he was the one who'd been ringing the *Challenger*, I pretended we'd made an appointment for the following morning and he'd not turned up. It was all a pure accident, provoked by his violent and abusive behaviour.'

The version Pascoe believed in was that Sharman had had time to cool down before he met Vollans. His unwillingness to be specific plus his colour had eventually irritated Vollans to the point where he became abusive. *These nigger perverts are animals, they've no right to be treated like humans* was a phrase in his with-drawn confession. Whether he'd deliberately run over him or not was the only point at dispute. Wield was certain he had,

Pascoe tended to go along with this, but Watmough was happy to settle for Vollans's version as this had at its centre the idea that Sharman had invented all his allegations about the police with a view to extracting money.

In the end, the lawyers would decide all that. Meanwhile, Vollans was safely locked up, Miss Keech was safely horizontal in a hospital bed, and though the full details of that case had not yet been released to the Press, Watmough was looking forward to taking the Committee into his confidence during the forthcoming interview. Purely by chance he had found himself the previous night sitting next to the Committee's Chairman, Councillor Mottram, at the dinner to inaugurate Eden Thackeray's Presidency of the Gents. He had not missed the chance to prime Mottram so that he could ask the right questions this morning. Yes, fate was certainly shaking the golden fruit into his lap at the moment. Mottram had told him that they'd just had word of the withdrawal of Stan Dodd from Durham, adjudged by the makers of books and by Watmough himself, to be his arch-rival. A heart attack. Poor Dodd. He must remember to send him a get-well card.

All he had to do now was wait. The Committee was meeting at County Hall. Interviews of the four surviving candidates would take place at hourly intervals from nine o'clock. At one, the Committee would debate its reactions over lunch. And as soon as may be thereafter they would announce their choice. Watmough's interview was the final one, at midday, the prime position. The gods had even given him the best initial.

With such complacent thoughts he drove slowly to Police Headquarters which he now viewed fondly as his own. Entering, he returned the greetings of those he encountered with a friendly (but not too friendly) wave, imagining their surprise to see him turning up for work on this most important of days, and their admiration, even envy, of his *sangfroid* and sense of duty.

But his attendance was not simply a gesture. He wanted to be right up to date with all aspects of the Force's work when he turned up at County Hall, particularly of course with the fine details of the two murder cases.

And there at the centre of his desk was a large buff envelope with his name printed on it in a hand which was unmistakably Dalziel's.

Why did the name Belshazzar suddenly flit into his mind?

He opened the envelope and withdrew its contents slowly.

First was an internal memo. He began to read it.

TO: DCC
FROM: Head of CID
SUBJECT: Sexual deviancy in Mid-Yorkshire CID.

He paused here to brush his fingers across his eyes as though to remove an impediment to his vision. Then he read on.

As per your instructions (copy of relevant memorandum attached) I have consulted with Dr Pottle of the Central Hospital Psychiatric Unit concerning possible m.o. for detecting sexual deviancy in CID officers. Enclosed is draft questionnaire for your approval.

He let the memorandum flutter from his fingers and turned to the questionnaire. It consisted of four sheets of A4 size, alternating blue and pink in colour.

The first was headed CONFIDENTIAL, addressed to ALL C.I.D. PERSONNEL and gave as its issuing authority DCC.

There was a blurb.

This is a multi-choice questionnaire aimed at rounding out file information for use in assessing promotion, location and designation of personnel.
Tick only one box in each section.

He let his eyes move trance-like on the pages, focusing on questions at random.

> *(3)   As a baby were you (a) bottle-fed? (b) breast-suckled?*
> *(c) don't know?*
> *(9)   Were you ever interfered with by a relative? (a) yes (b) no*
> *(15) Did you ever masturbate (a) alone? (b) in company?*
> *(c) both?*
> *(29) Which do you prefer next to the skin (a) silk? (b) cotton?*
> *(c) leather? (d) blue serge?*

He read no further but sat for a while gazing at his Yorkshire Beauty Spots Wall Calendar. Today's date was ringed in red. This month's picture was a view of Fylingdales Moor with the Early Warning System prominent.

There was something else on the memorandum. His censorial eye had skipped it first time round, but his ill-divining soul had taken it in.

> *DISTRIBUTION: CC*
> *ACC (1)*
> *ACC (2)*
> *Chairman and members of Police Committee (as per DCC's directive CK/NW/743 on Consultation and Information)*

With an effort of will which might well have won him the job if the Committee could have seen it, he carefully replaced the questionnaire in its envelope and locked it in his desk. He found in himself a very great need for a drink and the bottle of thin sherry he kept for hospitality purposes had little appeal.

There was only one place he could get a proper drink at this time of day in safe and soothing surroundings. He left the Station with the same measured tread as he had entered it, only this time he acknowledged no greeting. It was not a long walk. Ten minutes later he was entering the door of the Gents.

"Morning, George,' he said to the steward in the vestibule. 'I'll have a large Scotch, in the smoking-room.'

'Yes, sir. Quiet day for crime, is it?' said the friendly steward.

Not quite understanding the remark, Watmough went through into the smoking-room, a haven of peace and repose, empty at this hour except for a single figure behind an outspread copy of *The Times*.

Even under stress, Watmough did not ignore the courtesies expected between gentlemen members.

'Good morning,' he said.

Slowly the paper was lowered.

"Morning, Neville,' said Andy Dalziel, beaming. 'Now isn't it grand to have a place like this to escape to when things get rough down at the factory?'

Only two mourners attended Cliff Sharman's funeral, his grand-mother, Miriam Hornsby, and Wield. It was a busy afternoon at the municipal cemetery—autumn was a good dying season as though ailing souls balked at the prospect of another winter—and a long back-up of cortèges blackened the curving driveway to the little chapel. The officiating vicar consigned the coffin to the grave as speedily as possible and spoke his parting condolences over his shoulder.

The silent mourners hardly noticed his departure. Here there were no residual resentments to be heaped on the coffin like hand-fuls of earth; here would come no dramatic interruptor to mar the time's solemnity; here was only grief and the futile self-reproach of those who did not know how they might have done other.

'Nineteen years,' said Mrs Hornsby. 'It's not much.'

'No,' said Wield.

'No time to do anything. And a lot of what he did do wasn't what you'd call good, was it?'

'I suppose not.'

'I did right to let him be buried up here, didn't I, Sergeant Wield?' She sought reassurance.

'Oh yes,' said Wield.

'And they'll put his dad alongside him?'

'I'll make sure they do.'

'Yes. Well, Mr Dalziel says he'll see to it too. He's a nice man, Mr Dalziel, isn't he?'

The idea was startling enough to penetrate the carapace of self-absorbed melancholy Wield had grown around him in the past few days.

'What? Oh yes.'

'And clever with it. He worked it all out, you know. He was telling me all about it, Dicky working at that same hotel and all.'

It had indeed been a small triumph of ratiocination which Dalziel had only mentioned to all those who had the ears to hear without the legs or the rank to run away.

With Commander Sanderson's help he had pursued Miss Keech through Army Records, Richard Sharman through tax returns and Mrs Huby through London hotel registers.

Miss Keech, now in hospital, had said nothing since the night she almost shot Lexie, so all scenarios were circumstantial. But the facts were that she had been an ATS corporal in 1944 posted to Maidstone, that there'd been an American negro unit stationed close by, that she'd married Sergeant Sharman and given birth to her black baby only six months later.

'She must've worked fast when she realized she was pregnant,' theorized Dalziel. 'Caught the poor sod desperate for a bit of romance before he went overseas. Did he really believe his divorce was final? Who knows? In them days, who cared!'

So had begun the course of events which was to start gathering its final momentum three years before when Richard

Sharman, arriving one morning for his job as a relief barman at the Remington Place Hotel, had glimpsed Miss Keech getting into a taxi with Mrs Huby after breaking their journey in London on their return from Italy. He thought he recognized his mother. Checking with the hotel register would have given him the women's names plus their Troy House address.

A man of action and impulse, he had caught a train north later that same day. By the time he found out where Troy House was, it was late evening. In any case, the women would have gone to bed early after their travels. Getting into the house would pose little difficulty as the animals had to be permitted almost total freedom of movement.

And so poor Sharman had wandered into someone else's receiving fantasy, just as Pontelli three years later was to be the victim of a situation he had neither created nor comprehended. It was a sad irony that he had almost certainly gone to Troy House in search of Rod Lomas, whose presence there had been revealed to him that same afternoon by John Huby, and who was at that moment keeping a vain vigil outside the Highmore Hotel.

Now Wield gently turned Mrs Hornsby away from the grave and together they walked back towards the chapel where the single funeral car waited. As they approached another car drew up behind it and Dalziel got out.

'Hello there. Everything go all right?' he asked.

'Yes, thank you, Andy,' said the woman. 'It was nice of you to send them flowers.'

'Think nothing of it. Will you excuse me and the sergeant here a mo?'

He took Wield a few steps into the chapel porch.

'You all right?' he said.

'Yes, sir. Look, I want to talk...'

'Not here, lad! Show some respect. You won't mind going back by yourself in that thing, will you?'

'No. But what about...'

'I'll look after Mrs Hornsby,' said Dalziel firmly. 'I thought I'd take her out, cheer her up a bit. Spend my winnings.'

'Winnings?'

'Oh aye. Haven't you heard. I collected from Broomfield. Dan Trimble from Cornwall got the job like I said he would.'

'And Mr Watmough?'

'Well, he didn't get the job,' explained Dalziel patiently. 'Seeing as there's only one Chief Constable at a time, I should've thought even a detective-sergeant could've worked that out.'

'Yes, sir. I meant, what happened...?'

'I think the Committee got the notion he had some funny hang-ups about gays,' said Dalziel.

Wield considered this, then said angrily, 'You're not saying that he didn't get it because they thought he was gay, are you?'

Dalziel regarded him curiously.

'That'd bother you, would it, lad?'

'From now on, that kind of crap'll bother me a lot,' said Wield grimly.

'Easy,' said Dalziel. 'Two things for you to remember, sunshine. Coming out the way you did doesn't qualify you to be a hero. What are you going to do? Wear red feathers and a tu-tu and demonstrate outside County Hall? Not your style, Wieldy. Second, it wasn't because someone thought Watmough was a crypto-queer he didn't get the job. Oh no. He sticks out a mile as a crypto-queer-basher, doesn't he? But he didn't know his committee! All these directives on cooperation and information, and he knew bugger all about Councillor Mottram, the chairman!'

'You mean Mottram...?' Wield looked at him in disbelief. 'But he's got a wife and two kids!'

Dalziel shook his head in sorrow.

'So had Oscar Wilde,' he said. 'Don't be so square, lad. And keep your mouth shut about Mottram. Just because you've come up on deck, don't rock the boat for them as prefer to remain down

in the hold. You didn't exactly make it with one mighty leap yourself, did you? Now I'd better not keep poor Mrs Hornsby waiting.
There's a lot of comforting needs done there.'

He moved away, then paused and turned.

'By the by, your sick leave's over, as of today. I'll expect you
at your desk tomorrow morning. Don't be late!'

He glanced towards Mrs Hornsby and grinned ferociously.

'On the other hand, don't start ringing the hospitals if I am!'

Pascoe nursed Rosie in his arms.

'It's all over, kid,' he said. 'All done. All sorted out with
precious little help from me, I might add. I mean, what did I
do? Like the Fat Man said, I got absorbed with peripherals, with
intellectual speculation, moral problems and the romantic past.
Only he didn't put it like that, did he? What he said was... No,
I won't tell you, kid, even though you've got your eyes shut and
you're snoring. You never know about subliminal hearing and I
reckon between us, me and your mum will do enough to mess you
up without feeding you the gospel according to Andy Dalziel at
such a tender age. Not that I think he was totally right. Once or
twice I got close to things, once or twice I got close to being the
wise, witty and wonderful dad you're going to imagine I am till
one day it hits you that really I'm as much of a child as you are,
and then suddenly the child is truly father to the man and you'll
rather sadly leave me to my silly play and sally forth yourself to
save the universe.'

His perambulations with the sleeping baby had brought him
before a dressing-table mirror, up-tilted so he could look down at
his reflection.

He regarded himself seriously, then said, 'Excuse me,
Inspector, there are still a couple of things I don't understand...'

EPILOGUE

Spoken by Peter Pascoe

The child is father to the man

Wordsworth: *My heart leaps up*

Statement made by Detective Chief Inspector Pascoe P. on the something of whatsit in the presence of a cassette-recorder and a bottle of Scotch, half full or half empty depending which way you're going. Statement made voluntarily, without duress or Dalziel, which some allege are indistinguishable at dusk with the light behind them.

Statement begins. But where? Two years is a long time in a cop's life, almost as long as two minutes in politics. Better start with the Italians. Most things start there except for them as start with the Greeks. So. The Italians.

At the time, the Italians weren't very happy about one of their nationals getting shot dead in England and no one getting his wrist slapped for it.

Dalziel said, 'Tell 'em the silly bugger died of bad parking. They'll likely understand that.'

The trouble was, Miss Keech ended up as one of Pottle's patients in the Psychiatric Unit, far beyond confession or interrogation. We told the Italians that the bullets that killed Pontelli and Richard Sharman came from the same gun, but despite the condition of Venice, they obviously like things tidier than that. Perhaps in revenge, they pursued our initial request for information about Pontelli with slow thoroughness, and long after I'd forgotten all about the Huby will, a bulky envelope dropped on my desk.

It contained a detailed account of Pontelli's life and activities. The curious thing about it was that to all intents and purposes it began in 1946 and didn't thicken out till the mid-'fifties. Before that it was all hearsay—in other words, what other people had heard the not very forthcoming Pontelli say. On his childhood there was nothing, not even any documentary evidence to support his claim to have been born in Palermo, though the Sicilian investigator made the point that many records were destroyed during the German occupation and the Allied invasion.

I was getting the message now. Some Florentine joker was dropping a super-subtle hint that perhaps Pontelli really wasn't their concern after all!

I went to Dalziel with the report.

He said, 'It's nearly eighteen months, Peter! I don't have time to be bothered with things that happened eighteen days ago.'

'What shall I do?' I asked.

'It's dead,' he said. 'Bury it.'

Next day I went to see Eden Thackeray.

There was a new girl in his outer office, sleek, smart, elegantly made-up, sitting in front of a word-processor. The alterations extended into Thackeray's own room. Dark oak and red leather were out. It was now a silky white and shiny chrome temple of hi-tech.

'I thought, to hell!' he explained rather shamefacedly. 'If the old customers didn't like it, I'd got newer richer ones who did!'

'What about Lexie Huby? Didn't she fit the new image?'

He grew indignant.

'She's doing a law degree at Leeds University! Do you know, she got A grades in all her advanced levels, doing them at nights without referring to anybody? I have high hopes of that girl, very high.'

I said, 'Does she still see Rod Lomas?'

He shrugged and said, 'How should I know?'

He always looked a bit embarrassed when the Lomas side of the family was mentioned. Rod and his mother had consistently denied any knowledge of Pontelli's trip to England or his plans to claim the estate, though acknowledging that the late Arthur Windibanks might have put him up to it. As for the woman's firm identification of the maple-leaf birthmark, she had become very vague about that, smiling sweetly at Dalziel and saying, 'One sees so many behinds that they all begin to blur into one, don't they?'

Our hopes of getting them on a fraud charge arising out of their misappropriation of the rental from the Villa Boethius vanished when Eden Thackeray refused to cooperate.

'We have the reputation of the estate to consider,' he said primly to Dalziel in my presence. 'Full restitution has been made.'

The fat man just regarded him closely for a moment, then said, 'You randy old bugger! I never knew what restitution was till now!'

And poor Thackeray, attempting to look indignant, could only raise a blush.

I showed him the papers from Florence and said he was welcome to them if they were any use.

He thanked me gravely and said he would keep them safely filed though he could see no way in which they could be helpful.

'There's still a couple of things unexplained,' I said provocatively.

'And so they shall remain,' he said. 'This business has brought farce where there should have been decorum, and tragedy where there should have been delight. Soon there shall be an end.'

'Soon?' I said. 'The Court of Chancery's still considering the case, isn't it? Doesn't that mean another ten years at least?'

'The days of *Jarndyce and Jarndyce* are long past,' he said. 'It will be months at most; perhaps even weeks.'

I smiled disbelievingly. On my way out I waved dashingly at the new girl, who nodded back as coolly unimpressed as Lexie Huby had always been. I was glad to see one of her long eyelashes fall off and come to rest like a weary earwig on her damask cheek.

That night I had a confused dream about that eyelash and Thackeray's office and the whole Huby affair. It was silly. It was ancient history. The intervening months had been crammed with all the long tedium and sharp excitements which make up a CID man's work. But it was only this case which invaded my dreams. I told Ellie. She said, 'Guilt.' I said, 'What?' She said, 'You're a sucker for it. It's people like you that make repressive religious regimes possible. You're always like this when you reckon you've missed something.'

She was, of course, right. She usually is. It's one of her least attractive characteristics. But she compensates by going wildly wrong when she tries to be too clever.

'The earwig on the damask cheek is the clue,' she said in her best Freudian manner. 'It's the worm in the bud, you see. Conscience, the curious mole, nibbling away. Something you've left undone.'

'Bollocks,' I said with confidence, for suddenly I knew all about the earwig on the damask cheek. Or thought I did. I had to send for Seymour the next day to be sure. He thought I was mad but was bright enough not to let it show too much. Also under pressure he turned out to have something like perfect recall. I'd noticed this before when he made reports. I complimented him fulsomely and he went away bewildered but content.

Now I had a theory but nothing to test it in. Then three months or so later, I read in the *Post* that the Chancery judge had indeed pronounced as quickly as Thackeray had forecast. He had ruled that the waiting period in the Huby will was inequitable. PAWS, CODRO and WFE could have their money instantly.

Ellie went into her indignant harangue about the iniquities of giving vast sums to cats, officers' widows and fascists. I made a few phone calls and a week later I was sitting in a small stuffy room next to the office of George Hutchinson, general manager of the Leeds Head Branch of the Yorkshire Commercial Bank.

I felt curiously nervous and when the door opened, I jumped to my feet like a twenty-year-old in search of a loan for a motorbike.

Hutchinson said, 'Would you mind stepping in here, Miss Brodsworth? There's someone who'd like a word.'

A young woman stepped inside and regarded me incuriously with hard blue eyes. Behind her, Hutchinson caught my eye and beckoned, but I didn't want to be diverted at that moment and I closed the door firmly in his face.

Then I faced Sarah Brodsworth. With her tight blonde curls, rosebud lips and blouse-straining bosom, she should have been very attractive, but I did not find her so.

I reached forward and gently squeezed her left breast.

'Hello, Lexie,' I said.

The breast felt very real and for one awful moment I thought I'd got it wrong. My mind was already accelerating through apologies to Brodsworth, explanations to Ellie, and pleas in mitigation to the judge, when the girl replied, 'Hello, Mr Pascoe. And what can I do for you?'

I said, 'Let's sit down.'

We sat opposite each other on either side of a small desk.

I said, 'Lexie, I'm sorry.'

I don't know why I said it, but it was what I felt.

She said, 'How did you know?'

'I should have known two years ago, I ignored evidence.'

'What evidence?'

'The evidence of my own eyes, for a start. First time I saw your sister, Jane, she was wearing a low-cut sweater. What I saw down there had to be real! Then my constable found the wig and the falsies...'

'He was in my room? Illegally, of course,' she said.

'Let's say accidentally. And he thought it was Jane's room. But I should've known when he said he'd found the stuff behind some books. Jane doesn't look the booky type to me.'

'That sounds a bit élitist,' she said. 'Everyone reads.'

'Milton, Byron, Blake, Wordsworth, a History of Grand Opera?' I said. 'My constable was amazed at what he could recall when I prodded him. I could have checked with Jane, of course. But I didn't want to worry her.'

'Instead you lay in wait for me here today and squeezed my tit? That was brave of you.'

I said, 'Do you want to tell me about it, Lexie.'

She shrugged and said, 'If you want to hear. I had a poke around Thackeray's not long after I started there. They thought I was a bit of an idiot, so no one took much notice if I popped up in odd places. Just thought I'd got lost. I went through Aunt Gwen's file. I'd been hearing about her fortune all my life so I thought I'd take a look and see how much there really was. I was amazed, I've got to admit. I'd thought there'd be a few thousand, but I could see at a glance there must be over a million! Then I saw where it was going. PAWS, CODRO, WFE. It didn't seem fair somehow. In fact it seemed wrong. Especially WFE. I'd heard Aunt Gwen mention them and I knew what they were about.

'I thought about it a long time. Then I rang Mrs Falkingham. I invented the name Sarah Brodsworth and told her I was a student and that I'd heard about WFE and thought it sounded interesting. She was delighted to have someone to talk to and invited me to tea. It struck me I'd better change my appearance. It'd be daft to find that Aunt Gwen had shown her a photo of me or something. Not that that was very likely, but it was silly taking risks. All I did that first time was to clip dark lenses over my specs, put on a lot of make-up, wear a beret and stick a lot of tissues into my bra! I felt really stupid! But as things developed between me and Mrs Falkingham, I started to do the job properly. I even got tinted contact lenses, which I realized after was silly as I couldn't use them normally. But at least there wasn't much chance of my being recognized, was there?'

'No,' I agreed. 'There wasn't. So you infiltrated WFE?'

'That's not a word I'd use,' she said. 'I joined and started helping the old lady. I quite liked her. She was daft but harmless, and a lot nicer with it than Great Aunt Gwen. Yes, I liked her. I was sorry when she died last year, but it did make things a bit easier.'

'Easier to rob her, you mean?'

Lexie Huby regarded me curiously.

'There was no question of robbing her,' she said patiently. 'The money wasn't going to Mrs Falkingham and she was far too scrupulous ever to have used a penny for herself. No, all I meant was that after she died, I was left solely in charge of WFE. I had only myself to worry about. No one could get at her any longer.'

'You mean like Henry Vollans and White Heat?'

'That's right.'

'You knew about Vollans?'

'At first I just thought he was a nosey journalist. That was worrying enough. Then I began to get a sense that it wasn't just a story he was after. He was sounding me out. So I sounded him out too.'

'And finally, you reached an understanding,' I said.

'Why do you say that?'

'He didn't mention you when he did his deal with the law, did he?' I said, not without bitterness.

In my opinion, Vollans should've been done for murder. But in the end he'd pleaded to manslaughter and got sent down for seven years. There is no such thing as plea-bargaining in English law, but the list of White Heat members covering all four estates which Vollans had provided must have influenced somebody somewhere.

'He wanted us to stay friends,' said Lexie.

'You write to him in jail.'

'You've checked? Yes, the occasional note.'

'And he sits there looking forward to getting out and sharing the loot, is that it?' I said.

'I expect so. Why do you sound so put out?'

'Because I think that, having got the money, you're going to be Lexie Huby again full time and Vollans is going to find that his friend Sarah Brodsworth has vanished from the face of the earth! In time he may even work out that it was you who turned him in.'

'You think so?'

'Who else could it have been that rang Mr Dalziel?'

She nodded.

'You're right, of course. I'd got a date with Vollans the night the coloured lad was killed. He didn't turn up. Then I found out he was the reporter due to meet Sharman the next day and I got to wondering.'

'How did you find out all this stuff?' I asked.

'I was Eden Thackeray's secretary, remember? Everything that came into that office came through me. I led Vollans on a bit. He always thought I must be fronting for some other extremist lot, so when I started swapping nigger-bashing stories with him, he wasn't surprised. He as good as admitted killing Sharman. So I rang you lot and let you sort it out.'

'Like a good citizen,' I said. 'And also it got Vollans out of the way of your little scheme, didn't it? Very handy.'

'Yes,' she said calmly. 'Having him sniffing around didn't make it any easier for me to make sure I got full control of the money.'

'Yes. At last. The money. Why did you do it, Lexie?'

I realized I was hoping she'd find some form of excuse for herself. I was even willing to hint a couple of possible mitigating factors. I said, 'Was it because you felt your family had been cheated? Was it to help your dad?'

'Oh no,' she said, amused. 'I warned Dad he were daft to rely on any money coming from the old girl, but he never paid any heed to anyone else, least of all me! But I wasn't worried about him, not even when he went ahead with all them extensions on borrowed money. I know my dad better than anyone, Mr Pascoe. If he doesn't get what he wants one way, he'll get it another. No use going against him. I learnt that early on. Have you been out to the Old Mill recently? Most of the work's finished now, without a penny of Huby money to help him. He's bullied and bribed and done half the work himself but he's got there and the place is doing well, believe me. You know what really brings the people in? It's Dad himself! He's rude, he's vulgar, he's sometimes downright abusive, but they love it! What the regulars like best is watching newcomers' faces when he gets on about Aunt Gwen's will and ends up by booting Gruff-of-sodding-Greendale up the chimney. They think he's still really mad about it, but he got past that long ago. It's part of the show now. He's even had Gruff reupholstered twice to keep him looking realistic!'

Her pride in her father was touching. Also it struck me how like him she herself was. If she didn't get a thing one way, she had the drive and wit to get it another, whether it was higher education or her great-aunt's money.

'I'm glad he's doing well.'

'Yes. And now he'll be getting the money Mr Goodenough promised him if the will got overturned,' said Lexie. 'So everything's grand down at the Old Mill.'

'So,' I said, 'the money is just for you. How did you think you could get away with it?'

'With what?'

'Fraud.' I spelt it out. 'Misappropriation of funds. I'm sure the Fraud Squad will have half a dozen other charges. Not forgetting impersonation.'

'By me? Who of?'

'Sarah Brodsworth,' I said.

'But she is me,' said Lexie. 'I even changed my name by deed-poll when I got to eighteen. There's no problem. I'm officially Alexandra Sarah Brodsworth-Huby. How can I impersonate myself?'

'Don't quibble,' I said. 'It doesn't become you. Your aunt had a purpose for this money. There is no way in which you will be able to claim that it came into your possession legally.'

'You're right,' she said. 'There wouldn't be. But it's not in my possession.'

'Transferring it to a Swiss account isn't going to alter matters, Lexie,' I said. 'Who advised you? Lomas?'

'Why do you mention him?'

'I just thought he might have inherited some of his father's expertise about fund-laundering,' I sneered.

She said, 'How'd a nice lady like Mrs Pascoe get herself married to a mind like yours?'

For the first time I got angry.

'Don't try to be smart with me, young girl,' I said grimly, launching into my Dalziel impersonation. 'You think it's all a game, don't you? A little play with you in the lead? You should've been the family actor, Lexie. From what I've seen of Lomas you could knock him into a cocked hat, which is probably where he belongs! Well, your next big part will be in court. What's it to be? Simple little Lexie Huby, the office mouse? No, that'll hardly do, not now you're almost a fully-fledged solicitor. How about, clever Miss Huby, the self-educated working lass, who's overcome all obstacles and reads poetry and listens to opera? But when I tell them that behind the poetry and the opera, there's a blonde wig and a pair of false boobs and a sharp little, greedy little mind at work, they'll look closer at you then, Lexie, and save their applause for the judge who sends you down.'

She said, amused, 'My wig's better than his, I think. But you've not got it quite right, Mr Pascoe. The poetry and the opera, yes, I acknowledge that, and I couldn't live without 'em. But I've known for a long time that behind the poetry and the music there's a world full of horrible, ugly things that can't be disguised, that can hardly be avoided.'

'Unless you've got the money to build a big enough barrier,' I concluded for her. 'And that's your justification?'

'What do I need with money?' she snapped suddenly. 'I need money like my dad needed it. It was thinking he needed it that nearly ruined him. Knowing he wasn't getting it just put him on the right road. Like Rod. He'll never be a great actor, mebbe, but unless someone gives him a lot of money, he'll have to work so hard he'll become a very good one.'

'And you?' I said, somewhat taken aback.

'Oh yes. Money'd spoil me too,' she said. 'I don't need to cheat to get it, Mr Pascoe. I can't see any trick to making a lot of money if that's what you want. It's a talent I'll have to be on my guard against as long as I live, I suspect. Here, take a look at this. I've got a class to go to, and I've wasted too much time here already.'

She thrust a piece of paper at me.

On it the Yorkshire Commercial Bank, acting on behalf of the East African Famine Relief Fund acknowledged receipt from the accredited representatives of Women For Empire of six hundred and eighty-nine thousand, three hundred and seventy-four pounds and thirty-eight pence.

'Do me a favour,' she said. 'Stick it in this envelope and post it for me, will you? I'll not have time to get down to the Post Office now you've made me so late.'

She handed me an envelope, I glanced down at it.

It was addressed to Henry Vollans, c/o HM Prison, Wakefield, Yorkshire.

'Lexie,' I said. 'I'm sorry. I thought that…'

'Yes,' she said, and grinned. It was like an internal light being switched on and for the first time through the outer layer of disguise I could see the unmistakable and true Lexie Huby.

I said, 'Was this what you planned from the start?'

'Planned? No plans, Mr Pascoe,' she said. 'I'm getting to the age of plans now, because that's how adults get things done. I wasn't an adult when all this started. I don't know. Mebbe it started when I was a child and I first heard about Alexander, about him being dead, and not dead. I never liked Great Aunt Gwen but I could see how desperately she wanted Alex not to be dead, and I thought of all the other mothers who wanted their children not to be dead, well, not thought, because that means plans, doesn't it, but imagined, that's the child's way, imagination, play...'

'But death?' I said. 'What could death mean to a child?'

She said, 'Death? Not much. Not then; not now. What is it? You here, I there; you stopping, I going on? Unimaginable! But I can imagine dying and the fear of it. The love of it too. I can imagine...'

Pascoe pressed the stop button and then ran the tape back to the beginning. He'd listened to it three times already and the final section was still as harrowing as it had been when first he'd heard it in that stuffy bank office. Lexie had seemed almost to be speaking in a trance induced by the intensity of her own imaginings. It struck him that this power to project herself so deep into the minds and feelings of others might prove a double-edged weapon. To a child, such imaginings were principally play; to an adult, along with valuable insights, they must bring a terrible vulnerability. He would watch little Lexie Huby's progress with interest and with concern. Meanwhile he found himself vulnerable to a question of conscience.

This was, did his approval of the direction in which Gwendoline Huby's money had been diverted give him the right to conceal his knowledge of its diversion?

He knew what Ellie would say. 'Right? It wasn't a matter of *right*. It was your *duty* to do nothing!'

He could guess what Dalziel would say. 'Bury it. But if that lass is going to practise law round here, don't let her forget she owes you a favour!'

Sod 'em all! When it came down to it, there was only one person whose judgment he could rely on absolutely.

He pressed the erase button on the cassette, locked the whisky bottle in his desk, and went home to talk to Rosie.